THE LINGFIELD POINT KILLINGS

An absolutely heart-pounding crime thriller

C.J. GRAYSON

DI Max Byrd & DI Orion Tanzy Book 3

Originally published as *No One's Safe*

JOFFE BOOKS

Revised edition 2023
Joffe Books, London
www.joffebooks.com

First published in Great Britain in 2021 as *No One's Safe*

This paperback edition was first published in Great Britain in 2023

Cover art by Nebojša Zorić

ISBN: 978-1-83526-112-5

Monday evening
Napier Street, Darlington

Danny Walters finished the washing-up, put the tea towel over the sink, and sighed. He was glad to be home with his family. After they had eaten, he'd put Mark and Peter to bed, kissed them both good night and started on his chores. They always demanded a bedtime story which he relished, as he too loved books, although it was sometimes the last thing he wanted to do after a long, hard day.

He heard someone shout something from upstairs. It sounded like Peter, his youngest son, aged seven. He'd been having bad dreams over the past year but recently these had become worse. More graphic. More real. Walters had lost count of how many times he'd woken suddenly, finding Peter standing by the bed, virtually camouflaged in darkness, staring at him.

'Coming,' he said towards the dining room, hoping the sound would travel up the stairs to Peter's room.

His eldest son, Mark, had just turned eleven. He was in his bedroom playing on his Nintendo switch, no doubt with his headset on, so Walters knew he wouldn't be the one shouting; the game console was all he needed.

Walters's wife, Jessica, was out with her friends for a few hours. Late night shopping or something, she'd said.

He left the narrow kitchen, made his way through the warm dining room, feeling the heat from the gas fire they were using to dry clothing as their boiler was broken.

After he reached the top of the stairs, he looked along the narrow landing. Mark's door, the nearest on the left, was closed. The door beyond that was his and Jessica's room. Peter's door, straight ahead of him, was slightly ajar.

'You okay, Peter?' Walters approached the door, his footsteps creaking on the old floorboards below.

'Dad . . .' a soft voice said from inside the room.

Walters opened the door and stepped into the darkness. The landing lamp offered enough light to allow him to see Peter in his single bed with his covers held tightly up to his chin.

'What's the matter, dude?' Walters asked, lowering to the bed.

'Dad, I'm scared,' he whispered.

'What you scared about, son?'

'I keep hearing noises.'

Walters could see the fear in his bright blue eyes, even in the dim conditions surrounding them. He placed a palm on the side of Peter's face and stroked his cheek with his thumb.

'Don't worry about a thing. You're safe here.'

Peter looked away for a moment, unsure.

'What happened in the last house will never happen again, especially not here.' He fell silent and continued stroking his cheek. 'Go to sleep.'

Peter managed a small nod, turned onto his side and closed his eyes.

'Good boy.' Walters stood up. 'I'll see you in the morning. Good night.'

'Good night, Dad.'

Walters edged Peter's door closed, padded along the landing and opened Mark's door. The boy was hunched over on his bed, his attention on the Nintendo down in his hands.

'You okay, Mark?'

Mark glanced up briefly. 'Yeah, Dad.'

'Ten more minutes on there, then shower, okay?'

Mark nodded again.

Walters closed the door and made his way downstairs, all the dark thoughts he'd previously banished slipping back into his mind. Shaking them off, he went over to the kettle, turned it on and sat down at the breakfast bar.

Waiting for the water to boil, he thoughtfully ran his fingers over the burns on his left forearm, memories of the horrific fire flooding back to him. He remembered kissing Jessica good night and turning over to go to sleep when the fire alarm downstairs had gone off. The smoke had drifted in beneath the door, his sons had coughed and cried, and moments later, banged urgently on the wall, desperate for help.

Once he'd woken Jessica, they had dashed out onto the landing, grabbed Peter and Mark and glared down the stairs into the black smoke and dancing orange flames. There had been no way out.

Returning to Peter's room. Walters ran to the single-glazed window and used his elbow to break the glass. He'd grabbed one of Peter's T-shirts, wrapped it around his knuckles, and punched out the remaining shards, so that they could crawl through safely. Jessica went first, climbing down onto the kitchen roof and turned, waiting with open arms for Peter and Mark to be lowered.

Last to go through, Walters looked back at the landing from the window. The smoke was now thick, black. The fire had caught hold of the landing carpet and as he had turned towards the panicked faces of his wife and two terrified sons, a sudden explosion threw him forward, the force sending him through the window onto the kitchen roof, where he had landed on his arm, and broken his ankle. His family had been thrown off the roof into the alley below, suffering several broken bones. By this time the fire brigade had been alerted, and safely lowered Walters down from the roof. They were all admitted to hospital, where Walters spent some time in the burns unit from the severe burns to his back and left arm.

No one had ever been able to determine the exact cause of the fire.

Walters blinked the memories away. He made himself a cup of coffee and checked his phone. Apart from a message from his friend, Mick, the rest was social media posts. People he didn't know who'd "friended" him and thought he should know what they'd made for dinner or where they were going that night, expressing the exciting lives they lived.

Moments later, the front door opened. Jessica walked into the kitchen with several bags and dumped them on the counter.

'Hey,' Walters said. He nodded at the bags. 'Spend much?'

The smile she'd been wearing disappeared. 'Listen, it's on my card. I'll pay it all back next month.'

Walters returned to his phone, telling himself to be patient. After the fire, in which they'd almost died, she was determined to live life to the fullest, unfortunately meaning buying the things she wanted with often no consideration that money doesn't grow on trees.

'It's just clothes,' she said. 'Oh, and I got us a nice new clock for in here.'

He looked beyond her to the clock she had bought only two months ago and sighed. 'There's nothing wrong with that one.'

Jessica unpacked the bags and showed him her purchases, proudly holding up a black shirt she'd bought him for the weekend. He thanked her and she bent to kiss him.

She stood back. 'Okay, what's wrong?'

'Oh, nothing.'

'Come on. We've been married six years, together for twelve. I know when something's the matter.'

'Well, it's just that Peter said he was scared earlier. He's okay though.'

She smiled sadly. 'Mark on his Nintendo?'

He nodded. 'He'll be finishing in a minute.'

4

'Have you found your key yet?'

Walters shook his head. 'God knows where that is. It must have unclipped itself when I was out earlier. Good job you were in, and we have spares. I'll get more cut tomorrow.'

They chatted for a while about their day, and then Jessica went upstairs to kiss the boys goodnight. She stood at their bedroom doors, watching her children, the landing light falling across their innocent sleeping faces.

Walters came upstairs, passed her and went into their bedroom. 'You coming to bed?'

'In a minute,' she whispered. After a few minutes she pulled their doors to, and quietly tiptoed into their room.

'Everything locked up?' she asked, climbing into bed.

Walters nodded and picked up a book from his bedside table. He didn't read for long before his eyes were sore. He placed the book on the side and fell asleep.

Something woke him.

The sliver of light that always fell through the door had darkened, something or someone was blocking it.

He turned over, rubbed his eyes, sat up and swung his legs off the bed. Behind him, Jessica was sleeping soundly. He stepped out onto the landing.

'Peter?'

Peter was standing in the middle of the landing, facing away from him. 'Peter, what are you doing?'

Peter stayed perfectly still.

'Peter?' Walters said, approaching him slowly, in case he was sleepwalking, something he'd started doing in the past few months. Walters made his way towards him, the carpet wet under his bare feet. It wasn't the first time Peter had wet himself. One memorable time they had woken to find him standing at the wardrobe with the door open, urinating all over their clothes.

Walters placed a hand gently on his shoulder.

The carpet was saturated, but it would clean; it always did. It was a shame they'd only cleaned it the day before.

'Come on, son,' he whispered. 'Let's get you back to bed.'

Walters slowly turned Peter around and guided him back to his bedroom. He changed his pants and put him back into bed.

He turned back to the landing, frowning down at the carpet. It seemed too wet for one of Peter's occasional accidents. The carpet was drenched. which was odd. They had had all the carpets cleaned yesterday and the chemicals used had left a slight odour, but the cleaner had said it would disappear in a day or two.

Now the smell was stronger.

'This makes no sense,' he muttered, leaning to look down the stairs and into the dark hallway below. The stair carpet was also soaked. He glanced back along the landing towards his bedroom, thinking hard.

'It doesn't make sense at all.'

He peered back down the stairs and froze. Someone was standing at the bottom, looking up. In the gloom, Walter could just see that he was smiling.

Walters was speechless.

In the man's hand was a lit match. Then it dawned on him. It wasn't Peter's urine on the stairs, it was petrol. The staircase and landing carpets had been doused in petrol.

Every hair on Walters's body stood on end. He stood, frozen, unable to move.

The man at the bottom of the stairs smiled, dropped the match on the bottom step and laughed as the flames raced up the stairs.

Walters dashed frantically back along the landing but even before he reached the door of the first bedroom, his skin was burning.

2

Tuesday early morning
Napier Street, Darlington

DI Orion Tanzy turned off the engine, yawned, and looked through the windscreen at the house. An ambulance, a fire engine, and three police cars were parked on the road outside the house. Officers nearby spoke with each other. The narrow, terraced street had been cordoned off at both ends.

He stepped out, locked the Golf and made his way towards the crime scene tape where people were watching what was happening. On his approach Tanzy heard a lady in her mid-twenties, dressed in a white dressing gown, asking PC Josh Andrews what was going on. Andrews, a tall, good-looking police constable holding a clipboard, told her that information couldn't be given out just yet. Tanzy stepped around the small cluster of people and smiled at PC Andrews.

'Morning, boss,' Andrews said, turning away from the woman.

'Hey, Josh.' Tanzy, wearing a thin black jacket, black jeans, and black shoes, ducked under the tape. 'Is Max here yet?'

'Yeah, he's inside. Arrived a few minutes ago. He's beaten you again.'

Tanzy smiled. 'Thanks.'

The senior forensic officers, Jacob Tallow and Emily Hope were outside the front door, wearing their standard white paper overalls and their masks pulled down under their chin. A few familiar PCs were close by. Tanzy noticed PC Amy Weaver positioned at the end of the street, guarding the other cordon.

Tallow and Hope glanced Tanzy's way as he approached.

'Morning, you two.'

'Morning, Orion,' Tallow said, nodding. Tallow was tall and thin, just over six foot four. He made Tanzy, who was over six foot himself, seem small. Tallow hadn't shaved for over a week, which was unusual for him. In his hand, there was a small clear plastic bag with something black inside.

'Hey, Ori.' Hope smiled politely. She was thin, had short blonde hair and excessive tattoos that gave the impression she didn't give a shit.

'What's happening?' Tanzy asked.

Tallow sighed heavily.

'That bad?'

Hope nodded. 'It's tragic, Ori. We've come out, we needed a breather.'

Tanzy looked beyond them at the small crowds and vehicles parked in the centre of the road. People who lived across the road were looking out their windows at the commotion as if they had nothing better to do.

'Where's Max?'

'He's upstairs, Ori.'

'Who was the first responder?'

Tallow turned, pointed a few houses down. DC Anne Tiffin was speaking with a man Tanzy didn't know, probably a neighbour, noting things he was telling her on a notepad. Moments later, she smiled and nodded at the man, folded her notepad and made her way towards Tanzy.

'Hey, boss.'

Tanzy smiled. 'First here?'

She nodded.

'You were quick.'

'I was heading to Stanhope Road, so was very close.'

Tanzy frowned.

'Someone reported their car stolen. Some yobs hanging around in the early hours, the lady said.' She smiled, opening a sheet of paper and grabbing a pen. 'I'll sign you in, sir.'

'Here,' Hope said from his left. She lowered to her bag, picked up some overshoes, and threw them at him. 'Put these on.'

A thickset fireman stepped through the front door, down onto the path. He smiled courteously at Tanzy as he was putting the shoes on, and headed to the fire engine.

'You'll need this too,' Hope added, grabbing something else from her bag. 'The smell is horrendous in there.'

Smiling, he took the face mask and hooked it around his ears. 'I'll see you in there.' He took a deep breath and stepped up into the house.

3

Tuesday, early morning
Napier Street, Darlington

Tanzy could smell it as soon as he stepped inside the hall. He couldn't describe it but gagged in his mask as he moved forward, his feet slowly crunching on the black, crispy floor below. He studied the stairs which had been scorched to charcoal.

He heard voices upstairs, and recognised his colleague DI Byrd and the crime scene manager, Tony McCabe. He moved closer to the base of the stairs and, to his right, stopped at the doorway to the living room. The fire had barely touched it. The leather sofa against the wall looked new and the carpet was untouched. Moving on to the dining room, he peered in, noticing everything a foot below the ceiling was as it should be. Two single leather chairs were against the right wall with a small table in between, a small, tidy desk with a flat-screen monitor and computer unit was tucked in the right alcove, and a rectangular dining table with six chairs neatly placed around it sat in the middle of the room. Everything within a foot of the ceiling was black, meaning the flames must have burned through the ceiling but spread no further.

There was a crunch to his left. A fireman walked into view, presumably coming from the kitchen.

'Hello,' he said to Tanzy. His voice was hoarse, which Tanzy guessed was either from smoking or entering countless burning buildings. He stood short and stocky, his shoulders rounded. He had a thick black moustache and dark, brown eyes. Tanzy didn't recognise him which he thought was odd as the fire station was located next to the fire department.

'Hey,' said Tanzy. 'Bad one, eh.'

'No kidding.'

The fireman stopped and studied the ceiling for a moment.

'I'm Detective Inspector Tanzy.'

'Roger Carlton,' he replied, looking away from the ceiling and extending his hand.

'What are you looking for?'

'Just damage really.' He focused upwards again.

'Did it make it through there?' Tanzy asked, pointing towards the kitchen.

He continued to stare at the ceiling but knew where Tanzy meant, and said, 'No.'

Tanzy wasn't an expert on fires and didn't possess the qualifications to investigate one, but he understood the basics. 'Where was the origin?'

The fireman looked at him. 'The stairs. I'll show you.' Tanzy stepped back into the hallway, allowing him to pass through the door.

'It started on the stairs.' Roger pointed to the third step. 'See this.'

Tanzy leaned forward. The step was jet black and brittle.

'This is our point of origin. I don't know if you can smell it but petrol has been used. See how the third one differs from the second? Then it trails up the stairs in a kind of snake motion. The burning is different on the walls compared to the carpet.'

Tanzy nodded.

'Nasty work,' Roger said, before he returned to the dining room and out of sight.

'Thanks for the input.'

'Happy to help,' replied Roger, disappearing into the kitchen.

Tanzy gingerly climbed the stairs one at a time. The paint on the walls and skirting boards had been fiercely stripped, leaving ashy plasterboard, crispy flaking paint and exposed shrunken wood.

The higher he went, the worse the smell became. It was a mixture of burnt wood, paint, petrol, and human flesh. He had smelled burnt skin before; it was a scent that always knocked him for six.

When he reached the top, he turned right and stepped up until he reached the landing. The carpet had vanished, leaving exposed wooden floorboards with holes dotted around where the petrol had helped the fire burn. The walls had been stripped of plasterboard, exposing singed brickwork, copper pipes, and curled up singed electrical wiring. Tanzy guessed the house was probably built in the 1930s, and although there was no doubt that the solid structure had resisted the fire compared to modern-day stud walls, evidently, it hadn't been enough.

Up ahead, there were three open doors.

Tanzy moved along the landing and stopped at the first door on the left. The smell from inside was horrendous, causing him to gag. Tony McCabe and DI Max Byrd stood a few feet into the room, talking about something, pointing to various parts of it. Both had their masks lowered under their chin, likely accustomed to the stench that surrounded them.

'Hey,' said Tanzy, from what was left of the doorframe.

Byrd glanced his way. 'Hey, Ori.'

Tanzy absorbed the room in horror. It was black from floor to ceiling. Everything inside had been burnt, including the male lying in the middle of the floor and a smaller body curled up below the window at the far end of it. The sun shining through the window indicated how the flames had heavily scorched the window.

'They had no chance, did they?' Tanzy noted.

Byrd looked his way and shook his head sadly. 'No.'

Tanzy frowned, hearing something above him. 'What's that?'

'One of the firemen is up in the attic,' Byrd said, pointing. 'See that door?'

Tanzy turned to where Byrd was meaning. On the landing, he spotted a burnt door open an inch. 'It leads to the attic.'

Tanzy nodded, looked back and focused on the room they were in, studying the figures in front of them. 'Father and son?'

'Looks that way.' McCabe focused on the boy under the window. 'He's probably no older than ten. Imagine the pain they endured.'

'Unimaginable.' Tanzy exhaled heavily, gazing around at the sea of charred items: single bed, table, chair, television, games console. If not for the shape, the items would be unrecognisable. 'Just the father and son?'

Byrd turned to him. 'No. Come this way.' He stepped around Tanzy out onto the landing and took a left into the front bedroom. In the corner, were two figures crouching down holding each other. They resembled black mannequins you'd see in a shop window, though the skin wasn't shiny and smooth, it was crispy and rough.

'Jesus. The whole family gone like that.' Tanzy looked down for a moment. 'Who the hell did this to them?'

McCabe walked in. He was short but stocky with shoulders like boulders. His younger years spent boxing hadn't helped his looks but had certainly given him that rough, don't-take-shit-from-anyone attitude. 'Some evil bastards. I heard the origin was at the bottom of the stairs. My guess is that the father heard something and went out onto the landing. Then someone lit the stairs and he fled into his son's room. The other child came out of his room and came in here with Mum. Judging by their windows, it would have been impossible to get out and that would have been the only way.'

The small area of the window at the top looked like it could open but there'd be no way to climb up and safely get down.

'Do we know who the family are?'

Byrd nodded. 'According to a neighbour, the husband was Danny Walters. The wife was called Jessica. And their two sons were Mark and Peter. They were eleven and seven.'

Tanzy didn't say anything, instead looked down sadly at Jessica and one of the boys.

They spent a few minutes in the room and decided to make their way back to the landing.

Tanzy pulled the charred door open and peered up, seeing a wooden ladder leading to an open hatch. The attic was well lit by natural daylight judging by the colours. 'You all right up there?'

'Yeah,' replied a male voice.

'I'm coming up.' Tanzy stepped inside the small space and climbed the ladder. The attic was spacious with only a wardrobe and pale blue carpet.

'See anything?'

The fireman shook his head. 'Was checking for fire damage.'

Tanzy studied the room and went over to the wardrobe. After finding only old, unused coats and hanging clothes, he closed it and went back to the landing. Byrd and McCabe were heading down the stairs as Tanzy stepped on the landing, so he followed them.

Harry Law, the senior fire investigator, entered through the front door. He was a big man in stature, nearly towering over Byrd who wasn't short himself at six feet.

The detectives shook his familiar hand. They'd worked with him on previous cases, unfortunately under similar circumstances.

'The origin was here.' Tanzy pointed to the third step behind him.

Law frowned. 'It is. I didn't know you were so clued up, Detective?'

'One of your men told me before I went upstairs. The guy with the moustache. Carlton.'

'Carlton?' Law asked.

'Roger Carlton. He showed me before.'

'We don't have anyone here named Roger Carlton.'

It was Tanzy's turn to frown. 'He — he was just here before. He headed that way, which I'm assuming is the kitchen.'

Harry Law checked the dining room and the kitchen, finding both of them empty.

'I've been outside talking with Forensics,' Law said, turning back to Tanzy. 'No one has come out.'

'If he didn't go out the front, then he's gone out the back.' Tanzy pointed through the French doors that led into the small, narrow yard.

Law peered through the glass into the yard, seeing the back gate was wide open.

4

Tuesday, early morning
Napier Street, Darlington

The man who called himself Roger Carlton had seen what he wanted. What he was looking for wasn't there.

He had heard someone enter the house and stop at the base of the stairs. He thought it would be better to leave the kitchen, pretend he was looking at something on the dining room ceiling.

Good job he did.

A detective named Tanzy had taken him for a fire investigator and asked him about the fire. If he hadn't been responsible for pouring petrol on the stairs and igniting the fire, he wouldn't have been able to tell him where the point of origin was. Obviously, he wasn't as clued up as a fire investigator, but he believed the detective bought the story.

Dressed in the firefighter uniform he'd purchased from eBay, he exited the house through the back gate, took a left, and at the end of the alley, he went right towards Duke Street. He crossed the road and glanced behind him to check no one was there, searching for him.

He took a left into East Raby Street and saw his car parked up ahead. The street was quiet. It was before eight. He imagined the people inside the houses as he passed them, just waking up to another normal day, the kids off to school, the parents off to work, all eating their cereal around the table with their heads over their iPads, not knowing what had happened last night only a few streets away. They might have heard the fire engine late last night, but people only care if it affects them directly. The man approached the car, smiling, knowing the media would soon be there, with their eager reporters and happy snappy photographers. He couldn't wait to see it on the news later.

He used a fob from his pocket to open the car and got inside. Once there, he took off his helmet and placed it on the seat next to him. He then carefully took the fake moustache off his upper lip and dropped it in the passenger footwell.

He started the car, put the gear in first, and edged out, making his way to the bottom of the street, where he took a left and went back up Duke Street. At Larchfield Street, he went right, idling along until he reached Napier Street and slowed to a crawl, peering at the sea of police and firemen beyond the small crowds of people. Among the people standing near the door, he spotted the Detective Tanzy who he'd spoken to in the dining room, looking confused.

He smiled, focused forward, and whispered, 'Fire, fire, fire,' over and over again until he arrived home.

5

Tuesday, early morning
Napier Street, Darlington

Tanzy and Byrd approached DC Tiffin, who they knew was the first responder at the scene, standing a few feet from the front door of the house.

'Anne,' Byrd said. 'Is there anyone called Roger Carlton on that list?'

She frowned, looked down at the paperwork.

'No, he's not listed here.'

The fire superintendent, Harry Law, walked out of the house a moment later, and looked their way, looking for an update on the imposter.

'So why was he in there?' Tanzy said to no one in particular.

They heard footsteps behind them and turned to see the two senior forensics, Emily Hope and Jacob Tallow, dressed in their white disposable coveralls and face masks. They both took off their masks, relieved to finally breathe some clean air.

'How's it going?' Byrd asked them.

Harry Law, a tall, overweight man with a goatee — the kind you would see standing outside a pub as a doorman you wouldn't want to mess with — turned towards the senior forensic officers, interested in their answer. From the years he had been doing it, he had seen his fair share of fires and the damage they had caused. Seldom had he walked into something like this: a family of four burnt to a crisp. It was tragic, to say the least.

Hope sighed and dipped her shoulders looking towards Tallow, who met her gaze with a sad smile. Tallow knew Hope's body language indicated she didn't want to discuss it with Byrd and Tanzy. Seeing the events unravel in her mind was bad enough, but to speak of them was different.

'I think you know roughly what happened,' Tallow started, 'but from what we've seen so far, Danny Walters was affected first, probably on the landing, judging by his position in the back bedroom. I think he spotted the fire and went in to save his son, then died halfway across the bedroom, probably more from the pain than the burns. He probably passed out.'

'Vasovagal syncope,' said Byrd.

Tanzy frowned at him. 'Vaso what?'

Byrd smiled thinly. 'When a person is subject to intense pain, the brain informs the body it can no longer withstand it and temporarily shuts down. I can't imagine the pain he and his family went through.'

Tanzy nodded but said nothing.

'Someone's been reading,' commented Hope, tilting her head.

Tallow continued. 'The fire no doubt took the whole room and got to his son who'd hidden in the corner. I noticed scratches on the window where he'd clawed at it. He probably wasn't strong enough to break the glass.'

Byrd winced, picturing the scene in his mind.

'The mother and other son found in the front bedroom tried to stay out of it, but I think, judging by the markings on the floor, that both bedrooms had been covered in petrol beforehand.'

'How can you be sure?' Tanzy asked, his brows furrowing to the centre of his forehead.

'I'm not one hundred per cent sure because I'm no fire expert.' She turned to Harry Law for support, who was listening to her theory. 'But a material burns differently when covered with something flammable. To me, it appears both rooms were doused in petrol, and they didn't stand a chance.'

Byrd looked towards Law. 'Does that sound right?'

Law gave a confident nod. 'I agree with your colleague here.'

'So, this so-called Roger Carlton walked into the house,' Byrd said, 'went into their bedroom, covered the carpets in petrol without waking anyone up?'

Law and Hope and Tallow all shrugged, unsure if that would be feasible.

Byrd focused at the floor, then back to Tallow. 'Are there signs of a break-in?'

'We haven't got around to that yet,' he explained. 'We need to check the windows and the doors.'

'Guys, have a look out the back,' a voice said behind them.

They turned. DC Leonard was standing on the front doorstep.

'When did you get here?' Tanzy asked him, frowning.

'Minutes after you did,' Leonard said. 'Come have a look.'

'What have you found, James?'

'I'll show you.'

6

DC Leonard led them down the hall, through the dining room and into the kitchen. To the right, was an open door which led them into the narrow yard. A nice little space filled with various plant pots and trellis along the furthest wall. The sun rose brightly from the east, hitting the yard from the left, already warming it up.

Leonard walked halfway down the yard and stopped.

Byrd, Tanzy, Hope, Tallow and Harry Law stopped behind him, wondering what he'd found so important enough to show them.

'What is it?' Byrd asked, studying the yard but couldn't see anything obvious.

Leonard pointed at the far corner of the yard. Everyone looked. Three bikes were locked up under a slanted roof which had been built purposely to keep them dry during wet weather.

'What are we supposed to be looking at?' Tanzy asked him.

'You see it?'

Tallow nodded. 'I can. The camera just under the roof?'

Leonard nodded.

Tanzy stepped forward, searching for any wires attached to it. It didn't take him long to spot something trailing across the wall at the back until it hit the brickwork and went through into the house.

'We'll be able to see Roger Carlton leaving if it still works,' Tanzy noted, thinking logically.

'Good spot,' Byrd praised him.

Byrd and Tanzy turned and stepped into the kitchen, looking for a wire coming through the internal wall at a similar height.

'Where is it?' Byrd was having no luck.

Tanzy shrugged, also unable to spot anything.

There was a closed door at the end of the kitchen. Tanzy opened it to reveal a bathroom so small it made him feel claustrophobic. You couldn't even swing a cat in it. The toilet was on the right, a small basin opposite, and a narrow, short bath against the far wall, with minimal floor space, most of which was taken by a shower mat. Up on the wall to the right, he saw a wire protrude through the plasterboard and run horizontally along the wall, painted with the same colour as the walls.

'There.'

They followed it until it dropped vertically, then a metre off the floor, it went through to the kitchen. Tanzy backed out and looked in the corner of the worktop, noticing a small black electronic box, roughly the same size of a wireless router, plugged in but there was no power.

'It's dead.' Byrd realised the plug was on, but the device's green light wasn't.

'The DB is probably under the stairs. Will have been destroyed in the fire.'

Byrd tilted his head. 'The DB?'

'Distribution board. The main electrical box or consumer unit.'

Byrd pushed his lips out at Tanzy's terminology. 'If we took it, we could give it to Mac at the Digital Forensics Unit.

He should be able to get it going, or at least find out what happened before the fire.'

Tanzy nodded. They met with Leonard and the forensics, who were still out in the yard. 'We're gonna head back to hopefully see what's on here. If Roger Carlton or whoever he is, left through that gate, we'll identify him.' He turned to Tallow. 'Will you guys be okay?'

Tallow nodded. 'We'll be here most of the day. There's loads to do.'

Byrd and Tanzy both knew what was involved in forensic work and would catch up with them later back at the station. DC Tiffin signed them out when they exited the house using the front door and took a few steps away from the house.

Byrd took off his mask and held it in his hand. 'Where you parked, Ori?'

Tanzy pointed along the street at his Golf.

They walked side by side back to their cars. 'How's Claire doing?'

Byrd nodded. 'She's good. She's getting really big.'

'Must be coming up six months soon, is it?'

'She calls it weeks. Twenty-five weeks.' He smiled. 'Roughly six months.'

'See you back at the station. I can't wait to tell Fuller all about this one.'

Byrd smiled and got into his car.

7

Byrd and Tanzy hung their coats on the back of the chairs at the rear of the long, rectangular office. The six rows of desks were split by a walkway down the middle, leaving two desks on either side of each row. Tanzy and Byrd were seated at the back on the left-hand side. Directly behind them was DCI Martin Fuller's office.

No doubt he'd heard what had happened early this morning and would be expecting both Byrd and Tanzy to inform him as soon as they returned.

Byrd knocked on his door and waited for the usual 'Come in' before he opened it. Tanzy followed. They both took a seat at his desk.

'Morning,' Fuller said.

He was a thickset man with short dark hair and possessed a look of impatience about him. He wasted no time getting to the point and didn't care if his peers liked him or not. Being a DCI meant having to get on with things and manage people in a certain way. Fuller had a lot of responsibility and things moved fast. He'd been the DCI since the departure of DCI June Thornton and ran things differently to the way she had, but everyone in the office seemed to be getting used to him, although they didn't agree with his methods. He had a scar on the right side of his face from a knife attack when he was only weeks into his training. It didn't improve his looks, that's for sure.

'Tell me . . .' he said to them.

Byrd sighed. 'House fire, boss.'

Fuller waited, stared hard at them.

Byrd continued. 'Looks like arson. Petrol was used. It wasn't an accident.'

'How many dead?'

'Four. Father, mother and two sons.'

It was Fuller's turn to sigh. He looked down at the desk and stayed silent for a moment. The detectives waited.

'I knew it wouldn't last,' he said, shaking his head.

'What's that?' Tanzy asked him.

'We've had three great months, three.' He held up three fingers. 'Darlington was on the rise. Our figures have been great compared to what happened a few months ago.'

Byrd felt his skin warming but decided to keep silent. It was all about the figures to Fuller. All about how his team weighed up against the other constabularies. God, it wasn't a bloody competition and it bloody pissed Byrd off.

'What do we know?'

'Fire was started at the base of the stairs, and it took no time to spread up them because the carpets were covered in petrol. There's evidence to suggest the bedroom carpets were also covered in petrol. Harry Law agreed with that theory.'

'So, whoever did it, had gone into the bedrooms while they were sleeping?'

'Seems so,' Tanzy said.

'Jesus. Takes balls that.'

'When I was there, I spoke to a guy who called himself Roger Carlton. He was looking at the ceiling in the dining room and told me about the fire. Turns out, after speaking with Harry Law, that no one by that name works for the fire department but when we went looking for him, he'd gone. The back gate was open.'

'How on earth did he just walk in?' Fuller frowned as he picked up his coffee and sipped it.

'We don't know,' Byrd said. 'But we found something.'

Fuller waited.

'DC Leonard found a camera at the end of the yard. We traced the wire back and found a little black box at the end of the kitchen. Fortunately, it doesn't look like the fire had reached the kitchen. We've handed the box to Mac in DFU. He said he'd check it out straight away. We'll head over when we leave here.'

'What do we know about the victims?' Fuller leaned back into his chair.

'So far, not much. We need to do some digging.'

'Forensics?'

'Still at the house.'

Fuller nodded. 'Keep me updated.'

Byrd and Tanzy stood up, left the office, and returned to their desks. According to a neighbour, they were informed the victim's name was Danny Walters, so searched that first. Several results came up, so they narrowed the search to Darlington. There was only one specific to that location and that Danny Walters was forty-one years old.

A little later, after several cups of coffee, they'd built up a profile for him, noting he worked at B&Q as a customer service assistant and had no previous convictions. He was nothing out of the ordinary according to the profile; nothing stood out to explain any reason why he and his family were subject to such brutality.

'Why him, though?' Tanzy read over the facts on his screen. 'No previous trouble, not even a parking fine. He did a level six diploma in Business Management and used to work in the engineering sector as a commissioning engineer. He seems pretty normal.'

'They always do, Ori.'

Determined, they continued to dig.

'How are Pip and the kids?' Byrd asked.

'Good. She hasn't touched in ages. She received her badge last week and came home with the biggest smile on her face. She's feeling much better about herself and life in general.' Tanzy's wife, Pip, had had issues with drinking and had constantly been hitting the bottle over the past few years. She put it down to her father, the way he used to treat her and her mother. Violence. Sexual abuse. Byrd knew the stories weren't pleasant.

'The kids are great too,' Tanzy went on. 'Jasmine will be eleven soon. Still knows everything.'

Byrd smiled.

'And Eric is loving his Lego. He built a tower for me last night. Told me he wanted to put it beside my bed so I could wake up to it every day. It's honestly *this* big.' Tanzy raised his hand from the desk and indicated a level above their heads.

Byrd was still grinning. 'Kids, eh.'

'You'll soon find out, Max.'

'I will. It won't be long.' Byrd clicked his mouse a few times. 'How's the judo going?'

'Good. They're coming on.' By "they" he meant his students.

Tanzy had done judo since he was six years old and had recently started tutoring beginners at the Dolphin Centre, often helping out tutoring the more advance classes too. At six foot two, weighing barely twelve stone and a six-pack that every man envied and most women desired, he was a hit with the ladies. His short — almost bald — hair took no maintenance and trimmed goatee enhanced his beautiful narrow face.

Byrd, however, wasn't as fortunate with his looks. His hair was much longer, in need of a trim and he was clean-shaven. Months ago, Byrd had been overweight. He knew that himself, as he had continually been feeling lethargic and slow, but playing football twice a week and eating the right things — plenty of greens Tanzy had told him — the two stones he'd lost a few months ago had stayed off. And he felt amazing. He had never had the six-pack that Tanzy had, nor did he care, but he'd settled on being content.

'You fancy it?' Tanzy asked him.

'Judo isn't for me, Ori.' He shook his head. 'I'll stick to football.'

Tanzy threw a smile his way, knowing it was a previous topic they'd discussed.

On the desk next to Byrd, the phone rang. He picked it up.

'It's Mac. I've had a look at the camera footage from Napier Street.'

'Anything interesting?'

'You need to see this.'

8

Tuesday afternoon
Police station

Byrd and Tanzy immediately went to see Mac in his office. There were two chairs positioned next to each other in front of the computer screen when they entered, so they made their way around and sat down.

'How's Mac?' asked Byrd.

Mac was approaching the age of forty. He'd been doing digital forensics for nearly twenty years; there was no one in the force with his skill set. He'd put on weight due to the nature of his job, which involved sitting at a desk for most of the day and not much physical activity. They'd often seen him eating chocolate bars or noticed empty crisp packets on his desk.

Byrd noticed the black box they had retrieved from the kitchen earlier that morning on the desk next to his keyboard with a wire plugged into it from the computer.

'Mac's good.' He clicked several times. 'Watch this.'

On the screen, there was today's date. Mac clicked on the time bar at the bottom and dragged it just past 8 a.m. The camera had the ideal view of both the French doors leading to the dining room and the back door leading to the kitchen. A minute later, the man who called himself Roger Carlton stepped out quickly and headed towards the gate then vanished.

'Go back,' Byrd said. 'Pause it on his face.'

Mac did. Byrd looked at Tanzy.

'That the guy you spoke with?'

'Yeah.'

'How tall was he?' Byrd asked Tanzy.

Tanzy thought for a moment. 'He wasn't six foot. Maybe five ten tops.'

Because of the yellow composite helmet he was wearing, they couldn't see his hair properly but could tell it was long. The visor on the helmet was pushed up, shielding his eyes but the moustache stood out like a sore thumb.

'Is that tash real?' asked Byrd.

'It looked real,' said Tanzy.

'Tom Selleck would be proud of that,' Mac noted.

'What time did you speak with him?' Byrd asked.

'Just after eight.'

'Go earlier this morning, see what time he got there.'

Mac had already done this before calling the detectives and stopped the time at 7.49 a.m., then pressed play. Roger Carlton appeared on the camera a moment later, coming from the right where the back gate was. He walked up to the back door, pulled out a key, and opened it.

'Where did he get the key from?' Tanzy asked, frowning.

Mac smiled, closed the video, then hovered his mouse over another file, and clicked open. 'Now watch this.'

They both frowned at the time and date at the bottom of the screen, indicating it was two days earlier.

'Why have we gone back two days?' Tanzy asked.

Mac pointed at the screen. At 2.03 p.m. on Sunday, the back door opened, and a man stepped out with some kind of cleaning device. It was roughly two feet high and a foot wide. Most of it was made of see-through plastic. The liquid inside was black. Byrd and Tanzy knew it was Roger Carlton as he stood in the corner of the yard near the back door pulling off the top of the unit and tipping the contents down the drain.

'What on earth is he doing?' said Tanzy, leaning forward an inch.

'So, he was there two days ago?' Byrd ran a hand through his hair.

'It certainly looks like him,' Mac said, with a shrug.

Roger turned and before he went back into the kitchen, they got a view of his face, clearly seeing his moustache and thick mop of black hair.

Mac scrolled the time back and they watched it multiple times.

'Why was he there cleaning the carpets two days ago?' Tanzy asked, glancing at both Byrd and Mac as if looking for the answer.

'That's when he must have taken the key,' said Byrd. 'Did Harry Law say what time they'd got to the house?'

Tanzy nodded. 'He said just after five. A call came in by a neighbour opposite. Said they got up to go to the toilet just after half four and had seen the flames through the front bedroom window.'

'And Roger returned just before eight a.m.?'

Mac nodded. 'There's something else . . .'

The detectives waited, both intrigued.

Mac closed the video screen, found another file in the folder and double-clicked. The screen opened, showing the same shot of the back yard. The only difference was the date told the detectives it was two days further back, making it four days ago. The time was 8.13 a.m.

'He was there on Friday, too?' Byrd pursed his lips, trying to fathom why.

Again, Mac nodded and focused back on the screen. Roger Carlton entered the screen from the right and made his way to the back door. He pulled out a small case, lowered to his knee, grabbed a tool and used it to open the lock. Once the door opened, he went inside for approximately seven minutes before he came back out.

'He's got some balls, this guy,' Tanzy noted, shaking his head.

Silence grew around them for a while.

'So, no one, apart from you, saw him in there?' Byrd asked Tanzy.

Tanzy shrugged. 'I don't know. Why?'

'Surely if one of the firemen had seen him, they'd have known he wasn't one of them. It's almost like he knew when to come back.'

'He could have been around the front, watching them going in and out of the front door.'

'It's possible he knew they wouldn't be in there at that exact time. And it's possible he knew who Harry Law was.'

'But the question is,' said Tanzy, leaning back a little, 'why he was there. What was he looking for in the kitchen? I don't know how long he was in there, but now I think of it I'm sure I heard the sounds of drawers opening and closing. Then he appeared in the dining room and started looking at the ceiling.'

Byrd frowned, thinking hard.

'This makes no sense to me,' said Mac, raising his brows. 'Why was he cleaning the carpets on Sunday?'

Byrd smiled.

'What's funny?' Mac asked him.

'Maybe he was there cleaning the carpets.' Byrd looked their way. 'But whatever substance he used, whether a chemical that cleaned carpets or something that acted as a fire accelerant, the Walters wouldn't have known any different. He probably told them to ignore the smell and that it would pass in a few days. He didn't need to go into their rooms and pour petrol in the bedrooms because he knew the bedroom carpets would burn fiercely.' Byrd sighed. 'He only needed to pour petrol on the stairs to get things going. This attack had been meticulously planned.' Byrd looked away from the still shot of Roger Carlton. 'We are dealing with someone very dangerous here.'

9

Tuesday afternoon
Police station

The detectives returned to their desks with the notes they'd made. Mac had taken several screenshots of Roger Carlton leaving the house and while he was there on Sunday afternoon, specifically shots of him emptying the contents of the cleaning device into the drain. He emailed the images to both Tanzy and Byrd.

The detectives opened the images and had another look. Neither of them had seen him before nor did he look familiar. They both concluded that the moustache and his hair were both fake — no one would be walking around in public with a moustache like that.

Byrd picked the most concise and clear photo of Roger Carlton and emailed it to their media representative, making sure he included DCI Martin Fuller in the email for transparency within the team. The faster they got this on the news, the quicker someone would get in touch with any information.

The time ticked on. Tanzy had phoned the senior forensics, but they'd not picked up their lab phone. He decided to walk down, finding the lab empty apart from the forensic trainee, Amanda Forrest, sitting at her desk.

'Hope and Tallow not back yet?' Tanzy asked her.

She told him they hadn't returned from Napier Street and would be a few more hours. He thanked her and went back to the office. Before he found his desk, DC Leonard called his name as he passed.

'What is it?' Tanzy walked over to Leonard's desk.

'I've done some digging on the name Roger Carlton. There are only fifteen people in the UK with that name. It shouldn't be too long to narrow it down.'

'Good.' Tanzy nodded in hope. 'Check everything. You know the drill. Social media and such.'

Leonard nodded and continued clicking and typing. Tanzy returned to his desk and told Byrd that Tallow and Hope were still not there. It was an extensive job analysing a crime scene from a forensic point of view. Everything took time. Tallow and Hope were very meticulous and methodical in the way they did it and worked superbly together. It hadn't always been like that. When they were first matched up, all they had done was argue and disagree with each other. Most likely because they were opposites but, in the end, opposites seem to attract. Emily Hope was single, liked getting tattoos, drinking too much and listening to loud music. She took no shit and wouldn't bat an eye if she upset anyone. Jacob Tallow was the polar opposite. He led a quieter life, always had. He had a wife who worked at a local DIY store and was equally as bland as he was. However, his plain persona was a good trait because he didn't waste time talking shit and got straight to the point. Everything was black and white. He focused on the facts and did his job as thoroughly as anyone. They shared a similar work ethic and had learned to enjoy each other's company, eventually building an unbreakable bond.

Tallow would always take a video of the crime scene upon arrival so they could analyse the scene as it was before they started working, potentially moving important items and interfering with evidence. After that, they would get to work. In this case, finding the four burnt victims in a house fire didn't make the cause of death very difficult to work out. Because the bodies had been involved in such a horrific crime, they would be sent to the basement of the hospital where pathologists would study further to determine anything beyond the burns. Byrd and Tanzy had informed them they'd been in touch with the lead coroner of County Durham, Peter Gibbs, about what had happened. He told them he was currently in London attending a medical conference and to ensure Forensics had taken their usual video and a vast selection of photos so he could review them at his next opportunity. Peter had plenty of faith in both Tallow and Hope, knowing they'd get everything he needed to put together a comprehensive report.

For the areas of the house that hadn't been affected by the fire, such as the front door and back door, they'd check for fingerprints on the handles, footprints inside and outside the house, fibres of clothing that had fallen off the suspect, bodily fluids, such as sweat, urine, or blood, that may be found. It was a demanding, lengthy process.

Tanzy sat down at his desk, noticed Byrd typing away on his keyboard. 'Doing your report already?'

'Yep. Best doing fresh in my mind.'

Tanzy pulled himself in, moving the mouse to awaken his screen. 'Pointless us still doing them.'

'It's what they want, Ori.'

Tanzy turned to him. 'No, it's what DCI Thornton wanted. Not Fuller.'

Byrd smiled quietly.

'What?'

'Just get it typed up.' Byrd finished typing a sentence. 'It helps put things into perspective.' He nodded. 'Higher up probably told Fuller to continue it — it isn't a bad thing, Ori.'

Tanzy sighed and paused. 'Coffee?'

'Not right now. I need to finish this.'

Tanzy shook his head, got up, went to the canteen and shortly came back with a coffee. With no time like the present, he placed his coffee by his keyboard and followed Byrd's footsteps by typing up his report, agreeing it was better fresh in his mind. The office was loud, busy with PCs at their desks, some talking into phones, others typing away. The fire at Napier Street had certainly got people moving around and chasing things up.

Just as Tanzy had finished his report, he heard footsteps to his left and looked up to see PC Amy Weaver standing there with a concerned look on her face.

'Amy, what's wrong?' Tanzy asked her.

'You both need to see this,' she said, her tone serious.

Frowning, Byrd and Tanzy stood and quickly followed Weaver back to her desk.

10

When Byrd and Tanzy approached Weaver's desk, they saw DC Leonard, DC Cornty and DS Stockdale standing there, staring at the screen. Stockdale moved back to allow Weaver to drop into her seat and eyed Tanzy a certain way so he knew whatever they were about to be shown was very serious.

Tanzy and Byrd stopped next to Stockdale and focused over Weaver's shoulder at the computer screen.

'What's happening, Amy?' Byrd asked.

'This has been uploaded to YouTube, sir,' she explained quickly. 'It has over twenty-five thousand views so far. It's been shared across all social sites, including Facebook, Twitter and Instagram. It's a video.'

Byrd frowned. 'A video? Amy, we don't have time for this.'

'Sir, you might want to watch this one,' DI Leonard said matter-of-factly.

Byrd regarded his tone and turned towards the screen. 'Okay.'

Amy moved the mouse cursor around the screen and double-clicked to enlarge the video so it filled the whole screen. The still shot was dark. There was a small silhouette of a figure in the long, rectangular window. A tiny hand was pressed against the glass. The features of the face couldn't be seen in the shot, nor could any great details of what the image was.

PC Weaver pressed play.

Tanzy and Byrd watched it for the first time with wide eyes and didn't say a word throughout. It was the fourth time the others had seen it and they were just as disturbed as they were the first time around. The video lasted for forty-five seconds. When it finished, Byrd breathed deeply and asked her to play it again.

'Jesus,' Tanzy said, then gasped.

The title of the video was "Element One".

'What on earth is Element One?' Tanzy asked no one in particular. They all shook their heads in confusion.

Amy looked back at him and said, 'Read the comments, boss.'

Judging how the others didn't lean in meant they'd already read them, so moved back for Tanzy and Byrd to have a read. Their eyes scanned the dozens of comments in the thread.

Jay89 — Rest In Peace little person.
Dom454 — Jesus, someone said this was Darlington — anyone confirm this?
ElaineJef01 — What an awful way to go.
RuthDal — Oh God, can you imagine how that would feel?

Byrd slammed the desk with the side of his fist causing everyone, including Tanzy, to jump. 'Is this what I think it is?'

Weaver shrugged, not wanting to say anything to further his anger. Leonard and Stockdale stayed silent. Seldom had they seen anger from Max Byrd before.

'Did this bastard do this and then video it from the fucking alley?' Byrd asked.

Again, no one spoke.

'Does anyone know?' He slammed his hand on the desk again.

'We don't know, sir,' Weaver said quietly.

'Play it again,' Byrd instructed her.

She turned with sad eyes and scrolled the time bar back to the beginning. At the start of the clip, it showed the small figure, who Byrd and Tanzy could only assume was one of the sons, clawing at the window frantically. Behind him, the room was glowing colours of red and orange, energetically dancing on the walls and ceiling behind him. Through the speakers, they could hear his high-pitched screaming, his desperation to escape but not having the power to do so. With nowhere to go, the only thing he could do was wait until the flames consumed him. As the window got brighter, the boy hit the window for the final time before his little body disappeared. The glass then illuminated with an orange flare and the whole room shone like the sun. His crying then stopped and all that could be heard was laughter from the person who recorded it. Then a voice said, 'Fire, fire, fire, fire . . .' repeatedly.

They all felt physically sick. Byrd and Tanzy both knew from being at Napier Street earlier how horrific this crime had been and if they were in the same position, how awful it must have been to be inside and to feel the severe pain they'd endured. To see the little boy clawing at the window and hearing his shrieking built a fit of anger in them they hadn't felt in a very long time.

'Jesus Christ!' Byrd screamed, turning, and punching the wall behind him. The whole office became deadly silent. Everyone glared at him, wondering what on earth was going on.

Tanzy turned and took a few steps towards Byrd, taking hold of his wrist 'No, Max.'

Byrd breathed heavily, his chest rising and falling quickly as he rested his forehead on the wall near where he'd damaged it.

'Are you all right?' Tanzy said softly, resting a palm on his back.

Byrd turned slowly, opened his eyes, and noticed everyone looking at him. The ones who had stood up abruptly to see what the commotion was about sat back down immediately when his gaze fell on them. Byrd looked at Tanzy and gave a small nod.

'I'm sorry for that, guys, I . . .' He shook his head and said nothing else. Tanzy looked back at Weaver and asked her the name of the user that had uploaded it.

'*RCarl20* uploaded it,' she said.

'Okay, we need to find this fucker ASAP,' he said, addressing Weaver, Stockdale and Leonard. They all nodded and listened further. 'I've emailed the still shot we have from the camera positioned at the back of the yard that picked up the guy calling himself Roger Carlton. We need this on the news.' He looked at Weaver specifically. 'Get this out on our Facebook, Twitter, and news update accounts.'

She nodded. 'Sir.'

The others dispersed towards their desks, leaving Tanzy with Byrd, who looked like he was going to be sick, his body slightly bent forward.

Tanzy put a hand on his shoulder again. 'You okay, Max?'

Byrd took a deep breath, stood up straight and managed a nod. 'Yeah. It's just the thought of Claire and I bringing a child into a world with sick bastards like this around.'

Tanzy forced a smile and looked him in the eye. 'We'll get him. We always do.'

Byrd half smiled and, with a new lease of motivation, he said, 'Right, come on, let's find him.'

11

Tuesday afternoon
Police station

DCI Fuller had been informed about the uploaded video and had been straight to see Byrd and Tanzy. Unfortunately, with nothing to offer yet in the way of explanation or who *RCarl20* was, he left disappointed, storming back into his office and slamming the door.

'Dickhead,' Tanzy muttered under his breath.

The time was approaching 3 p.m. Mac, the DFU guy, had asked them to give him until then to see what he could come up with.

Byrd and Tanzy logged out of their computers, stood up, and made their way across the office towards the opposite side, where they entered the corridor, and a minute later, opened Mac's door. He was sitting at his desk to the right of the small room. His workspace was cluttered with empty chocolate bar wrappers and two empty coke cans. The bin underneath the desk near his feet was full and needed emptying.

He coughed, quickly grabbed the wrappers and threw them into the bin.

'You had enough time?' Byrd entered the room, noticing the mess of it. Not only did the desk define the word clutter but the whole room lacked the TLC you'd expect it to have. Byrd spotted containers with bits of food in placed on the shelving unit behind him and winced, shivering at the thought of how long they'd been there. In the past, Byrd had commented on the state of the office, advising he should keep it tidier as it wasn't very professional. But for now, the detectives had more pressing issues.

'Yeah, yeah. Come in,' Mac said, waving them in.

He edged back a little, allowing Byrd and Tanzy to stop in the centre of the room once they'd rounded his desk and were positioned in front of the three computer monitors. Mac's set up was a gamer's dream. On the right screen, was the YouTube clip they'd seen earlier of the footage recorded from the man who called himself Roger Carlton, the bottom of the clip indicating the username: *RCarl20*.

The middle monitor contained some complicated digital graph that neither Byrd nor Tanzy understood, and the left screen was a word document featuring several paragraphs of text, but the detectives weren't close enough to read them.

'You look well,' Mac said to Byrd. 'Kept the weight off?'

Byrd nodded. 'I have. I told you I would. How's your fitness campaign?'

Mac smiled sadly, staying silent. Byrd didn't need an answer; Mac's rounded shape and the empty chocolate wrappers in the bin gave Byrd all the answers he needed.

Moving on, Byrd asked, 'What have you found?'

'Well, the username *RCarl20* is a new user. It subscribed to YouTube only two weeks ago. It has no display picture or any attached information to the account. The video had been uploaded at 5.36 a.m. this morning.'

Tanzy asked him how many views the video had had now, remembering the vast number it had already reached.

'On the channel itself, nearly seventy thousand.'

'Shit. That is not good.'

'No.'

'I'm surprised that YouTube hasn't taken it down yet?'

Mac to towards Tanzy. 'They will soon. However, I can see the digital patterns of the algorithms. They tell me it's circulating on Facebook, Twitter and Instagram mainly.'

Byrd frowned. 'Is it possible to trace the IP address of the user *RCarl20*?'

'It certainly is. I have the IP address of the phone it was uploaded on. Here, have a look.' Mac leaned to the left and pointed to the furthest screen. The detectives squinted at the number which meant nothing to them. 'I have tracked the IP to the service provider. They told me it was uploaded from a Samsung S10 device.'

'Who's the owner of that phone?' Byrd said.

'Roger Carlton.'

'From the IP address, can we see the location of the device when it was uploaded?'

'We can, but . . .' Mac paused.

The detectives frowned at him and waited.

'The upload came from Oldbury, in Birmingham.'

'Birmingham? How is that possible?' Tanzy wanted to know.

'Two ways. Either the video had been sent to the device registered of Roger Carlton which was in Oldbury at the time of the upload, or he's used some kind of IP diverter.'

'IP diverter?'

Mac nodded twice.

Byrd sighed. 'We need to get on to Leonard, see where he is with these profiles.'

Tanzy agreed with a nod and focused back at the right screen. 'Does the video look right?'

'What do you mean?' Mac asked.

'It's real, isn't it?'

He nodded confidently. 'Without a doubt. I often see videos that have been tampered with. You can tell if it's fake. Any little mistake stands out to someone who knows what they are doing. To make sure for my analysis, I ran it through

Vidreel — an app that savvy techs use to check a video's authenticity — and can confirm it's real.'

'Okay. Let us know if you find anything else,' Byrd said, standing.

They backed out, walked towards the office and, as they entered, Tanzy veered off to the left in the direction of DC Leonard, who was concentrating on his computer screen wearing his new silver-framed reading glasses. The continual headaches he'd been getting, according to the doctor, could be down to needing glasses. So, when Leonard had struggled with the basic eye test at an opticians, he wasn't surprised to be told that he needed them. Tanzy hadn't got used to him in glasses yet.

'Jim.' Tanzy pulled out a chair out and sat down beside him. 'What have we got?'

'From the fifteen registered names of Roger Carlton, the closest we have is in Hull.'

Tanzy squinted. 'Hull?'

Leonard glanced his way. 'Yeah. Only one of them is in the PNC. He's thirty-nine. Attacked two teenagers in a park last April.'

'Where?'

'Westminster, London. His registered address is in Crawley, West Sussex.'

'Any from Oldbury, near Birmingham?'

Leonard shook his head, wondering what was so important about Oldbury.

Tanzy looked defeated. 'What about the PND?'

The Police National Database is a large database of people the police have previously investigated but from their findings, no arrests had been made. The PNC would pick up someone who, in some form, had committed a crime and had been arrested.

'Five of them,' Leonard said. 'Closest one is Oxford.'

Tanzy thought for a moment. 'Do some more digging. I want to see pictures. When you have them, send them over. I want to run them through facial recognition in and around Darlington. If one of the fifteen is our guy, we'll get him.'

Tanzy headed back to his desk and emailed a photo of Roger Carlton over to the media team, who would inform the local news channel and the *Northern Echo* so it made tomorrow's paper. The sooner the public saw the image of the man, the sooner they'd find him.

'I wonder how Tallow and Hope are getting on?' said Byrd, glancing down at his watch, noticing it was just before 8 p.m.

'I'll see if they're back.' Tanzy stood, leaving Byrd focused on his computer. The less time Tanzy spent as his desk reduced the chance of seeing DCI Fuller appear from his office. So far, they hadn't seen him leave so assumed he was still in there. He'd been in such a foul mood all day, no doubt getting it in the neck from higher up regarding what progress had been made. Tanzy knew one thing: he wasn't looking forward to the morning meeting tomorrow.

Tanzy knocked on the forensic lab's door and slowly opened it. 'Anyone here?'

'Yeah. Come in.' The voice sounded distant.

Tanzy entered the cool lab, closed the door courteously, and spotted Jacob Tallow sitting on a stool, leaning over a microscope, studying something at the far side of the room.

'When did you get back?' Tanzy gazed around. No sign of Hope.

'An hour ago. We have all the samples we need. We'll have reports ready for the morning.'

'Emily gone home?'

'Just left, Ori.' Tallow sat straighter and turned his way. 'Hoping to catch her for anything?'

He shook his head. 'No, nothing important.' He padded further into the room. 'Tough day, today, huh?'

'We've had better.' Tallow's tone suggested he seemed distracted from the conversation and allowed his focus to fall on the substance under the scope.

'What's that you're looking at?' Tanzy stopped beside him and leaned to the side to get a better view of the sample under scrutiny. It was dark grey and appeared an ashy texture.

'I've collected it from the carpet in the back bedroom.' Tallow sat straight again, sighing. 'I'm hoping it indicates what chemicals were used. I'll do some chemistry in the morning which should give us a better idea.'

'Thanks.' Tanzy turned and headed for the door. 'See you tomorrow, Jacob.'

Tanzy returned to the office which seemed quieter than before. The late shift workers were out patrolling the streets and dealing with a list of issues that had backed up during the day. He could see the top of Byrd's head on his approach to his desk, surprised he was still there. Only when he rounded the end computer, could he see he was on the phone.

Byrd lowered the phone, placed it on the desk, and sighed. 'Been a long day, Ori.'

'Never a dull day.' Tanzy pulled out his chair and sat down. 'Who was that?'

'Harry Law from the fire department. Confirming the fire origin being on the stairs.'

Tanzy nodded, turning to him. 'Tallow is studying something from the carpets. Hopefully he'll let us know what the chemical Roger Carlton used was by the morning.'

Byrd smiled. 'Can't wait.' He stood up, put on his jacket and pushed his chair in. 'That's enough fun for one day. See you tomorrow.'

12

On the desk in front of him there were dozens of photographs clustered in no particular order. He ran his small, dark eyes over them, slowly switching from photo to photo, absorbing each scene in detail. The colour of their clothing. The shade of their skin tones. The way they moved, especially the eldest son, who shuffled with a slight limp. The way the sunlight shone down on their innocent, clueless faces. The brickwork of the house behind them had stood there for decades, not knowing the next day would be a witness to a horrific murder.

He then looked down at the photo in his hands. It was the last photo he'd taken of them. They had no idea it would be their last ever smiles captured in the still shot, which he'd keep tucked away forever.

Watching the house for a couple of days, he had got used to their routines and their little habits. Friday morning, he'd watched Danny Walters head to work just before eight. That was the benefit of the summer months; the mornings were nice, warm. There was no getting up earlier to de-ice the windows and get the car warmed up. Minutes after Walters had left, his missus, Jessica, and their sons, Mark and Peter, had come out. They had walked a few paces before they got into a red Renault Clio, then a moment later, they had gone.

The man had got out of his car and locked it, then made his way to the bottom of the street and taken a left up the alley. He'd counted the houses along to make sure the numbers matched up and he had the right house. Luckily, the gate wasn't locked, so he'd walked in and made his way to the back door. He'd lowered to his knee, used his tools to open the door, and gone straight through the dining room and up the stairs into the bedroom at the front. From his pocket he'd pulled a small, sealed plastic bag filled with black liquid, slid the lock across, and poured half of it on to the carpet, spacing the drops to cover a decent area. He then went into the back bedroom and did the same. Once satisfied he'd gone downstairs and placed a business card on the front doormat as if it had been posted like any other letter, then turned, made his way back through the house, locked the back door with his tool and gone back to his car.

Later that day, he'd had a phone call to asked if he'd go round and see if he could clean their carpets. The leaflet he'd left on their doormat advertised a carpet cleaning service he was confident would do the trick. So, he went there to have a look at the awful mess in the two bedrooms, watching the confusion on Jessica and Danny's face, wondering where these marks had come from. He told them he'd need some strong chemicals and would return on Sunday to do the job. When he'd gone back, he'd taken the back door key and checked there were no locks on the gate when he was emptying the cleaning unit in the outside drain.

It was simple really.

He placed the photo on the desk, then leaned to his right, grabbing a piece of paper printed with four empty boxes. Each one bore the heading "Element". He took up a pen and placed a cross in the first box, whispering 'Fire, fire, fire . . .'

He fastened his gaze on the next empty box, staring at it for a long time. Soon, he'd be able to put a cross in that one too.

13

Tuesday night
Low Coniscliffe, Darlington

Byrd slowed the car and pulled up on to the kerb outside his house. He was shattered. It was only nine o'clock. He sniffed. The car was filled with a delicious aroma, rising from the package on the passenger seat beside him. He couldn't wait to get inside to eat it.

He removed his shoes once he was through the door and made his way into the kitchen. Claire was sitting at the kitchen table reading her Kindle. Byrd placed the bagged food down on the worktop to the right and went over to her, bent down and kissed her forehead.

'How're my favourite people?' Byrd asked.

Tiredly, she smiled and lowered her Kindle to the table. 'He's wearing me out.' She rubbed her pregnant belly with her hands.

Byrd placed a hand over hers.

'What's in the bag?' She looked past him to the contents on the worktop.

'Your favourite. I didn't know if you'd had something to eat but I got it anyway.'

'I have already eaten, but I'm eating for two now, so . . .'

Byrd smiled and kissed her again. He went over to the cupboard, pulled a plate out and plated her some food up. Since she became pregnant, Claire had developed a desire for chicken parmesan, which was strange, as she'd not eaten it very often before. It was weird how women could develop cravings while they were pregnant that made no sense at all. When she told Byrd about her new hunger, about the food she'd usually turned her nose up at, she explained that her mother had told her when she was pregnant with her, she had been obsessed with mint imperials. And when she couldn't get them, she'd chew on chalk. They'd both laughed at that one.

Byrd poured a dollop of sauce on the side of her plate, made her a drink, and carried them both over to the table. She tucked into the food as if she hadn't eaten in days.

'What are you reading?'

She chewed her mouthful of food, and said, '*Recursion*. Blake Crouch.'

'Crouch?' Byrd asked, standing at the worktop, filling his own plate. 'Like the footballer?'

Claire frowned. 'No . . . American guy. Sci-fi. One of the best reads this year, apparently.'

Byrd took a seat opposite her. 'Is that so?'

She smiled and forked a load of food into her mouth. They ate in silence for a few moments. 'You had a good day?'

Byrd wiped his mouth with the back of his hand and shook his head. 'No, not really.'

Claire didn't have to ask. She'd been with Byrd for two years now, and each time he walked through the door after his shift, the look on his face alone would indicate if his day had been good or not.

'Wanna talk about it?' She knew he wouldn't, but felt the need to ask.

'Not really.' He smiled. 'Thanks, though.'

She continued eating.

Byrd glanced up at the clock to his left; the time approached 10 p.m. He told Claire he was getting a quick shower then going to watch the news.

'I'll do the washing-up and meet you in the living room.'

By the time he walked in wearing his dressing gown, he noticed through the window, the sun had almost dipped behind the houses opposite leaving the street in the falling dusk.

'Ready?' asked Claire, holding the remote. She knew Byrd would be longer than a few minutes and had paused it. Byrd sat down and she pressed play.

'Good evening,' the female news reporter in the blue suit started. 'Our first story takes us to Darlington and the tragic deaths of four family members during a house fire near the centre of town. The police and fire service, based on the evidence so far, suspect arson. The victims are confirmed to be forty-one-year-old Danny Walters, his wife, Jessica Walters, aged forty, and their two sons, Mark and Peter, aged eleven and seven. This news comes as a massive shock to the town and police have sent us a photo taken from a camera at the property which shows an individual who visited the house on three separate occasions. Police believe this man to be responsible for setting the fire.'

The enlarged photo which Tanzy had sent to the media team filled the screen. The still shot had captured the man walking back towards the rear gate, his long mop of dark hair and ridiculous looking moustache plain to see.

'If anyone recognises this man,' the reporter continued, 'please get in touch with Durham Constabulary with any further information. They believe this individual goes by the name of Roger Carlton.'

Claire muted the sound and looked at Byrd, who was focused on the screen. She now knew why he hadn't had a good day. Usually, he'd phone her several times during the day, but today he hadn't. And when he didn't, Claire knew he was busy with something very important.

'Wanna talk about it?' she asked softly, placing a palm on his shoulder.

He looked down at the carpet under the television. 'It was awful, Claire.'

She rubbed his shoulder but didn't say anymore, knowing him well enough that if he wanted to talk about it, he would.

Byrd leaned in, kissed her, stood up and went upstairs to bed. For the first time in nearly six years, he'd fallen asleep within a minute.

Then he woke at 2.30 a.m. when he heard something. He shuffled up, his heart beating quickly, and looked around the dark room. A sliver of light crept in through the curtains from the streetlight outside. To his right, Claire was sleeping peacefully on her side, facing him.

For a moment, he thought he'd woken from a dream, imagining the sound was something to worry about. But the longer the silence continued, he was convinced it was nothing. He tiredly lowered his head to the pillow and closed his eyes, hoping he'd fall back to sleep.

Then he heard it again. The sound of someone downstairs.

14

When Tanzy walked through the front door, Eric and Jasmine both hugged him as if they hadn't seen him in weeks. Tanzy put his bag down near the door, lowered to his knees and put his arms around them. Eric excitedly told him he'd been sewing at school, then grabbed the square of fabric from the unit near the stairs to show him. It was a flower made from four different colours. Tanzy didn't have a clue how to sew, so with Eric being only ten, he was very impressed.

'That looks brilliant, mate,' he said, kissing his warm cheek. 'Have you showed Mum?'

He nodded, smiling widely.

Tanzy turned to Jasmine, who told him about a game she played with her friends at dinnertime. Similar to stuck in the mud, but they had to crawl under their legs instead of their outstretched arms.

'Mum has a surprise for you,' Eric said, laughing, nodding his head back and forth, his dark curls rocking on the top of his head.

'She does, does she?'

Eric and Jasmine both nodded shyly.

'Where is Mum?'

Jasmine turned her head quickly, her long dark hair whipping the air, and pointed to the kitchen. Tanzy found his feet and smiled, wondering what it could be. In the kitchen, Pip finished washing the last plate and placed it on the draining board. She was wearing her grey tight-fitting jogging pants and a short-sleeved purple T-shirt.

'Hey,' he said, happy to see her.

Jasmine and Eric followed him in.

She turned and smiled. 'Hey, yourself. How was your day?'

'Well, we'll talk about it later.' He glanced behind him, spotted the kids looking up at him with mischievous eyes. 'What's going on?'

Pip moved across the kitchen floor, her bare feet silent on the tiles, and hugged him tightly. 'I have a surprise for you,' she whispered in his ear. Her emerald eyes glistened against the modern lighting under the cupboards to his left. Her dark, shiny hair rested on her shoulders.

'Do you?'

'Well, it's from me and the kids.'

'It isn't my birthday until next month.' He smiled and rubbed his perfectly trimmed goatee.

'Kids, go and get it for Daddy.'

They left and returned a few moments later with a rectangular box covered in *Toy Story* wrapping paper.

Eric handed it to him. 'Open it, Daddy.'

Tanzy lowered to his knees and placed the box on the floor. He excitedly ripped the paper off and was surprised to see a Makita cordless drill.

'A drill?' he said, unsure why they'd bought him a drill.

'Well, you did mention that you couldn't finish the project in Eric's room because your drill broke,' Pip explained. 'So, I ordered one from Amazon for you. Hope it's the right one.'

Tanzy stood up and studied the photo on the outside of the case. It was pretty much the same one as he owned. And she was right, he did need a new one. After seeing something in one of her fancy magazines, Pip decided it would be good to build Eric a den in his room. Roughly head height, nestled in the corner with a ladder he could climb to access, a great place for him to go to read or watch films on his iPad. Tanzy had been building it for a while now, mainly in his spare time, but it seemed to be taking forever.

'Now you can finish his den.' Pip smiled.

Tanzy grinned and looked behind him, noticed Eric clapping his hands excitedly. 'Yeah, that's great,' he said to him, although his words weren't filled with as much enthusiasm as they could have been.

'Daddy will soon have it done for you, Eric,' Pip said to him.

Eric hugged Tanzy and ran off upstairs, thrilled. Jasmine left too, returning to the dining room where she'd been watching the television before Tanzy arrived home.

Tanzy and Pip talked about their day, leaving out the descriptive details. What they'd witnessed at the house fire was beyond words. He told her how Max had punched the wall in the office.

'That's not like him,' she said.

'I know. I think the stress of the baby is catching up with him.'

'What did Fuller say about it?'

'He said he'd have to pay for the damage.'

Pip made a fair-enough face and flicked the kettle on. She made coffees and they both sat down.

Tanzy looked at her and said, 'How are you doing?'

'Yeah, I'm good.'

'No, I mean, how are you doing?' he said seriously.

She frowned at him, unsure what he meant. In the cupboard behind them, Tanzy had noticed a bottle of vodka at the back. It was a bottle that had turned up no later than last week. When Pip started back at AA, Tanzy had made sure that they had no alcohol in the house so nothing could tempt her. He knew all too well how easy it was to have a bad day and turn to drink. The months of hard work and effort gone in a single vulnerable moment. But he'd noticed this bottle four days ago, and a day later, he noticed there was less vodka in it than the day before. Then yesterday, there was even less. He knew this because he'd made a thin pen mark on the side of the glass, just thick enough for him to see it.

'I'm okay,' she said, but her slouched body language told a different story.

He nodded slowly, stood up, went to the cupboard and opened it. After moving some tins and jars aside, he pulled out the bottle of vodka, returned to the table and placed it down in front of her.

He watched her throat bulge and her eyes widen as he took a seat on the chair. It didn't take long for the silence to become uncomfortable.

'I er . . .' she muttered.

'What?'

She fell silent and looked away from him.

'Six months, Pip.' He stood up, went over to the cupboard, pulled out an empty glass and placed it next to the bottle. 'You really want to go back to this? Go ahead. We'll move the kids out, send them to your mum's. I'll stop at Max's, and you can drink all of it, Pip. Every single drop to yourself.'

She frowned at him. Her eyes became glassy.

'You've been doing so well. Don't fuck this up now. But if this is what you want, go ahead.' He pushed the glass towards her. 'Go on.'

She stared at him, then at the bottle.

'I'll leave it up to you.' He stood up, leaned over to kiss her forehead. 'You're better than that, my love. But the decision is yours.' He left the kitchen and went upstairs for a shower. After he got out, he checked on the kids, then returned to an empty kitchen. He checked the living room and dining room. She wasn't there either.

'Pip?' he shouted.

He opened the front door and looked out, seeing her car still on the driveway. Back inside the house, he went down the hall, through the living room and opened the back door to the garden. At the recycling bin, Pip stood, gazing out on the garden.

Tanzy slowly approached.

Near her feet, he noticed the paving stones were soaked. He silently reached past her, opened the bin lid, and inside, found the empty vodka bottle. He closed the lid and held her close.

'Thank you,' he whispered.

They went inside, sorted the kids, and settled on the sofa to watch a film. Before midnight, they climbed into bed and held each other, Tanzy spooning her and stroking her dark hair. Pip slipped a hand around her back and started rubbing Tanzy until he was hard. She turned over and climbed on top of him. After they were finished, they went to sleep.

At 2.30 a.m., Tanzy's phone beeped, waking them both. The text message was from Byrd.

'Who's that?' Pip said, groggily.

He read it. 'A text from Max. He says there's someone in his house, and if I don't hear from him in five minutes, I need to ring the police and head over.'

15

Tuesday night
Low Coniscliffe, Darlington

Without waking up Claire, Byrd silently got out of bed, grabbed the dressing gown from the back of the bedroom door and put it on. He took a few steps towards the bed, leaned over, and opened his bedside drawer, the sliding mechanism moaning in the darkness, but it wasn't enough to wake Claire. He grabbed the truncheon and torch, placed them on the bed while he picked up his phone and slipped it into his dressing gown pocket. He opened the bedroom door and tiptoed out onto the landing, the truncheon nestled firmly in his right hand, the torch in his left.

He leaned over the banister to look downstairs. It sat in darkness. The sounds that woke him up were louder now, he was sure, but couldn't work out where it was coming from or what it was.

The past couple of weeks Low Coniscliffe had been subject to a few break-ins. As it wasn't a congested, busy place, everyone knew each other. So, when people had knocked on Byrd's door asking what was going on or who was responsible, he didn't have an answer. He'd lived there long enough to know the majority of the folk who lived here and surmised it was someone outside their little community responsible, but went around knocking doors regardless. One of the neighbour's cars had been taken, and other people had had jewellery and laptops stolen. Whoever it was had worn gloves and overshoes, leaving no prints at all.

Several people had bought security cameras to protect their property, while others had fixed their broken burglar alarms. The small village hadn't seen its share of crime, so people were now wary of this once very quiet place.

Byrd stopped at the top of the stairs and listened hard. The noise was coming from the kitchen. A thumping sound? He directed the light down into the hallway, illuminating the darkness as he took the first step, then the second, followed by the third. The sound, if anything, was getting louder. His truncheon was extended to its capacity, raised slightly, in case he needed to suddenly swing it. Once he reached the wooden floor he peeked around the post at the bottom of the stairs, peering down the hall towards the kitchen, seeing the moonlight cast a haze of dull grey light through the closed blinds, giving the table and kitchen appliances a look of mystery about them.

With the noise still present, he tiptoed along the hall, his torch shooting its beam of brilliant light into the space ahead.

The noise stopped dead.

'If anyone's here, make yourself known,' Byrd said. 'You are on the property of a police officer who is not afraid to use the weapon in his hand.'

He stopped a few feet from the open kitchen door. The light at the end of the torch didn't show anything unusual in the narrow section of the kitchen he could see. He stepped in, hitting the switch on the left, the space lighting up under the six bright spotlights above.

It was empty. He looked to his left towards the back door. It was closed. He could see the sliver of the lock in place, knowing it hadn't been breached.

He frowned in confusion and looked around.

'Hello?' he said again.

He quickly turned around, shining the torch back into the hallway, feeling there was something behind him. Apart from the coats hanging on the hook and the shoes on the low-level rack next to the door, it was empty.

Moving closer, light on his bare feet to the centre of the kitchen, his eyes flitted left and right as he tried to remember the sound; he was sure it was a thumping sound. Everything was in its place. Nothing had moved.

He was about to relax and go back upstairs when he heard it again and froze. It was coming from the garage. With a sudden wave of anger, he dashed to the garage door, flicked the lock open, and barged it open with his truncheon held high.

An array of tools and garden furniture were under the focus of his torchlight, but the thumping sound came from the left. He aimed the light towards the sound and suddenly stopped, his heart beating hard and fast.

Then he smiled, laughed quietly to himself.

He flicked on the garage light and noticed the timer had thirty-four minutes left of the cycle. The clothes he'd put in before were meant to start in the morning, so Claire could take them out and hang them out to dry. He must have set the timer wrong.

He did a quick visual around the well-lit garage. The door at the back, leading to the garden, was closed, as was the garage door itself at the front.

Happy there were no monsters in his house, he locked the garage and turned the kitchen light off. Before he climbed the stairs, for peace of mind, he checked the handle on the front door and froze, immediately feeling the icy fingers crawl up his spine when the handle dipped and the door opened inwards.

'Jesus!' he whispered in panic.

As well as putting the wrong timer on the washing machine, he'd left the front door unlocked too. What was he thinking? He shook his tired head, had a quick peep outside onto the dark street which sat silent and still. He closed the door, grabbed the keys from the small table and locked it.

Before he went upstairs, he checked the living room and dining room, then tiredly made his way back upstairs.

As Byrd reached the top and turned for his bedroom, the person crouched down behind the living room door sighed and smiled to himself. He'd wait until Byrd went back to sleep before he made his move.

16

Wednesday morning
Darlington

Tanzy was late out of the house and told Byrd he'd meet him at B&Q just after 8 a.m. He hadn't slept well, especially after being woken at half two when Byrd had told him someone was in his house. A few minutes later, he'd received a text message saying there was nothing to worry about and went back to sleep.

Tanzy stepped out of his Golf, closed the door, and paused to admire his new purchase. Similar to his last car, but this had all the mod cons and was a darker shade of grey. Pip was envious but to compensate, she drove his Mercedes CLS 350 when he was at work. Other than taking the kids to and from school, she didn't use it much, so Tanzy wasn't too concerned about her racking the mileage up.

He was surprised to see how full the car park was as he walked towards the entrance. He spotted Byrd's X5 near the entrance in one of the 'load and go' bays.

The sun was up and shining brightly, a sea of reflections from angled car windscreens and polished roofs. It had been warm over the past few weeks and according to the weather reports, would only get warmer. It would be a record for the month of May, the experts had predicted.

As he approached the black X5, he made eye contact with Byrd through the driver's wing mirror. Byrd who was wearing black trousers and a very thin dark-blue jacket, opened his door and stepped down. His hair had been gelled and his moisturised skin shimmered in the morning light, although noticeable dark semi-circles sat just under his eyes.

'Morning, Max.'

'Morning, mate,' Byrd replied.

'You look shattered.' Tanzy stopped in front of him.

'I am. I kept hearing things all night. Didn't sleep well at all.'

'Thanks for waking me at half two.'

They shared a smile.

'Don't know what's wrong with me, Ori. My head feels like it's all over the place. I went to go back upstairs then heard something again, even thought I'd checked the house. I randomly tried the front door handle and I honestly couldn't believe it — it was open! I'd forgotten to lock it. After the local break-ins, I don't know how I missed it, Ori.'

'You know what that is, don't ya?'

Byrd waited, frowning.

'Old age,' Tanzy said, and winked.

Byrd pressed his lips together, realising the seriousness of it, before they turned and headed for the entrance. At the reception desk, a small woman in her fifties, with blonde hair and a wide smile showing coffee-stained teeth asked them how she could help.

Byrd took charge. 'Can we speak to the manager, please?'

'Sure. Can I ask what it's regarding?'

'It's about one of your employees. Danny Walters.'

Her smile faded quickly. 'Oh. Okay, I'll call him.' She picked up the phone to her right and told the person on the other end that the police were here to speak to him about Danny. She placed the phone back on the receiver and told them he'd be a few minutes.

Byrd and Tanzy smiled and stepped back, spending their waiting time looking at the deals strategically placed on the low-level stands near the entrance door. It wasn't long before a short guy in his late twenties appeared with a practised false smile.

Byrd extended his hand and shook it firmly. 'Can you spare a few minutes to speak about one of your employees Danny Walters?'

The man nodded several times. 'Of course, anything we can do to help.'

From his response it was obvious he was aware of what had happened to Danny. He led them from one end of the shop to the other and went through a door near the trade entrance and climbed some steps, took a left then, a few metres down a narrow corridor, opened a door to an empty room. There were a couple of chairs and a table, but other than the clock on the wall, it was empty. Most likely used for one-to-one or small staff meetings.

He introduced himself as Chris Gilbert, then sat down, waiting for the detectives to speak first.

'So, I'm sure you're aware,' Tanzy started, taking the only seat on that side, 'that Danny and his family tragically died in a house fire?'

Chris nodded. 'Yes, I watched it on the news. We are devastated. He was a lovely man. Been here longer than I have.'

'How long is that?'

Chris explained he'd been the manager for almost four years, and Danny had been there at least ten years before that. 'He worked in the plumbing aisle. Did his time as a plumber but work had dried up and he got a temporary job here until it picked back up, but said he enjoyed it and liked the people.'

Byrd nodded. 'Can you tell us if he'd ever mentioned any problems he'd had outside work? I'm sure you know we are treating this fire as arson.'

Chris thought for a moment. 'I can't say he ever did. We talked most days that he was here. He was an upbeat guy. Everyone liked him.'

'What was he into, any interests?'

'He said he liked his online games, used to play a lot with his friends. I don't see the fascination, but I know many people his age do. It isn't unusual. Have you found anything that can help in finding who did this to him?'

The detectives considered the question.

Tanzy said, 'We have a few leads we are chasing. Do you know anyone here who was friendly with him?'

'I'd say just about everyone. As I said, everyone liked him.' Chris shrugged, indicating he could offer no more on the matter.

Byrd and Tanzy both stood, then Tanzy handed him a card. 'Please get in touch if you think of anything that might be important.'

Chris nodded.

'Anything at all,' added Tanzy.

Chris led them back to the shop floor, so they took a left through the door to the car park. The sky was bright blue and there wasn't a single cloud in the sky.

Byrd didn't say much on the way back to the car and it didn't go unnoticed.

'You okay?' asked Tanzy, looking his way.

Byrd held his gaze. 'Yeah. Why?'

'Just don't seem yourself.'

When he stopped at the car, he turned to Tanzy. 'I'm just nervous about the baby, I think. It upsets me that . . . ahh it sounds daft. I—'

'You don't need to be all macho for me, Max. What is it?'

'My mum and dad won't get to see him. It upsets me the way the world is, that I'm bringing a baby boy into this mess.'

Tanzy placed a palm on his shoulder. 'The world is the way it is. It will never change. I'm telling you that having kids is the best thing you'll ever do. If you're worrying it will be hard, I can promise you it will be, but I can also promise you it's amazing.'

Byrd nodded, appreciating his encouraging words. 'Let's head back to the station, see what mood Fuller is in this morning.'

When Byrd got into his car, his phone rang in his pocket. He leaned to the side, pulled it out and noticed Claire was ringing him. It was unusual because she'd always text when he was at work unless something was wrong.

'Claire?'

'Max, did you go out the back door this morning?'

Byrd thought quickly and remembered he didn't. 'No. I got a quick shower, grabbed a bite, and went straight out the front door. Why?'

'Because my laptop isn't here. And the back door isn't locked. I think someone's been in the house.'

17

Once they'd spoken with Hope and Tallow, Byrd and Tanzy had learned all the evidence had been collected from the house fire at Napier Street. After DNA had been taken from the four bodies, they had been transported to the undertakers. The need for detailed post-mortems was unnecessary considering the nature of their deaths, they'd decided.

Peter Gibbs, the lead coroner for Darlington and Durham, had been on the phone, going through what had happened again. House fires like these fortunately didn't happen very often, and it was unusual for a family of four to die in this way, so when he returned from the medical conference in London, his first port of call had been the house to have a look at the scene himself.

Hope had told Byrd that, after analysing the samples taken from the house, due to the fire, there wasn't any other DNA found, which surprised Byrd as Roger Carlton had been there several times. Byrd had asked about prints on door handles, knowing he'd opened and closed the back door several times when cleaning the carpets on Sunday. But, looking back at the camera footage, the man had covered his tracks, wearing gloves to minimise his trace.

They did find something.

A footprint.

Located at the back door near the mat, they cross-referenced the pattern and found it didn't match up with any of the family's footwear. She told Byrd she would find out the type of the trainer and get back to him once she knew.

DCI Fuller popped his head through his office door, informing both Byrd and Tanzy he wanted a word with them. They stood up, went inside, and sat down in the two chairs on the other side of his desk.

'Updates please, gents?' he asked, wasting no time.

They filled him in on the footprint that had been found and said they were waiting on Forensics to find the model.

'Keep me updated with that. What else?'

'That's it for now, sir,' replied Byrd, itching his chin.

'Where are we on the missing women?' pressed Fuller, clearly agitated.

Four days ago, on Saturday night, four women had left the Grange bar in Darlington's town centre and had got into a taxi. It was the last time they had been seen. A string of queries had come in a day later from worried family and friends, saying they hadn't arrived home. The police had managed to come up with a list.

Theresa Jackson. Lisa Butterwick. Sarah McKay. Lorraine Eckles.

Byrd and Tanzy had spoken to the husband of Sarah McKay, who said Sarah had texted him saying she was leaving the Grange but was heading to Lisa's house afterwards for a few drinks. When he woke the following morning she wasn't there, so he tried ringing her but her phone was off.

Byrd had got in touch with the manager at the Grange, who checked the CCTV, and had seen four women matching their descriptions leaving the bar just after 2 a.m. With that information, Tanzy had spoken to Jennifer Lucas at the Town Hall control room who had followed them on the nearest camera, watching them climb into a blue van with the registration plates removed.

'No one has seen them, sir,' Tanzy said. 'We have obtained their pictures and as you know, the media have shown the public but nothing yet. We've updated our Facebook page and Twitter feed with it multiple times. We are receiving messages about how sad the situation is but there's nothing to go on.'

Fuller sighed heavily and sat silent for a moment. Then he said, 'Have we found Roger Carlton yet?'

'According to our data, the closest Roger Carlton lives in Leeds.'

'Facial Rec?'

Byrd shook his head. 'Nothing.'

'He may be wearing a wig and a fake moustache,' added Tanzy.

Fuller forced a smile and dipped his shoulders into the back of his chair. 'At least his photo and name are on the news. Hopefully we hear something soon.'

The door behind the detectives opened. They both turned.

DC Leonard was standing at the door. 'Sir, someone thinks they know who Roger Carlton is.' It was aimed at Tanzy, more so than Byrd or Fuller.

'They still on the phone?'

He shook his head. 'She's waiting in reception, boss.'

18

Byrd and Tanzy entered the small reception at the front of the building, where a woman, in her early thirties, dressed in a black pencil skirt, a white blouse, a black blazer and high heels, stood before them. If she had told them she was a lawyer, they wouldn't have second-guessed it. Her straight dark hair sat nicely on her shoulders, either side of an attractive, stern-looking face. Maybe she was a lawyer after all.

Byrd stepped forward and extended his hand. 'Hi, I'm Detective Inspector Max Byrd.' He turned and used his hand to indicate Tanzy, who stepped forward. 'And this is my partner, Detective Inspector Orion Tanzy.'

After she shook their hands, she told them her name was Samantha Verity.

'We have been made aware that you may know Roger Carlton?' Byrd asked.

She nodded several times. 'Is there a place where we can talk?' Whatever she wanted to say, she knew it would take a while to do so.

The detectives led her through a door, down a corridor, and into a room on the right. It was a box room, with a table in the centre of it, two chairs on either side. There was no window and didn't feel very welcoming.

'Please, take a seat,' Tanzy told her, motioning either seat with his hand.

As Samantha sat, Byrd, who was still standing, asked, 'Can I get you a coffee?'

'Yes, please. Milk. No sugar,' she replied, followed with a smile.

Byrd nodded and left the room.

She settled herself in and looked a little nervous. Tanzy waited until Byrd returned with three coffees and placed them all down on the table.

'So, what can you tell us, Miss Verity,' Byrd asked, not wasting any time, knowing Tanzy would have waited.

She blinked a few times. 'I heard about the fire in Napier Street, about how the family all died. I recognised the man in the photo. The name Roger Carlton doesn't exist. At least not that I know of.'

The detectives frowned, unsure where she was going with it.

She noticed their confusion. 'Sorry, I'm not explaining myself well. A few years ago, I went out with a guy. He was obsessed with this American TV series.' She rocked her head back and looked at the ceiling. 'God, I can't remember the name. There was a character in it called Roger Carlton. The guy I used to date loved it. He always watched it. He always said if he could change his name it would be to Roger Carlton. From the photo on the news, he was wearing a wig and a fake tash. The character in the American show did the same.'

'What's he called? Your previous boyfriend.'

'Adrian Dilton,' she replied clearly.

'Does Adrian Dilton have an address? We'd very much like to speak to him urgently.'

'He used to live on Victoria Embankment when I knew him. I fell pregnant with his baby but we lost it when I was six months along.'

Byrd gave her a sad smile, uncertain if she regarded it as a good thing or a bad thing.

'Oh, don't worry, it was for the best. I can promise you that.'

Her words insinuated she had more to tell.

'I'd been seeing him for a couple of years. Things were going okay. We'd spoken about marriage and having a family but then things got weird — he got weird.'

'Weird how?'

'He started spending a lot of time on his computer. He didn't want to go out and have fun anymore. He completely shut me off. All he cared about was his stupid computer.'

'What did Mr Dilton do for work?' asked Tanzy.

'He worked for an IT firm based somewhere in Newcastle. He's got a degree in some IT thing, I'm not sure the name. Programming or something.' She waved her hand, expressing little understanding or interest.

Byrd and Tanzy absorbed her words.

'I'm not sure if it was because we lost the baby, but we lost interest in each other and finally called it a day. It wasn't that he was a nasty man, it's just . . . he didn't prioritise his things well. And his obsession with his computer, well, that got too much for me.'

'What did he do on his computer?' Tanzy asked, curiously.

'Games, I think. But then sometimes, I think he did things he shouldn't have been doing.'

'What makes you say that?'

'A few times, I walked in without knocking or without him knowing I was there, and he went ballistic, telling me to eff off and that it was his time. I'm not entirely sure, but he became obsessed with it. A few months before we split up, he started getting this look in his eye. A dark look. As if there was another side of him that he hadn't shown me yet.'

'Had he ever shown any violence towards you?' Byrd said, leaning forward, placing his palms on the desk.

She shook her head. 'No.'

'When was the last time you saw him?'

She narrowed her eyes in thought. 'About six months ago. I passed him in the street. He saw me but looked the other way as if he was ashamed of what he'd become. We stopped seeing each other two years ago.'

'Does he have any family living in Darlington?'

'Not that I know of,' she said. 'He has a sister that lives somewhere down south and a brother who lives in the Midlands. He didn't see much of them when I was with him, so I don't know if that's still the case.'

'Do you still have his mobile number?'

'Unfortunately not. I deleted it. Sorry.' She genuinely looked apologetic.

'What number on Victoria Embankment did he live?'

She told them. Byrd took out his phone and made a note.

'Is there anything else that could help?'

'Not at the moment.'

Byrd leaned to the left, pulled a card from his right pocket and handed it to her. 'In case anything does come to mind.'

'Thank you.'

She rose to her feet. Tanzy walked her to the reception and watched her leave through the main doors. Back in the office, they knocked on Fuller's door and mentioned they were going out. They stepped out into the sun and made their way over to Tanzy's Golf.

19

Wednesday afternoon
Victoria Embankment

They knocked on the door where Samantha Verity had told the detectives Adrian Dilton had lived. They waited and knocked again. With no answer, they took a step back, peering in the window to the right, then into the windows upstairs. There was no movement or sudden twitching of curtains.

The front door belonging to the house to the left opened. A man in his seventies stepped out with a thick coat, ready for winter, with a walking stick that looked older than he did.

He peered at them through bottle-bottom glasses. 'Can I help you?'

Byrd smiled. 'We're looking for Mr Dilton. Do you know if he's in?'

'Oh, Whack-job Willy?'

Byrd frowned. 'Who?'

'It's not his real name. It's a nickname we have for him — my wife and me. He was a strange one.'

'What makes you say that?'

'He didn't speak much. Spent a lot of his time inside playing on his computer. His bedroom must have backed on to our room.' He pointed upwards towards his bedroom in case the detectives weren't sure where that would be. 'And he used to keep us up most of the night. We complained on several occasions but it didn't make a difference. He carried on as he wanted.'

The elderly man gingerly made his way to the black, iron gate and slowly pulled it towards him, then stepped down carefully onto the path. He lifted his free hand up to his face to shield it from the blinding sun.

'Can you tell us any information about him — where does he work?'

'He worked from home I think. Something to do with that stupid computer of his.'

'Did he have many friends? Or a girlfriend maybe?'

'From what we saw of him, I don't think so. He hardly came out of the house. Only for shopping, because every time he came back, he had bags in his hand. And, he wasn't the type to stop to say hello. To be honest, I don't think he was all there.' He raised a finger to his temple and made small circles with it.

The detectives nodded, waiting for more.

'Oh, there was a woman who used to visit him,' the man said. 'Only came a handful of times while he was there. Could have been a girlfriend, although I can't be sure.'

Tanzy raised the notepad, ready to write something. 'Did she have a name?'

The old man told them he didn't know it but she had blonde hair and wore glasses, which Tanzy quickly jotted down.

'So, what time does he usually return home? We can pop back later,' Byrd said.

The old man smiled. 'You'll be waiting a while. He hasn't lived here for six months. The place is empty now.'

Byrd sighed heavily. 'Great. Does a landlord own it?'

The man shrugged. 'How am I supposed to know? Anyway, I need to go. She'll be wondering where the meat is. She's cooking dinner later. I'm not missing it. And I can't be arsed with the earache.'

'Appreciate your help, sir,' Byrd said, with a forced smile.

The elderly man and his stick headed along Victoria Embankment towards town. Wherever he was going, judging by his pace, it would take him a while.

Byrd turned back to Tanzy. 'Well, that's great. Back to square one.'

Tanzy was going to reply but his phone rang in his pocket. He plucked it out to answer. 'Hello?'

'Boss, it's Amy.'

'What's happening?'

'I found the trainer the man who called himself Roger Carlton was wearing at Napier Street.'

'That was quick.'

'It's an Adidas Samba trainer.'

Tanzy closed his eyes, knowing they were sold in hundreds of shops from here to London and no doubt all across the globe. 'Okay. We'll be heading back soon. We'll catch up then.' He put his phone away and headed towards the Golf. Byrd followed.

'So,' Byrd said, putting on his seatbelt, 'we have four missing women, a house fire that has killed four people, a missing man who is very likely the man responsible for it, and an address which he doesn't live at.'

'You're missing the Adidas Samba trainers.'

'Oh yeah, the trainer that could have been bought in any shop in any town in the whole country.'

'We'll check with the Land Registry, see who the house belongs to.'

Byrd nodded toward Tanzy. 'Good shout.'

'Other than that, the investigation is thriving . . .' Tanzy turned on the engine and edged out, made his way towards Victoria Road. 'How's Claire, you spoken to her?'

'Yeah, she's okay. Just shook up a little. I popped home to see her in my dinner break and made sure all the doors were locked and nothing else had been taken.'

'Haven't there been some break-ins in your village?'

'A couple. I've knocked on most doors, asking if people had seen anything. Whoever is doing it is a ghost. I'm going to buy more locks today and put them on when I get home. The last thing we need is her worrying and not feeling safe. Won't do the baby any good at all.'

20

Although it was summer, the large room was cold and dark. There wasn't a single speck of light from anywhere, not even from the small, one-way window on one of the walls.

The floor was cold and hard. One of them had mentioned it felt like concrete to touch, but the others weren't sure.

There were several bed covers laid out for them along one side of the room, which they'd spent the majority of their days sitting on in silence. The covers weren't thick but it kept them off the cold floor.

In the first few days, after waking up and realising they were without their phones or any possessions, they had investigated the room in darkness. They'd learned many things. The room was square-shaped. The walls were made from concrete. In the centre of the room, there was a plastic bag with items inside. Packets of crisps, drinks and chocolate bars. When hunger got the better of them, they had had little choice but to tuck in. Item by item, the bag became lighter, so they rationed their supplies, unsure how long they'd be there for. There were still a few drinks inside and other wrapped goodies and they had decided to only eat when they were starving.

When they had first woken up, they'd all panicked, and it had taken them a while to finally calm each other down. One of them recalled their last memory of getting into the van they assumed was a taxi, but after that their memories are blank. Then they had woken up here, panicking and flustered, kicking and screaming and punching the walls in desperation but they were tired and had nearly given up. Each day, their cries for help were

absorbed by the cold, dark, damp, unforgiving room.

'I can't feel my feet,' Lisa said.

'Me neither,' said Sarah.

'You awake?' Lisa asked the other one.

'Yeah, I'm here,' Lorraine replied weakly, shuffling a little to get comfortable.

It had been three days since they'd heard from Theresa. Lisa had realised that Theresa hadn't been talking much, so had called her name and received no answer. They'd checked the whole room in the dark, using their searching hands to feel the cold floor and walls but it soon dawned on them that Theresa was not there anymore. Somehow, she'd vanished. None of them could remember when or how. They realised they weren't getting out and had accepted their fates on the sixth day.

On the opposite wall to where their makeshift beds were, they used the wall and floor area for the toilet. The foul smell, along with the damp brickwork, had worsened as the days went on, but they'd become immune to it. Even their individual bad smells had almost become a comfort to one another. Strange how only last week, they were leading their own lives.

It seemed like a lifetime ago.

'I need to pee,' Lisa said. She used the wall's surface to aid herself up. Because she hadn't moved in a while, her bones felt like they were brittle and her muscles had almost forgotten how to function. She padded across to the other side with her arms outstretched until she reached the opposite wall, then pulled up her skirt. The sound of her urinating echoed in the large, empty space.

She returned to Sarah and Lorraine, tiredly dropping on the floor near them.

'We're not getting out of here, are we?'

Lorraine leaned over, blindly reaching for her hand, and finally found it. 'I don't think so,' she whispered.

Lisa shuffled in and held her friend tight, battling against the cold that wasn't giving up, and started to cry.

* * *

Through the small rectangular window high on the opposite wall where they were crying, two men watched them. The glass was one-way, appearing jet black on the room's side, not allowing anything in, so the women couldn't see or know they were being watched.

'Which one are they going to pick this week?' the man on the right said, rubbing his chin. He was thin, wore glasses, had eyes darker than the midnight sky. He ambled back over to the desk, sat down, and placed his hand on the desk, gently tapping the wood near the keyboard with his long fingers.

'I'll check the votes,' the other said, pulling himself closer to the computer and taking hold of the mouse. He was taller and wider. The run-around, the one who did the leg work. The muscle. He clicked on the voting panel to check the scores.

There were three pictures on the screen. The images had been duplicated from their social media accounts. They needed the players and watchers to see what they were looking at. Under each picture was a percentage, and because they were down to three, their score was split three ways.

'They seem to like Lisa,' said Brad, checking the figures. 'They like watching her cry. Her vote is low. They want to keep watching her.' Up in the corner of the room was a night vision camera recording twenty-four seven.

Mitch took his focus off the window and glared at Brad and the computer screen.

'Looks like it could be Lorraine?' Brad said.

Mitch leaned in. 'Lorraine's got forty-six per cent. Right, start the gas. Let's get her prepped for Friday.'

Brad stood, left the desk and went over to the wall. He took hold of the gas valve and turned it on. Soon they'd all be asleep, and he'd go in to get Lorraine.

21

Wednesday evening
Low Coniscliffe

Claire, tired after she'd finished the ironing and washing-up, went straight to the sofa. She picked what she wanted to watch, settled in, and focused on the brand new fifty-inch TV they'd recently bought. Byrd had listened to her moaning about how she couldn't see it properly from the sofa, telling him they needed something new. Something bigger. Whether that was the case, or whether it was her friend, Mary, who'd told her *they'd* just bought one, and she was feeling jealous.

Byrd had decided to join her, sitting down on the other sofa in the bay window.

'Are you watching with me?'

'Nothing else planned.' He smiled. Byrd seldom spent his evenings watching the TV but figured it'd be nice to spend some time with her. Watching her, it melted his heart how she subconsciously rubbed her belly.

Her son. *Their son.* Alan.

He felt emotional. The thought of bringing a child into the world and not having his parents crushed him more than words could describe. Not only for the support they'd provide, but for the happiness they'd feel to see their first grandchild. It was a shame they would never feel that love.

It also pained him that his sister had been taken twelve years before and hadn't been given the chance to give them a grandchild either. Poor Anna. She was two years younger than Byrd. All of his life he'd protected her. Any issues with boyfriends in the past, she'd gone to Byrd first.

He thought back for a few moments, reliving their childhood in his mind, how they used to go out on days with Mum and Dad, spend their time in the car arguing about the next song they'd listen to. Then, when she was twenty-seven and he was twenty-nine, he got the phone call.

He remembered as if it was yesterday, standing in the kitchen when his mobile rang. It was Tanzy, who informed Byrd he'd discovered his sister, Anna. With multiple stab wounds to her stomach and chest. Byrd had taken a week off work, roaming the streets, knocking on doors, and becoming obsessive. It had certainly changed him in a couple of ways. He appreciated his life more. Each day he woke, he tried to remember that Anna hadn't, and that he should be grateful for another day to live. Eventually, a few leads had led him to the man responsible. He'd cornered him in an alley. Just the two of them. The rage inside him had made him want to grab the man's head, smash it off the cobbles on the ground below, but he had been determined not to throw his life away. He had cuffed him, dragged him to the station, and the man had been sentenced to twenty-five years. Byrd hadn't been allowed to interview him due to his involvement but he had learned the killer hadn't had a motive for the attack. He was just a nutcase, which in a way, made things worse, because Anna had died for nothing.

He pushed the thoughts from his mind and absorbed what was happening on the screen. Claire was intrigued with sci-fi — not spaceships and aliens' kind of sci-fi, more strange happenings type of sci-fi. They both watched a little boy holding a teddy anxiously walk into a cave in the middle of the night.

'Do you think he'll come back?' she asked, keeping her attention on the screen.

Byrd looked over to her and pondered the question, unsure whether she meant the boy on the screen or the person that had broken in and taken her laptop.

'The doors are secure,' he replied, assuming she meant the latter. 'Are you sure you haven't misplaced your laptop?'

She turned her head to him and frowned. 'I'm not stupid, Max.'

'I'm not saying you are, but everyone misplaces things,' he said, his voice even.

'I've looked all over. You have as well. It's been taken. The back door was open.' She sighed, then focused back to the TV.

Byrd didn't reply. Instead, he thought hard about whether he'd locked the door last night. He was sure he hadn't gone out.

'You need to get the cameras working again,' she said, matter-of-factly. And she was right. Byrd had a camera fixed above the door, looking down the driveway, but for some reason, it hadn't been working properly. He'd checked the wiring. To him, it looked okay, not that he knew much about electrics.

'The house is safe,' he said finally. 'No one is getting in.'

22

Thursday afternoon
Police station

Byrd and Tanzy were at their desks. They'd already had lunch and spent much of their morning speaking with Forensics about the house fire in Napier Street. There'd been nothing new found, and no further leads. The most promising lead had been Samantha Verity giving them Roger Carlton's real identity. Adrian

A team had been looking for Adrian Dilton. There were seven in the whole country. It wasn't a very common name at all, which worked better for the police, because one of the Adrian Diltons did have a criminal record. Several counts of suspected murder down in Essex from seven years ago. So far, he hadn't been caught and was still out there, hiding somewhere.

Was it the same man?

Last night, when Byrd had left Tanzy's house and got home, he had watched the news, where the reporter had updated viewers on the name "Adrian Dilton" and requested that anyone who knew him or his whereabouts, should let the police know immediately.

Byrd had spoken to the Newcastle-based IT firm where Samantha had told them that Adrian had worked. The manager there, a Mr Jonas Black, had told Byrd that Dilton was a quiet man, who kept himself to himself and had handed in his notice around six months ago. Didn't give a reason. Byrd asked him what address they had for him, and it turned out to be the same address they'd already visited.

The door behind them opened and Fuller popped his head out. 'You two. In here.' His tone wasn't very positive, nor did it give them a feeling it was going to be an uplifting conversation.

Byrd and Tanzy locked their computers and went inside the DCI's office. They took a seat in the two chairs opposite him.

'Updates, gentlemen? Start with the fire.'

Tanzy spoke first, telling him there were no further leads from a forensic point of view. He mentioned the trainer that PC Amy Weaver had matched to a pair of Adidas Sambas but also stated that they could have been bought in hundreds of shops anywhere in the country.

With nothing else to update, they left the office and returned to their desks. Byrd sat down while Tanzy stopped at his desk chair and decided to go and speak with DS Stockdale for any progression on the four-missing-women case.

The office was full. A wave of mixed conversations danced from wall to wall. Keyboards were tapping, mugs of coffee and tea being raised and lowered back on desks.

DS Phil Stockdale sat at the opposite end of the office to where Byrd and Tanzy sat. On his row of three computers, his desk was the closest to the wall. Through the window next to him, he had a nice view of St Cuthbert's Way.

As Tanzy rounded the last row of desks, he noticed Stockdale was hunched over his phone, focusing intently on something. It was obvious he hadn't heard Tanzy approach because when Tanzy spoke, he jumped and fumbled with something in his hand.

'Oh, hi, boss.' His face reddened suddenly. 'Didn't see you there.'

Stockdale had short black hair, was clean-shaven and thickset. When people learned he used to play rugby, it didn't come as a surprise to them due to his stature.

Tanzy stopped in front of him and eyed him curiously. 'What are you up to?'

He looked at his phone and shook his head, then placed it into his pocket. 'Ahh, nothing.'

Tanzy was aware that Stockdale had had issues with gambling in the past. It had almost ruined his marriage after the thousands of pounds he'd wasted, digging himself further into debt. He'd promised his wife and Tanzy that he wasn't gambling anymore.

'How — how can I help, sir?' The colour of his face returned to pink again.

'Any updates on the four missing women?'

Stockdale sighed and looked up with his green eyes. 'No, sir. Not yet. I need to make some calls.'

Tanzy nodded. 'Phil . . .'

'Yeah?'

'If you need help with something, you only need to ask me. As well as your supervisor, I'm here to help you as a friend. With matters inside and out of work. You know that, don't you?'

Stockdale nodded appreciatively and watched Tanzy return to his desk. Stockdale pulled out his phone and unlocked it, then immediately logged out of the site and deleted his internet history.

23

Jane Ericson smiled at her reflection in the vanity mirror in the bedroom of her fourth-floor "Luxury Apartment", approving her make-up and outfit choice. When advertised, the flat had been labelled "luxury" but it was nothing more than a new flat with fancy sockets and light fittings. Of the two bedrooms, her bedroom was the biggest. The other bedroom, almost half the size, was filled with open rails of clothing and sealed boxes. Hanging dresses, T-shirts, and garments filled one wall, and the other wall contained a shelving unit filled with folded items, such as skirts and jogging bottoms.

Her phone pinged with a text message on the vanity unit in front of her. She'd been waiting for the reply and smiled. She picked it up and noticed it was from Suzie, who was confirming she'd meet her in William Steads at 7.30 p.m. with the others.

It had been a few weeks since they'd all been out together, and it promised to be a good night. She knew most of them from school, and even now, eight years on, most of them were friends and made the effort to see each other on a weekly basis.

The time was 4.30 p.m., so she had a few hours to kill, bearing in mind she'd already showered and put her foundation on. She stood up, made her way over to the bed, and sat down, pulling her closed laptop towards her. She opened it, logged on, and waited for the ancient thing to boot up.

Once the internet page loaded, she clicked on her bookmarks and found the page and waited nervously. It was the second time she'd done this and hoped it would excite her as much as it had the first time. The screen came up.

There she was, sitting in the chair.

Up in the corner of the screen was a small list of usernames; people that were joining the session. She noticed her name, *Ericj4*, second on the list, although the list didn't indicate any relevance of order.

After the session ended, she sighed heavily and slumped a little in awe. Then she went back over to her vanity unit and finished her make-up before making a quick phone call to her friend to ask when she was picking her up. Once ready, she checked her bag a few times to make sure she had everything for her night out.

When the time was 7.15 p.m. she stood at the front door of the flat and checked herself in the long vertical mirror, ensuring her choice of the dark purple maxi dress complemented the black high heels. Her dark hair had been curled, ringlets nestled over her shoulders and down her chest. Her ocean-blue eyes stood out against the jet-black eye shadow and eyeliner.

Somewhere outside, a car horn beeped several times. Then a text message pinged on her phone in her small bag from her friend, telling her she was outside. Jane grabbed her keys, opened her door, locked it, then got in the lift in the hallway.

* * *

As soon as Jane stepped inside the lift, she pressed the button, turned to face the front and waited for the lift to take her down to the ground floor.

Adrian Dilton watched her through the camera up in the corner of the lift. He'd hacked into the flats' CCTV system and had taken control. Usually, the cybersecurity of such a modern building would be a tough nut to crack but whoever had set it up, hadn't done the best job to make it safe.

Judging by her choice of outfit, it wasn't hard to guess where she was going. He'd seen the purple maxi dress in her small bedroom when he was there yesterday, checking the electrical wiring that had played up the day before. Fancy the chances of her electrics not working properly and him putting a business card in her letterbox the same day. *What* a coincidence.

Roger Carlton electrics.

Yesterday he'd looked around the flat, aimlessly checking the sockets and switches, pretending to know what he was doing. When she received a phone call and went into the kitchen, he'd taken out his listening device and placed it under the desk where her laptop was. Then, being the hero he was, he checked the main supply from the consumer unit on the ground floor, flicked the switch, and *voilà*, the power came back on. The visit to her flat was also useful to discover if she lived alone.

The time on the office wall clock told him it was nearly 7.30 p.m. He got up, went to his bedroom to put on a shirt, jeans and some shoes. He then headed out, into town, in the direction of William Steads.

* * *

Hours later, Jane stumbled home, disorientated, stuffing cheesy chips into her mouth from the white Styrofoam container in her hands. Garlic sauce dripped down her chin onto her maxi dress, but she was too drunk to notice. She'd had a really good night.

She turned left into Trinity Road and staggered up the incline as if she were a baby learning to walk, struggling to stay in a straight line, her strides not quite in sync, feeding chips into her mouth as she went.

Stanhope Park sat in darkness on her left. A few eerie murmurs came from somewhere in the park, but she ignored the sounds, not bothering to look. Whoever they were, if they stayed out of her face, there wouldn't be a problem. Without looking for approaching vehicles as she came to the end of the path, she crossed the road on Vane Terrace, then stepped up onto the kerb in the direction of her flat.

* * *

Adrian Dilton waited on the corner of the small road that led to her flat entrance, peering around the side of the building, watching her stagger towards him. The darkness around him was a blessing, although, in her current state, her blurred vision would probably mistake him for a tree if he remained still enough.

He watched until she was only metres away, then hid back in the shadows and waited until she passed. He could hear her breathing heavily through the struggle of walking and eating at the same time. The smell of her perfume still lingered around her like an invisible bubble, albeit not as strong as it was when he was standing next to her in the Green Dragon a few hours before. She'd spotted him at the bar and shouted, 'Hey, you're the electrician!' They idly chatted for a little bit before she introduced him to a few of her friends, who smiled because that's what people did to be nice. Each pub and bar she and her friends went to, he was there, watching from the shadows.

Waiting.

Waiting until she made the short walk home.

She unevenly made her way to the front door but stopped before it, remembering she'd need a key to get inside. She closed the half-eaten chips container and fumbled with her bag, lifting the flap too quickly, causing her phone, keys, and several coins to fall out and cause a racket on the ground.

Dilton stepped out from the dark and made his way over to her.

She didn't hear him coming.

24

'Let me help you with that,' Dilton said.

Jane Ericson wearily turned after hearing the voice behind her and squinted as he approached. Although she was plastered, there was a flash of recognition. She'd seen him somewhere before.

He bent down, picked up her items and handed them carefully back to her, apart from her keys of course.

She grunted something inaudible.

'Sorry?' he said.

''Trician . . .' She hiccupped violently, which threw her body forward a few inches, then she smiled, remembering their playful conversations earlier that night when she'd seen him in town. 'You electrician . . .'

'That's right. I'm just walking home. I saw you walking and thought I'd catch up and say hi. Do you want me to open the door for you?'

She nodded three times, her head feeling loose on the top of her shoulders like it wasn't connected properly. Like a Churchill dog on a car's parcel shelf. He slowly moved around her and used her key to gain access to the entrance hallway. He held the door open for her, then jumped forward to grab her when she tripped over and started laughing. Some of the chips fell out onto the carpet near the door.

'Silly me,' she muttered.

Leaving them, he guided her in and allowed the door close, conscious of people up in the windows of the surrounding flats. There was no one around.

The corridor was familiar. The lift was to the right. Beyond that was a cupboard.

He guided her toward the lift and pressed the button. 'Wait here.' He moved over to the cupboard, opened it, and leaned inside.

'Was that?' she slurred, leaning against the wall, looking down at the bag in his hands. It was the type you'd take to the gym, long, narrow, black in colour.

'Oh, this? I forgot it earlier,' he said, with a smile.

She stared at him, her eyes glassy and half-open as if she could fall asleep at any moment. The lift door pinged open, the sound echoing in the silent building.

'I'll be okay from here,' she slurred, staggering into the lift and pressing the button.

'If you're sure?' he asked, watching her lean back against the lift wall, unstable on her feet.

She nodded twice, her head swooping in huge uncontrollable arcs.

As the doors started to close, he stepped forward, placing his hand between them, causing them to ping open again. He entered the lift with his bag, keeping an eye on her. She was so drunk, she barely registered his presence.

He placed the bag on the floor, unzipped it, and pulled out a full head mask; it had a built-in filter around the mouth area with a large space for the eyes made from glass. The top and rear of it was made from thin flexible rubber.

'Wazzz that?' she asked, frowning now, unsure what she was looking at.

Ignoring her, he pulled out a spray can. It was the size of a WD40 can but instead of having a push spray mechanism at the top, it had some kind of circular pin. He placed his forefinger into the ring and yanked it upwards.

It didn't take long for the green gas to come out of the top and start filling the lift.

Jane looked confused, seeing the green mist start to fall and pool in the bottom of the lift.

'I don't like this,' she muttered, shaking her head. 'Let me out…'

'Have you ever suffocated?' Dilton asked her.

Her eyes narrowed and she shook her head. 'No. I want to get out.' Her words were becoming more incomprehensible.

She moved forward towards the lift doors and coughed a few times until it become continuous. Dilton stepped out of her way. Worried, she hit the lift doors with clenched fists, dropping her small bag in the process. Unable to breathe, she put both her hands to her mouth.

Dilton watched the panic in her eyes. Her frantic eye twitching, her sudden body jerking forward and backward realising she wasn't getting the air she needed to breathe. It was only getting worse.

'You can't breathe, can you?' he whispered. 'You're getting no air.' His eyes wrinkled at the edges as he smiled behind the mask.

She lowered to a crouched position and clawed at her throat, willing it to open up to allow some clean air inside. But the green mist was up to their chests now and completed covered her in the green haze, depleting the level of oxygen inside the small space. She cried out as the green mist filled her mouth and she took one last breath before she collapsed on the lift's floor.

25

When the lift reached the top floor, the doors opened. Before committing to fully stepping out, Dilton leaned out to check the small corridor.

No one there.

Absolute silence. He grabbed the bag and threw it out first, then went back, placed his hands under her armpits and dragged her out slowly. Placing her down, he went back inside the lift and gathered the items she'd dropped and put them in her bag.

He removed her keys from his pocket and unlocked her flat door.

Once inside, he pulled off the mask and dropped it, then went back out for his bag and dragged Jane inside before closing the door. The short narrow hallway lit up with cold, bright light as he flicked the switch near him. He remembered the flat's layout from his visit yesterday.

Leaving her curled up on the floor in the small hallway, he walked into the kitchen and went left, over to the French doors that led out to the small, rectangular balcony.

The area was only two feet out, four feet wide. A viewing point at best, surrounded by a black, metallic railing. Dilton imagined it would be the perfect spot to stand and drink a cup of morning coffee, watching the town wake up, the noise gradually growing with early morning commuters on their way to work. He turned the lock and gently pulled the double doors towards him.

Night air gently slapped his face, noticeably cooler compared to how it felt on the ground level. He closed his eyes, took a lungful, and slowly breathed out like he had all the time in the world. He had to admit the view was amazing. Although it was just after 3 a.m., he could see the sun waiting to creep up over the skyline for another hot summer's day.

He studied the balcony railing for a moment, made up of thin cylindrical metal poles fixed to the base of the balcony, spaced three inches apart, going vertical to the handrail, which was flat, roughly three to four inches wide.

Finally, he nodded, happy about his decision.

He went back into the hallway and picked Jane up, using her armpits to drag her flaccid body across the living room. He lowered her for a moment on the balcony floor to readjust his stance and picked her up again, this time higher, towards the height of the railing.

'Jane?' he whispered.

No response. She was still unconscious.

He smiled, then very carefully, lifted her over the balcony railing, placing one of her arms over the outside of it, then did the same with her right leg, so the top of the balcony rail was against her chest, stomach and in between her legs. Her head was tipped to the left towards the flat, so, to balance her weight, he shuffled her centre of gravity to the outside of the railing.

Once he was sure she was balanced, he took a step back to observe. One wrong decision could be fatal.

Her left arm and left leg were hanging over the inside, and her right arm and leg over the outside edge, four floors up.

'When you wake up, Jane, don't panic,' he whispered. 'Or you might just fall.' He went inside, grabbed her phone from her small bag and placed it on the floor of the balcony. He switched it on and saw it had plenty of battery remaining.

He locked the French doors and, on his way out of the flat, turned off the light and shut the front door. He exited the building at 3.34 a.m. He looked up to see Jane still balanced on the railing. Deciding his work was done, he smiled.

* * *

At 6.01 a.m., DI Byrd's phone rang. His eyes flickered a few times until he realised what it was and sat up quickly, rubbing his eyes from the morning sun that had crept around the edge of the half-closed curtains.

It was DC Phillip Cornty.

'What the hell does he want?' he muttered.

He accepted the call. 'Phil, do you know what—'

'Boss. You need to come. We have a very delicate situation on our hands.'

26

Byrd pulled up at the address which Cornty had given him, red-eyed and tired. He hadn't slept well; kept hearing noises downstairs at home and, on several occasions, had investigated to find a quiet house with no intruders or monsters lurking in the shadows. The whereabouts of Claire's laptop were still unknown, and she'd claimed on her insurance that it had been stolen. He checked all the doors and windows before he left, happy Claire was safe inside, asleep upstairs, nestling their baby boy who, in three months, would be here. Whoever had entered his home the other night, if that's what it was, wouldn't be getting in again. He'd managed to fix the cameras which he could access remotely on his phone, the installed app informing him of anyone approaching the house which gave both of them peace of mind.

Trinity Road was a quiet road with random cars scattered along the street on either side, their windows reflecting the bright morning sun. As he unclipped his seat belt, the movement of Tanzy's Golf pulling into the road up ahead caught his eye. Tanzy angled over and stopped just in front of him. They made eye contact and nodded, then stepped out. Byrd, although it was a Saturday, had dressed in his usual smart trousers and shoes, but instead of a shirt, he'd put on a black T-shirt and worn a thin black jacket over the top. His hair had been dampened and brushed to the side.

'You going to a funeral?' Tanzy said.

Byrd winced. 'Let's hope not.'

Tanzy was more casual, wearing trainers, blue jeans, and an open thin, dark-blue jacket, showing a tight white T-shirt. He wouldn't look out of place in a fashion magazine with his trimmed goatee, piercing blue eyes and tanned bald head.

They both walked along the small, narrow road towards the entrance of the flats that Cornty had described, peering up, trying to see what had been explained to them but struggled in the low sun that dominated the morning sky.

When they arrived at the pillars of the entrance, they noticed a cluster of people standing in the middle of the car park in front of them, close to the building's front door, all with their heads tipped, focusing on something above them. Each face showed a look of serious concern.

Tanzy and Byrd stopped at the small crowd and looked up, using a palm to shield their eyes from the sun.

'Jesus,' Byrd whispered, spotting the woman balancing on the handrail.

DC Cornty heard the detectives approach and came over from their right.

'Morning,' he said. 'We got a call from a runner who spotted her from the road just over half an hour ago. Just hanging like that.'

Byrd and Tanzy craned their necks to look up again.

'Is — is she dead?' Byrd asked, squinting in the morning glare.

'We don't know. When dispatch received the call, the woman explained what she could see and cleverly advised the operator not to use their sirens in case the loud sounds woke her up.'

Byrd nodded. It made perfect sense.

Tanzy gazed around at the people watching. 'Where are these people from?'

'The guy in the suit lives on the third floor. Was on his way out when he saw the runner standing in front of him, looking up with a worried look on her face. He said he doesn't know her but has seen her around, coming and going.'

Near the short chubby guy in the suit, there was an old lady, dressed in running gear but holding a small dog on a lead, who seemed to be itching to finish his run, doing small energetic circles around her feet.

There was another couple in their fifties, probably on a morning walk, and just beyond them, a bald guy dressed in shorts and a hoodie.

'We need to get something set up,' Tanzy said to Cornty. 'If she's alive and wakes up, we need to make sure if she falls she lands on something soft. Or at least clear these people away so they don't get hurt. Has the fire department been notified?'

Cornty shook his head.

'Get on it,' Tanzy instructed, disappointed with him. Cornty nodded, pulled his phone out and made the call.

'What on earth is she doing up there?' Byrd said. 'Is she drunk?'

Tanzy shrugged. 'We need a negotiator down here. If that's what her intentions are.' He looked over to Cornty, who had his phone pressed against his head. He focused on Byrd. 'Max, we need the fire lads out, get an extended ladder up there. If we can't get through that door, that'll be the only way.'

Byrd agreed. Tanzy then went over to the man in the suit from the third floor, holding a black briefcase and looked like the banker or lawyer type. 'What floor is she on, the fourth?'

The man, who Tanzy guessed was in his fifties judging by his hairline, turned. 'Yeah, the fourth. I'm on the third.'

'Can you let us in the building? We need access to her flat.'

'Sure.'

Tanzy turned his attention to Cornty, who'd finished on the phone. 'What's happening?'

'Backup is coming now. I've told them to approach quietly.'

'We need to move these people back. If she falls now, she'll land on them.'

DC Cornty moved forward, and quietly insisted that everyone moved back. Tanzy spotted Byrd on the phone and went over as Byrd ended the call and slipped his phone into his pocket.

'Negotiator is on his way,' Byrd informed him.

Tanzy nodded. 'The guy in the suit will let us in.'

'Cornty can control people down here. If we can get in her apartment and open that door, we could pull her back before she wakes.' Byrd and Tanzy went over to the short guy in the suit. 'Can you let us in now, please?'

The man nodded, pulled his keys from his pocket, and shuffled over to the front door of the building. Once he let them in, he went to the lift and pressed the button. Within seconds, the doors pinged open and they stepped inside.

They got out on fourth floor. 'Judging by her window, this should be the door.' He angled over to the door on the right.

'Do you know her name?' Byrd asked him.

He squinted. 'Could be Lorraine. Or Jane. I'm not one hundred per cent certain.'

Tanzy took out his phone and phoned the station, telling them to check the occupant of an address and to update them on their intentions of getting inside her apartment.

'Yeah, I'm sure it's this one.' The suited guy moved back, allowing Byrd and Tanzy to stop at the door.

Byrd tried pushing the door, then tried the handle. It was locked but worth a try. He checked Tanzy wasn't directly behind him, took a few spaces back, then lunged forward with his right foot into the left side of the door where the lock was. The door shook with a loud bang but it stood firm. He tried again and failed.

A door to their right opened. An elderly man appeared, frowning. 'What on earth is going on?' He wore a long, blue dressing gown and thick-framed glasses sat on the end of a thick nose. It seemed they'd interrupted his newspaper reading judging by the folded *Northern Echo* in his hand.

'I'm sorry, sir,' Tanzy said. 'Don't worry, we're the police. We need to get inside. The woman is in danger.'

'What's wrong with Jane?'

'She's on her balcony. We need to get inside to help her.'

He eyed them suspiciously for a moment. Although he recognised the suited man as someone who lived on the floor below, he asked, 'Can I see some ID? You don't dress like you're with the police.'

The guy had a point. Tanzy looked ready for a catwalk and Byrd looked like he'd been to his gran's funeral. Tanzy pulled his ID from his pocket to show him. Once satisfied, the elderly man said, 'Don't kick that door again. You might break it.'

'But we need—'

'I have a spare key,' he said, stopping Tanzy short.

'Thank you.'

The guy went inside. It felt like three hours had passed before he came back and handed Tanzy the key. It was a single key linked to a keyring with a photo of Benidorm's seafront.

'What's her full name?'

'Jane Ericson.'

Byrd pulled two pairs of latex gloves from his pocket and handed a pair to Tanzy. They used the key to open the door, and Byrd went in first, followed by Tanzy. The man in the suit waited at door, unsure what to do.

Immediately to the left they spotted the French doors and saw Jane positioned on the balcony. From inside her flat, they could see how perfectly balanced her weight must have been, and it wouldn't take much for her to become unbalanced.

Byrd tried to slide the door open but it wouldn't budge.

'The lock,' Tanzy said, pointing to the mechanism near the handle. Byrd, for a moment, felt stupid, then flicked the lock down, and very slowly slid the door open. Just as he did, a loud ringtone rang out, coming from a phone positioned on the floor of the balcony.

It was so loud, Jane stirred and murmured something. She opened her eyes suddenly and stared wide eyed at the phone below her.

Byrd froze and watched her, listening to the ringtone. He didn't want to speak or disturb her or call her name, knowing it could cause an unfortunate sudden movement that could literally tip her over. But she panicked, realising she was on her balcony handrail.

Then it happened so fast.

Byrd lunged forward to grab her left hand but missed.

And she fell four floors down to the concrete below with a sickening thud, the awful sound followed by a string of screams and panic from the people on the ground.

27

Saturday morning
Police station

'You missed her?' DCI Fuller asked Byrd after hearing what had happened.

Sadly, Byrd nodded. 'It happened too fast. But yes, I missed her.'

Fuller leaned back, sighed heavily and looked up at the ceiling. Byrd and Tanzy didn't say anything. Fuller hadn't intended to come in today, but after Byrd had phoned him less than an hour ago, informing him about Jane Ericson, he had no bloody choice. He didn't look amused about it either, not that it was Byrd or Tanzy's fault.

The sunlight shining through the window that overlooked St Cuthbert's Church to the left had warmed the office. So much so that Fuller looked hot and bothered in his coat, but for some reason, he hadn't taken it off. A simple phone call and an emailed report would have done. He'd promised his missus and kids they were going to the beach and weren't pleased to hear he'd have to go down to the station to be personally updated about another death in Darlington.

'We don't need this shit.' Fuller's tone was grim and straight to the point. 'So, as well as a house fire that killed a family of four, and four missing women who haven't been seen in nearly a week, we now have this?'

Byrd and Tanzy said nothing. There was nothing to say.

'Please talk me through this again,' Fuller said, seeming like he had other things on his mind. 'You managed to get into the flat using the key from her neighbour, then saw her on the balcony. Then as you opened the door, the phone rang on the balcony and woke her up?'

Byrd nodded, confirming his analysis so far.

'But she panicked, realising she was balanced on the handrail and went over?'

'Yeah.'

Fuller thought for a moment. 'Who phoned her?'

'This is one of the reasons why I phoned you,' said Byrd. 'I needed to tell you personally.'

'Go on . . .'

'The number in her phone was saved as Roger Carlton.'

'The same name linked to the house fire, who we suspect could be Adrian Dilton?'

Tanzy and Byrd both nodded in unison.

'Sonofabitch . . .' Fuller dipped his head and looked down at the desk. 'We need to find this fucking Adrian Dilton. He's playing games with us. Do we know how she got up there?'

'Not yet. There are several possible scenarios,' said Byrd, who'd discussed this with Tanzy earlier at the scene after she'd fallen. Fuller waited for it. 'We'll be able to determine if she had consumed alcohol after the tox report, meaning she could have been out in the town, came home, and for whatever reason, collapsed in that position.'

Fuller made a face, unsure if that story had any truth to it.

'I know. It doesn't seem likely,' admitted Byrd. 'Or . . . she was taken home, knocked unconscious, and carefully positioned there for her life to be determined whether she woke and leaned to the left or the right.'

'Where is Jane now?'

Byrd informed Fuller she had been taken to the hospital for the pathologists to have a look at her. It was obvious, judging by the nature of what happened and the state of the body, the fall had caused her death. But they needed to check to see what happened before then. Had she been drugged? Excessive levels of alcohol?

'Does the building have cameras?' asked Fuller.

Byrd nodded. 'We spotted a camera in the lift and in the entrance door. DC Cornty is speaking with the maintenance team to see the footage from last night and early this morning.'

'Why did the phone ring when it did?' asked Fuller. 'Seems a coincidence it was when you almost reached her?'

Tanzy nodded several times as if something had clicked. 'It's as if whoever did it, was watching, waiting for that exact moment, knowing that ringing her would wake her.'

'Are Forensics there?'

'Yes. Forensics are checking the apartment for any prints. Tallow and Hope said they'd be in touch later. Tallow wasn't happy he had to come in.'

'Nature of the beast, unfortunately.' Fuller shrugged, implying he wasn't pleased to be here, either. 'Good work, you two. See what the cameras tell us and see what Tallow and Hope find.' He then noticed something on Tanzy's face. 'What is it, Orion?'

Tanzy turned to Byrd. 'Remember the people watching below, the people near us?'

Byrd bobbed his head.

'The bald guy in the shorts and hoody, remember him?'

Byrd said he did.

He rarely missed anything.

'Didn't Samantha Verity, from seeing the clip from the still shot on the camera at Napier Street, say she was certain that Roger Carlton was Adrian Dilton, and she was one hundred per cent sure he was wearing a wig and a fake moustache?'

Byrd nodded. It finally clicked. 'Same height, same features . . .'

'I knew when I saw his face, there was something familiar about him. I'd spoken to him on the morning of the house fire. When I saw him this morning, he recognised me. But he didn't have dark, brown eyes. He had bright blue eyes. And a thin goatee.' Tanzy fell silent for a second. 'They were contact lenses. He was in disguise. Adrian Dilton was there, standing with us, watching Jane.'

'He knew exactly when to make the call,' Byrd said. 'As soon as he saw me at the French doors from below, he phoned her, knowing the call would wake her and there'd be a good chance she'd panic and would fall.'

28

Claire was tired, slumped on the sofa in the living room, her eyes barely staying open as she watched the television fixed to the wall above the fireplace. Little Alan had started moving in her belly more recently and she hadn't been sleeping very well during the night.

The front door opened. Byrd, standing in the hallway. 'You okay, Claire?'

She smiled and looked back at the television. 'Has anyone seen anything?'

He padded a few steps in but didn't sit down. 'No, no one. Rick and Mary down the road have a camera that shows much of the street, but we couldn't see a thing. No one has heard anything in a few days. Nothing else has gone missing. Probably just a passer-by, trying his luck.'

'Hope so,' she said slowly. 'Can I have something to eat?'

'What would we like?'

'Up to the head chef. Surprise me.'

Byrd smiled, turned and left the living room. He removed his shoes and positioned them near the front door under the piles of coats. It had been a long day. He went into the kitchen, took a pasta bake from the freezer and put it in the oven to cook.

His phone rang in his pocket; he was expecting the call.

'Hi, Jacob,' answered Byrd.

'Hey, Max,' replied Tallow, the senior forensic.

'All done at the flat?'

'Yeah, we finished a little while ago.' Tallow paused a moment. 'In the way of prints and traces of DNA, there's nothing out of the ordinary that stands out. Have you seen the camera footage yet?'

'No, we're still waiting on the maintenance man to call.'

Byrd leaned over to check the pasta in the oven.

'We did find something interesting in the bedroom though,' Tallow went on.

'What's that?'

'Under her desk, there was a bug stuck to the underside.'

'A bug?'

'A listening device. Something you guys know all about.' Tallow explained what it looked like and Byrd agreed it was very likely a remote listening device. 'There was also a business card positioned on top of her closed laptop.'

'What type of business card?'

'An electrician's card with the name Roger Carlton on it.'

'Roger Carlton?'

'Yeah.'

Byrd fell silent for a few moments, thinking hard. Without seeing the cameras and finding out if Jane Ericson had gone up to her flat by herself, it was obvious that Roger Carlton aka Adrian Dilton had been in her flat at some point. If so, there was a similarity with the fire at Napier Street and his frequent visits there before the actual murder. This had been planned, similar to the last one. And not only that, Adrian Dilton had been there at the scene with them, same as he was in Napier Street, posing as a member of the fire department. It was like he was checking his plan had worked.

'There's something else,' Tallow said. 'On the back of the Roger Carlton card, it said to look at the laptop.'

'Jane's laptop?'

'Assume so.'

'Where is the laptop?' asked Byrd.

'Orion told me to contact Mac from DFU, who said he was at the station, so we left the laptop with him, mentioning Tanzy had requested for it to be checked.'

Byrd frowned, surprised that Tanzy hadn't mentioned it.

'Okay, thanks for letting me know. Good work, Jacob. Enjoy the rest of your weekend.'

'I'll try.' Tallow hung up the phone and the line went dead.

Byrd slipped the phone back into his pocket.

A little while after, he plated the pasta bake for Claire. He entered the living room and found her sound asleep. He smiled, placed the plate down onto the coffee table with some cutlery and stood for a moment, watching her, the way she held her belly, holding their son, comforting him as he grew inside of her. He leaned down, placed a palm on her stomach and kissed her forehead. He couldn't wait to meet baby Alan. His only regret was that his parents wouldn't have the chance to see him but that's something he'd have to get over.

29

Adrian Dilton sat at his desk, his hand on the mouse, clicking and scrolling, with a deep focus in his eyes. When he concentrated, nothing distracted him; he knew what he wanted and knew how to get it.

Danny Walters had been straightforward. Everything had gone to plan. Killing his family in the process was unfortunate, but he wouldn't dwell on it too much. It was all Danny's fault.

Jane Ericson had been a breeze too. As long as he continued to stay focused and prepared, the plans would fall into place.

But, he had to admit, he was cutting it fine.

Earlier that morning had been the second time that DI Tanzy had seen him. Whether or not the detective inspector had noticed him was a different matter, but he knew it was a dangerous game to play, being there at the scene, involving himself when, perhaps, he didn't need to.

The difference was he wanted to make sure his plan had worked.

After his preparations, he needed to check they were dead. When DI Byrd had opened the French doors four floors up, Dilton had called Jane's phone, knowing the ring-tone he'd set up would startle her.

And boy did it.

As soon as the phone rang, he saw the anxiety in Byrd's serious face when pathetically attempted to reach for her and Jane suddenly panicked and fell over the edge. In less than a second, she hit the floor with a sickening splat.

Even he admitted it wasn't pleasant.

But when everyone jumped back in terrified shock, he casually placed his phone into his pocket and walked away. Everyone had been too concerned with Jane's mangled body down on the concrete to notice him disappear.

For a moment, he stopped what he was doing, looked at the printed sheet of paper to his left with the boxes and names underneath Danny Walters and Jane Ericson. He went through the names in his mind, thinking about who was next, and how he'd implement his plan. It needed to be right.

He decided he'd come back to it later and finish editing the video on the screen. Once he'd made several tweaks, he watched it over and over, happy it was ready to go.

He opened YouTube and logged in. He wasn't worried about being traced because he'd protected himself and his location, his IP address changing every ten seconds, bouncing around the globe, making it almost impossible for the most intelligent of IT wizards to trace.

He clicked on UPLOAD and sat back, waiting for the download bar to reach one hundred per cent. He leaned back, smiled and closed his eyes. He couldn't wait for the havoc it would cause.

30

A few hours later, Claire woke up, feeling hungry. Byrd warmed her food, brought it into the living room and placed it down on the coffee table in front of her.

'There you go,' said Byrd. 'How are you feeling?'

She shuffled up to a sitting position and leaned forward to grab the bowl of pasta bake. 'I'm tired, Max.'

He took a seat next to her, smiled and rubbed her back for a moment. 'I can't wait to see him, you know. I wonder what he'll look like?'

'I bet he's a chunk, like you!' she said, with a playful grin.

'I'm actually categorised at an ideal weight now,' replied Byrd. And he was right. After losing two stone he was doing well, though he didn't have a lot of muscle. He wouldn't be on the cover of *Men's Health* magazine, or modelling swim-wear, nor would he ever be as finely tuned as Tanzy, but certainly, an improvement on what he was like six months ago. He felt better, felt sharper, fitter. He enjoyed football, being able to run longer and quicker.

'I know,' said Claire, rubbing his thigh lovingly. 'You've done so well. It's my turn to be a fatty now.' She patted her stomach with her free hand.

Byrd leaned to the side to check his phone.

'You expecting a call?' Claire frowned at him. 'It's nearly nine.'

'I'm waiting for someone to ring me about the cameras at the flat today.' Byrd had told Claire the basic story of what happened earlier this morning, but missed the not-so-pleasant details, like Jane Ericson bouncing on to the hard concrete with a stomach-churning smack. He knew, after weeks of feeling sick because of the pregnancy, it wouldn't help her cause. She seemed to be worse in the morning, frequently waking, feeling nauseous when she woke.

Claire nodded and turned back to the television.

On cue, Byrd's phone rang. He didn't have the number saved, but stood and left the room, then answered it as he wandered into the kitchen.

'Hi,' the voice said, 'is this Detective Inspector Max Byrd?'

'That's me.'

'Hi, my name is Joseph Peters. The maintenance man for the flats at Trinity Road.'

'Hi, Joseph.' Byrd glanced up at the kitchen clock and wondered what had taken him so long to call.

'Apologies I am calling you now. I've been having issues with my phone. Only got it working over an hour ago and heard the awful news about what happened earlier. Is it true you want to see the footage from the cameras?'

'Please, if that is possible.'

'Well, it is possible. But I'm afraid they won't be of any help.'

Byrd frowned. 'How so?'

'Both cameras — the one in the entrance door and the camera in the lift — don't show anything between 3 a.m. and 4 a.m.'

'You're joking?' Byrd hung his head and pressed a palm to the side of his temple.

'I wish I was. As soon as the clock on the screen goes to 3 a.m., it immediately changes to 4 a.m. There's an hour missing. I don't understand it myself. I can't explain it. It's never happened before.'

'Okay. Can you send the footage over as soon as possible. We'll need it to analyse ourselves.'

Joseph Peters stayed silent for a while.

'Can you access the cameras now where you are?'

'Yes, I have access to the cameras from my home. What is it you need?'

'Are you able to email over the footage for every camera in the building from the last three days?'

'Erm, yeah, I suppose I could.' His tone suggested he wasn't too keen, obviously knowing it would take a while.

'How many cameras are there?'

'Just two. One in the lift and the other covering the entrance and exit door. I'll put the files together and email them straight over.'

'Great, thank you,' said Byrd. 'That would be a great help.'

'My pleasure, Detective,' he said, now sounding more upbeat.

Byrd placed his phone down on the kitchen worktop when the call ended and sighed heavily. Just as he was about to pick the phone up and head towards the living room, it rang, the ringtone echoing in the silent kitchen.

It was PC Amy Weaver. He frowned. It was unusual for her to be phoning him at this time, especially when she wasn't on shift. 'Amy?' he answered.

'Sir. Sorry to bother you.' She sounded flustered.

'What is it, Amy?'

'There's another video on YouTube. My God, you need to see this.'

31

Byrd immediately went upstairs to his small, quiet office and closed the door. He dashed to his desk and opened his laptop and sat down, his heart pumping in his chest.

'You at your computer?' Amy Weaver asked through the phone.

'Yeah. Hold on.'

'I've emailed it to you,' added Weaver. 'The link will take you straight to it.'

'How did you find it?' Byrd tapped the desk surface, waiting for the screen to load that seemed to be taking forever.

'It was on Facebook. A friend tagged me.'

'Jesus.'

Weaver stayed on the line waiting for him to open the link — just above the email offering him penis enlargement pills and diet shakes for "great" results. He clicked on the link.

For the next minute, he remained silent, watching carefully. At the end of the clip, he realised he'd held his breath and let it out suddenly. 'Jesus Christ, Amy.'

'I know, Max,' she said quietly.

'Thanks for letting me know. I need to ring Ori.'

Byrd hung up and watched the video again. He then found Tanzy's number and pressed CALL.

'Max, what do I owe—'

'Ori, I'm sending you a link. It's a video. You need to stop whatever you're doing and watch it.'

Tanzy didn't reply for a moment. He knew by Byrd's tone it was something important. 'Hold on.'

There were sounds of shuffling through the phone. Tanzy said, 'Okay, the laptop is open. How've you sent it?'

'Check your personal emails.'

Tanzy opened the email and clicked on the link.

'Tell me when it starts,' said Byrd.

'Yeah, it's started,' Tanzy informed him.

Byrd pressed play and they watched it together on their screens. At the bottom of the video, the title of the video was "Element Two".

'What is element two?' said Tanzy.

The video looked like it had been edited and didn't flow perfectly, clearly showing different times of the day and background activity. The camera positioned high up in the corner of the dimly lit lift picked up the man who stepped inside, carrying a holdall of tools. He then leaned forward and pressed a button on the control console, then took a step back, revealing his thick head of hair and ridiculous moustache, which Byrd and Tanzy now both knew, was fake.

'That's Dilton!' noted Tanzy. 'See the time, Max. 4.30 p.m. the day before.'

'I see it.'

The next scene showed Jane Ericson walk into the lift, dressed up ready for town, wearing a purple maxi dress, her dark, curly hair resting on her slender shoulders. It wasn't long before she disappeared. The time was just after 7 p.m. the night before.

'Max, what—'

'Just watch, Ori.'

The video changed to another scene inside the lift. This time, it was 3.10 a.m. earlier that morning. Jane Ericson stumbled inside, carrying a half-eaten tray of chips and her small handbag. She used the wall of the lift to steady her weight, which didn't take a detective to work out she was drunk.

To the right of the screen, an arm came into view and placed a black holdall down onto the lift floor. Judging by the size of the arm it looked like a man wearing a shirt. Unfortunately, they couldn't see a face. A few seconds after, the figure lowered to the area where he'd placed the bag and pulled something out.

'What's that?' Tanzy asked.

When the man moved in full view of the camera, Byrd and Tanzy noticed he'd put on a mask, covering the whole of his face and top of his head.

'What the hell is that?' Tanzy whispered.

The man leaned down, picked up some variety of can, unscrewed the lid and green mist started to fill the lift. Jane Ericson didn't seem fazed at first. If anything, her drunken state found it amusing, judging by the smile curling up the side of her face. Very soon, the entire screen turned green and the mist eventually took over.

'What on earth is that, Max?'

'I have absolutely no idea, Ori.'

In the next scene, it was daylight. Outside. The camera or recording device was angled up to the sky, showing Jane Ericson balanced on her balcony. Somewhere off the screen, the sound of beeping was heard, then a final beep. The video then showed the balcony door open on the fourth floor and, out of nowhere, the phone rang.

Jane Ericson then fell to the ground with a splat. The video captured every second of it. Then a voice said, 'How unfortunate,' before it cut off.

Byrd's face grew hot.

'So, he recorded it, then put it online for the world to see. Again!' shouted Tanzy. 'We need to stop this before it goes viral.'

'It's already gone viral, Ori.'

32

Tanzy made two coffees, brought them over to the kitchen table, placing them both down, and took a seat opposite Pip. She smiled thanks and looked down, scrolling through something on her phone. The kids were outside playing in the garden. Eric was kicking the football against the side wall of the garage, the repetitive banging borderline annoying, and Jasmine was playing with a water set that Pip had bought recently, the sound of water splashing onto the decking every so often.

As Pip continued to scroll at whatever she was looking at, Tanzy's phone rang. He plucked it out from his jogging bottoms and answered it.

'Ori, it's Mac,' the voice said.

'Hi, Mac.'

'I've been looking at Jane Ericson's laptop.' He fell silent as if he was doing something else. 'I need to show you something.'

'Okay, can you email it over? I can have a—'

'I need to show you now,' Mac said, cutting him off. 'Are you at home?'

119

Tanzy frowned. 'I am . . .'

'Good. I'm near yours. See you in five.'

* * *

Tanzy curiously opened the door to Mac, who stood there with a laptop under his arm, looking a little scruffier than usual, in a faded jumper a size too small and jeans with a tear at the knee which looked years old.

'Hey, Ori,' he said, with a thin smile.

'Come in,' Tanzy said, who stepped back and motioned him inside.

It was the first time Mac had been to Tanzy's house. Whatever Mac was going to show him, Tanzy knew was important, otherwise it could have waited until the following morning.

'Just through there,' said Tanzy, pointing to the kitchen. 'Can I get you a coffee?'

Mac told him he would love one and pulled a seat out at the table. Pip had gone outside with the kids, ensuring they stayed there. Mac opened the laptop on the table and without asking, took the half pack of biscuits and helped himself.

No wonder you're in the obese category, Tanzy thought.

Tanzy brought the coffee over and took a seat next to Mac, who explained to him he'd found something weird.

'Weird?' asked Tanzy, frowning.

'Well, when you know where to look, you can see how long people spend on certain websites. Behind the scenes, if you like —' he waved it away rather than getting too technical — 'and the data tells you that.'

Tanzy gave a gradual nod, not really following. 'Okay . . .'

'There's a certain website that she'd visited. The problem with the site is that, apart from an empty word box near the top of the page, there's nothing else. The site itself carries a huge source of data.'

Tanzy held up a hand. 'Hold on, hold on. I'm lost, Mac.'

Mac smiled. 'Have you got Wi-Fi?'

'Who doesn't,' said Tanzy. 'You want the password?'

Mac nodded.

Once connected, he said, 'Let me show you.' In the blank bar at the top of the page, he typed in the address and tapped ENTER. The site came up immediately.

'At the end dot com?'

'Yeah,' said Mac, nodding. 'But look.' He angled the laptop so Tanzy could see it clearer. 'See this page. It's a black screen, apart from that log-in bar.'

'Yeah?'

'But a page like this, with no additional drop-down menus or no visible linked pages, should have a small internet presence. The data volumes coming from that server should be minimal.'

'But . . . ?' Tanzy said, unsure.

'It has the capacity to run a large page with multiple drop-downs and a mass amount of media, such as videos and images.'

'So, why is there only the username and password log-in option?'

'That's what I was wondering,' admitted Mac. 'Whatever she was up to, she needed a password to access, which I assume, would take her beyond this page and on to whatever is lurking behind this page.'

'Is there a way to get past it?'

'I've tried dozens of words and phrases. Every time I press enter, the search bar clears and I have to try again.' He pulled the laptop closer to him. 'What I have done, though, is search for the site on Google. There are a couple of forums that came up. Here, have a look.' He pushed the laptop closer to Tanzy, who read the comments in several threads.

He frowned, worriedly. 'What on earth was she watching on that site?'

33

Most of the team were aware what happened over the week-end regarding Jane Ericson and waited nervously in room 103, a long rectangular room with windows on one side that allowed a substantial amount of daylight in. A whiteboard filled most of the wall near the door, with a projector fixed to the ceiling just above it for presentations or videos.

The morning was going to be used for just that. An update on the latest news and current affairs.

The tables in the room were positioned in a 'U' shape. Fuller had said that it made everyone feel important and part of the team. In previous roles, he'd implemented such ideas instead of rows of desks, experiencing that people at the back didn't involve themselves as much as the ones at the front.

As the detectives stood at the front, Byrd noticed the morning sun shining brightly through the windows, illuminating most of their tired, squinting faces, so he went over and used the pull cord to lower the blinds a little.

On the tables furthest away from them was DC Cornty, DC Tiffin, PC Andrews and PC Weaver. The right side was filled by DC Leonard, PC Grearer, DS Stockdale, and PC Timms. On the left side, were the lead forensic techs, Jacob Tallow and Emily Hope. Next to them, the forensic trainee tech, Amanda Forrest. Beside the forensic team, closest to the door, was DCI Fuller. He didn't always attend the meetings but after the events from the weekend, he'd made sure he was present, ensuring his team was up to speed with current affairs. It also gave him the opportunity to hear their views and ideas on how to solve them, which he enjoyed.

Byrd returned to the centre of the wall and stopped near Tanzy, who had set up the laptop with a presentation they'd both put together earlier.

'We'll make a start,' Byrd said, grabbing the small black remote from the table. Tanzy pressed a button on the laptop and the whiteboard filling with a page titled "Current Affairs" and the date underneath it.

'As most of us know, Jane Ericson, a twenty-six-year-old female, fell from the fourth floor of her balcony to the ground. She died immediately.'

The slide on the screen showed everyone the area of concrete where she'd landed, covered in a small, faint pool of dried blood. The next image was a photo taken of the balcony from ground level, indicating the height of the fourth floor to give them a clear perspective.

'That's a long way down,' DC Cornty commented.

'In addition to this, another video has been uploaded to the internet. Some of you may have seen it, some may have not. Hands up who's seen it?' Half of the hands went up. 'We managed to save it before it was taken down. For those who haven't seen it, here goes.' He looked back at them. 'Viewer discretion is advised.'

Most of them nodded, readying themselves. The video was the same one Tanzy and Byrd had watched yesterday, starting with Jane Ericson entering the lift, glammed up ready for town up until the early morning when the green gas filled the lift until they couldn't see Jane anymore.

'What on earth has just happened?' DC Anne Tiffin asked, the first time she'd seen it.

Byrd or Tanzy didn't respond and continued to watch. The next part was taken from ground level, looking up at Jane, who was balanced on the handrail of the balcony.

When Jane hit the ground, Tiffin covered her mouth with her hands.

'That is a long way . . .' DC Cornty whispered.

Tanzy said, 'So, we have a similarity here, guys. We have two murders and we have two videos. Investigating the scenes, we can also confirm we have the name Roger Carlton too. As we also know, a female called Samantha Verity came forward informing us she'd had a relationship with Roger Carlton who, in fact, is called Adrian Dilton. She said he was obsessed with an American show where one of the characters was called Roger Carlton. She also said he was strange and there was something off about him. The first time we came across Roger Carlton was at the house fire at Napier Street. I spoke with him — he was posing as one of the fire investigators, but after speaking to Harry Law, their supervisor, he didn't know the name or see the man in question. Secondly—' he looked over to Forensics — 'thanks to our forensic team, we found a business card on Jane's laptop. It was an electrician's business card with the name Roger Carlton.'

DC Tiffin raised her hand.

'Yes, Anne?'

'If the videos were uploaded to the internet, can we not trace it? Or the IP address of the device that uploaded it?'

Byrd and Tanzy both smiled, appreciating her train of thought.

'Unfortunately not,' Byrd answered. 'We spoke with Mac in DFU and he said he did his best to trace the IP address with the ISP but the—'

'The ISP?' questioned DC Leonard.

'The internet service provider,' answered DC Cornty. All eyes fell on Cornty for a moment, so he elaborated.

'Everyone is assigned an IP address by their internet service provider.'

'That's true,' continued Byrd, 'however the IP address was never fixed and the service provider didn't recognise the address of the upload.'

Leonard frowned. 'Meaning what exactly?'

'That Roger Carlton, a.k.a Adrian Dilton, found a way to make sure his IP address was untraceable. Mac said he's come across it but only on rare occasions. The address seemed to bounce across providers, leaving no fixed location. We are assuming he's based here in Darlington, but according to his IP address, he could be in India, then ten seconds later, in America.'

There were a few confused faces but no one said anything on the matter.

'Do we have any intel on the whereabouts of Mr Dilton, yet?' asked DCI Fuller over from the left, sitting casually with one leg over the other.

'Not yet, sir,' responded Byrd. 'We spoke with the company he worked for, an IT firm up in Newcastle.' Fuller was aware of this but appreciated it was for the benefit of the team.

'Did Samantha Verity give an address for Adrian Dilton?'

'She did. Orion and I went there. House was empty. We spoke with a neighbour who said he hadn't seen him in months. Turns out, judging by the information I received from the Land Registry, that the house isn't owned by Adrian Dilton anymore. A guy called Geoff Adamson purchased it. I spoke with him on Friday and he bought the house from Mr Dilton but didn't have any contact details. I tried checking with the solicitors who'd been involved in the sale but they folded and no longer exist.'

Fuller nodded but it was clear by his facial expression he was less than impressed with how things were going.

'Anything on the fire at Napier Street?' DS Stockdale asked.

Byrd turned towards the forensic team, who all shook their heads.

'What about the four missing women?' Fuller asked.

Byrd and Tanzy had heard him on the phone in his office to the superintendent, Barry Eckles. Judging by their heated conversation, it appeared Eckles was pressing him hard and didn't hold back in expressing his disappointment so far. The call had ended by Fuller saying 'I understand' before he hung up the phone.

'No sign of them, sir. I've spoken to their families over the weekend to give them updates, a way of informing them they are our priority.'

Fuller gritted his teeth and pushed his lips out. It wasn't looking good. And judging by what was going on in Darlington, they all thought the same thing: it wouldn't be long before another body turned up or went missing.

34

Monday morning
Essex, south of England

Linda Fallon made coffee and toast, then sauntered into her conservatory, placing them both down on the small table next to her chair. She grabbed the TV remote and settled into it. The sun was up and high in the sky, brightly shining through the glass windows of the conservatory. She'd had it built three years ago, ready for her retirement.

It wasn't long before Rusty, the black lab she'd had for eight years, came bouncing in from the kitchen, no doubt smelling the toast lingering in the air. He loved toast. It was his favourite.

'Good morning, you!' She leaned forward and rubbed under his chin and top of his head. There was nothing but love in his dark, brown eyes as he looked up at her waiting patiently. 'You want your breakfast?'

He moved his head eagerly as if he understood.

'Here you go . . .' She grabbed a slice and fed it to him. It was gone within seconds, but he seemed happy. Rusty was a brilliant dog. She'd bought him as a puppy when her husband, Gary, was alive. They used to go walking with him over the fields and down by the river. Rusty was Gary's idea. He knew cancer would take him eventually and wanted Linda to have company when it was his time to go. And he wasn't wrong. Neither were the doctors. Six months after getting Rusty, Gary passed away. Liver cancer. The only saving grace was that, in the end, it happened quickly.

Rusty looked happy and lowered to the floor, dropping his head between his front legs, looking towards the television. He did this most mornings. It was their routine. Linda had always wondered what he could see on the television, or whether it was just colours but either way, he enjoyed it, and no doubt enjoyed her commentary about what was happening.

Using the remote she found the news saved in her recordings and pressed play. She liked the national news; liked to know what was going on around the country, not only in and around Essex.

She watched the news desk reporter inform the public about a killer in Darlington, who'd set fire to a house, murdering a family of four, and was now the likely suspect in the death of a young woman who had fallen from her balcony from the fourth floor.

She raised a hand to her mouth. 'God . . . that's awful, Rusty.'

She grabbed her iPad from the arm of the chair and searched for murder in Darlington. A string of results came up. She slowly scrolled down the list and clicked on the link with the headline: *House Fire — Family of Four Burns to Death*. At the bottom of the page, it mentioned a YouTube video, titled "Element One", explaining that it was live footage recorded from the scene of the fire. She opened up YouTube and typed it in. Nothing came up. It had been taken down.

She pressed return and found herself on the list of results again, seeing headline: *Woman Falls to her Death* underneath. She clicked it, read up on Jane Ericson to learn exactly what had happened to her. Due to further investigation from the forensic team after seeing the deadly gas from a camera inside the lift, they assume it was most likely an asphyxiant gas that depleted the level of oxygen inside the small space. The green colour could have been added for effect.

There was mention of another video posted to the internet, titled "Element Two". Linda opened her app and searched for it, but it was either blocked or had been deleted.

'Never mind, Rusty,' she said to the dog. 'It isn't there.'

When she finished watching the rest of the news, she stood up, went to the kitchen and made a coffee. On her way back to the conservatory she stopped to stare at the dozens of photos on the wall, her focus on the one of her and Chief Constable David Gilling, when she'd received an award of recognition at the annual Police awards from several years ago. She was so happy and proud. Single-handed, she had interviewed and successfully got inside the mind of Tony Crawley, the man who'd kidnapped and killed multiple teenage girls, but had given the name of the last victim who he'd kept alive. Because of her, sixteen-year-old Bethany Tate had been found and sent home to her family, safe and sound, albeit with a few scratches and a story she'd remember forever.

After the award she had retired to settle down for a quieter life.

She had been thinking about it all morning and made the decision to pick up her phone and call the number she memorised.

'Hi, my name is Linda Fallon. I'm wondering if I can speak to one of the lead detectives who is dealing with the recent murders in Darlington?'

'Hold on,' the operator said, 'I'll put you through.'

'Thanks.' Fallon waited.

'Hi. This is Detective Inspector Max Byrd of Durham Constabulary. Who is calling?'

'My name is Linda Fallon. I'm a retired criminal psychologist.'

'How can I help you, Mrs Fallon?'

'You can't,' she said. 'But I have a very good feeling I can help you.'

35

Monday evening
Darlington

Lisa Butterwick and Sarah McKay were cuddled together on the dark, cold floor. They had got over the fact they wouldn't see Lorraine again. It had been four days since she'd been there. Four horrendous days that, without any awareness of the time or light inside the dark space, had felt like weeks. They had tried to keep count of the days but were tired, dirty and hungry. They still didn't know how they'd got there and had stopped trying to work it out. One minute, they were getting into a minibus to take them to a party, the next, they woke up in this dark room without the ability to see or even begin to understand the situation they were in.

After two of them had vanished, their confusion worsened, understanding less about what was happening.

Watching them through the one-way mirror high up on the wall, were the two men responsible for putting them there. Mitch and Brad.

* * *

'They've given up, haven't they?' Brad said, standing at the window, peering down on them.

'What do you expect, Brad?' replied Mitch. 'If I was in there, I'd have given up too.'

Brad shrugged, turned and made his way back over to the desk where the computer screens were positioned, dropping into the empty chair. 'Who are they wanting next?'

Mitch focused on the computer monitor. 'Votes are really close so far. See what it's like on Thursday.'

'I think we should mix this up a little,' suggested Brad.

'How?' Mitch swivelled on his chair, curious about what he had in mind. 'What ideas do you have?'

'Nothing yet, but people will start to get bored if we keep things the same. We need to mix it up every so often. Maybe throw in a curveball of some sort. It'll get them all excited, won't it?'

'I'll think about it,' considered Mitch.

Both men focused on the screen for a while, looking at the various profiles. A message popped up in the lower right-hand corner.

'Ooh is that another one?' asked Brad, recognising the notification sound.

'Looks like it. We need to keep it quiet. It can't grow too quickly. I'd love it to, but it will attract too much attention.'

Reluctantly, Brad nodded his head.

'We'll put them on the reserve list for the next lot. There's so many to choose from.' Mitch smiled widely. 'We'll pick a selection when the time is right.'

'Sounds good,' agreed Brad, then he dropped his head. 'Mitch, we won't get found out will we?' Mitch smiled and shook his head. 'This is untraceable. Trust me. No one will get beyond the firewall. Have you seen the film *Inception*?'

Brad squinted, wondering where he was going with it. 'I have . . .'

'It's like that. A dream within a dream within a dream. This site—' he jabbed a finger towards the computer screens — 'is like that. Even the best IT wizards won't find it.'

Mitch's eyebrows shot up. 'They're paying through bitcoin. Trust me, it's untraceable.'

Brad nodded at Mitch's words. 'How does bitcoin work?'

Mitch waved it away. 'You don't need to worry about a thing. It's a safer way of doing things, Brad.'

Brad wasn't sure but nodded again. He pointed to the screen. 'How's it looking?'

'The vote's tilted. They want Sarah now.'

Brad grinned. 'How many votes is that so far?'

'Three hundred and six.'

Brad smiled wider. 'We're doing well.' He stood up and went over to the window again. 'Seeing as Danny and Jane aren't going to be joining us anymore, are we going to let two more players in?'

'We are. I'm checking their profiles now. I'll pick two of the voters later. But for now, I need to go to work. How long are you staying?'

Brad looked down at his watch. 'Not long, the missus will be expecting me home soon. By the way, have the three remaining players voted?'

'Two have. The other is online but they haven't decided yet.'

Standing up, Mitch yawned and stretched. 'Can't be bothered with work tonight. When you leave, turn off the lights and make sure you lock up. Leave this system on. Might be good to keep playing the video from Friday. It'll keep them entertained.'

Brad nodded. It made sense. 'When are we getting some more?'

'Have a look around town on Saturday night. With a little persuasion and charm, you'll be able to pick up a few drunks in town that would be happy to go to a house party.'

'You got it, boss. See you tomorrow.'

* * *

Brad was still there an hour later, watching the women down on the floor through the glass. Through the microphones he could hear their tired, exhausted whispers.

He moved over to the left, stepping around the desk and, reaching for the valve fixed to the wall, he opened it. Through the vents gas silently filled the room, and after three minutes he turned off the valve, grabbed the plate of food they'd prepared earlier and headed down the stairs to the room. Before entering, he picked up the mask from the floor, put it on, and unlocked the door, then went inside with the tray, smelling the rancid scents of urine and faeces. He gently placed the tray of food on the floor near them and locked the door on his way out.

36

Tuesday morning
Police station

Tanzy and Byrd went to DCI Fuller's office and gave him an update on current investigations. Fuller barely said a word, clearly less than impressed with how things were going.

The only links between the two murders were the posted videos to the internet and the name Roger Carlton, who they knew to be Adrian Dilton.

'Have we located Dilton yet?'

Byrd shook his head. 'We've searched and searched. His picture is with the media. His last known employment was working for the IT firm up in Newcastle.'

Fuller sighed and leaned back. He was wearing a thin black jumper, something that fitted him better when he was a little slimmer.

'So, what's the plan?' asked Fuller.

'We may have someone who can help us,' said Byrd.

'Go on.' Fuller seemed sceptical.

'I spoke with a woman called Linda Fallon from Essex. A retired criminal psychologist. Seems to think she can help us with the investigation regarding Adrian Dilton and the videos posted to the internet.'

Fuller frowned and said nothing.

'What is it, sir?' asked Tanzy, noticing a flash of recognition of the DCI's face.

'I'm sure I've heard that name before,' Fuller said. 'Have you checked her out?'

Tanzy nodded. 'I phoned Essex police, spoke with a male colleague of hers by the name of PC Garling. Said she worked there for years and most recently as a criminal psychologist. He mentioned she had retired.'

Fuller nodded, absorbing the information.

'I've also looked her up,' Tanzy went on. 'Spent a lot of years working her way up the ranks to our level and decided a change in career, using her degree to get into the psychological side of things, as her ex-colleague PC Garling confirmed.'

Fuller nodded, leaned to his left and wiggled his computer mouse. The screen came to life, and he typed in her name. 'Yes, I thought the name was familiar. She received an award a few years ago from the Chief Constable of Essex for her hard work and diligent efforts in finding a missing victim. The killer had confessed to her whereabouts, and the girl was saved.'

Byrd and Tanzy nodded their approval.

'And she thinks she can help us track our guy down?'

'That's what she says.'

'Are you going to send her some information about our current findings, see what she comes up with?'

'Better than that, she said she's coming up.'

Fuller seemed surprised. 'From Essex?'

Byrd nodded. 'Told me she'd be here sometime this morning.'

Fuller smiled thinly, feeling a trace of hope inside. 'Good. Hopefully, we can make some progress with—'

There was a knock on the door.

Fuller said, 'Come in.'

PC Amy Weaver entered. 'There's a Linda Fallon here to see you, Max.'

Wasting no time, Byrd, Tanzy and Fuller stood and went through to the office to find a very slender woman with long, well-kept blonde hair, who Byrd assumed, to be in her fifties. Despite the warmth of the summer morning, she wore a long brown cardigan that went down to her knees, black jeans, and high brown boots. She had a very attractive, thin face, with prominent features: high cheekbones, and a thin nose that sat below bright blue eyes.

Byrd extended a hand. 'I'm Detective Inspector Max Byrd.' She had something about her; charisma and confidence that Byrd found attractive.

'It's nice to meet you, Detective Byrd. I am Linda Fallon.'

Fallon then shook Tanzy's hand, then Fuller's, who both introduced themselves with the professional courtesy when addressing someone in the force you didn't know.

There was an uncomfortable silence, then Fuller checked the time on his wrist. 'I have a meeting I need to attend to. I'll leave you in the very capable hands of our detective inspectors, Max and Orion.'

'Thank you, DCI Fuller.'

Even without knowing she was from Essex, her accent was a giveaway.

'Thank you for coming all this way,' Byrd said, with a smile. 'Can I get you a coffee or tea? Water?'

Byrd headed to the canteen to make the coffee while Tanzy took Linda to meeting room 101, going through the office, attracting the curious stares of personnel who hadn't seen her before.

Tanzy motioned to a chair across the desk when they entered the room. Fallon took off her cardigan, revealing a long-sleeved black T-shirt that enhanced her slim physique, and hung it on the rear of the chair before she sat down. They made small talk, discussing what time she'd arrived in Darlington and where she'd stayed last night. She even told Tanzy about leaving her dog, Rusty, with her next-door neighbour.

It wasn't long before Byrd came back holding a small tray. He placed the coffees down on the table and asked if she wanted a biscuit. She said she didn't, which didn't surprise Byrd, judging by her figure.

'I'll waste no time, Detectives. It seems like we don't have much of it,' she said. 'Have you heard of the four elements?'

37

Tuesday morning
Police station

'The four elements?' Tanzy asked, a frown lining his tanned forehead.

Fallon sat with one leg over the other, nodding.

'You mean fire, air, water, and earth?' said Byrd.

'That's right.'

Tanzy glanced to Byrd, feeling like he was missing out on something very important.

'I'm aware of there being four natural elements in the world,' said Byrd. 'Everything is made up of the four elements. I'm no expert, though.'

Next to Byrd, Tanzy looked lost. 'You need to tell me what you're talking about, Max.'

Byrd said, 'It originated from the ancient Greeks, who believed that everything was made up from four elements. Air. Water. Fire. And earth.'

'That's right,' Fallon agreed. 'But more importantly, this theory had developed in scientific terms and the meaning that it gives to our earth. For example, the air is a gas, water is a liquid, the earth is a solid, and fire is plasma.'

Tanzy frowned.

'You're both wondering why I'm telling you all this?'

They nodded in unison.

'Well, the first victims died in a house fire. The Walters. That's our first element. The second victim, from reading it correctly, fell from four floors up onto the concrete. She—'

'So that's earth?' Tanzy asked, jumping the gun.

'I could see how you would think that. Because she hit the ground, which, as we know, is solid. But reading the report, she was gassed inside the lift beforehand, wasn't she?'

Byrd frowned, glancing at Tanzy for a moment, then back to her.

'How do you know that?'

'Because I read the report, Detective.'

'How did you read the report?' Byrd exchanged a look of confusion with Tanzy. 'Our reports are only for us to see, not the general public.'

'I asked someone to request it.'

Byrd leaned back a little. 'Who?'

'A friend of mine.'

'I thought you were retired?'

'I am,' she admitted. 'But I still have friends in Essex.'

'Why did you feel the need to access the report. This, as you know, happened in Darlington. What interest would you, or anyone else from the Essex police department have to request the report?' Byrd's tone had turned sour after learning what she'd done, unsure of her motives.

She held up her palms. 'Listen, I can see how this looks. After seeing both videos on the internet about the fire and the fall, I needed to know if the fall was because of the earth. As it turned, out the victim was gassed in the lift beforehand, so I'm assuming it's the air element.'

Byrd didn't reply straight away, wondering who'd authorised it.

'What are you saying, Mrs Fallon?'

She looked at Byrd. 'Please, call me Linda. Mrs Fallon seems too formal for someone who speaks the way I do.'

She had a point.

'What are you saying, Linda?'

'I'm saying that's two of the elements down. There are two to go. Water and earth.'

'Why do you think that?'

'Well, Detective Byrd . . .' She hung her head for a moment before lifting her gaze to meet his.

'Because I've seen this happen before. And I'm not letting the sonofabitch get away with it again. Not this time.'

'What happened?' asked Tanzy.

'Let me start from the beginning,' she replied.

38

Tuesday morning
Darlington

Rachel Hammond hadn't been awake long. She'd finished at 3 a.m. and once she'd got home, had taken a quick shower and gone straight to bed.

She went downstairs and saw a leaflet on the doormat. It was unusual because the post didn't normally arrive until the afternoon, so she assumed it was a pointless leaflet, someone trying to offer another useless service. She picked it up and made her way down the narrow hall and through the dining room with it in her hand.

The first thing she did when she woke up, regardless of the time, was make a coffee. She needed it to wake her up and get her mind going. She decided on a caramel latte from the selection and grabbed a mug from the side, placing it on the ledge under the nozzle.

While she waited, she turned back and noticed the flyer on the worktop. She leaned forward to have a look at it to pass the time.

'That's cheap,' she muttered to herself, then pulled her phone from her dressing gown, found her friend's number, then pressed CALL.

'Hey, it's Rachel . . .'

'Hi, what's up?' said the voice on the other end.

'You know last night we were talking about getting a hot tub for my birthday this weekend?'

'Yup?'

'Just got a leaflet through the door. A company renting out hot tubs on short notice?'

'How short is short notice?'

Rachel carefully lifted her mug from the holder and placed it on the side. 'I don't know. I'll ring the number. If I can get one for Saturday, I'll have you lot round.'

'Brill. Let me know what they say.' Her friend hung up.

Rachel typed the number into her phone and pressed CALL. 'Hi, I'm ringing about hiring a hot tub.'

'Hi. When's it for?' It was a man's voice.

'This weekend. Saturday. A party on the night.'

'Yeah, there's a couple available. How many people is it for?'

Rachel thought for a moment. 'Five, possibly six.'

There was a long silence.

'We have one available. I can pop over on Friday to set it up so it's all ready for the Saturday. Would that work for you?'

'That would be great. I have the Friday and the whole weekend off,' she said excitedly.

'Great. Can I take a name and address?'

She told him.

'I'll be there Friday morning.'

'See you then, Roger.'

Adrian Dilton smiled and hung up the phone. Roll on Friday, he thought, smiling to himself.

142

39

Byrd and Tanzy gave Linda Fallon their undivided attention, desperate to know how she could help them with the investigation.

After she took a sip of coffee, she carefully placed it down on the table in front of her.

'Nearly seven years ago, I was involved in something similar. Actually, at the time, I was a detective inspector before moving into the psychological side of things. As well as my degree in criminology, I went on to study psychology. The way the mind worked and what made people tick excited me. My peers suggested combining them would be a career I would thrive in. I'll be honest, I loved being a DI, running my small team. As you guys know, every day is different and, let's just say, every day can be very interesting.'

Byrd and Tanzy smiled and nodded, knowing exactly what she meant.

She continued. 'It all started with the fire. It was horrific. A father, mother, and daughter were burned. Similar circumstances. Days after, we witnessed a drowning. The victim had been drowned in the bath, left there for several days until a concerned friend, who had arranged to do something with her the previous night, was suspicious when she couldn't get hold of her, then went into her house using the spare key she had for emergencies, she found her in the bath, still with her eyes wide open, staring up at the ceiling. Several days after that, a man was found inside his car after leaving work after a late shift. Just after midnight, we learned that a man had crept up behind the car and climbed into the back seat just as the engine had been turned on, a deadly gas, according to the forensic team, had been released. The victim died quickly.' She stopped for a moment. 'And lastly, a male victim was found by a dog walker who passed him one morning, partially buried in the woods.'

Byrd and Tanzy absorbed her serious words.

'Where did these events occur?' asked Byrd, narrowing his eyes.

'Places close to Essex.'

Tanzy nodded. 'So why do you think they are linked?'

'Not only can I see the four elements here, but there's a bigger similarity.'

The detectives waited.

'They were uploaded to the internet a day later for the world to see. Our best IT guys tried to track it but couldn't.'

Byrd took a deep breath. 'Did you identify the suspect seven years ago?'

She shook her head again. 'Unfortunately not. But the username of the person who uploaded it was *Rcarl20*. The name will always stay with me. Since then, I've looked for anything about fires, drownings and people being gassed. When I saw the article on the house fire and the woman falling that happened in the same town within a few days, it got me thinking. Then when the article mentioned the videos that had been uploaded, it's all I thought about. The last thing I wanted to do was get involved. I have a quiet life now, I'm retired. I've put all the crime scenes and insane people this country has to offer behind me. But . . .' she stopped, looking at the table for a moment. She went on.

'I can't let the man responsible get away with this again. If it is him, he's ruined so many lives and I can't let him do it again. So, detectives, what I want — or should I say, need — is for you to believe that you have witnessed the fire and the gas. Very soon, you may well be witnessing water and earth.'

'In what way?' Tanzy asked curiously.

'That I don't know. But if what I believe is true, then you're going to have more deaths on your hands very soon.'

Byrd hung his head, lost for words. Tanzy didn't say much either, letting the silence fill the room, which was broken when there was a knock on the door. They all turned towards it when it opened.

'Boss?' It was DC Leonard, breathing heavily.

'What is it, Jim?' Tanzy said.

'Something has been found on the A66, in the middle of the road. We need to go.'

40

Tuesday late morning
A66, outside Darlington

Before Byrd and Tanzy had left the station, they went to see Fuller, telling him what they'd been told. He immediately logged off his computer, jumped up, and left the office. Byrd, now responsible for Linda Fallon, had mentioned to Fuller about her going along; maybe she could assist in assessing whatever they were about to see.

They joined the A66. Byrd put the X5 into third gear and put his foot down. Tanzy was riding shotgun, holding the phone to his ear, speaking with DC Leonard who was already there. Fallon was in the back, sitting in the middle, leaning forward, anticipating the road ahead.

'Only a mile or so from the roundabout,' Tanzy said, relaying the info from Leonard before he ended the call and lowered the phone to his lap.

Byrd maintained a steady sixty, passing a temporary sign at the side of the road saying, *Incident Ahead — Route Diverted.*

Down the road, Byrd could see two marked Peugeots parked diagonally to prevent any traffic getting through, with a large sign positioned in the centre of the road, stating

Diversion with an arrow pointing to the left, diverting traffic towards Sadberge. By the sign, PC Amy Weaver stood with her arm permanently outstretched towards the village to reinforce the message of the diversion sign.

Byrd slowed gradually, angling over into the right lane and came to a gradual stop just before the sign. Weaver immediately recognised his car and moved to the left so she could direct the cars that came behind him.

'We stopping here?' Fallon asked from the back seat, staring through the windscreen at the tape set up and the diagonally parked cars.

Byrd turned off the engine and opened his door. Tanzy climbed out of the passenger door and stepped down onto the road. They turned, looking back along the A66, watching the cars approach and slow under PC Weaver's instruction and the diversion sign. Byrd, Tanzy, and Fallon moved around the driver's side to evade any traffic and peered down the road. Byrd noticed Fallon appearing a little apprehensive, unsure if she'd be witnessing the third kill they had mentioned.

From one of the parked Peugeots, PC Josh Andrews opened the door and smiled their way as they approached.

'You got here fast,' Tanzy said to him.

'Not fast, ya last.'

Tanzy smiled at the small joke between them.

Andrews was a tall guy and in good shape from recent gym visits. He was good-looking, his hair was always gelled and brushed over. His clean-shaven face made space for his square jaw and good posture.

'What's the story?' asked Tanzy.

'Just up ahead, sir. A call came in from a man who was driving along with his missus. The rear doors of a van that was driving in front of them opened and something hit their windscreen. They almost veered off the bloody road. The guy got out and found the object that hit them.'

'Where is he now?' Tanzy asked, looking around, seeing no sign of the man and woman in question.

'Parked at the petrol station further down the road. Anne is speaking with them.'

'How far down is the road shut off?' Byrd asked, knowing there was a turn off not far away.

'We've blocked off Stockton Road that joins the A66. For the moment, we don't know how far down we need to look.'

Byrd agreed that should be a sufficient distance.

Tanzy peered around him and saw the rear of the Forensics van that was parked further down. 'Who's here?'

'Tallow, Hope and Forrest. DC Leonard and DC Cornty. Think Cornty got here first.'

Tanzy nodded and turned, hearing footsteps behind him. He introduced Linda Fallon to PC Andrews, who shook hands briefly and shared polite smiles, although Andrews had no idea who she was or the reason for her being there.

Byrd, Tanzy and Fallon ducked under the loose plastic cordon and passed the cars before walking down the empty road. It was surreal in a way, the road that was usually filled with speeding cars was silent and still. The sun was shining above them, beating down in waves.

Once they reached the forensic van, they noticed Jacob Tallow thirty metres further down, dressed in white coveralls and wearing a face mask, kneeling at the right side of the road, his attention on something near the kerb. Byrd and Tanzy could see the object but not quite make out what it was.

Beyond him, roughly twenty metres further, on the opposite side, were Emily Hope and Amanda Forrest, dressed the same. Hope was bent over with Forrest standing beside her, a camera in her hand, snapping whatever Hope was looking at down on the road.

A hundred metres along, Tanzy noticed DC Leonard and DC Cornty ambling along the edge of the road, one either side, inspecting the grass verge.

'What have they found?' Fallon asked Byrd and Tanzy, intrigued by the sight of Forensics. She then stopped, her posture changing.

'What's up, Linda?' asked Byrd, noticing she'd stopped.

She stayed silent. 'I feel sick for some reason.'

Byrd turned and approached her. 'We don't know what's here yet.'

She smiled. 'I know. It's — it's been a while, that's all.'

Byrd nodded. 'Come on. You'll be fine.'

They joined Tanzy and made their way along the road.

On their right, the senior forensic tech, Jacob Tallow was still kneeling at the side of the road. He heard footsteps and looked to his right, eyed Byrd and Tanzy, then noticed Fallon a step behind them.

He stood up and stepped away from the grass.

'Max. Orion.'

'Pleasant day for it,' commented Tanzy, stopping near him.

'Just got a whole lot better, believe me.'

Byrd smiled at his sarcasm and turned towards Fallon. 'This is Linda Fallon, a retired criminal psychologist from Essex Police.'

Tallow nodded and pulled down his mask. 'A pleasure to meet you.'

Under different circumstances, they would have shaken hands, but they were both professional enough to understand the situation they were in and that formalities could come after.

'What have we got, Jacob?' Tanzy focused on where Tallow had just been kneeling.

'See for yourself,' he replied.

Byrd and Tanzy both edged forward to see the cylindrical object. It was a foot wide and at least ten inches long. The outside part was pale white, but the ends were more of a pink colour with specks of dark red and white hard bits.

'What is it?' asked Byrd, frowning.

'Pathology will have a better idea but, if I were to guess, I'd say it was the top of someone's leg.'

41

Forensics had collected a total of fourteen body parts; each part had been photographed in the exact position they'd been found and carefully picked up and bagged for further testing.

Knowing each part could potentially make up the anatomy of a human body, Tallow cleared a space in the rear of their van and placed a plastic sheet down. Then placed each body part in the position he thought it might go.

So far, they had both feet, both calves, one knee, both thighs, both hands, two separate pieces of flesh that resembled the stomach, another piece resembling a forearm, and two upper arms.

'What's missing?' asked Byrd as he reached the rear of the van.

Tallow looked down at the separated body. 'The head. One of the arms. Chest. Shoulders.'

Byrd said nothing. Mainly because he was speechless. Who on earth would do this?

'Can you see a similarity here, Mrs Fallon?' asked Byrd, turning his head towards her.

'Please, call me Linda.' It was the second time she'd said that. Byrd could hear by her tone she didn't want to say it a third time.

'Sorry, I'm used to formalities.'

They exchanged a brief smile.

'No, Max. If I'm being honest with you, I can't.' She looked back to the neatly positioned parts in the back of the van, then at Tallow who studied them for a moment. The sun beat down hard, reaching mid-twenties but it didn't deter Tallow's concentration.

She angled her gaze back to Byrd. 'Can I have a word?'

'Sure.' They stepped away from the van far enough so their conversation was only between themselves. Tallow left the van and wandered back down the road; there were still missing parts to search for.

'What is it, Linda?' asked Byrd.

'There's no link here to what happened in Essex.'

'How can you be sure?' Byrd frowned at her. Not in a questioning, I-don't-believe-you way, but more in a curious way, hoping she'd explain.

'I can't see the elements here. As we know, we've seen fire and air. There's no water or earth here. This is something entirely different.'

Byrd nodded, but he'd always focus on the facts, disregarding presumed speculations, which more often than not, led them down the wrong path.

'We'll see how DI Tanzy is doing down there.'

She nodded and followed his lead, passing Hope and Forrest rummaging through the grass verges down on the left. Further down, PC Timms and PC Grearer were over to the right. They waved a hand as Byrd passed.

A few hundred metres down the road, they took a left into the petrol station. It felt strange doing it on foot and gave Byrd the feeling that a car would appear behind them at any second.

Tanzy was over to the left, speaking with a man and woman standing in front of a car. Byrd spotted the red blood on their windscreen as he approached with Fallon. Tanzy, with a notepad and pen in his hands, turned and nodded at him.

'This is Detective Inspector Max Byrd,' Tanzy said, introducing them. In turn, they shook Byrd's hand and told him their names. The man who introduced himself as Rick was Byrd's height and had a shiny, tanned skinhead. He was muscular and thickset. The small, thin woman beside him told him she was named Paula.

They had told Tanzy they'd been driving behind a blue Volkswagen Transporter when the rear doors opened and something fell and bounced up, hitting their windscreen. Byrd figured that was the mark he'd noticed on his way over.

'Did you manage to get a registration plate?' Byrd asked.

The man sighed. 'I've already told your colleague,' he said, indicating Tanzy. 'It all happened so fast.'

'Where do you guys live?' asked Byrd.

'Darlington. Just off North Road.'

'Where are you heading?'

'Billingham. I have family there,' replied the man sharply, a sign he was becoming impatient. 'Listen, can we go now? We've answered all the questions you've asked. We need to get to Billingham. Our family is waiting to go out for dinner, and they'll be wondering where we are.'

Byrd smiled briefly and moved over to get a better look at the windscreen, seeing the registration plate. He pulled his phone from his pocket and texted someone at the station to run the plate.

'What are you doing?' Rick asked. 'Your colleagues have looked already.'

Byrd turned to Tanzy. 'Have Forensics taken a picture and a sample of the blood?'

'Yeah. Tallow has been down.'

Byrd nodded and took a few steps back, turning to give them his full attention. He was about to say something when his phone pinged. He excused himself for a moment and looked at the text message. Rick and Paula sighed heavily and eyed him disapprovingly.

'I'm sorry about this,' Tanzy said to them, knowing exactly what Byrd was up to.

Byrd opened the message. The information about the car was legitimate. The car belonged to a Rick Jacobs. It was both taxed and tested. Byrd turned back and pulled a card from one of his pockets. 'If there's anything else you can think of, give us a call. You're welcome to go. Enjoy your dinner with the family. Sorry to have kept you.'

Rick forced a smile and wasted no time getting into the car. Paula traipsed around the other side and got into the passenger seat.

The detectives and Linda Fallon walked back up the quiet road towards the Forensics' van. They looked up to see if there were any cameras on their way back but couldn't see any.

'Do you think you could have a word with Jennifer Lucas at the Town Hall?' Byrd asked Tanzy. 'I know it's out of her range but she'll have contacts in Teesside won't she? See if we can trace the blue Transporter.'

'I'll get in touch with her.' Tanzy plucked his phone from his pocket, found her number and made the call.

Byrd looked at Fallon. 'How are you holding up?'

'It's hot today.' A thin film of sweat lined her forehead. 'But I'm okay.'

Tanzy spoke for a few minutes on the phone, explaining to Jennifer Lucas about the situation. She told him she'd get back to him with any footage that could help with their investigation.

Back at the van, Tallow and Hope were discussing something. Hope nodded several times, then turned when they heard the detectives approaching.

Byrd noticed their confusion about something. 'What have you found?'

'We haven't found the head yet, if that's what you're wondering,' Hope replied. 'But it doesn't make sense.'

'What doesn't?' Tanzy said, intrigued.

'I don't want to speculate,' she said. 'But we'll see what pathology has to say.'

42

Tuesday
Outskirts of Darlington

Brad heard the loud noise behind him and peered through the rearview mirror. The van's back door had swung open.

'Shit!'

He focused back on the road in front, almost ramming into the rear of a car which for some reason had suddenly slowed.

'What are you doing?' he shouted at them, having to undertake them in the left lane. It was an elderly couple driving an old Micra.

He looked in the side mirror to see what was going on. The car behind had come to a sudden halt, objects dancing on the road before it, bouncing on the tarmac, going in every direction.

Instantly he felt sick. What was he going to do? He couldn't stop the van in the middle of the A66 and walk back up to collect the body parts. He had to get away.

'Shit!' he shouted again, banging his hand so hard on the steering wheel, the horn blasted for a few seconds. He put his foot down and reached eighty, then took the next left turn near Long Newton, taking him around to the left and

154

over the bridge. At the mini-roundabout, he took a right, and a hundred metres down the road, he pulled over, put his hazards on and jumped out quickly. He raced to the back of the van and stared through the open doors.

'Oh . . . no,' he whispered as he pressed both hands on his head, knowing most of the body parts were now missing. He started to shake. A car whizzed past, startling him from a second, then the road fell deadly silent as the car disappeared into the distance, leaving the sound of his thumping heart and the pounding in his ears.

He'd messed up big time.

There was no way he could go back.

The police would be on their way.

With shaking hands he pulled the phone from his pocket, found the number and pressed CALL.

'Yes, Brad . . .'

'We have a big problem, Mitch.'

'What?'

Brad explained what had happened.

'You, Brad, are an absolute fucking clown! Go back to HQ and don't do anything until I get there.'

43

Linda Fallon had been granted full access to the files on the murders in Essex that she believed were linked to the recent happenings in Darlington. After speaking with DCI Fuller, Byrd and Tanzy had both decided she could be an asset and were happy to keep her there with them.

It was undeniable that Byrd and Tanzy were capable detectives but even the best detectives missed things.

Fallon used one of the empty computers at the back of the room, just across from Tanzy. She accessed her emails and forwarded the information she'd received from Essex to both of them. They read through the reports on the murders that Fallon had briefly spoken about yesterday, and Byrd and Tanzy noticed the similarities between them, although a different location, and seven years apart. They understood Fallon' desperation in catching the man who got away from her.

It had just turned 9 a.m. Byrd and Tanzy were standing at the front of the meeting room ready to brief everyone on yesterday's events. Fuller was sitting in his usual chair, the one closest to the door.

Byrd pressed the button on the black remote and the first slide came up.

DC Cornty asked, 'Sir, I was wondering — probably the same as other people here — who's the lady?' He pointed to Fallon who was sat next to Fuller, with one leg crossed elegantly over the other.

Byrd narrowed his eyes at his smart comment, and said, 'The *lady* is—'

Fallon stood up abruptly, interrupting him. 'This lady is called Linda Fallon. She was a criminal psychologist who retired a year ago, and prior to that, spent seven years helping Essex Police get into the minds of criminals and killers. Prior to that, she was DI, with nearly thirty years' experience in police and criminal activity, predominantly for Essex Police. She is here because she believes the house fire and the woman falling from the flats are linked, not only to each other but to previous murders that happened seven years ago in the Essex area.'

The room fell silent immediately. Byrd and Tanzy couldn't help but smile at each other before gazing over at Cornty, along with everyone else. The smug look on his face was replaced with embarrassment. Fallon sat back down, happy with herself.

'That a good enough explanation for you, Phillip?' DCI Fuller asked him.

His cheeks reddened so much that Tanzy and Byrd felt sorry for him.

'Yes, sir,' he replied quietly, looking away to avoid eye contact with anyone.

'Okay,' Byrd said, 'glad that's settled then.' He focused on the board behind him. 'We know the current situation with the missing four women. And we know about the fire at the Walters' house, and Jane Ericson falling from the flats. The focus of this meeting is about what happened yesterday on the A66. As some of you know, a couple were behind a blue Volkswagen Transporter near the Sadberge turnoff, when the rear doors of the Transporter opened, and something hit their windscreen. They stopped to check it out and found a human thigh.

Byrd was about to continue but noticed DC Cornty looking down at his phone. He waited for a few seconds. Cornty heard the silence and looked up at Byrd, who scowled at him.

'Are you finished, Phillip?'

Cornty apologised and put his phone back into his pocket.

'Hope, Tallow and Forrest, with the help of Eric and Donny, found fourteen body parts scattered around the area. Forensics are currently working with the pathology department at Darlington Memorial Hospital to find out who the body belongs to.'

Byrd pressed the fob. The next slide was a photo of the top of someone's leg. The following slide showed various body parts.

'No head?' DS Stockdale asked.

'Not yet. We believe we have found all the pieces that had fallen from the back of the van.'

DC Anne Tiffin raised a hand.

'Yes, Anne?' said Tanzy, looking her way.

'Do we have any information on the van?'

'Not yet. I contacted Jennifer Lucas from the Town Hall yesterday. She works in the control room and monitors the CCTV devices in and around the town. She's checking and will get in touch when she has an update.'

Tiffin smiled.

'So, now it's time to formally introduce Linda Fallon.' Byrd motioned her forward with a hand. She stood, moved past Fuller and joined Byrd and Tanzy at the front of the room.

She looked directly at DC Cornty as she spoke for a few moments then scanned the faces in the room. As she'd already introduced herself when Cornty had made his comment earlier, she cut to the chase, explaining her theory that each murder involved one of the elements. Fire, water, air or earth. She answered a string of questions from Cornty, who Tanzy and Byrd surmised was being awkward, followed by more sensible ones from DC Tiffin and PC Weaver. She explained the videos being uploaded online were the reason she firmly believed this was the killer that the Essex Police hadn't caught.

'I've given Max and Orion full access to the files and reports Essex have on the murders in case they may come in handy. We need to find this man.'

She received several supportive nods around the room.

'And rest assured,' she added, 'I'll do everything I can to help and make sure we catch this sonofabitch.'

44

Byrd and Tanzy arrived there just after 1 p.m. They made their way across the busy car park towards the entrance door under the high, hot sun. According to the weather forecast, it would reach thirty degrees but if anything, without the breeze, it felt hotter.

A woman in her mid-forties was standing a few feet from the entrance door, dressed in a pink fluffy dressing gown, with a cigarette in her hand. In the other hand was a phone pressed against her head. She spoke loudly, complaining about the doctors and nurses who she felt weren't doing a good enough job for her. Byrd knew patients or personnel weren't allowed to smoke on hospital grounds. It was common courtesy for everyone else to obey but they had bigger issues to deal with.

Byrd went through the sliding doors first, followed by Tanzy. The air con in the corridor was cool and welcoming as they passed a handful of doctors and nurses who were walking the opposite way, some of them looking down at clipboards with furrowed eyebrows as they went, while others were on the phone. Some, the detectives knew, were consultants, dressed in tightly fitted shirts and smart trousers.

The pathology department was down a long corridor and to the left. They stopped at the small desk to see an attractive, thin, dark-haired woman in her early thirties, look up from her computer over the top of her glasses.

'Can I help you?' Her voice was soft.

'Here to see Arnold Hemsley,' Tanzy said.

'Do you have an appointment with Doctor Hemsley?' she said, raising her eyebrows.

'He's expecting us. I'm Detective Inspector Orion Tanzy of Durham Constabulary. This is my colleague Detective Inspector Max Byrd.'

'One moment, please,' she replied with a smile and returned her focus to the screen. A moment later, she pointed to the double doors to their left. 'Through there.'

'Hello, Arnold,' said Tanzy, once they were inside the doctor's office.

Hemsley was a slight man in his fifties with a bald head, appearing hardened by a lifetime of working long hours and eating very little. His teeth were tainted with cigarettes and coffee when he smiled. The crow's feet lining his eyes made him appear older.

'Detectives,' he said, standing.

'Come this way.' He led them along the corridor and through the double doors into the lab. Tallow and Hope were dressed casually, standing at the rectangular table where the neatly positioned body parts they had found yesterday had been placed. There was no sign of the forensic trainee Amanda Forrest. Most likely, she was back at the station lab or with the crime scene manager, Tony McCabe, going over her reports. On the opposite side of the table was coroner Peter Gibbs.

The detectives had attended numerous post-mortems but never had they seen a dismembered display such as this.

The room was square-shaped and as clean as any other lab. A clinical smell hung in the cool air which was kept cold from the conditioning unit fixed to the ceiling.

Along the back wall were two low-level sinks, with emergency cleaning fluids and an eyewash station fixed to the wall. Next to the sink, was a metal tray used to place objects such as body parts or other not very pleasant materials on.

'Let's begin,' said Hemsley, stopping at the table next to the coroner Peter Gibbs.

'Do we have a name?' asked Tanzy.

'We do. It's Lorraine Eckles. One of the missing four women we are looking for,' Tallow said.

When the four women had gone missing, Byrd and Tanzy had requested samples of their DNA to be taken from their homes with the permission of their family, to hold on the database in case they potentially found something they could match it with.

Hope and Tallow moved along to make room for Byrd and Tanzy. They all focused on Hemsley.

'After inspecting these parts yesterday and running our tests,' Hemsley said. 'I can confirm these parts belong to the same person. The interesting thing I found was, as Jacob and Emily pointed out, is that this is very unusual.'

Byrd frowned. 'Unusual how?'

'Well, let me start by what we know. It's a woman. Without having the head here or the pelvic bone, I know this because of the size of the hands. They belong to a female who's somewhere between a teenager up to her thirties. It's fully grown and the skin also tells me her age.'

'How have the parts been cut, Doctor?' asked Byrd.

'The cut lines indicate an electric cutter or something you'd used to cut meat. Not your average household cutting device but something stronger to get through the bone. Each part has been cut the same way. Slow, methodical. The killer wasn't rushed.'

Tallow and Hope had assumed something similar. They weren't experts on dismembering parts of the body but they were aware and fully understood the science and process behind it.

'But . . . each part is different. Each part tells us something unique.'

162

'How do you mean?' asked Tanzy, with a quizzical frown.

'This person has been tortured before they were cut up,' Hemsley replied. He then leaned over, pointing to one of the hands. 'See that mark?'

Byrd and Tanzy leaned closer.

'This is a burn mark. It looks like it's been done with some kind of blowtorch.'

'Something a plumber would use to heat and solder a joint?'

Hemsley looked up at Byrd. 'Exactly. And this part.' He pointed to a piece of flesh. They remembered from the scene where Tallow had said it could have been the top of someone's leg. 'This has been crushed.'

'Like a vice?' Tanzy said, tilting his head.

A nod from Hemsley. 'Something like that, yes. The skin is stretched and the muscles have elongated. And see here . . .'

The detectives looked at where he pointed. 'Bruises on the skin,' he went on. 'This, which we know is the forearm, had been strapped. I doubt the victim wore her watch that tight. She's been tied down to something while this happened to her.'

Byrd sighed heavily and hung his head. 'So, we've found one of them.'

'Question is,' said Tanzy, 'will we find the others in time before they end up like this?'

45

Wednesday afternoon
Police station

When Byrd and Tanzy returned to the station, they grabbed a coffee from the canteen and made their way to their desks. They found Linda Fallon sitting across the walkway at the desk she was temporarily using, speaking quietly on the phone. They heard a little of the conversation which sounded like she was giving someone instructions on what time to feed a pet.

She ended the call and put the phone down. 'Hey. How was it?'

Because she wasn't officially employed directly by Durham Constabulary, Linda hadn't been allowed to go to the hospital to see the body parts, so had stayed at the office to do some research.

'How you getting on?' asked Byrd as he placed his coffee down on his desk.

She stood up, went over to them and placed a sheet of paper on a space between their desks. 'I've made a list of places.'

'What's this?' said Tanzy, leaning over.

'Well, as I believe we are waiting on earth and water, I've made a list of ways someone could die by water. The most obvious is drowning. I've listed the rivers and ponds in the local area.'

'Must have taken a while,' said Tanzy.

She nodded. 'I've also been in touch with Jennifer Lucas at the Town Hall asking if these places are monitored with the town's CCTV system.'

Tanzy was impressed, going through the places on the list.

'What did Jennifer say?' Tanzy asked her, noticing ticks next to some of them.

'The ones with the ticks have CCTV in the nearby area.'

'Good work,' Byrd said to her. It was refreshing to see someone doing something off their own back instead of being asked. 'I'm going to see the rest of the team, give them an update on what the pathologist found.'

'Anything about the four elements?'

'Vic had been burned in various places. Other parts suggested they'd been squeezed or compressed in some way. Apart from that, no.'

Fallon nodded and Byrd walked away. He came to DC Leonard's desk first, who was sitting on the right, tapping away at his keyboard. He pulled the seat out and sat down, gave a quick recap of what happened at the hospital. When he finished, he got up and went to DS Stockdale who was sitting a few rows past Leonard.

'Phil. Have you done your report?'

'Not yet. Just doing it now, sir.'

'Show me . . .'

'Show you?'

'The report you said you were just doing?' Byrd edged closer. Stockdale didn't move. It was obvious he wasn't doing his report and was trying to come up with something quick. 'You weren't doing a report. You were on your phone. So don't lie to me.'

Stockdale's face reddened.

'How's the gambling?'

Stockdale sighed a little, his shoulders giving away the answer before he spoke. He said, 'I'll be honest . . .'

'That's what we want, Phil.'

'Not good at the moment. I bet most days. The missus is talking about us separating and me finding somewhere else to live. If I don't change.'

Byrd smiled sadly. 'We can offer you help, Phil, if you feel you need it. If it's affecting your health and mental well-being, we can get you help. You know the number, don't you?'

Stockdale nodded. It was well known that almost half of the police force, had taken sick leave due to a mental illness at some point in the previous few years. Policing was both demanding and stressful, seeing and witnessing potentially traumatic situations daily could take its toll, driving individuals to do things they wouldn't normally. However, although everyone knew help was available, many in the police saw it as a sign of weakness to seek it. Byrd hoped Stockdale wasn't one of them.

'Don't hesitate to call it. You have mine and Orion's support.' Byrd stood up. 'Once you finish the report, send it to Fuller. He's wanting to read it, okay?'

'Boss,' he replied with a nod, then pulled himself in to start the report.

Byrd patted his back and moved on, looking across the office. He was about to get DC Cornty's attention but PC Weaver walked towards him from the right, carrying a cardboard box, roughly a foot by a foot in size.

'Boss, this is for you,' Weaver said.

Byrd frowned. 'What is it?'

'I don't know. I can't see through the box, sir.' Weaver smiled.

'Where's it from?'

'Receptionist handed it to me when I walked in. Just been delivered.'

Byrd frowned and noticed his name and the address of the station on the label. He wasn't expecting anything. 'Thanks.'

Weaver nodded and returned to her desk while Byrd carried the box back to his.

* * *

Tanzy hung up the phone after speaking with Jennifer Lucas about the mysterious blue van. Unfortunately, nothing had been spotted so far, but she would continue working with Cleveland Police.

Byrd came back with the box that PC Weaver had handed him. 'What did Jennifer say?'

'She hasn't located it yet. Said there are no cameras where it happened. She's spoken to a woman who'll be in touch when they find it.'

Byrd placed the box on his desk to the right of his keyboard and pulled his chair over to sit down.

'What's in the box?' Tanzy frowned. It wasn't often they got deliveries.

'Weaver has just handed it to me. I'm not sure. It's quite heavy.'

The cardboard box was sealed at the top with Sellotape.

'Ooh, I'm excited,' Tanzy said, edging closer.

Byrd peeled off the tape and opened up the flap to look inside. He immediately took a step back.

'What is it, Max?'

Byrd didn't reply. He just stared inside.

'Max, what's in the box?'

After Byrd didn't reply again, Tanzy pushed his chair out, stood up, and leaned in to have a look. 'Here, let me have — Jesus Christ!' Tanzy stumbled back a little and gasped. 'What the hell?'

46

'I think we need Tallow and Hope . . .' whispered Byrd. He took a step back, grabbed his phone and made the call. 'Jacob, we need you and Emily in the office right now.' He then explained to him what was inside the box and Tallow told him not to touch anything and they'd be straight there.

* * *

The back end of the office, apart from Tallow and Hope, had been cleared. Fuller, Byrd, Fallon and Tanzy had moved to the front and informed others what they'd found in the box. Weaver gasped and placed her hands to her mouth, disgusted she'd handled the box before handing it to Byrd.

'Who does it belong to?' DC Leonard asked them.

'I don't know,' Tanzy said, who seemed to be in a daze.

'I think it's her.' Byrd pointed down at Weaver's computer. 'Get up the pictures of the missing women. The one we sent over to the media.'

Weaver nodded, pulled herself into her desk and typed with trembling hands. The four images appeared on her screen. She slid along to make space for Byrd and Tanzy who leaned forward to study them.

'It could be her . . .' Tanzy said.

Byrd stood and looked over to his desk. Tallow waved him over.

'Max, we'll take the box to the lab,' said Tallow when he was close enough.

Byrd stared in the box at the human head. She had long, matted dark hair. The cut had been just under the chin, showing thick clots of blood and multiple severed tendons.

'Let us know what you find.'

Tallow nodded and, with gloved hands, carefully picked up the box and made his way through the office back to the Forensics lab. All eyes were on Tallow and the box in his hands.

Tanzy returned to his desk and asked Byrd, 'You all right?'

Byrd nodded. 'Yeah. What the hell is going on in this town?'

'Never a dull day in Darlington, Max, you know that.'

47

Wednesday evening
Low Coniscliffe

Byrd entered the living room, dressed in a T-shirt and shorts, and went over to Claire who was slouched on the sofa. He bent over and kissed her forehead. 'Thanks for tea.'

The curtains were drawn but the room was still well-lit from the daylight creeping in down the side.

'Are you all right?' Byrd asked. 'You look a little pale.' He placed a hand on her cheek. 'You're quite warm.'

'I don't feel very good, to be honest.' She pushed out her bottom lip. 'I haven't felt right all day.'

Byrd offered to run her a bath but she declined. 'I'm comfy here. Maybe later.'

'You let me know and I'll go up and run one for you.'

Byrd took a seat beside her. 'What are you watching?'

'*Lost*. Some plane crashes on an island and everyone's trying to survive. Just started it.'

Byrd smiled and sat with her for a while, noticing the colour in her face.

'You sure you're okay?'

She turned her head slowly to him and managed a thin smile. 'I'm fine, Max. Just tired I think.'

'I can take you to bed if you want. You can watch the television up there?'

'I'm fine, thank you.'

As they were coming to the end of the pilot episode, Claire made a strange sound.

'What's wrong?' Byrd sat up a little.

'I feel dizzy. I'm going to be sick.' She attempted to shuffle up. Byrd rose and gently grabbed her arm to help her up.

'Here, let me,' he offered.

'No.' She frowned at him. 'I'm fine. I can go myself.'

'I'm trying to help, Claire.'

'I don't need help,' she said quickly, brushing his hand away.

He edged back and held his palms up. 'Okay. I'm here if you need me. Just tell me what you want.'

It wasn't like her to be abrupt, but Byrd put it down to the pregnancy hormones and certainly wasn't going to push it. He was learning when to pick his fights and silently trailed her out of the living room and stood in the hallway and watched her struggle up the stairs. The bathroom door closed, followed by the sound of heavy retching that filled the house.

He returned to the living room to check his phone. There was a text from one of his friends about five-a-side football at the weekend and a few emails he needed to respond to. He was so focused on one particular email he hadn't heard Claire return to the room.

'Max . . .'

From the sofa, he craned his neck to look up at her.

She was standing, hunched over with both hands on her stomach. Below, around her groin, there was blood. A lot of it.

'God . . .' he said.

'Max, I think something's wrong with the baby.'

48

Thursday morning
Police station

Tanzy arrived just after 7 a.m. and parked up. The space to his right, the one Byrd normally parked in, was empty. He frowned, knowing he could count on his hand how many times in the last year he had arrived earlier than Byrd.

Tanzy entered the building through the sliding double doors and passed the receptionist, Julie, who looked up and gently waved.

'Morning, Julie.'

'Good morning.'

Tanzy grabbed two coffees from the canteen and made his way through the office, stopping to speak with DC Leonard, DC Cornty and DS Stockdale, who were at their desks, located a few metres apart. They told him that Jacob Tallow was already in the lab and had obtained fingerprints from the box they found the head in yesterday.

'Brilliant,' noted Tanzy. 'We're getting somewhere with this. I'll go see him now. Is Linda here?'

'She is.' Leonard pointed towards the back of the office.

Tanzy walked down the central walkway and placed a coffee beside her. 'Brought you a coffee.'

Her eyes widened in pleasant surprise. 'Thanks, Orion.' She picked it up and took a sip.

'Where's Max?'

Tanzy shrugged. 'He normally gets here before me.'

He took off his thin, dark-blue jacket and hung it on the back of his chair. 'What time did you get in?'

'Just after seven, Ori.' She pointed to the screen. 'Been looking for Adrian Dilton. Had no luck yet. The last known address is where you and Max went — Victoria Embankment. After that, nothing. No jobs after working for IT company in Newcastle. No social media profiles. It's like he's just vanished.'

Tanzy nodded.

Seven years ago, Fallon hadn't known it was Adrian Dilton she was looking for. She had, however, known the name, Roger Carlton. It was the name of the uploader who put the videos online seven years back.

'It's only a matter of t—'

Fallon stopped talking and frowned at Tanzy, noticing he'd pulled his phone from his pocket and froze.

'What is it, Ori?' Her eyes narrowed with intrigue.

'Shit.'

'What is it?'

'Max texted me last night. I've only just seen it now. He took Claire to the hospital. She wasn't feeling very well.' Tanzy fell silent and reread the message. He didn't want to mention the part where Byrd had told him she had been bleeding and feared there might be something wrong with the baby, so didn't mention it to Fallon.

'Oh, no . . . I hope she's okay.'

When Tanzy didn't reply, she slowly turned back to her screen, continued typing, and moving her mouse cursor across the screen.

He pressed CALL and put the phone to his head.

'Hey, Max. Sorry I didn't text you back last night. I've just seen the message now.'

'It's okay, Ori.' Byrd sounded flat and tired.

'Is — is everything okay, Max?'

Byrd didn't answer straight away and Tanzy waited.

'She was bleeding pretty bad so we went to the hospital. The doctors had a look at her and did a scan. Luckily, the baby is still there and his heart is beating so that's the main thing.'

'Aww thank God, Max.' Tanzy tilted his head back and sighed in relief.

'But they don't know why she bled in the first place. So we're here now, doing more tests. And until the results come back, we have to wait here.'

'Okay, Max. Hope she's okay.'

'She's okay in herself. Just pain in her belly. She's been given some tablets. I spoke to Fuller early this morning so he's aware.'

'Is there anything you need me to bring?'

'No, we're okay, thanks, Ori. We're in our own room. There's a shop downstairs if she wants anything and I can go home to get anything else she needs.'

'Well, if there is, let me know, Max.'

Byrd thanked him and hung up. Tanzy put the phone back into his pocket and looked over to Fallon, who was staring at her screen, but Tanzy had the feeling she was listening to his side of the conversation. 'They're at the hospital now. She's staying in for tests to make sure things are okay.'

She smiled and crossed her fingers.

Tanzy left the office in the direction of the Forensics lab. He knocked on the door and opened it. Inside the lab, Tallow was hunched over his desk at the far side, typing away. After he finished whatever he was doing, he looked over and waved Tanzy in.

'Morning, Jacob.'

Tanzy pulled out a chair and sat down near him. 'Are the results back?'

174

Tallow nodded and slid along a few inches to the left to pick up a piece of paper from the desk. 'The blood and DNA came back matching Lorraine Eckles. The head is currently at the hospital with pathology.'

Tanzy nodded. 'No relation to the superintendent, Barry Eckles, is it?'

Tallow smiled thinly and shook his head.

'What about prints on the box? I know Amy handed it to me, so I'm assuming hers will be on it.'

'Max, yours, Amy's, Phil's, and Julie's.'

Tanzy studied the list. 'Julie from reception?'

A nod from Tallow.

'Which Phil?'

'Cornty.'

Tanzy nodded. 'I suppose if you were to send a suspicious box to the police station addressed to a detective, you'd most likely wear gloves.'

Tallow smiled. 'Well, that's what I'd do . . .'

Tanzy stood. 'Thanks, Jacob.' He looked around at the empty room, unable to see Emily or Amanda. 'Where are . . .?'

Tallow jumped in. 'Emily is getting coffee in the canteen. Amanda isn't here yet.'

'How's she getting on — Amanda?'

'She's coming on well. This job takes time, a lot of time. Tony is happy with her so far, so that's all that matters really. How's the great DCI Fuller coping in the big office?'

'He's . . . okay.' Tanzy winced a little. 'Under a lot of pressure from Eckles at the moment. He's always on the phone. As you know, Max and I sit right near his door, so when he comes out, raging, he can vent his frustration on us.'

Tallow laughed. 'I bet.'

'Anyway, thanks, Jacob.'

Tanzy left the lab and made his way back down the corridor, through the office and took a seat back at his desk. The office was warm, the morning sun shining through the windows to his right. Not long after he sat down, DC Cornty appeared at his side, wearing a black tight-fitting shirt and black trousers. His hair was gelled slightly different today.

'Morning, boss,' he started, looking down on Tanzy through his square-framed glasses. 'Did you see Forensics?'

Tanzy looked away from the computer screen and nodded up at him. 'I did.'

'Who does the head belong to?'

'Lorraine Eckles. One of the missing four women. The one whose body parts were laid out on the A66.'

'What about the prints on the box?' asked Cornty.

'No good. Mine, Max's, Amy's, Julie's from reception, and yours.'

Cornty dipped his head and gave a beaten sigh. 'Never mind.'

'What are you doing now?'

Cornty explained he was looking for blue Volkswagen vans in the local area. 'I have a small list. There are three in Darlington. Going to knock on some doors later this morning, hopefully speak to the owners of them.'

'Take Leonard with you.'

Cornty was going to ask why but nodded instead. 'Okay, he's aware of what I'm doing so I'll let him know when I head out.'

'What's he doing right now — Leonard?'

Cornty frowned and looked down the office, seeing the top of Leonard's head where his desk was located. 'He's doing a report.'

Tanzy smiled. 'How about DS Stockdale?'

'I — I don't know,' Cornty said. 'I haven't seen him for a while. He was on the phone earlier, speaking with someone at his desk. Not sure who, though.' Cornty was about to turn but stopped, appearing as though he had something on his mind. 'Excuse me for asking, boss. Why the questions?'

Tanzy looked up at him. 'No reason, Phil.'

49

Thursday morning
Darlington

Brad locked the blue van and carefully looked around, making sure it was clear. He walked along the side of the building, rounded the corner and went to the front door. He was told to keep the van out of sight in case anyone noticed it from the road. He used a key to open the yellow double metal doors, pushed them open, the hinges creaking and moaning. Once inside, he closed and locked them.

He flicked the switch on the right-hand side and the wide hallway flooded with harsh bright light. He walked down the hall, his boots echoing off the hard wooden floor, until he reached a door on the right and entered the room where the two computers were.

He turned on the light, dropped into one of the seats at the desk and looked at how the votes were going so far.

'Ooh, interesting,' he whispered.

Sarah had fifty-six per cent and Lisa had forty-four.

When the phone rang, he pulled it out. 'Hello?'

'How are things going there, Brad?'

'Okay. Gonna be close on votes I think.'

'How they doing? They still alive?'

Brad concentrated on the screen.

'They're awake. Sat against the wall. Not saying much, though.'

'You fed them yet?'

'Just about to.' Brad went back over to the chair and sat back down. 'Hey, I was thinking . . .'

'Yeah . . .'

'We'll be okay, won't we?'

'How do you mean?' replied the voice.

'I mean about the van, you know. 'Cos I messed up with the body parts. Think the police will trace us?'

The person on the phone didn't answer him, which sent butterflies through Brad's thick gut.

'I mean—'

'They're fake plates anyway, Brad. Don't worry about it.'

'Mitch isn't happy about it,' said Brad.

'I can't blame him. Let's make sure that doesn't happen again, Brad.'

Brad gulped. 'They can't track us, can they?' He pointed to the computer screens in front of him.

'Mitch has been doing computers all his life. There's no way the site can be traced, never mind traced back to you, me or Mitch. It doesn't work like a normal website.'

'How do you mean?'

'You heard of the dark web?'

Brad frowned. 'Yeah?'

'It's like that.'

'Okay . . .'

'Don't worry, big fella.'

Brad smiled. 'Good. Just concerned for a moment there.'

'No need to be. Listen, I need to go. I'll speak with you two soon.' The voice hung up quickly and Brad stared at the phone for a few moments before placing it down on the desk. He wanted to call Mitch, wanted to see if he was still in his bad books. Maybe give him an update on how the scoring was going so far. He hadn't known Mitch very long. They'd met a few months ago in the Green Dragon pub in town. It was a Friday night, the place was busy with loud music, fancy disco lights, and a DJ who didn't make much sense when he spoke but played some classic dance tunes when he finally put the mic down. Brad had gone for a smoke in the busy smoking area. Groups of men were laughing and joking nearby and Brad had occasionally chipped in with a word or two. When the group had gone inside and he was alone, a man approached him and introduced himself as Mitch. He asked if he wanted a job. As he was out of work, Brad had said yes.

On cue, Brad's phone rang. He answered it. 'Mitch, how—'

'Are the girls fed yet?'

'No, not yet, I—'

'Go feed the girls. I'll get over there this afternoon at some point. Remember, only two more to go and we'll have enough money for ages, Brad.'

Brad placed the phone down on the desk, went over to the valve on the wall and turned it on. When Lisa and Sarah slid down the wall and fell asleep, he turned the gas off and turned on the fans to clear the room before he entered.

He grabbed the tray of food from a desk to the left, made his way through the door and down the set of steps illuminated with the blue neon handrail and into the dark room. With Sarah and Lisa in a deep sleep, he placed the tray of food down on the floor near them and walked out.

'It'll be the last meal for one of you,' he said then walked out and locked the door.

50

Thursday evening
Dolphin Centre, Darlington town centre

Usually, the police held their press briefings at Darlington Business Centre but tonight would be different as two days earlier, a small, rowdy crowd that had been there had caused damage to the walls and furniture.

This evening they were using a function room at the Dolphin Centre, which had enough space and would do as a temporary measure.

Reporters, members of the public and town officials were sitting in the rows of chairs in the middle of the room, focused on the two figures seated behind the top table.

DI Tanzy felt nervous and did his best to slow down his breathing. Beside him was a man representing the PR department of Darlington Borough Council, who'd asked to sit in, wearing a plain, black suit with a black tie.

A woman dressed in a blue suit standing to their left raised a palm to quieten the idle chatter until silence descended on the room.

'Thank you all for coming here this evening,' she started, her experienced voice loud and clear. 'I can only apologise it isn't in our usual place. I've been told they are renovating.' She paused a moment, looking down at the clipboard in her hands to collect her thoughts. 'This meeting is concerning current events in Darlington. We, as the people of this town, should know that this town is safe and that our police force is doing everything they can to keep it that way. Tonight we have Detective Inspector Orion Tanzy from Durham Constabulary with us, to explain what's been happening, and to hopefully reassure us that our town will soon be safe to live in.'

Her words hovered over the crowd.

Tanzy felt his blood pump around his body and his cheeks warm, knowing it was his turn to stand up as soon as she sat down. He hated these things, hated the spotlight.

He slowly stood, feeling the stares of the people watching him. The cameras clicked, quickly illuminating the room in stabs of lightning. He took a breath and introduced himself first, then said, 'I'd first like to say that Durham Constabulary are doing everything they can to catch the person responsible for the murders of the Walters family. We believe the same killer was involved in the unfortunate case with Jane Ericson. We think—'

'Is it true a detective should have reached her but missed, which led to her death?' a reporter said, sitting in the middle, two rows back. It was a woman with ginger frizzy hair, holding a recording device out in front of her at arm's length to pick up the clarity in Tanzy's response.

'I'm not sure where that information came from. Unfortunately, Jane Ericson panicked and lost her balance. Regardless of who was standing at that apartment door trying to grab her, she'd have fallen either way.'

'What leads have you got on the person responsible — it's an Adrian Dilton you're looking for, isn't it?' The question came from a man in his early sixties with wispy grey hair and whose face was blotchy with red skin.

'We are led to believe, by a witness who came forward, he's called Adrian Dilton. We have been to his address and been notified by a neighbour they haven't seen Mr Dilton for six months now. The address in question, according to the Land Registry, doesn't belong to him anymore.'

'Is that all you have on him?' the same man asked, disappointed.

Tanzy shook his head. 'Mr Dilton's last known job was for an IT firm based in Newcastle. I've spoken with the manager there who confirmed Mr Dilton was in their employment but hasn't been seen for the last six months. The address given by the member of the public who came forward was confirmed with the IT company.'

'What did Dilton do at the IT company?' a voice asked but Tanzy couldn't place it.

Tanzy looked in the general direction where the voice came from and said, 'He was a software expert.'

'Is that why you aren't able to track the videos he uploaded?' asked the same voice. Tanzy shifted his head but he still couldn't see who asked the question.

Tanzy sighed, feeling frustrated. 'Whatever he's done, he's made it very difficult for our IT employees to track it. But we believe we are getting very close.' Tanzy didn't want to go into details about how the IP addresses kept shifting every so often, making it almost impossible to trace. And the fact that they were nowhere near locating him. 'On a positive note, we also have help from a former employee from Essex Police force, who believes there are similar links to something that happened in Essex seven years ago. I'm not willing to go into details but informing you things are moving forward.' Tanzy fell silent and swept the rooms with his eyes, searching for the next question.

'What about the four missing women?' the ginger-haired reporter asked, still holding the device out in front of her.

Tanzy took a deep breath, carefully thinking about an answer.

'Whose body was found on the A66?' a man then asked, his face serious. 'Why aren't the police telling us what's going on?'

Tanzy forced a thin smile and scratched the top of his tanned, bald head. 'I can assure you we are doing everything we can. Please—'

'Who does the body belong to?'

Tanzy didn't think this was public knowledge yet, wondering how they were aware of the body falling from the van on the A66. He knew it would only be a matter of time before word got around in this town. 'We haven't clarified the identity of the body yet, sir. We need to speak to Forensics and the pathology department at the hospital. We're still waiting on official identification. As soon as we know, we'll inform the public.' Tanzy then nodded, indicating he was ready for another question.

'In your opinion, Detective, are the public safe?'

Tanzy thought long and hard about the answer. 'I think we all need to remain very vigilant.'

51

Thursday evening
Darlington

Adrian Dilton picked up his phone from the kitchen table and called her.

'Hello . . .'

'Hi, is that Rachel?' he said in a chirpy, upbeat voice.

'Yes . . .' she sounded hesitant.

'It's Roger Carlton. I'm just confirming you still require the hot tub for tomorrow evening. I've had a couple of calls from potential customers who are wanting some tubs over the weekend, but as you are booked in, I'm just confirming your slot.'

'Oh, hi, Roger.' Her voice softened. 'Yes, please. I'll need it for Saturday night. Did you say you'll pop by tomorrow to set it up, to make sure everything is working?'

'That's right,' Dilton said. 'It'll be late morning.'

'That's fine. I'm in all day.'

'Great. See you then.'

Dilton hung up, placed the phone on the table and made his way over to the worktop. He opened the zip of a bag and peered inside to check the contents under the bright cupboard lighting so he'd have everything he needed for tomorrow.

Needles. Two knives. Thin clear tubes. A mechanical pump. Several coiled hoses. Sheeting. Rope. Two jugs. An extension lead. Duct tape. Two small boxes. A catheter with a pre-lubed needle and case.

Happy, he zipped it back up, then lifted the bag over to the back door and dropped it carefully down near the large plastic tank.

Minutes later, he was up in his office, sitting at his desk with his laptop open, looking at a social media profile for Rachel Hammond. He'd been looking at her photos from this year. By the looks of it, she'd been all over the place. Egypt. Cyprus. Turkey. Spain. It was only bloody June.

Dilton was jealous. The last time he'd been on holiday was Greece over ten years ago. A small place called Lindos on the island of Rhodes.

His phone rang. He pulled it from his pocket and answered it.

'Hey.'

'How you doing?' asked the voice.

'I'm good. How are you?'

'I'm great, thank you. How are things . . . progressing?'

'So far, so good,' he said. 'Fire and air are both done.'

'I know. What's next?'

'Water.'

'When?'

'Tomorrow,' he said, proudly.

'Will it work?'

'Yes. Everything is planned. It will work. They will get what's coming to them.'

'You've done yourself proud.'

'Thank you.'

'Good luck, Adrian. I'm praying for you.'

Dilton smiled to himself. 'Don't pray for me. Pray for *them*.'

52

Tanzy kissed both Eric and Jasmine good night and returned downstairs to find Pip in the kitchen clearing away the dishes. A smell of lavender hung in the air from the plug-in on the worktop that lingered with her sweet perfume. He stopped in the doorway to observe her beauty. Her slim physique, her curvy hips, her long, dark, straight hair that tickled the base of her spine as she moved, putting the clean plates away.

'They asleep?' she asked, knowing he was standing there, watching her.

He walked in and pulled a glass down from the cupboard. 'They soon will be. They're shattered.'

'Thanks.'

Tanzy filled the glass with water and drank it all. Then, as he turned, Pip got in his way, stopping him from moving away from the sink.

'Wha—'

She placed her finger on his mouth. 'Shh, Ori . . .' She then took the glass from his hand and placed it beside him on the worktop, then slowly pulled his shorts down to his ankles, and lowered to her knees.

'Pip, what are—'

She silenced him when she took him in her mouth. It wasn't something she'd normally do but he wasn't going to complain or interrupt her. Instead, he leaned back against the worktop and closed his eyes.

* * *

After Pip had showered, she returned to the kitchen to find Tanzy sitting at the table, focusing on his laptop.

'Do you ever stop?' she asked.

He shook his head. 'I don't. I need to finish this report. Today has been manic. Did you see the news?'

'You looked as handsome as ever.' She grabbed a snack bar from the cupboard, sat down opposite him and removed the wrapper.

'Eric has been asking about his den.'

Tanzy pulled his focus away from his laptop to look at her. 'I haven't started yet. I've been so busy with work and everything going on.'

'He won't be happy with you.'

Tanzy rolled his eyes, knowing his ten-year-old son all too well.

'How are Max and Claire?' she asked.

He'd told her about Byrd not being there today because Claire had been bleeding and they'd gone to the hospital. Pip was going to text her didn't want to appear to be nosey.

'As far as I know, they're still there. Max hasn't told me what's happening yet. He said the baby is fine though, which is the main thing, but they've done some tests and are waiting on the results coming back. You know how long these things can take.'

Pip nodded. 'Let's hope things will be okay.'

* * *

After *CSI New York* had finished, Tanzy picked his phone from the arm of the chair and decided to ring Byrd for an update on Claire.

'Hey, Ori,' Byrd answered.

'How're things?'

'We're home now. Just got in actually. Walked through the door fifteen minutes ago. Was going to ring you.'

'Long day.'

'Longer for Claire.'

'How's she doing?'

'The results came back. Doctors say she has got uterine fibroids.'

'What are they?'

'Tissue around her uterine wall. Says the tissue could have expanded during her pregnancy which has caused the heavy bleed.'

'What happens now?'

'She has to see a specialist. Because of where they are, the fibroids could affect the pregnancy if they grow too big. She has to go in every week to have them checked. If they grow too big, she'll have them removed.'

There was a moment of silence.

'Well I'm just happy things are okay, that the baby is, you know . . .'

'Makes two of us. What's been happening in the office then? Oh — how was the dreaded conference?'

Tanzy could tell there was humour in Byrd's voice, who was well aware of Tanzy's public-speaking fear.

'As good as any other time. Bloody dreadful. Whatever happens, you're doing the next one.'

'You got it.' Byrd laughed. 'Any updates?'

'I have two from today. First is we got the fingerprints from the box with the head in. No other prints than ours. The second is confirmation of the head belonging to the body parts we found on the A66. Lorraine Eckles. You back tomorrow?'

'Yeah. I'll be there.'

'Okay. See you bright and early.'

53

Friday morning
Elton Road

Rachel Hammond had enjoyed her lie in because she seldom got one. She rose just after nine, had breakfast with a cup of strong coffee and jumped in the shower. She was in her office — a small spare room with a desk and a laptop — by 10 a.m.

She slid across the room and peered out of the window while her laptop booted up, spotting Mr Weller next door, tinkering in his garden, dressed in only shorts and a cap. For sixty, he had a terrific figure from running three times a week, which he'd done for years. When a ping came from the laptop, she slid back across, settled at her desk and logged on to the website. And there they were. Two of them. Awake, sitting against the back wall, in silence.

The votes could be seen on the right-hand side of the screen. Lisa had fifty-three per cent and Sarah had forty-seven. It was going to be a close one because not everyone had voted yet. It showed the three players who were online, including herself.

RCarl20.
Spork11.

And herself. *Hammr33*.

Where were the other two players?

DWalt66 and *EricJ4*.

She didn't know these people personally but knew their usernames. They were a part of something together, but the rules of the game dictated they couldn't contact each other directly.

Above the usernames was a tab saying "watchers". Next to this, the number 488 was highlighted in brackets. She couldn't see any information on them but knew they were there, waiting for the next game.

Outside, she heard an engine, and slid away from the desk. She peered through the window and spotted a white van parked directly outside her house. She closed the lid of her laptop, left the office and made her way downstairs to the front door.

'Hey,' she said when she opened it.

A stocky, clean-shaven, bald man in his late thirties, wearing a pair of shorts and a tight-fitting top was standing there. His dark brown eyes were unusual, almost so dark, they sucked you in for a moment too long when you looked into them.

'Rachel?'

'That's me. Are you Roger?'

'I am. Sorry I'm a little earlier than I said. I like to get a head start on the day.'

She playfully waved his comment away. 'Oh, that's okay.' She was sure she'd seen him somewhere before very recently, but she couldn't think of where. She frowned. 'Do I know you?'

He smiled. 'I'm not sure. You don't look familiar. Darlington is a small place though, so we've probably crossed paths at some point.'

She grinned.

'Would it be possible to see where you want the hot tub first to make sure there's enough space?'

She opened the door fully. 'Yeah, no problem. Follow me.'

He stepped up into a wide hallway and she closed the door. He noticed the stairs were up to the left. At the end of the hall he could see through to the kitchen. There were a couple of doors going off to the right, presumably the dining room and living room. The decor was simple yet modern with shades of whites and greens mixed. A large rectangular mirror was fixed to the wall on the right, positioned above the radiator.

'Please, this way.' She headed towards the kitchen. He followed, watching her tanned, muscular legs contract as she walked. She sounded sexy on the phone and her appearance didn't disappoint.

'Mind the mess,' she said. 'I'm about to clean up.'

Dilton smiled as he followed her. People always said the same when you went into their house, regardless of whether they hadn't cleaned in a week, or they'd just finished.

'So, have you got many booked in for today?' she asked.

He stared at the back of her head, watching her closely, pulling out one of the needles from his pocket. 'Yeah, I have seven.'

She turned and made a "wow" face. 'That's good. Just through here.' As she stepped one foot on the lino she felt the needle go into the right side of her neck. She quickly slapped at her neck, assuming it was some type of wasp or bee sting. Dilton threw his strong left hand around her and pulled her close into him, her feet leaving the floor for a moment, and pushed the liquid into her neck. Helplessly, she shuddered and wriggled, struggling for several seconds until she lost consciousness.

Dilton removed the needle and dropped it on the floor. Keeping hold of her, he carried her into the dining room and lowered her onto the carpet.

'This will be perfect.'

He admired her for a moment in her unconscious state. A minute later the front door opened.

'Hey, Rach.' A man's voice. 'I'm home.'

'Shit,' Dilton whispered.

54

The man closed the door and looked down the hall, hoping to see Rachel in the kitchen, but the house was unusually silent. Usually, Rachel had music on and could be heard singing from somewhere.

'Rachel, you here? I'm back from judo.'

He took a few steps down the hall and looked upstairs. 'Rach?' He carried on down the hall and found something on the floor. 'What the —?'

He picked up the first needle on the floor. 'What the fuck is this?' he said. 'Rachel, where on earth are you?'

* * *

Dilton's heart pumped quickly as he waited in the doorway of the dining room, hearing the footsteps approach. It would only be a matter of seconds. He had the element of surprise but would need to act quickly. As the side of the man's face appeared Dilton threw himself through the threshold with the syringe in his outstretched arm, stabbing the man in the chest, using his size to take him to the floor. He managed to inject the liquid into him, the effects almost immediate as the man's body softened and went placid.

Dilton finally let out the breath he'd held in.

'Jesus,' he whispered. He slowly got off him, grabbed the man's hands, dragged him into the dining room and placed his body next to Rachel. He sighed heavily. When she'd asked him if she knew him after she opened the door, he'd panicked a little, hoping she wouldn't realise it was him that had trailed her around Morrisons a few days ago and overheard the conversation she'd had with a friend about renting a hot tub this weekend.

* * *

Rachel woke up first. She tried to move her arms but realised she couldn't, as if they were secured somehow. She opened her eyes and looked down, noticing they were secured to the chair she was sitting in. She peered up, seeing him in the chair opposite. His head was tilted back, his eyes closed, his body totally still.

'Aaron?' she whispered. She frowned, unable to comprehend why he was tied to a chair. There was a strange smell in the air, like a cleaning fluid, but she hadn't cleaned. There was a slight draught too, but the French doors to her right were closed, the curtains were pulled across, leaving the room darker than it should have been.

'Aaron. Aaron. Wake up.'

She felt groggy and sick, unable to remember what had happened. A surge of pain formed in her temple each time she blinked.

Aaron was positioned on the chair facing her. There was a gap of two metres. The doorway to the hallway was behind him. His arms were tied to the chair with a thick rope and there were several loops of rope around his chest and stomach which seemed to go around the back of the chair numerous times. His legs were also tied together in several places.

Then she noticed the tubes.

'What the fuck?' She frowned at her unresponsive boyfriend.

In his forearm, there were several tubes connected to what looked like catheters. She followed the tubes down to the floor, along to a little metal block on the carpet. On the other side of the block, there was a rubber pipe, similar to a hosepipe, which ran a few feet to the left side of a mechanical pump. A tube from the back of the pump that went to a large, black plastic box but it was unclear what was inside.

She then noticed the hose pipe connected to the right side of the pump which came down under the table towards her, joining another metal block, which split off into smaller tubes. The smaller tubes went along the floor and up into two catheters that were fixed into her own forearms.

She gasped. 'What the fuck. Help me!'

She wriggled and fought against the ropes, but they were too tight.

In her hand was a small black box, with a button on it. She stared at it in confusion.

'Roger?' she whispered, suddenly recalling he was the last person she had seen. 'Oh, God. What happened?' She remembered walking into the kitchen to show him the back garden, then woke up here, tied to the chair, with tubes sticking out of her arms.

'What the fuck is this?' she screamed, her anger filling the silent house.

She looked around for Roger Carlton. She spotted something out of the corner of her eye and turned her head. There was writing on the wall in a thick black marker pen. It covered most of it, nearly filling it from the ceiling to the floor.

It read:

Hello Rachel. I'm sorry things had to be this way, but you did this to yourself. You have sinned and it's up to me to put things right, so you can't harm again. As you may have noticed, there are tubes fixed to you. These tubes are connected to a mechanical pump which is connected to the large plastic tank over to your right. Inside the tank there is water. Just ordinary tap water, which isn't very good for you, believe it or not. Every seven minutes, the pump will turn for a few seconds and will pump approximately half a litre of water into your body. Now, this doesn't sound like much, but have you heard of water intoxication? Maybe you have. Maybe you haven't. This is when the body gets too much water which causes it to break down and not function. If water intoxication is severe, you will die. Because too much water causes the sodium levels in your body to dilute, leaving the sodium lining on your cells vulnerable, allowing water to penetrate them. If this happens to your brain cells, let's just say your brain will swell and prevent the flow of blood and oxygen to your head. First you'll get a headache, then you'll feel sick, then be sick, and let's just say the whole thing isn't a pleasant experience. In your hand, you have a small remote. This remote, if you press the button, will turn on the pump, sending water into your boyfriend's body instead of yours. If you don't press the button, then every seven minutes, half a litre will be pumped into both of your bodies until one of you dies. And I can guarantee that will be you because he's bigger, and it'll take more water to kill him. Choose wisely. I'll be watching. Roger.

'What the fuck?' she whispered, looking down at the tubes, pump, and plastic tank. 'Is this a joke?' She looked around the room and noticed the small white camera on the table facing them. There was a red light flashing every few seconds, indicating whatever it was, it was probably recording them.

As she reread the handwritten message on the wall for clarity, just before the last line, the pump to her right kicked in for a few seconds.

'Shit! Shit!'

She started shaking, feeling the liquid being pumped into her arm. It was a surreal feeling.

Aaron jerked wide awake in the chair opposite and opened his eyes wide. 'What the fuck was that?' he mumbled, trying to move his arms and body but realised he couldn't. 'Where is he — where—?'

He noticed Rachel in the opposite chair, also tied up, with the tubes in her arms.

'Rachel — what the fuck is going on?' He clamped his eyes shut for a moment and tipped his head back. 'My head is banging.'

'Aaron, don't panic.'

'Don't panic? What is this?'

Rachel started to feel a headache coming on. According to the writing on the wall, it was the first sign of the body breaking down.

'I — I don't know, Az. I woke up like this.'

He moved his head around, trying to work out what was going on, absorbing the tubes and mechanical pump. 'Why are we — who did this?' He shook violently but the ropes held him secure.

'It was a man, he—' She trailed off, thinking hard. 'Roger — he's called Roger!'

'Roger?'

She explained about the hot tub.

Near them the pump whirred.

Aaron screamed, feeling the liquid enter his arms. 'Aah, what is that?' He tried to thrust forwards, but the ropes restricted any form of movement. 'Rachel, I don't feel well.'

She clamped her eyes closed, feeling the liquid fill her body. Her head started to pound. She didn't want to believe the words on the wall, but could she take another shot of water?

'Just hold on,' she said, maintaining his eye contact, hoping he wouldn't see the writing on the wall, but it was so clear, it was impossible to miss. He looked to his right and started reading it. When he reached the bottom, he glared at Rachel, then down to the black box in her hand. 'Rachel, why do you have that?'

She focused on him with tears in her eyes and knew there were a few minutes until the pump would rotate and inject water into her veins again. Would she die before Aaron?

This had to be some kind of sick joke.

Who would set this up?

'Rach — don't press that button. Please! My head is going to explode.'

She took a deep breath and considered how long since she'd heard the pump. It would only be a matter of time. 'I'm sorry.'

'Don't you fucking dare press it!' he spat at her. 'Don't you dare.'

She pressed the button, and the pump came on.

'Rachel — turn it off!' He could feel the liquid pouring into his arm, filling his body slowly. It wasn't long before he was sick, the liquid covering the front of his T-shirt and shorts.

Rachel winced but held her finger on the button, the pump continuously going.

His skin started turning white. 'Rachel . . .' His voice was weak now. Then he was sick again. 'Rach — turn it off, pl-please.'

She didn't want to do it but if it was a choice, she had to look after number one. If she didn't press it, he'd survive longer, meaning he'd live. She had to keep the button pressed.

He clamped his eyes shut and rocked his head back violently. 'My head. Please . . .'

Tears rolled down her face as she kept pressure on the button. She knew it was something she had to do and cried loudly to mask the wails of his pain.

Nearly half an hour later, Aaron was still, his head cocked to one side, his eyes bloodshot, looking down at the floor. His almost albino-like white skin had swelled and bubbled. She finally let go of the remote and dropped it on the floor.

Her head pounded from the excess water and crying. She sat still, without the energy to move, then angled her

head to the writing, reread the part where it said *choose wisely.
I'll be watching.*

'Hello?' she said, barely audible. 'Roger . . .'

After seven minutes had passed the pump kicked in for a few seconds. Her eyes widened, feeling more liquid injected into her body.

She started screaming, realising this was a game neither of them would win.

An hour later, she was dead.

55

Friday late afternoon
Police station

Tanzy was sitting at his desk with Linda Fallon, who'd logged on to Byrd's computer to save them shouting across the walkway. Fallon had been, for most of the day, looking over her old files from Essex Police concerning the murders that happened seven years ago, searching specifically for water and earth.

Fallon had found the files on a drowning and another file for a burial.

'I have a list of victims from seven years ago, Ori.' She handed over a list she'd handwritten on some plain paper.

At the top, it said "fire", followed by three names. Norman Peters, Anna Peters and James Peters. Man, wife and child.

Then below, it said "water" and named a female who'd been held under the water in her bath to drown. Tess Forgan.

The third was "air" followed by a male victim who had been gassed out inside his car. Lewis Phillips.

And lastly, "earth", followed by another male victim who'd been buried in the woods. Donald Cramer.

Tanzy's eyes narrowed at the list. 'Did you figure out a link between these people? Something they shared in common. Or did it appear random?'

'I looked into every victim. Who they were. What they did as jobs. Their interests. But we couldn't see a pattern. It frustrated us like nothing before. It seemed a random list of people. I studied this list for months on end, sure I was missing something. It drove me insane. My super, at the time, had mentioned taking me off the case because it was all I was doing. I'd stay up all night, obsessing over it. I didn't have an image of what the man looked like. I remember making up my own image of him in my mind, and having dreams about being at home and hearing something come up behind me and I'd feel his breath on the back of my neck and wake up in a sweat.' She sighed and shook her head a little as if reliving the pain and effort she'd been through.

'There must have been something which linked them?' Tanzy picked up his coffee, took a sip and placed it back down by his keyboard. 'Someone doesn't just go and kill six people on four different occasions.'

She shrugged. 'It's the first killer to ever elude me.'

'Do you think it was some type of ritual?'

'The four elements?' she said, frowning at him.

He nodded.

'I don't know. Perhaps.' It was her turn to sip her coffee, then silence descended on them. The other end of the office was busy. DC Leonard was at his desk, speaking with someone on the phone. DS Stockdale was on the right-hand side at his desk, looking down at something. Probably his phone, Tanzy thought. PC Weaver, Andrews, Timms and Grearer were dotted about, tapping keyboards, and discussing various things, keen to make some form of progress.

'Where did Max go?' Fallon asked.

'He had to go home to see Claire to make sure she's all right.'

'How is she?'

'Taking things easy.'

'She needs to. Carrying the baby and all.'

Tanzy agreed and stood. 'Excuse me a minute.'

Fallon nodded.

Tanzy rounded the desks, joined the central walkway and headed towards the opposite end. He noticed DS Stockdale walking towards him.

'Hey, Phil.'

'Are you going somewhere? We've just got back. Wanted to let you know about the vans.'

Tanzy nodded. 'I was coming to ask about that actually.'

They both stopped and Tanzy waited.

'A man called Jeremy Simms in West Crescent owned one. Had it for a few years. All kitted out with the works. A bed, toilet, sink, shower. Looked really good.'

Tanzy wasn't interested and Stockdale saw that in his face.

'Did you get a reg?'

'Yeah. It's clean.'

'Where did he say he was on Tuesday morning?'

'Told us he and his wife had been to the Lake District. Been camping for a few days. Got back Wednesday night. His wife confirmed it.'

Tanzy said, 'What about the other one?'

Stockdale nodded. 'Another owned by a twenty-seven-year-old, blonde-haired female who bought it last year. Doesn't use it very much. Bought it for more of a memento to her father who was obsessed with them. When he died, she thought she'd get one to remember him by.'

'There was a third one?'

Stockdale nodded. 'There was. Mrs Anderson, in her sixties. It was strange because when we asked about the van, she started going crazy, asking why we hadn't found it yet. Said it was stolen last week.'

Tanzy scowled. 'First I've heard about that one.'

'I know. I said I'd look into it and update her on the situation.'

Tanzy thought for a moment about why CID wasn't aware of her missing blue VW van; the likely van that had the body parts in on Tuesday morning.

'Interesting.' Tanzy pressed his lips together. 'Keep me informed, Phil.'

'Sir.' Stockdale turned and made his way back toward his desk but didn't turn into the aisle, instead heading for the door, probably either the canteen or the toilet. Tanzy went to see Leonard.

'Jim.'

Leonard had noticed Stockdale speaking with Tanzy from his seated position at his desk. 'Did he tell you about the van?'

'He did.'

'I've been in touch with Jennifer at the Town Hall,' Leonard said. 'She said it's on the system, so if there's a hit, she'll get back to us.'

'Good.' Tanzy said nothing for a while.

'Everything okay?'

Tanzy narrowed his eyes and leaned in. 'How's Phil?'

'How — how do you mean?' Leonard leaned into him, making sure his voice was also low.

'I . . . don't know. He's not himself. He doesn't seem as focused.'

'Maybe having a tough time at home,' answered Cornty, who was sitting on the other side of Leonard, clearly eavesdropping. Tanzy peered over Leonard's shoulder. 'Heard he's been on his phone a lot,' Cornty went on. 'Also, heard him talking to Donny about a bet he put on and nearly won but never.'

'Okay. Where's Donny?'

'Canteen with Amy. One last coffee before the weekend.'

Tanzy stood up, turned, and came to a halt when Weaver dashed towards him, holding her phone out to him.

'Where's the coffee?' Leonard complained, seeing no coffee.

Weaver ignored Leonard and focused on Tanzy. 'Sir, you need to see this.' She stopped next to him and showed him what was on her phone.

'What is it?'

'Another video has been uploaded by *RCarl20*.'

They watched it on her phone.

'Jesus,' Tanzy said.

56

Tanzy had asked Weaver to forward the video clip to Leonard. Leonard opened it up. Everyone stood behind and focused on his computer, seeing the video on a bigger scale, feeling sick in the pit of their stomachs, apprehensive about what they were about to see. The camera was positioned roughly a metre high off the floor, showing a man and a woman sitting on two chairs, facing each other. They were tied securely to the chairs. They were both non-responsive, both quiet and still.

Behind them, black writing covered most of the wall.

'What does that say?' Tanzy said, pointing from over Leonard's shoulder.

Leonard double-clicked the screen to enlarge it, but the writing was too small and blurry.

'I can't see it properly.' Leonard leaned closed and squinted.

'No way of zooming in?' DC Cornty suggested.

'Someone get Mac,' Tanzy said to no one in particular.

Weaver took a step back and dashed down the corridor towards Digital Forensics.

'Print screen it and save it,' Tanzy told Leonard. 'Hopefully, we can enhance the shot to see the words better.'

Leonard saved the still shot into a location he'd easily remember.

'Watch it again,' Tanzy said.

It was clear the video had been edited. The time in the bottom right corner of the screen kept changing, progressing forward as the video did. The whole video should have been nearly three hours long but had been compressed to thirteen minutes. The woman was on the left and woke first, and it didn't take long for the panic to set in.

'What's with the tubes in her arms. Where do they go?' Cornty said, seeing the two small, clear tubes going towards and off the bottom of the screen.

'I have no idea,' Stockdale said. 'Are they going into her arms?'

'Like a catheter?' added Tanzy, nodding.

Weaver returned to the office with Mac, who, judging by the crumbs on his T-shirt, had been eating crisps. Again. Tanzy asked him to sit and watch the video.

'Jesus, what's this — is this him again?' Mac asked, noticing the uploader username *RCarl20*.

Tanzy came from Mac's right and pointed to the screen. 'Can you see what's on the wall behind them? It looks like writing, but we can't fathom out what it actually says.'

Mac leaned closer to the screen and focused trying to make out the black writing.

'Is there a way you can enlarge it?' asked Tanzy.

Mac used the mouse to copy and paste the address and fired an email over to himself. He told Tanzy he'd get straight on it and get back to him when he knew what the words said.

The woman on the screen woke up a little startled, sighing and getting her breath back. It took a few seconds for her to recognise the man — and the situation — in front of her. It wasn't long before a mechanical sound was heard.

'What the hell is that?' DC Leonard asked, furrowing his brows up at Tanzy, then to Cornty.

'Doesn't sound good, whatever it is.' Cornty shook his head and peered down over his glasses, with folded arms.

They watched on.

Linda Fallon appeared in the walkway. 'What's happened?'

'Your man is at it again,' Tanzy said, indicating the events on the screen.

She stopped beside Tanzy and watched.

It wasn't long before they learned the man's name was Aaron and she was called Rachel. Aaron kept telling her not to push the button, and it wasn't long before the detectives noticed something in her right hand, the hand nearest to the camera.

'Is that some kind of remote?' Tanzy wondered out loud.

Aaron then screamed, jerking his body back and forth, as much as the rope holding him in place allowed. The sound of the pump continued while she kept the button pressed.

'Whatever is happening, it isn't good,' noted Tanzy.

'Is *she* doing this to him?' Leonard asked.

Tanzy wasn't sure so stayed silent.

'Does Max know about this yet?' Cornty asked.

Tanzy shook his head. 'He'll be back soon. He had to pop out for a little while.'

Footsteps were heard behind him. It was Mac, carrying a piece of paper in his hand. 'Hey . . .' They all turned. 'I took still shots and zoomed in.' Mac handed the paper to Tanzy, who took it to read.

'Those tubes are pumping water in their veins . . .' Tanzy told them after digesting what it said.

'Water?' Leonard frowned. 'Why water?'

'Here, read this . . .' Tanzy handed the paper to him.

A moment later, Byrd turned up, wondering why they were all standing behind Leonard, watching something on his screen.

'What's the big commotion?' Byrd asked.

Tanzy turned to him. 'Max, there's another video.'

Byrd sighed and placed both hands on his head.

'Not only that,' PC Eric Timms said as he dashed over from the other side of the office. Byrd and Tanzy frowned, eager to hear what he had to say. 'There's someone on the phone. She says she knows the woman on the video. She's Rachel Hammond, aged twenty-seven.'

'Does this person know Rachel's address?'

'Yeah. She does.' Timms handed over the slip of paper with the address on.

Byrd glanced down. 'Looks like we're heading out. Come on.'

57

Friday late afternoon
Elton Road

Byrd took Tanzy and Fallon in his X5 and Cornty went with Leonard in his Vauxhall Insignia. Stockdale said he'd travel alone and would meet them there.

Byrd turned into Elton Road, drove a hundred metres before he slowed to focus on the house numbers. When he reached the number, he pulled over on the right and stopped at a semi-detached property with a brown-painted door.

The street was quiet.

Byrd stepped out onto the grass verge while Tanzy opened the passenger door and stepped down onto the road. Fallon climbed out too and followed them towards the driveway. They'd been discussing on their way over how to stop Adrian Dilton. Fallon had expressed her concern they had already experienced "water" and it would only be a matter of time before he used "earth" to kill someone.

The house looked well-kept and carried unique character, similar to others in the street. The low wall at the front of the boundary protected a modest neatly trimmed garden. The bay windows, on both levels, looked brand new.

They walked up the driveway. A two-year-old Renault Clio was parked, facing the road, its yellow, polished paintwork glistening in the late afternoon sunlight.

Tanzy knocked on the door.

Behind them Leonard and Cornty parked up and joined them.

Tanzy tried knocking again and when he got no answer, tried the handle. The door opened. In his hand was the baton he'd grabbed from Byrd's glovebox.

'Hello?' Tanzy shouted as he entered.

Byrd from the doorstep turned and directed Leonard and Cornty around the side towards the brown gate which spanned the width of the drive. He then told Fallon to wait at the front door until he deemed it safe for entry, who nodded in understanding.

The hallway was wide. The walls were white but tinted with green to give it colour.

'Hello?' shouted Tanzy. He peered up the stairs then down the hall into the kitchen. He moved forward with the baton in his right hand, ready to attack if he needed to use it. Byrd was a step behind him. By the time they reached the dining room, Tanzy noticed Rachel and Aaron in the chairs.

'Jesus,' said Byrd in the doorway, looking inside the dim room.

They were still tied up. The tubes and catheters were still in place, fixed to equipment down on the floor. There was a large, plastic tank next to the table — a similar size to a water tank you'd find in the attic before Combi boilers had taken over — with what looked like a pump in front of it, being powered by an extension lead that ran to a socket in the alcove.

The writing on the wall to their right was clearer and much bigger than when they saw it on the video. Byrd entered the room and skimmed over the words while Tanzy went to the victims. The carpet was saturated with water, causing a squelching sound each step they took.

Linda Fallon had ignored Byrd's instruction and entered not only the house, but the room they were in. She gasped when she saw Aaron and Rachel sitting lifeless in the chairs.

Byrd turned. 'Hey, I said for you to wait, Linda.'

'The skin . . .' Tanzy whispered.

Intrigued, Byrd turned his way.

Fallon grew closer, moving past Byrd to get a better look. The skin on the back of Aaron's neck was white, almost translucent. 'The water's changed his skin,' she said.

Byrd finished reading the last few lines and turned to see what Tanzy and Fallon were meaning. It was true. Their skin colour had changed, almost becoming see-through and bloated. Byrd was about to comment on it when the mechanical pump whirred near the table.

Tanzy raised the baton quickly and faced the sudden sound.

'Easy partner,' mused Byrd, knowing what it was after reading the words on the wall.

Water seeped from every visible orifice — their mouths, nose, ears — as if their bodies couldn't absorb any more, like a sink overflowing. It was the strangest thing Tanzy had ever seen. 'This is fucking weird.'

They both watched Fallon bend down to take a closer look at Aaron's forearm.

'We need Tallow and Hope in here,' said Byrd.

Tanzy picked his phone from his pocket and rang Jacob Tallow, telling him the situation.

'Jacob said he's on his way with Emily,' Tanzy told them when he hung up and pushed his phone back into his trousers.

'I'm going to have a look around,' said Byrd, who turned slowly, leaving the dining room.

Tanzy made a call to coroner Peter Gibbs, to inform him of the situation. He was sure Peter would like to visit the scene for himself; it was certainly something Tanzy hadn't seen before. The police would need to contact their family members to formally identify the bodies once they moved them to the hospital, away from the crime scene, once Forensics were happy for them to be moved. Once the identities had been confirmed, the pathologists would need to confirm their suspicions that water had been used, although, judging by the scene before them, it seemed pretty obvious.

Once Byrd had swept downstairs, he went upstairs, the sound of Tanzy's conversation with Linda fading as he reached the landing.

He angled right and peered into the empty bathroom, seeing nothing out of place or anything that caused concern. He backed out and went into the rear bedroom. A single bed was against the left wall, a chest of cheap-looking drawers against the far wall and a wardrobe was to the right, next to the long, wide window.

He stepped back onto the landing, made his way to the bedroom at the end and opened the door, finding a much smaller room with a desk over to the right. A business card was positioned on the top of a closed laptop.

He picked it up with gloved hands.

Roger Carlton Hot Tubs.

'Crafty bastard.'

Byrd sighed heavily and tipped his head back. He could have screamed but didn't have the energy. Roger Carlton — or Adrian Dilton as they knew him to be — had used another excuse to get into someone's home. A valid, sneaky excuse to lure someone in thinking he was a normal guy doing a normal job.

A carpet cleaner.

An electrician.

A guy who rents out hot tubs.

Under his name, there was a handwritten message saying, "Look at laptop!"

Byrd dropped the card on the desk, found his phone and dialled Mac.

'Mac, you remember the laptop from Jane Ericson's apartment that you looked at?'

'I do.'

'I need you to do it again, please. I'm currently at the house where we saw the couple on the video. There's a card with handwriting on telling me to look at the laptop. I believe there could be something on it.'

'Okay, Max. Would you be able to bag it up and drop it off at some point?'

'I'll bag it up and drop it off very soon.'

'How soon?'

'As in I-want-to-catch-this-fucking-killer soon. Probably within the hour.'

Mac sighed, as if he had plans, but said, 'Okay . . .'

Byrd wasn't impressed with his attitude and hung up the phone. He picked up the card again and looked at the back. His eyes widened. This card was different from the others. There was a number on it with a handwritten message: *Call me.*

Byrd typed the number into his phone, pressed CALL and put it to his ear.

'Hello, Detective . . .' answered the male voice.

'Roger Carlton? Or should I call you Adrian Dilton?'

'Call me whatever you like.'

'I'll call you Adrian Dilton as that's your real name.'

'Suit yourself. How's the investigation coming on, Detective?'

'We're very close . . .'

'No, you're not. You're a million miles away. And let me tell you something . . .'

'What's that Mr Dilton?'

'It'll only get worse. Because I'm going to kill them all . . . one by one.'

'Kill who?'

'The ones who deserve it.'

'Deserve what?'

'I guess you'll have to wait and find out.'

Dilton hung up the phone and the line went dead.

58

Brad opened the door and carried two coffees over to the desk where Mitch was sitting and placed one down in front of him.

'Cheers.' Mitch picked it up and took a sip.

Brad removed his coffee from the cardboard holder and threw it at the bin over to the right but failed miserably, hitting the wall instead. He took a drink of his salted caramel latte and closed his eyes for a moment. 'Unbelievable.'

He turned to Mitch and noticed the look on his face as he glared at the computer screen. 'What is it, Mitch?'

'*HammR33* wasn't online last night.'

'She wasn't?'

Mitch lowered his coffee and shook his head. 'No, she wasn't.'

'The others?'

'*Spork11* and *RCarl20* were there.'

'How many were watching?' Brad asked.

Mitch grabbed the mouse, clicked a few tabs and found the figure. 'Just over a thousand. The most so far.'

Brad felt tingling in his chest and his smile widened. 'It's all working out, isn't it?'

Mitch smiled in agreement but it didn't look convincing. 'Why are players not turning up? Now it's *HammR33*. I don't understand.'

'As long as we get paid who's bothered, Mitch?' noted Brad, greedily rubbing his hands together.

Mitch gave a fair-enough shrug and focused on the screen that showed the camera view of inside the room below. 'I wonder how long it takes her to realise she's alone?'

'She probably already knows.'

'Where's Lisa?'

'She's in the van,' Brad replied. Their eyes met for a moment. 'I'm not stupid, you know, Mitch. I'll make sure the van's doors are locked this time.'

Mitch looked away from him and rolled his eyes. He knew Brad wasn't stupid, but he was a long way from Britain's next top scientist. He studied the list of players.

Spork11.

RCarl20.

'We'll open the table tonight and allow another three to play.'

'I think we should up the price too,' said Brad. 'It's clearly popular with so many watchers waiting for their turn.'

Mitch silently turned back to the computer and considered the idea. If they could make more money, then why not. To the right of the screen in the bottom corner, another notification popped up.

'They're coming thick and fast,' Mitch said, smiling.

Brad rubbed his thick hands together again, this time quicker. 'It's making the rounds.'

Each time someone clicked on *www.attheend.com*, a notification in the form of a small rectangular box came up in the bottom corner, with an IP address, and underneath it, an option for either Brad or Mitch to press "Yes" or "No".

He hovered the mouse over the box and decided to click "Yes" to another potential customer. He leaned back and sighed lightly, tilting his head into the leather of the high-backed chair.

'What's going to happen after Sarah is dead?' Brad asked as he watched the screen. Sarah was sitting against the far wall with her knees tucked under her chin, shivering.

'We need more women. Preferably in their twenties. Nothing older.'

'When by?'

'This time next week,' Mitch told him. 'We'll need another four. Doesn't matter where from.'

Brad looked over to him and nodded, understanding what was needed. He knew Mitch was the brains behind this and he was just the muscle. He would collect women against their will and bring them here, ready for the show.

They'd started so well.

The first group had been successful.

From the group of four women, three of them were now dead. They'd made thousands of pounds so far through people signing up as "players" and the others as "watchers". For this to continue, they'd need to stay clever and patient and not allow it go to their heads. Obviously, it was something they couldn't do forever but for now, they'd cash in whatever they could get. The ones unfortunate enough to be involved were collateral damage as far as Mitch was concerned.

'Right, Brad. I need to head off soon. Feed Sarah and get rid of Lisa. Remember —' he turned to him and pointed — 'no excuses this time.'

'I know!' Brad spurted quickly.

Mitch nodded and smiled. 'Good.' He stood and pushed his chair in. 'Have a think about the next four, Brad. I'll leave that up to you. I'll be in touch.'

59

Saturday afternoon
Police station

The office was quiet for a Saturday. The sun had blazed through the windows all morning and had created a hot box because the air conditioning was only half working. The maintenance man had been called and said he'd come in today at some point to have a look at it.

Tanzy gazed across the office, expecting to see a few heads over the top of computer monitors but there weren't many volunteers this weekend. The weather had been hot through the week and according to the forecast, it was going to peak on Saturday and Sunday before getting colder next week so people were obviously making the most of the sun. Overtime looked good on those who volunteered, but it wasn't a mandatory requirement. Tanzy was in today to attempt to move things forward. So far, they'd come up short in terms of answers and hadn't located Adrian Dilton yet. He also had to start the appraisals for his team, as well as catching up with Mac, who was in possession of Rachel Hammond's laptop.

Tanzy sighed heavily, feeling the weight of the current workload. He was frustrated that he'd been less than a metre from Dilton when he'd spoken with him at the Napier Street crime scene and that he'd taken a video in the car park when Jane Ericson fell to her death.

It seemed like Dilton knew how to play them. He knew how to stay hidden. Judging by the screen stills of the camera at Napier Street where the house fire was, the wig and tash were obviously fake. They did know his height and build, and that he had, from what Tanzy could remember, dark brown eyes and a large nose.

Tanzy's phone rang. He looked at the caller.

'Hi, Linda,' He answered.

'Just checking in. I'm bored at the hotel.' Fallon had said she was going to pop into town today and would phone either Byrd or Tanzy at some point. She had booked a few more nights in the hotel where she was staying but wanted to get out for a while. Sometimes, she explained, it got too much for her, day after day — she wasn't used to it anymore.

'Nothing yet, Linda,' replied Tanzy. 'By leaving his card on her laptop, it's obvious he wants us to have a look at it. Mac is checking it now.' It reminded him he needed to pop along to see Mac. 'Are you enjoying our fabulous town?'

'I'm currently in the Cornmill Shopping Centre. Just been to Waterstones. I'm heading back to the hotel soon.'

'Good. Well, I'll let you know if I hear anything.'

'Speak soon.'

They both hung up and Tanzy placed his phone near his empty mug. He thought about the day before, finding the bodies that had been pumped with water, thinking about what it would have felt like to have water pumped into your body quicker than it was absorbed. Judging by the screams on the video it wouldn't have been pleasant. He also thought about how DS Stockdale had acted when he turned up. He had seemed fidgety, not quite himself. He'd been like that for a little while now, and no matter how many times Tanzy or Byrd had spoken with him, it hadn't improved. They knew he was having issues at home.

Tanzy stood, remembering that Stockdale had said he'd come in today to do his report. On his way down to see Mac, he noticed he wasn't at his desk. He tried calling him, but it went straight to voicemail, so he left a message asking to send over his report when he had the chance.

Tanzy knocked on Mac's door.

'Yeah . . .'

He opened it and went inside.

Mac was sitting at his desk with Rachel Hammond's laptop open in front of him. There were several wires from her laptop to Mac's computer and another wire connected to one of the screens on his wide desk.

Tanzy closed the door and thanked him for coming in. He replied saying it was no problem, but Tanzy knew by his tone he wasn't very excited about it. Tanzy too had plans with Pip and the kids. He had promised to be back by 3 p.m. as they wanted to go to Hardwick Park for a walk and soak up some sun before settling down for a film and takeaway later, so Tanzy wasn't here to waste any time either.

'What have you found?' asked Tanzy, straight to the point.

'Remember when I checked Jane Ericson's laptop and found that website that contained much more than it appeared to have.'

Tanzy took a few steps towards him and nodded. *'Theend. com?'*

'Attheend.com,' Mac said, correcting him. 'She's been on that site a lot, according to her history. The difference we have here in comparison to Jane Ericson's laptop is that when you go to the site, it comes up with a username and password option. Her username is already there. *HammR33.'*

'Spell that, please.'

Mac did letter by letter. 'We just need the password.'

'Can you get past it?'

Mac pushed his lips out. 'Usually, yes. But not on this site. The firewall protection is so good, MI5 wouldn't crack it.'

Tanzy considered his words for a moment, grabbed a chair from his left and sat down.

Mac leaned over, grabbed a pack of crisps from his desk, opened them and started munching. Loudly. The sound of people eating made Tanzy want to punch the wall. He breathed slowly, trying not to let it bother him.

After Mac had finished, he threw the empty bag on the desk near another empty bag. Tanzy decided to not mention it. He was there to find out what was on Rachel's laptop, nothing more.

'So, what would you suggest we do with this then, Mac?'

The big man shrugged. 'I don't know, Ori. It's beyond my capability. Maybe we should send it away?'

'Okay. Yeah, maybe we'll need to. Thanks for having a look.'

Mac immediately stood and left his office without saying goodbye. Whatever he had planned was obviously more important than cracking this case. Tanzy shook his head a little and stared at Rachel's laptop screen, open on the website *www.attheend.com*. If only he knew the password to access the site.

Still in Mac's office, he decided to ring Byrd. When Byrd answered, he asked how Claire was doing.

'On the sofa, taking it easy.' Byrd fell silent for a moment.

'What's happening there, Ori?'

'Mac has looked at Rachel's laptop. He said Rachel has been on the same website as Jane Ericson went on.'

'Can he access it?' asked Byrd. 'I remember him coming stuck with it.'

'Same scenario. He said the firewall is too strong to get in.'

'So, we don't know what this website is?'

'We don't . . .'

'What is it?' asked Byrd, knowing there was more Tanzy wanted to say.

'Whatever it is, it's why people are dying.'

Byrd considered his words and had to agree with him. 'Very likely.'

'I wonder if Danny Walters had accessed the site, too?'

'His laptop would have been burnt in the fire. I didn't see any laptops there.'

'Or maybe it was there, but we didn't find it?'

'Maybe.'

'Leave it with me, Max. I'll go and find out.'

'Where are you going?'

'To Napier Street. Where this all started. If he had a laptop, it wasn't collected in evidence so it must still be there. I'll ring you if I find anything.'

'Good luck.'

Tanzy ended the call, stood up and put his phone away. He left Mac's office and headed along to the evidence room. After speaking with Rebecca and signing out the sets of keys that belonged to Danny Walters, he went outside in the warmth of the Saturday afternoon and walked over to his car.

It wasn't long before he pulled up outside the burnt house in Napier Street. He got and locked his car, then used the key from evidence to open the front door. The house was silent. Neglected. He could smell burnt charcoal as he made his way down the narrow hallway, snapping on a pair of gloves.

He took a right at the base of the burnt stairs and made his way through the dining room and entered the long, narrow kitchen. Drawer by drawer and cupboard by cupboard, he pulled them open, searching for a laptop. Seeing as the house had been checked when the police were there during the crime scene, he wasn't hopeful in locating the laptop, but he had to check; it must be somewhere. He sighed and returned to the base of the stairs, remaining positive it was in the house but hadn't been discovered yet. Looking up at the stairs, the smell of petrol and burnt flesh came back to him.

He gingerly climbed the stairs and entered through the second door on the left into the front bedroom. The image of the mother and son who'd died in there appeared in his mind; the way they held each other in the corner, the way the mother's eyes had frozen, looking down at her small son, all bloodshot and black.

He shuddered, imagining they were still there inside the room, watching him, begging him to find something that would help figure out who did this to them. The first place he checked were the wardrobes. There were two of them, one on either side of the chimney breast, built into the alcoves. He went to the left one, gently grabbed the metal handle, and pulled it towards him. Inside, he found nothing useful.

'Shit.'

He padded across the burnt carpet and checked the other wardrobe, finding more clothes, a large box filled with games, and a large plastic tub of toys which were blackened with smoke.

He left the bedroom and searched the other rooms, again finding nothing of value or anything that resembled a laptop.

Back on the landing, he noticed the door directly in front of him, the one that led to the attic they'd already checked. He sighed, pushed down the handle and pulled it open, seeing the same wooden ladder they'd seen the first time at the house. He leaned in and climbed the ladder, pushing the hatch upwards when he was close enough and pulled himself up into the attic, mindful of hitting his head on the angled roof.

Brightly lit with sunlight coming through the angled window, the room seemed bigger this time, spanning the full width of the house. The floor was covered with a pale blue carpet that had seen better days. With the window closed, the room was clammy, the air stagnant and hot. Tanzy gazed around. The room was empty apart from the old wooden wardrobe against the wall that backed on to the house next door. He went over and opened it, revealing a larger space at the top containing coats and unused jumpers and a smaller area at the base of it with narrow shelves.

He bent down, searching the shelves and pulled out a box from the second shelf but knew by its weight it was probably empty. He remembered DC Leonard doing the same. Other than unused clothing and the empty box, the wardrobe didn't contain anything of interest. With a beaten sigh and happy he'd covered the room again he ambled back to the hatch.

And that's when he spotted it. He frowned, noticing a faint crease in the carpet.

''What's that?'

He studied the crease and slowly dropped to his knees, pinching the surface of the carpet close to the skirting board with his fingertips and pulled it upwards.

'Interesting.'

Most of the exposed wooden boards were solid when he'd pulled back a section of carpet but there was a square of boarding roughly a foot by a foot in size that appeared to be randomly positioned. Tanzy noted it wasn't screwed down. He used a key to prise the board up.

'Bingo.'

There it was — the laptop. He carefully picked it up from between two joists and froze, sure he could hear something below. He couldn't be certain, but it sounded like footsteps. He listened, angling his ear to the open hatch.

It was probably something outside.

Then he realised someone was walking up the stairs.

60

Tanzy stayed perfectly still, staring at the open hatch, listening to the approaching footsteps until the house became silent. Had he imagined it? He slowly took a few paces towards the hatch with the laptop in his hand

'Orion?' he heard someone say.

He frowned. The voice wasn't familiar.

'Orion? Are you up there?'

He appeared at the hatch and looked down. 'What are you doing here? How did you know I was here?'

'I spoke with Max,' Linda Fallon replied. 'He said you were here. I tried calling but it kept going to answerphone.'

He pulled his phone from his pocket. 'I've had no missed calls,' he said. 'Ahh, I haven't got any signal.' He placed his phone into his jeans and gradually descended the ladder, careful not to drop the laptop.

'I was going to go back to the hotel, but when Max said you were here, I put it into my phone and realised it was only a few minutes away. What's that?'

'It looks like Danny Walters' laptop.'

* * *

They handed the keys over to Rebecca in the evidence lock-up when they returned to the station and headed for the office with the laptop. Tanzy searched the desks, seeing no sign of Stockdale, whose report he still needed to forward on to Fuller, who'd no doubt be looking for it first thing Monday morning.

Tanzy sat down at his desk, placing the laptop in front of him. Fallon sat on Byrd's chair and leaned in.

He opened the laptop and pressed the ON button.

Tanzy could smell her pleasant perfume; something familiar that maybe Pip had worn in the past. He glanced at her, noticing her blonde hair long and straight, her emerald eyes surrounded with dark mascara and light purple eye shadow focused on the open laptop screen. There was no denying she was attractive for her age. Tanzy had never felt attraction towards anyone in their fifties before.

'What?' she said, feeling his stare on her.

'Nothing.' He turned back to the laptop, which whirred a little before the screen came alive. 'Here we go,' said Tanzy. He navigated the laptop's mouse pad to connect to the station's Wi-Fi, opened the internet and checked the internet history.

The last visited address was *www.attheend.com*.

'Bingo,' he said. 'It's the same website Jane Ericson and Rachel Hammond used.'

The username *Dwalt66* was already typed in, no doubt saved from the last log-in, along with eight small asterisks.

'Is that the password?' Fallon asked, hopeful.

'Looks that way.'

'Go on it,' Fallon encouraged.

Whatever this site was, Tanzy knew it had something to do with the murders. It was the only link so far. He pressed the ENTER key and it went to the next screen.

A welcome message came up: *Hello, Dwalt66.*

'What the hell is this?' Tanzy whispered.

There was a box on the left showing a live camera feed of a dark room, revealing a woman sitting on the floor with her back against the wall. Near her were food wrappers and an empty drink bottle.

There was a box at the top of the page with the title "current players" and under the title were three names.

Dwalt66.

Spork11.

RCarl20.

He pointed to *RCarl20* and said, 'He's our guy. That's Adrian Dilton. That's the same user who uploaded those videos online. He's a part of—' Tanzy raised his palms towards the screen — 'this. Whatever this is.'

There was a title tab with "six days until next game" at the top of the screen so users were aware. Underneath that was a separate tab with "watchers" on, with the number 1023 beside it.

'Is that how many are watching?' Linda asked, frowning.

Tanzy silently pressed his palms on the top his head, trying to work it out. The heat in the office wasn't helping his focus and he could feel sweat running down his back.

'Is this some kind of game?' Fallon turned to him.

Tanzy didn't know what to say because he didn't fully understand it. He edged a little closer, trying to see the girl on the video feed better. Struggling to make out her details, he picked up his phone to ring Byrd. As the call connected, the screen on the laptop suddenly changed to a blank screen and a log-in box appeared.

Tanzy jerked back. 'No! Where did it go?'

Fallon scowled at the screen.

Username — Dwalt66.

Password — please enter…

'Shit. Where's it gone?'

* * *

Across town, Mitch had noticed a notification pop up, indicating *Dwalt66* had logged on.

'Hold on a second,' Mitch said quickly. '*Dwalt66* is online.'

Brad frowned and slid his chair over. 'He hasn't been on in a while.'

Mitch pulled himself closer to the desk. 'I'll find the IP address, see where it is.' Which didn't take long. 'Oh, hell no!' he shouted, quickly tapping the keyboard to log *Dwalt66* out of the system.

'What's wrong?' Brad said, unsure what was happening.

'It wasn't *Dwalt66* watching. It was the police.'

61

Tanzy was the last one to enter the meeting room and closed the door. He could feel all eyes watching him as he moved to the front of the room, including DCI Fuller's. He'd heard Fuller in his office earlier, speaking with someone on the phone. The tone of the call and the language used indicated it was far from friendly.

'Morning,' said Tanzy, addressing the room. He angled to Byrd and nodded to indicate for him to start the meeting...

Byrd pressed the button and the first slide appeared, telling everyone the day, date, and a title "Updates" underneath.

'I hope everyone has had a good weekend and had some valuable rest,' Tanzy started. 'This week will be a busy one. To the ones who don't know, we found Rachel Hammond dead in a property on Elton Road on Friday, tied to a chair sitting opposite her boyfriend, who was also tied up and also dead. There was a video posted online by *RCarl20*, the same user who uploaded the house fire video and the shocking footage of Jane Ericson falling from the flat, indicating it's his third victim and—'

'Sixth victim,' DC Cornty said, interrupting him.

Tanzy jerked his head towards him. 'I'm sorry, Phil?'

'It's his sixth victim, sir.'

Tanzy frowned.

'Four victims died in the fire. Then Jane Ericson. Now Rachel. That makes six. Actually seven, if we include her boyfriend, Aaron.'

Byrd sighed loud enough for only Tanzy to hear.

Tanzy took a deep breath. 'His third occasion, shall we say then?'

Cornty nodded his approval and smiled.

'So, we know Adrian Dilton left a business card on her laptop, claiming to be an electrician.'

Several heads bobbed.

'Eric, you wouldn't mind opening that window, would you?' DCI Fuller asked Timms, who was closest to it. 'It's too hot in here.'

Timms stood, went over to the window and opened it before returning to his seat.

'On Jane's laptop,' Tanzy continued, 'Mac found a frequently visited website called *www.attheend.com*. He tried accessing the site but said it was very strange, having layers upon layers of security he couldn't break through. I did some digging but didn't find a thing on *www.attheend.com*, so I can't be sure what it is. What I can be sure of is, when we found Rachel Hammond and after searching the house, there was another business card upstairs, on top of her closed laptop. The business card was *Roger Carlton Hot tubs*. Now we believe Adrian Dilton posed as a guy renting out hot tubs this time and got in her house that way.'

PC Weaver raised her slender hand. Her hair was different today. Curled. She looked stunning.

'Yes, Amy?' said Tanzy.

'So, he posed as a carpet cleaner, then an electrician, now a guy renting out hot tubs?'

Tanzy nodded.

'Seems so,' added Byrd.

Weaver gave a sad smile.

Byrd said, 'The business card that he left on her laptop had a number written on, along with a message asking me to call him.'

'And?' DCI Fuller pressed, for the purpose of the group.

'It was Adrian Dilton,' informed Byrd. 'He told me that he would kill them all.'

'Who?' Fallon said from the left, seated next to Fuller.

'He said everyone who deserves it.'

Silence swept the room, and no one said anything for a few moments.

'What did you find on Rachel's laptop?' DC Anne Tiffin asked.

Tanzy nodded. 'The same website as we did on Jane's laptop. But as before, we couldn't access it.' He turned to Byrd, who pressed the button, the screen behind them changing. 'It comes up with this.'

On the screen, it showed the log-in box on the entry page to *www.attheend.com*.

'What is it?' DC Tiffin asked, leaning forward.

'The site that both Rachel Hammond and Jane Ericson had been on.'

'Do you know the password or log-in?'

Tanzy shook his head. 'Unfortunately not.' He then took a few steps as if it would help release his thoughts. 'After seeing the same website, it got me thinking. What if Danny Walters had also been on this site.'

DC Anne Tiffin nodded in agreement, as did Amy Weaver.

'We didn't find a laptop in the house, Ori,' Tallow said.

'I know,' said Tanzy. 'But based on this information, I double-checked the house again. Remember the attic?'

'The attic was checked.'

'It was,' agreed Tanzy. 'I had a look up there.' He took a breath. 'But I had a feeling I'd missed something.' He informed them of the crease in the carpet and locating the laptop. He raised his hands. 'Totally my fault for not finding it first time around.'

Fuller nodded, appreciating this honesty.

'So, we had a look at it and found out that Danny Walters' last visited site had been *www.attheend.com*. His browser had saved his username and password so we logged in.'

The room suddenly became dead quiet, everyone listening to what was coming next.

'A small screen on the left showed a woman sitting on the floor of a room with her head tucked into her knees. The room looked big but empty. There was only her. Judging by her body language, she chose not to be there. On the right-hand side of the website was a tab with the word "players". There were three names. One of them was Danny Walters': *Dwalt66*. Another tab said "watchers" with a number over a thousand. Then it logged me out, taking me back to the first page. We couldn't get back in. But I did notice a notification saying it was six days until the next game. That was on Saturday morning.'

'So four days from now?' Fuller replied. 'Friday is the day. Whatever game this is, it's happening Friday.'

Tanzy nodded. He wasn't one hundred per cent sure but it was the only logical thing to assume.

'Do you think Adrian Dilton is behind this?' asked PC Weaver.

Tanzy wasn't confident and raised a hand to scratch his chin. 'If this is the link between Danny Walters, Jane Ericson and Rachel Hammond, which so far seems to be, then perhaps Dilton plays some part in it, considering the name *RCarl20* was one of the players.' Tanzy paused and frowned suddenly.

'What's the game?' Tiffin probed.

Tanzy could only shrug.

'So,' Fuller said, standing abruptly. 'In four days, there's a game?'

'Seems so, sir,' answered Byrd, unsure of why Fuller had stood up.

'Whatever this fucking game is, isn't good and will probably lead to another death. And I'll tell you something — after the conversation I've just had with Barry Eckles, it's something I can't let happen. It would be bad for all of us. And I *mean* all of us. Now, get your fucking acts together and find Adrian Dilton.' He turned, charged over to the door, opened it and went through, slamming it closed, the impact of the door with the frame causing vibrations through the room.

There was an uncomfortable silence in the room.

'Any questions?' asked Byrd.

62

Byrd and Tanzy quickly returned to their desks. Linda Fallon took a right, sat down on the desk across from them and logged on to the computer.

She caught Tanzy's eye and pointed towards Fuller's office. 'He doesn't seem very pleased.'

Tanzy offered a thin smile and raised his eyebrows, realising the pressure Fuller must be on from above. It went without saying a DCI either protected their team or allowed the shit to roll downhill. And, it appeared so far, during the course of this investigation, that Fuller had been protecting them, finally relieving some of that pressure.

'So,' Byrd said, sitting up with good posture, 'what's our plan, Ori?'

Tanzy rubbed his hands together, 'We need to find out what this website is.' He breathed heavily pulled himself in and started typing on his keyboard.

Byrd nodded and turned to his own computer.

Fallon wheeled herself over to them 'We've had water, fire and air.' Tanzy, closest to her, turned her way. 'Earth is next, I'm sure of it,' she added.

232

'Hopefully not,' Tanzy replied quietly to her.

She rolled back across the aisle to the desk she was using. 'I'll do some more digging on earth, Ori. See what I come up with.'

Tanzy checked his emails, checking the reports from the people who were at Rachel Hammond's house on Friday. He was still missing one report.

DS Stockdale's.

Narrowing his eyes, he stood up, peered over the desks, searching for Stockdale but was nowhere to be seen. He turned to Byrd. 'Have you seen Phil Stockdale today?'

Byrd thought for a few seconds. 'I didn't see him in the meeting.'

Tanzy checked the tracking system where employees swiped in and out.

'He didn't report in this morning,' Tanzy said. He turned his chair. 'Linda, have you seen DS Stockdale this morning?'

'Which one is that?' she replied, with a shrug.

'Never mind.' He stood. 'I'm going to look for him. I need his report on what happened at Rachel Hammond's house on Friday.'

Tanzy walked down the aisle towards the other end and found Stockdale's empty chair. He asked Leonard, who was sitting nearby, 'You seen Phil today?'

Leonard shook his head. He then asked Cornty, who replied the same.

Tanzy left the office, made his way down the corridor until he reached reception. Julie was sitting behind her desk, focusing on something behind her computer screen.

'Hey,' said Tanzy.

She put whatever she was focused on down on the desk and looked up, smiling. 'Hello, Orion.'

'Have you seen Phil Stockdale today?'

She considered the question and shook her head. 'I haven't. Has he swiped in?'

'He's not on the system, so assuming he hasn't. Could you double check, please.'

'Let me see,' she said, grabbing the mouse and edging closer to her monitor. Beside her Tanzy noticed a textbook on Criminal Law and smiled towards her. 'No, Orion, he's definitely not here.'

Tanzy thanked her and went out to the car park to check the cars, but he couldn't see Stockdale's. He picked his phone from his pocket, found his number and frowned at the notification at the top of the screen. He swiped down, revealing a missed call from Stockdale last night at 10.27 p.m. Tanzy couldn't remember receiving it or his phone ringing. It must have gone straight to the answerphone.

'C'mon, Phil. Where are you?' he whispered to himself.

Just before he put his phone away it rang. The number on the screen was one he didn't recognise and ended in two four seven. He accepted the call. 'Hello?'

'Is that Detective Inspector Orion Tanzy?' It was a woman's voice, sounding concerned.

'Speaking. Who's this?' Tanzy asked.

'My name is Joan Stockdale — Phil is my husband. I'm sorry for calling. I found your number in his notes for useful work contacts.'

'How can I help, Mrs Stockdale?'

Have you seen Phil today?'

'I — I haven't seen him today.'

Tanzy heard her sigh through the phone.

'I'm worried about him. It's not like him not to come home.'

'What do you mean?'

'He went for a walk last night,' she went on. 'Said he needed to clear his head.' She fell silent for a moment. 'Recently, he's…'

'He's what, Joan?'

'He hasn't been himself. He's been spending a lot of time on his phone and his laptop. I—' she sighed heavily — 'I think he might be gambling again. Has he mentioned anything?'

Tanzy thought hard, knowing Stockdale hadn't quite been himself but didn't want her to worry more than she already was.

'He hasn't, no.'

There was silence on the call for a long moment.

'You there, Joan?'

'Yes. Yes.' She started to sob a little. 'I just need to know why he never came home last night. We kind of argued so he went, saying he needed to clear his head. I went to sleep, thinking nothing of it, but when I woke this morning, he wasn't home. I've checked the house. He's not here.'

'Is his car at home?'

'Yes. It's still here,' she replied quickly. 'That's the weird thing about it.'

Tanzy pondered that. 'Let me make some calls, Joan. I'll find him. I'll be in touch.'

'Thank you.'

Tanzy hung up and called Stockdale again. It went straight to voicemail.

63

Sunday night (The night before)

'Please, just tell me what's wrong?' Joan Stockdale asked Phil, her hands out wide in desperation. She had just got out of the bath and was wearing a thin, blue dressing gown. Her dark hair was damp, tied up in a loose ponytail.

Phil was sitting at the kitchen table in a T-shirt and jogging bottoms, vacantly staring at nothing.

'Phil? Talk to me.'

'Nothing's wrong,' he said.

'Josh tried to show you something earlier and you weren't bothered. He's your son. You've never dismissed him like that before. Something's going on.'

She wandered over, dropped into the seat next to him and took hold of his hand. He edged away slightly, removing her hand.

'Please, Phil. Just tell me what's wrong?' she begged him.

He stared silently at the table.

'Is it the gambling again?' she said softly. 'Because if it is, we can get help again.'

He considered the question for a long moment, then shook his head slowly. 'No.'

'What is it — is it work? Is it too much?'

Again, the question seemed to take a while to sink into Stockdale's trance-like state. Something was obviously on his mind.

'Yeah. Work is hard at the moment. There's a lot of shit coming down from Fuller. We have our appraisals coming up soon.'

She smiled sadly at him.

'I'm not gambling again. I promise you that.' He slowly found his feet. 'I need some air. I need to get out.'

She frowned, looked up at the kitchen clock. 'Phil, it's after ten o'clock. Where are you going?'

'I don't know. I just need to walk.'

'It'll be getting dark soon.'

'I won't be long. I just need some air. You go on up to bed. I'll be back soon.'

He stood up, grabbed a thin jacket from a hook near the back door and put it on. From the table, she watched him with sadness, knowing she couldn't help him.

'I'll wait for you to come back.'

'I won't be long, Joan.' He left the kitchen, went down the hall and out of the front door.

Ten minutes after leaving the house, he found himself walking past Cockerton Green. It was quiet and still warm. The day's heat had stuck around but the sun was almost out of sight. He passed the row of shops and crossed near Cockerton Club, then continued along the path, crossing over Deneside Road.

Just before he reached the mini-roundabout at Woodland Road, a car slowed and stopped beside him. Stockdale turned to his right as he walked, and the passenger window lowered.

'Excuse me, mate,' the driver said, leaning towards the open window.

Stockdale stopped and took a few steps towards the car. 'Yeah?'

'Can you tell me where Pierremont Road is?'

Stockdale thought for a moment and pointed straight ahead. 'Take a left here and it's literally one hundred metres down. On your right or left, depending on where you need to be.'

The man in the car smiled. 'I knew it was around here somewhere.'

Stockdale frowned for a moment, realising the man looked somewhat familiar, but he couldn't place him. His big brown, dark eyes. The large nose. He'd seen him somewhere he was sure of it.

'Thanks, mate.' The man raised the window and checked the traffic behind before pulling out.

Stockdale continued to walk, thinking about the man. Then it clicked. He recognised him from the video from Napier Street. It was Adrian Dilton. He took out his phone, found Tanzy's number and pressed CALL. It went unanswered. As Stockdale rounded the corner and approached the tennis courts on his left, he noticed the Focus had stopped up on the left, just beyond the tennis courts, by the park entrance.

The lights were turned off. It appeared no one was inside.

As he grew closer, he heard footsteps inside the park to his left. Through the railings, he saw the man, walking along the path away from him.

'Hey, wait!' Stockdale shouted. He picked up his speed and entered the park. The high, surrounding trees blocked most of the remaining daylight, but Stockdale could vaguely track his movements.

'Hey!' he shouted, watching the man take a right and disappear.

Stockdale broke out into a jog, focusing down the dark path, which got murkier the further he went. Panting a little, he noticed the path branch off to the right, so went that way.

He opened his eyes wide but could see no one.

'Hello?' he said, quieter this time.

No response. The park was totally silent and, although he was a thickset man, it made him feel uncomfortable and vulnerable. He turned around, looking behind him, and grabbed his phone to find the torch app. The light was good but not bright enough to see very far.

'Where's he gone?' he whispered.

'Looking for me?' he heard from behind him.

He spun around and felt the sudden hard impact to the side of his head; a hot wave of searing pain like his head was on fire. Helpless, he fell to the ground and passed out.

64

Tanzy returned to the office, finding Fallon beside Byrd, both reading something on his computer screen.

'Stockdale's car isn't here,' said Tanzy. He stopped behind them and focused on the article on the screen. It was about the "earth" murder that had happened seven years ago near Essex; the case Linda Fallon had been heavily involved in. 'What's this?'

Fallon turned. 'An article written by a local paper about the guy who was buried in the woods.'

'Earth?' asked Tanzy.

She nodded. 'Yup.'

'Max, I've tried ringing Phil but it's going straight to voicemail.'

Byrd turned, pushing out his bottom lip. 'Have you spoken with his wife?'

'Funny you should say that.'

Byrd's eyes narrowed.

'She's just rung me asking if I'd seen him.'

Fallon stopped reading the article and turned her attention to Tanzy.

'She says he went for a walk last night to clear his head just after ten. But when she woke this morning, he wasn't there.'

Byrd's frown deepened. 'Where's his car?'

'It's at home. First thing I asked.'

'It isn't like him, this.'

Tanzy agreed.

The door opened behind them and DCI Fuller asked, 'Have you found DS Stockdale?' Tanzy told him about his conversation with his wife.

'And no one's seen him today, so far?'

Tanzy shook his head. 'I've checked with Julie at reception. She confirmed he hasn't clocked on today either.'

Fuller was about to comment on that but noticed DC Leonard dashing down the aisle towards them. Leonard looked alarmed, holding his phone out in front of him.

'Sir,' he said, addressing Byrd and Tanzy, not Fuller. 'Look at this.' He showed his phone screen to them.

'Is — is that Phil?' asked Byrd, frowning at the video.

'It looks like it,' said Leonard.

'Where the hell is he?'

65

It was a video uploaded to YouTube.

'Can we get it up on the computer?' Tanzy asked. 'Make it bigger?'

Tanzy copied the link and forwarded it to Byrd.

'I've sent it,' said Tanzy, nodding towards Byrd's desk.

Byrd sat down at his screen, found the link and clicked it open, tapping his foot impatiently on the floor. Tanzy, Fallon and Fuller waited impatiently behind him.

'What is it?' Fuller asked quickly, not needing to be a detective to figure out it was something very important.

The website opened on the screen, showing a close-up of Phil Stockdale's face, illuminated by a dim light. The camera was fixed in position. Judging by the way the skin sagged on Stockdale's face, it seemed like he was on his back.

Byrd noticed under the video the name of the uploader: *RCarl20*.

'It's him, isn't it?' Fuller said.

Fallon turned, nodded sadly.

'Bastard.' Fuller leaned forward a little to get a better view. 'What's he doing?'

Stockdale was on his back, his eyes darting around as if trying to work out what was happening. His upper body rose and fell with quick breathing. Panic had set in, implying whatever the reason he was there, it wasn't out of choice.

'Why is he moving like that?' asked Fallon.

'He's tied up?' Leonard suggested.

If he was tied up, it was out of camera shot.

'Is he in a box?'

Fallon turned to Byrd. 'Is it a coffin?'

Byrd snapped his neck at her as if realising something. 'Earth? Buried. It makes sense.'

'Where the hell is this happening?' Fuller shouted, his voice reaching the far end of the office. People looked up from their desks with curious eyes, wondering what was happening. PC Amy Weaver came over to join them.

'Jesus. Is that Phil?'

'Yes,' Byrd replied to her, keeping his eyes on the screen. He then looked up at Leonard. 'Jim, go get Mac!'

Leonard broke away from the desk and ran through the office, curious eyes following him. Once Leonard reached Mac's door, he opened it quickly but there was no sign of Mac.

'Shit.'

He checked the canteen and found a couple of PCs talking and having their lunch. He closed the door and made his way down the corridor, then down the flight of stairs, passing Jacob Tallow, the senior forensic, on his way back to the office.

'Have you seen Mac from DFU?'

Tallow shook his head. 'Haven't seen him all day. I've phoned him too, but he didn't answer, which is strange because he always answers.'

Leonard returned to the office. 'He isn't there,' he told Byrd and Tanzy before continuing to watch the video. Fuller placed his hand on his head, watching in horror, thinking about what they were going to do.

The video was ten minutes long. When it reached nine minutes, a voice spoke on the video.

'Hello, Detective Inspector Max Byrd and Detective Inspector Orion Tanzy. I trust you are watching and both listening.'

Byrd and Tanzy froze.

'How does he know your names?' asked Fuller.

'By now, you may have realised you are watching one of your own,' the voice continued. 'Detective Sergeant Phillip Stockdale. I'm sorry I had to do this to him, but it's the least he deserves for what he's done.'

Dilton's words played over in all their minds.

'What's he done?' Weaver asked, looking at them one by one but they ignored her, keeping their focus on Byrd's computer screen.

'As you may or may not see, Phil is tied up. He can't move. The enclosed space he is in, is in fact, a coffin. In approximately thirty minutes, the oxygen supply to the coffin will stop. And I don't need to tell you what happens when you don't get oxygen.' Dilton started to laugh. 'You can't breathe.'

Tanzy visualised him laughing and it boiled his blood.

'So, I hope you enjoy the show. Because as long as you keep enjoying it, the show will continue. Catch up soon, Detectives.'

After the ten minutes, the video stopped.

'In a coffin?' Weaver said. 'Why is . . .' she trailed off, battling with the million thoughts in her mind.

Byrd stood up abruptly, almost knocking into Fallon and went to the window, placing both hands on the top of his head and sighed deeply.

'What time was the video posted?' Byrd asked.

Tanzy used the mouse to source the video's information, indicating the video was uploaded at 1.14 p.m. He looked down at his watch. It was a little after 2 p.m.

'How long would you last inside a closed coffin without air?' Weaver wondered out loud.

Byrd turned from the window, his face dark, and shook his head. 'An hour maybe. Two at the most.'

'So,' Tanzy said, thinking hard. 'We need to think of the obvious. If he's in a coffin, he might be—'

'In a cemetery?' Fallon suggested, finishing his train of thought.

He nodded twice. 'Leonard, make a list of cemeteries in Darlington.'

'Okay, boss.' He left them, dashed down the aisle and sat down at his computer to make a list of cemeteries.

'We need to fucking find him!' Fuller shouted, smacking his hands together. Fallon flinched a little, unsure what the noise was initially. 'We don't have long,' he added, then returned to his office and slammed the door behind him.

A few seconds of silence passed. Tanzy took a deep breath, started the video again to see if he could spot something that could help. If it was true what Dilton had said, that Stockdale was inside a coffin, then the most obvious place he would be was a cemetery. It would certainly be the fourth kill, the one that Linda Fallon had predicted, being "earth".

'Where was that man buried, Linda?' Byrd asked, returning to his desk. 'The one in Essex?'

'In the woods.'

'Not a cemetery?'

'No. The woods. Nowhere near a cemetery.'

'If the coffin is a normal size, how long would it take to use all the air?' Byrd said.

'Hold on . . .' Weaver asked, pulling out her phone. She opened up an internet page. A few moments passed. 'The smaller you are, then there'll be more space for the air. The larger you are, the less space for air.'

Byrd pushed his lip out, knowing Stockdale was both tall and thickset.

'It says an average person under normal conditions could last up to five hours,' Weaver said.

'The problem we have,' said Tanzy, pointing at the screen, particularly at Stockdale's face, 'is that he's a large man, clearly panicking. The rise and fall in his chest indicate he's breathing quickly. That air, however much there is, won't last long.'

'Every breath he takes decreases the oxygen and increases the levels of carbon dioxide,' Byrd added.

Weaver glanced up and nodded, reading the same point on the site on her phone. 'That's true, Max. It says that here.'

A minute later, DC Leonard came back with a sheet of paper. 'Here.'

Tanzy took the paper and studied down the list.

There were three. West Cemetery on Carmel Road. East Cemetery on Geneva Road. North Cemetery on North Road. 'We'll need to split up to cover these — time is not on our side.' He turned to Leonard. 'You and Amy go to North Road. We'll go to Carmel Road.' He stood, glared over the top of the desks, grabbed PC Grearer's and PC Timms' attention and waved them over. They both stood and started across the office.

'What's happening?' Timms said when he reached him.

'You seen the latest video?'

Timms nodded.

'Can you both go to East Cemetery on Geneva Road?'

'What are we looking for?' Grearer asked.

'We think Stockdale is buried in the ground inside a coffin. Go there. Look for any areas which look like they've just been laid. If you see anything, ring me immediately. Go.'

Timms and Grearer both nodded and backed away, grabbing their keys and jackets, then left the office quickly.

Byrd said to Tanzy, 'Guess we'll start with Carmel Road?'

Fallon leaned over, noticing the top one. 'Where's Carmel Road?'

'Come on,' Byrd said. 'You can come with us.'

66

Monday afternoon
West Cemetery, Carmel Road

Byrd drove with Tanzy riding shotgun and Fallon in the back. Byrd reached the end of Park Place in seconds, took a left on to Yarm Road and put his siren on, going through the next red light at the bottom of Yarm Road. They overtook a string of cars, quickly making their way around the ring roads, joining Woodland Road and flew through the red lights at the crossroads of Greenbank Road.

At the end of Woodland Road, Byrd went left at the mini-roundabout, pushing through the gears, hitting nearly fifty going up the hill of Carmel Road North, veering around a handful of vehicles in the process. It wasn't long before he slowed and took a right into the cemetery, almost colliding with a car slowly pulling out, forcing Byrd to slam his brakes on. 'God . . .'

Fallon let out a quiet yelp as her belt dug into her shoulder and gripped the door handle to steady herself.

'Easy, boy!' Tanzy said, noticing Byrd's frustration.

The car moved and Byrd went through the large stone pillars.

'Jesus, this place is huge!' Fallon said as she observed the size of the cemetery. The rows seemed to go on forever. Through the front windscreen, she noticed the length of the road. 'Does it go all the way back?'

'I'm not sure,' Byrd admitted. He hadn't been there in a while. His parents were buried at North Cemetery.

He slowed the car, pulled it over to the side so other vehicles could pass. He knew there was a car park further down, but they had to cover all of it. 'We'll start here. See if there are any fresh burials.'

Tanzy jumped out. Fallon got out the back and closed the door.

They split up and started with the ones closest, taking a row each.

A man standing at the small building on the right, dressed in stained overalls, somewhere in his late sixties, stopped what he was doing. 'Excuse me?' he shouted over.

Byrd and Fallon were out of earshot, but Tanzy glanced his way.

'Who are you looking for? You can't park there.'

Tanzy jogged over and pulled his badge from his pocket. 'Detective Inspector Orion Tanzy. Are you in charge? Do you know if there have been any burials in the last day or so?'

The man with wispy hair and a short, grey stubble eyed his ID with furrowed brows. 'There've been three today.'

'We believe a police officer is in real trouble. We think he could be buried somewhere here.'

The man looked bewildered. 'We have names of all the people who have been—'

Tanzy shook his head quickly, silencing him. 'No. He's been buried alive.'

'Oh, God . . .' the man sighed, edging back. 'Here?'

'It's possible — are there any graves that have been dug, waiting for a burial in the coming days?'

The man looked around, thinking hard. There were multiple plots. 'There's a couple.' He turned and scowled down the long narrow road as if searching for the plot in his

head. 'If you go down the road. When you pass the crematorium, there are three spaces that have just been dug.'

Tanzy thanked him and started sprinting down the
road, his feet slapping the dry concrete as he ran.

Byrd heard the noise from the third row of gravestones
and glanced across the cemetery. 'Ori?'

'Where's he running to?' Fallon asked Byrd, studying
the row behind.

'I — I don't know.' Byrd had a quick look around at
the graves near him. They all looked intact and settled as if
they'd been there for years. 'Come on, let's follow him. He
obviously knows something we don't.'

Fallon met Byrd back on the narrow road and started
slowly trailing after Tanzy. She wasn't exactly dressed for
running in heels, jeans and a white long-sleeved T-shirt, so
Byrd settled at her pace, watching Tanzy run ahead but it
wasn't long before he disappeared from their view, taking a
left after the crematorium.

Fallon panted a few metres behind Byrd. He turned,
noticed her pace much slower.

'Keep up, Linda.'

'I'm trying . . .'

They passed the crematorium and Byrd glared to the
left, seeing a cluster of trees and more gravestones. But he
couldn't see Tanzy.

* * *

After Tanzy passed the crem, he kept going, his eyes frantically darting around, trying to spot the open graves the man
at the front had mentioned. It wasn't long before he spotted
them, about sixty metres down a walkway on the left.

But there weren't three graves. There were two.

There was a bald man in his late thirties, around six feet
tall, standing close to them. He had a stocky build and wore
a tight-fitting black T-shirt, blue jeans and white trainers.
He seemed focused on something particular. A freshly filled
grave with no headstone.

249

Tanzy slowed a little while watching the man, who must have heard his approach and snapped his neck in his direction.

When the man recognised Tanzy, he turned and darted across the grass towards the wall.

'Hey!' Tanzy shouted at him.

There was no doubt in Tanzy's mind it was Adrian Dilton. He remembered his face from the house fire in Napier Street, remembered the way he moved, his body shape. But his reaction and the way he bolted off confirmed it.

Dilton had at least forty metres head start, so Tanzy broke out into a sprint to give chase.

* * *

Once Byrd and Fallon rounded the corner, they saw Tanzy sprinting across the field, chasing someone in front of him.

'That's him!' Byrd shouted, pointing. 'That's Dilton.'

Fallon struggled for breath and followed Byrd's finger, seeing Tanzy on the field chasing Dilton towards the rear stone wall of the cemetery.

'Ori!' Byrd shouted, struggling for breath himself.

Tanzy heard his call and turned but kept running, pointing back at the walkway where he'd seen the buried grave.

Byrd shrugged, unsure what he meant.

Then his phone rang. It was Tanzy.

'Ori — what's happening? Who is it?'

'It's Dilton. I've got him.' Tanzy took a few short breaths. 'The guy at the front said there were three open graves. There are only two.' A few more quick pants. 'Stockdale could be in there, Max. Check it out. I'll get this bastard.'

Byrd slowed near the two open graves and put his phone away. He noticed the third one had been freshly filled, judging by the difference in colour to the ones near it. The others had settled to a lighter colour, no doubt dried by warmth and direct sunlight over time. This was a darker shade of soil as if just put down in the last day or so.

Byrd fell to his knees and took a deep breath, still tired from running the length of the cemetery, reminding him he needed to get even fitter. He turned to Linda. 'Go get a shovel, Linda. I'll make a start, but we'll be here forever doing it with our hands. Get two shovels if you can!'

Fallon remaining still, watching Tanzy running across the field. 'I'll help Ori,' she replied before she darted in that direction.

'Linda, wait,' said Byrd. He sighed, pulled his phone out and made the call for backup.

* * *

Tanzy was a few strides behind Dilton.

'Fucking stop now!' he barked.

Ignoring him, Dilton jumped and clambered up the wall, grabbing the top and heaving himself up. It was high, maybe six or seven feet. Tanzy made it in time and grabbed his left foot, preventing him from pulling himself all the way over.

'Get here . . .'

Dilton kicked a leg out and caught Tanzy hard in the chin. Tanzy stumbled back, startled by the kick that felt like a sledgehammer and saw stars before falling into a state of disorientation.

'Help me over,' he heard Fallon say behind him.

Tanzy felt okay and nodded, leaning up against the wall and interlocked his fingers for her to use as a step up. She got hold of the wall, used everything she had and pushed her foot into Tanzy's hands, using it to climb the wall.

'Wait for me on the other side. Don't move.'

'Okay.'

Tanzy took a few steps back and quickly ran at the wall, jumping and climbing it with ease. He dropped down on the other side with a light thud near Linda.

'You all right?' she asked.

He nodded and saw a path leading to an abandoned house.

They watched Dilton go inside.

'Come on, let's get this fucker,' Tanzy said.

67

Monday afternoon
West Cemetery, Carmel Road

Byrd was tired after only several minutes of strenuous digging. His hair, face, and neck were drenched in sweat and his hands were burning. He sighed heavily and pulled his jacket off, something he wished he'd done before he started. A minute later, he felt the lactic acid burning in his shoulders from the continual movement. He was about a foot down, give or take, and had opened an area of roughly two feet. His fingers were bleeding.

He pulled his phone from his pocket and found DC Leonard's number, pressed CALL.

'Boss?' Leonard answered.

'Are you here, yet?' he panted.

'We're close, boss. Any update?'

'Tanzy and Linda have gone after Dilton.' Byrd panted. 'And I'm digging a grave with my hands. Bring a shovel please!'

Leonard fell silent, no doubt wondering where to get a shovel from. 'Er, yes, sir. Be with you soon.'

He removed another few inches over the course of five minutes and sat up for a quick breather. His hands were stinging and bleeding more now.

'What on earth are you doing?' a voice said behind him.

He scowled towards to a man on the path. He didn't recognise him, but it was the same man Tanzy had been speaking with earlier, the elderly man with wispy hair near the front of the cemetery.

'Have you . . . got a . . . digger?' Byrd said, in between breaths.

The man stared. 'We have one in the shed. Want me to get it?'

'Byrd nodded twice. 'Please. I wouldn't be asking if it wasn't a life-or-death situation.'

The man absorbed his concern and gave a brief nod, then turned and broke out into a jog away from him.

Byrd turned back to the grave, knowing he was losing time.

'Come on!' he screamed to himself, fighting through the pain in his bloody hands.

Footsteps approached him.

It was PC Timms and PC Grearer.

'Jesus, boss,' Timms said, seeing how little he'd dug and the state of Byrd's hands.

'Someone's getting a shovel but for now, fucking dig boys. Quick!' barked Byrd, stabbing a swollen bloody finger at the ground.

They wasted no time following his order and both dropped to their knees, one either side and started clawing away.

'Quicker,' he told them.

It wasn't long before DC Cornty and DC Leonard arrived, both holding shovels.

'Got these from the caretaker,' Leonard said, dropping next to Timms and started digging the ground up. After a few minutes, they were making noticeable progress. Byrd was relieved but they still had a way to go. The coffin would be at least seven feet long and two to three feet wide. And God knows how deep it was. So far, they hadn't reached anything yet.

Nearby on the path, a couple in their fifties had stopped to watch them digging. They didn't say anything, just stared with their mouths open, wondering what they were up to. Behind them was the sound of a mechanical vehicle coming towards them.

'Move out of the way!' the man driving it said, waving a frantic hand.

Byrd and the PCs took a step back and watched the machine start removing the earth, its mechanical claw dragging up the soil and dropping it nearby. Byrd thought it would have been bigger, something you'd see on a construction site, but it seemed to be doing the trick.

'You all right, boss?' Leonard asked Byrd, placing a hand on his back.

After a few minutes of digging, the backhoe's claw hit something hard, making a clunk.

'What's that?' Timms shouted.

Byrd took a few steps forward and leaned over the hole. He could see wood. 'There it is,' he bellowed. 'Keep going. Keep going,' he told the man inside the digger.

The man gave a concentrated nod from behind the plastic viewing panel and continued playing with the levers.

'Where are Orion and Linda?' Leonard asked Byrd, realising they'd been missing a while.

68

The ruin Adrian Dilton had gone into was narrow, small and old. Although it had seen better days, the brickwork which was made up of different sized stones had stood there a long time, weathering through decades of seasons and stood proud in respect to the builders who had once put it there.

The front door would have been in good nick if it did indeed have a front door, not a gaping hole into a cold hallway made of a concrete floor leading to other open areas.

It was a place Tanzy hadn't seen before, just off the path, beyond the hedges and overgrown grass, probably belonging to a janitor of the cemetery from way back.

When Tanzy and Fallon stepped onto the short path leading to the front door, he placed his arm out, indicating for her to drop back to allow him in first. She slowed and nodded, dropping back.

He grabbed the truncheon he'd brought with him as he approached the ruin and focused through the open space with wide eyes, scanning for movement. The hard floor seemed to lead to a room out the back.

'Can you see anything?' she whispered, the fear clearly creeping into her words.

Tanzy shook his head but stayed silent, his heart racing too. His chin still throbbed from where Dilton had kicked it moments earlier, but he pushed the pain to the back of his mind and remained focused on catching this sonofabitch. If there was any truth in what Dilton had said to Byrd on the phone and what he'd said at the end of the video of Stockdale in the coffin, there was no doubt he would continue to murder.

Tanzy carefully and quietly stepped through the worn, neglected threshold, noticing several visible sharp edges they needed to avoid.

'Careful here,' Tanzy whispered.

In the hall, the stairs were to the left. The corridor ran along the right-hand side, leading to a room at the back, with another door off to the right. The doorframes had decayed, leaving exposed rocky brickwork, and the walls were bare, mostly down to the brick.

Tanzy slowed and peeped into the first room, which looked like where the living room would be. It was bare. Bits of rubble were scattered around the edges of the concrete floor and a cluster of flattened cardboard was in the corner with an old, brown stained sheet in one of the alcoves, indicating someone had slept there recently.

They backed out and checked the room at the end of the corridor. Exposed lead pipework was fixed under the window, all mangled and crooked, informing them it used to be the kitchen. To the left was another open void, leading to outside.

'Check upstairs,' Fallon said behind him.

He nodded twice. 'Come on.'

Silently, they made their way upstairs, Tanzy light on his feet, not only so Dilton wouldn't hear him, but so he didn't disturb the old, battered wood on the stairs that looked like it could give way any second.

Fallon slowly trailed him a few feet behind. Just before Tanzy reached the top, she misjudged one of the steps, catching the front of her right foot and stumbled forward into him.

'Linda . . .' he gasped. 'Careful.'

She gritted her teeth in apology and nodded.

Tanzy stepped up onto what was left of the landing. Gaps in the wood revealed aged joists and the musty hallway below. To his left was a small room with an old rusty bath inside and a sink pedestal that had come away from the wall. The toilet over to the right was brown rather than white and smelt heavily of urine. In fact, the whole place did.

He backed away, moving into the next bedroom which was brightly lit by the daylight coming through a window to the left. Again, the room was empty, apart from a box the size of a shoebox in the alcove, made from hardened leather. He would have gone over to see what was inside if it wasn't for the noise they heard from the next bedroom.

A creaking floorboard.

They both froze, making eye contact with each other.

Tanzy moved so he was in front of her, and carefully made his way across the incomplete landing, focusing on the doorway of the room they were about to enter, ready in case Dilton came flying out. He stepped inside, the truncheon tightly gripped in his hand, fully extended.

Adrian Dilton was standing in the furthest corner staring at him. He had nowhere to go. A window was to his left but wasn't open.

'Dilton . . .' Tanzy whispered.

Dilton didn't say anything and appeared very calm with a relaxed posture.

'You're coming with me,' said Tanzy as he stepped into the room.

Dilton slowly shook his head. 'I have more work to do, Detective.' His voice was rough, raspy, full of determination.

Tanzy smiled widely. 'You've done enough.' He held the baton high up behind him and cautiously made his way over, watching Dilton carefully, anticipating what he might do. There was nowhere to go. He was cornered.

Fallon held off a little, staying behind Tanzy, obviously scared of getting too close to him.

'I'm going to cuff you and take you in,' Tanzy said, edging closer and grabbing the cuffs from his pockets with his free hand.

Dilton smiled.

'You understand?'

His smiled widened.

'You have no—'

Tanzy felt the blow to his head a split second before he passed out and helplessly collapsed to the floor with a thud.

Dilton stared wide eyed at Fallon. 'Linda, why are you here?'

She dropped the brick she'd picked up near the door and smiled at him.

69

As soon as the man in the digger had cleared enough earth around the box, he jumped out, grabbed two long straps he'd collected from the shed and went to the open grave.

'Here, hold these,' he said to Byrd, who grabbed the ends of both straps. The man then carefully lowered himself into the hole and stepped to the side of the wooden box. It wasn't a traditional coffin by any means, rather something Dilton appeared to have made. The man attempted to lift the lid but it wouldn't budge.

'Here, pass me a shovel.'

Byrd handed him the shovel and he tried to use the edge of the blade to open the lid, but it appeared to the solid.

'Will it open?' asked Byrd.

The man sighed as he tried. 'It's tough.'

They all watched him attempt to break it until he eventually managed and lifted it to one side.

Inside, was DS Stockdale. He lay silent and still.

'Is he alive?' Byrd asked.

The gravedigger dropped the shovel, lowered his hand into the coffin and placed two fingers on the side of his throat to find a pulse. He looked back up and nodded twice.

'Right, let's get him out.' Byrd turned to Weaver. 'Amy, ring an ambulance, please.'

With tears in her eyes, she nodded and pulled out her phone.

The man in the grave took a hold of one of the straps that Byrd was holding and, although it was tough, managed to loop it underneath Stockdale around his back. He then looped the other around his thighs.

'Right, lift him up,' the man said, ready to guide the body. They all pulled gently on the ropes to lift him from the hole and lowered him on the soil beside the hole.

'Great work, guys,' Byrd said as he lowered to Stockdale and gently tapped his face. 'Phil?'

Stockdale's eyes flicked open for a second, but he didn't move.

'Amy, where's that ambulance?' shouted Byrd in her general direction.

'On its way, sir.'

Byrd nodded and looked back at Stockdale.

'Should we move him, boss? Get him out in the open?'

'Phil, are you hurt?'

Stockdale didn't respond.

* * *

Leonard told Byrd he would go and find Tanzy and Fallon to see if they needed help. Byrd agreed and asked Cornty to go with him. They ran across the field towards the wall that Byrd said they'd climbed and jumped over it, landing on a path on the other side.

'Where did they go?' Cornty asked, looking around. The path went under a cluster of trees in one direction, and in the other, bordered the stone wall until it went out of sight. In front of them, was woodland and clusters of bushes.

'In there?' Leonard said, pointing at the house Cornty had noticed through some hedging.

Cornty nodded and went first, stepping over the uneven ground and through the array of hedges until he reached the abandoned path leading to the house.

'Surely, they're not in there?' Cornty said, frowning at the ruin.

'Worth a check,' Leonard replied.

They stepped through the open doorway and heard something upstairs. Floorboards creaking. They froze for a moment and then went inside.

'Hello? Police here,' shouted Leonard, grabbing his truncheon from his trousers. Cornty grabbed his own, gripping it tightly in his right hand, a few steps behind Leonard as they went up the stairs. He reached the top and turned. 'Hello — is there anyone here?'

As he stepped onto the patchy landing, a shadow shifted ahead of him and someone stepped out from the front bedroom.

'Jesus, boss,' Leonard said.

Tanzy was unsteady on his feet, his right hand pressed firmly on the side of his head to stop the flow of blood coming from his head. Blood ran down his face.

'What the fuck happened, boss?' Leonard said, leaning in to have a closer look.

'Dilton. He was here,' Tanzy managed to say, wincing in pain.

'Where's Linda Fallon?'

Tanzy painfully shook his head. 'I don't know.'

70

Monday afternoon
West Cemetery, Carmel Road

'You okay, boss?' Cornty asked Tanzy, helping him away from the house. Leonard was on his other side. They reached the wall.

'Think you can climb it?' Leonard asked Tanzy, staring at the gash on his head.

Tanzy nodded. 'I'll be fine.' With the aid of Leonard and Cornty, Tanzy managed to climb over the high wall and drop down on the other side. His head was thumping in agony. Leonard and Cornty climbed over a few seconds after.

'What was Dilton wearing, boss?' Leonard asked, finding his feet.

Tanzy slowly stood up, the blow to his head affecting his balance and ability to move one hundred per cent. 'Black T-shirt and blue jeans,' he said, wincing at the pounding inside his head.

Leonard pulled his radio from his belt clip and spoke into it. 'We have a suspect in the nearby area of West Cemetery off Carmel Road, who we believe to be Adrian Dilton. He's just attacked one of our officers and is wearing a black T-shirt and blue jeans. Keep your eyes peeled.'

'How's the head, boss?' Cornty asked him.

Tanzy gave a slow shake of the head. 'Not good.'

'Can you remember where Linda went? Has he got her?'

Tanzy clamped his eyes shut as he struggled across the grass. 'She — she was behind me, and then I felt something hard hit me, then I was out . . .' Tanzy thought hard. 'There may have been someone else there.'

'Did you hear anyone else in the house?' Cornty asked. 'No.'

Leonard frowned, thinking of the possibility. If the only person who was there was Linda Fallon, could it have been her? What reason would she have to attack Tanzy? She'd travelled up from Essex to help them with the investigation. She'd shown them reports from a similar thing that Dilton could have been responsible for seven years ago.

It didn't make any sense.

* * *

Byrd heard what Leonard had said on the radio and told Weaver to wait at the car park they'd passed on their way in. It was about halfway up on the right-hand side. 'If he travelled here in a car, he might go back to it. Black T-shirt and blue jeans. Go keep an eye out.' He grabbed PC Timms' attention who was standing with PC Grearer. 'Eric, go with her, please.'

Timms nodded and together with Weaver, went back to the path and jogged along the narrow road to the car park.

Byrd looked away from Stockdale for a moment. 'Where's the ambulance at?' he asked no one in particular, then spotted Tanzy walking over with Leonard and Cornty. 'Ori . . .'

Everyone else looked over, noticed the blood on Tanzy's head and down his neck and arm.

'Jesus, Ori. What happened?' asked Byrd when he was close enough.

'I don't know.' Tanzy lowered his hand for a moment so Byrd could have a look.

'Nasty.'

'I had him cornered, Max. He was right there. Then something hit me from behind.'

Byrd considered his words. 'Where was Linda?'

Tanzy smiled sadly. 'Behind me . . .'

A frown found Byrd's face. 'You don't think?'

Tanzy shrugged. 'Why would she?'

On the road behind the sound of an ambulance siren was heard, gradually getting louder until it stopped on the grass to their right. Two paramedics jumped out, dressed in green, ran to the back and opened the rear door. The driver picked up a walkie talkie from the dash and said something into it. One pulled out a stretcher and the other grabbed a hip bag, looping it over his shoulder.

Byrd waved them over, pointing at Stockdale.

They ran over, one holding a bag, the other carrying a stretcher. The paramedic with the bag dropped to their knees beside him.

'Is he breathing?'

'Yeah,' said Byrd. 'He isn't in a good way, though.'

The paramedic assessed Stockdale and the other placed the stretcher down on the floor. They evaluated the position and well-being of Stockdale after checking his pulse and getting a rough story of why he was there, then placed a bag valve mask over his mouth and provided him with some desperately needed air. When he was more stable, they carefully lifted him onto the stretcher and transported him to the ambulance, followed by Tanzy and Byrd.

A third paramedic, who had waited at the ambulance, spotted Tanzy's injury. 'Let me have a look at you,' she said to him.

Tanzy lowered his hand to let him inspect the cut.

'What hit you — a brick or something?'

'Something like that,' Tanzy said quietly.

The blood was still flowing from the wound. 'Right, you need to come with us, too.' The paramedic turned to Byrd, assuming he was the man in charge. 'He's coming with us — we need to get this sorted. It's bad.'

Byrd nodded. 'Okay.' He looked at Tanzy. 'You want one of us to come along?'

Tanzy shook his head. 'No chance. Go find that sonofabitch.'

71

Monday afternoon
West Cemetery, Carmel Road

Weaver and Timms reached the car park halfway down on the right. It wasn't big with roughly thirty spaces, half of which were occupied.

A bald man with a black T-shirt and blue jeans.

That's who they were looking for.

A couple in their eighties were slowly dawdling along on the left with the aid of walking sticks. The man was dressed for the sun in a short-sleeved shirt tucked into grey trousers that appeared both too big and long for his legs. The lady walking beside him was slight, dressed in a blue two-piece and black tights. It made Weaver feel hot just looking at her.

'Excuse me,' Weaver said, slightly out of breath. 'Have you seen a bald man in a black T-shirt and blue jeans?'

The elderly couple looked at her strangely, then gradually shook their heads.

Weaver moved on, scanning the area.

'A bald man in a black T-shirt you say?' a voice said from behind.

Weaver and Timms turned to see a man standing on the grass verge near a row of freshly laid flowers, with a watering can in his right hand, wearing a pair of thin, white overalls. Looked to be a groundsman.

'Have you seen him?'

The man nodded twice. 'Sure. He was here a minute ago. Got into a blue Ford Focus.'

'You sure?' Timms asked, sceptical.

'Yes. He was running from down there.' The man pointed down the narrow road, back to where they'd just come from.

'Was he alone?' Weaver this time.

'Yeah. As far as I could see.'

'This blue Focus,' Timms said quickly, taking a few steps toward him. 'You didn't happen to see—'

'It was a twelve reg. Looked in good nick, apart from a scratch on the back passenger quarter.'

'You remembered that well?'

'As I said, he was running.' He smiled. 'Not much happens around here. The car was parked just over there.'

They followed his finger to the empty space, then thanked him. Weaver pulled the radio from her hip. 'We have a possible vehicle for Adrian Dilton in the area of Carmel Road. Twelve reg. According to a witness, there's a large scratch in the back quarter panel, passenger side.'

She put her radio back and returned to where they'd found Stockdale. The ambulance was parked up on the left with the rear doors open. DS Stockdale lay on a trolley inside with something over his mouth and a few wires coming from him. There was a jump bag fixed to a metal pole by his side, feeding him something but neither Weaver nor Timms knew exactly what. To the right side of the van, Tanzy sat upright with a bag of something cold wrapped in a cloth on his head to keep the swelling down.

They found Byrd, Leonard, Cornty and Grearer, who were talking about something but stopped when Weaver and Timms approached.

'Find the blue Focus?' Byrd asked.

'No.' Weaver frowned, wondering how he knew but then remembered saying it through the radio, which was fed to anyone that was tuned in to the same channel.

* * *

Adrian Dilton took a left when he came out of the cemetery and powered through the gears along Carmel Road. When he reached Hummersknott Avenue, he veered left, following the winding road a few minutes until he reached Baydale Road. He slowed and car and stopped roughly fifty metres down on the left and waited.

It was warm inside the car, so he cracked the window allowing mild air to seep in. Opposite, there were children playing in one of the front gardens, throwing a tennis ball between them. A boy and girl, a few years apart, likely brother and sister. He smiled, thinking about what life would be like with a brother or a sister. He hadn't had the most privileged upbringing, missing out on what some would consider a normal life and because of that, it had maybe shaped him into what he now was.

When the passenger door opened, he turned and watched her climb in quickly and close the door. She was panting for air.

'We need to ditch the car,' he told her.

'Why?'

He nodded at the police radio in his hand, one that she'd got for him. 'One of them said about a blue Ford Focus, twelve reg, with a scratch on the back.'

Linda Fallon sighed. 'We can just get another one.' She turned her head and looked through the front windscreen. 'Right, come on, Adrian. Let's get going. We have more work to do.'

72

Monday afternoon
Police station

Byrd turned the engine off and pulled his key out, sitting for a moment in deep thought. He picked up his phone, found Linda Fallow's number and called it. It went straight to answerphone.

'God's sake . . .' he whispered. His head was battered. He didn't know what to think. Why would she travel all this way from Essex to help them with this investigation and do something stupid?

But where on earth was she?

Had Dilton taken her? Killed her too?

Byrd had no clue, but he needed to know. Needed to find her. He pushed open the door and stepped down onto the tarmac. The day was hot, warmer than before. He was sweating profusely so removed his thin jacket and carried it in his dirty, bloody hand which he would need to clean when he got inside. The bleeding had stopped but it was maybe worth getting one of the first aiders to have a look.

He walked over to the entrance door and remembered what Dilton had said on the video he'd posted online. *They deserved it.* That *he* deserved it.

What had Stockdale done?

He opened the door of reception, stepped inside and smiled at Julie behind the desk before heading for the door on the other side. It wasn't long before he was at his desk. Weaver, Cornty and Leonard had made it back before him and were at their own desks. Weaver was telling another PC what had happened.

At his desk, Byrd hung his jacket on the rear of his chair and sat down. His first job was to ring PC Josh Andrews to ask for an update on Tanzy and Stockdale. He'd asked Josh to accompany them to the hospital and keep him up to date. He knew Tanzy's blow was bad but not life-threatening. Regarding Stockdale, he knew he'd been without oxygen for a while, so it could take some time before he was one hundred per cent. Following his recovery, questions would need to be asked about why he was there in the first place.

Andrews answered the phone on the second ring. They spoke for a few minutes before Byrd thanked him, hung up, and placed his phone down on the desk.

The door opened behind him. 'Max . . .'

Byrd turned to see a furious-looking Fuller.

'In here.'

Byrd nodded, stood up and went into his office. He closed the door, padded over to the desk and sat down on one of the chairs. Byrd spent the next ten minutes going over the events of the day.

'Where is Fallon now?'

Byrd shrugged. 'I don't know, yet. I'm going to the Premier Inn she's been staying at.'

A nod from Fuller. 'What about Dilton?'

Byrd shook his head slowly.

'Max, we need to get a lid on this.'

Before Fuller carried on, Byrd said, 'On my way back, I contacted traffic division to locate the blue Ford Focus. We only know it's blue and is a 2012 registration.'

Fuller nodded slowly, taking it all in.

'I've also contacted Jennifer Lucas at the Town Hall. She'll be our second pair of eyes watching and will get back when she knows something.'

Fuller didn't seem pleased, but it was a step in the right direction. They spoke a little more. Byrd explained how Tanzy and Stockdale both were.

'The question is,' Fuller said, 'why he was chosen. There must be a reason. I watched the video Dilton put online. I heard what he said at the end. That Stockdale deserved it.'

'I heard that, too,' said Byrd. 'Andrews is there with them both. They're on the same floor, so he's keeping in touch with the nurses regarding both of them.'

Fuller thanked him and asked Byrd to let him know when he found Fallon or heard anything back about the blue Ford Focus.

'Will do,' Byrd said as he stood.

Byrd sat down at his desk and sighed heavily. It had been one hell of a day and it wasn't over. Before he decided to go to the Premier Inn to find Fallon, he decided to make a call to Essex Police force. He needed to know who he was dealing with.

'Hello, this is Essex Police help desk. Clio speaking, how can I help?'

'Hi, Clio. My name is Max Byrd. I'm a detective inspector with Durham Constabulary in Darlington. I'm wondering if I can speak to one of your detective chiefs or maybe a superintendent? It's very important.'

Clio didn't reply for a moment, then said, 'Hold on one moment, please, Detective Inspector Byrd.'

There was a few moments of silence. Byrd looked around the office until he heard the voice.

'Hello,' said Clio. 'I'll have him call your switchboard at Darlington. Just to make sure you are who you say you are.'

'That's fair enough,' replied Byrd, a little frustrated time was being wasted. The call ended. Less than a minute later, his mobile rang, the call forwarded from the switchboard. He answered it.

'Hello, this is Detective Superintendent John Malice. Is this Detective Inspector Max Byrd?'

'Hi, John. Yes, I'm DI Byrd. I need some information, please.'

'Okay. What's the information regarding?'

'Linda Fallon. I believe she worked as a DI for so many years then went on to criminal psychology.'

A sigh from Malice.

'John?'

'Why do you need information on Linda Fallon?'

'We're looking for her,' Byrd explained. 'She came up last week to help us with a case we are working on. Something's happened. She's disappeared.'

'What happened, DI Byrd?'

Byrd explained.

'Detective Byrd, Linda Fallon didn't retire. Her employment was terminated.'

'What for?'

'Let me explain.'

73

'I have to admit I quite liked Linda,' Superintendent Malice said, 'but there was always . . . something different about her. And to say I'd never seen a change in her would be a lie.'

'How do you mean?' asked Byrd.

'She worked her way up to detective inspector after she did great in her previous roles. But I always had the feeling she wanted more.'

'A promotion?'

'Hmm, maybe not,' Malice said. 'I think that's why she went into criminal psychology for six years before we let her go. And she was good at it. She loved getting into the minds of killers and criminals to understand what made them tick. Why they did what they did. But she wasn't as — I don't know how to say this — as hard as she should have been.'

Byrd wasn't following.

'She always looked for a deeper meaning, why something was the way it was. Why a person would kill.' Malice paused a beat. 'So, as well as understanding why a criminal did what they did, she started to sympathise with them and understand their minds. She found a soft spot in her heart for them and their actions. I could never prove it, but I felt like she was often working against us.'

'How so?' Byrd was intrigued.

'She held things back. Information. Leads. She—'

'You mean on the four murders that happened seven years ago?'

'Yes. Particularly that one. She was a DI on that case. As a team, we'd come up with a few leads, but every lead she followed went cold. Every sniff we had at catching the sonofabitch was gone. Judging by what you've told me, it sounds like the same guy but, as you know, we never caught him. I blame Linda for that. But not only that, when she took the role as a psychologist, she advised us — and the criminals — on what to do. On more than one occasion, someone had heard her telling a murderer that they acted not on impulse but because of a deeper reason, a reason which, when explained sympathetically, would sway a court case against us. This happened too many times. We warned her, but she carried on. We'd had enough and had to let her go. She was getting in our way.'

'To summarise her, John, what would you say?'

'I'd say Linda Fallon is a very intelligent woman who always gets what she wants. I'd say don't be deceived by her but that's something we both know has already happened.'

Byrd shook his head, feeling stupid he'd allowed her to come to Darlington to search for Adrian Dilton, now knowing she'd fed back the information and aided him in many ways. 'Wish I'd spoken to you before we allowed her in. My colleague DI Tanzy called Essex a few days ago and spoken with a PC Garling about Linda.'

'What did PC Garling say?'

'Confirmed who she was but he didn't tell my colleague about anything you've just said.'

'Unfortunately, the reason why we let her go wasn't common knowledge. There was a good chance he didn't know what she'd been up to.'

Byrd sighed. 'Any idea where'd she'd go?'

'Not a clue. If I was a betting man, I'd say she's helping your man, Dilton.'

Byrd sighed and tipped his head back.

'Be careful of her. She's very unpredictable, Detective Byrd.'

74

Monday late afternoon
Police station

DC Leonard and DC Cornty had not only spent time doing their reports, they'd also got in touch with the train station and local airports to see if Fallon had booked anything. They'd also reached out to banks, asking if there was a Linda Fallon who had an account with them.

Barclays came back with a yes, confirming a Linda Fallon who was based in Essex had an account with them. But there'd been nothing booked in the past few days regarding tickets or flights or any transactions. After looking at her statements, which the bank was reluctant to hand over, they'd noticed regular household payments to utility companies and one for her phone. There had been several money withdrawals in the last month. It was also obvious to see she was very wealthy, her bank account over the two-hundred-thousand-pound mark.

'Someone's doing okay,' Cornty humoured when telling Byrd.

'Good work,' said Byrd. 'Keep going.'

It was getting late. The office was quieter than before, a few people had gone home. Byrd hung around and handed over the day's events to nightshift who were made up of several PCs and a DC who'd recently been promoted. Their task was to continue looking into Linda Fallon and Adrian Dilton in addition to whatever else the good town of Darlington had to offer.

On his way home, Byrd stopped off at the hospital to see Tanzy, who lay in a bed situated in the corner of the room, halfway down the corridor on the left, on the fifth floor. Byrd opened the door, spotted him straight away with a bandage wrapped around his head and went over, absorbing the amazing view of Darlington through the wide window at the back of the room. It was the first time he'd seen the town from up here, which appeared beautiful under the setting sun and clear cloudless sky.

'How are you holding up?' Byrd said to him.

Tanzy smiled. 'Top of the world, Max. Thanks for asking.' They shared a smile. 'Did you find Dilton?'

Byrd smiled sadly and shook his head.

'What about Linda?'

Byrd said he hadn't, then gazed out of the window for a moment to collect his thoughts.

'Some view, isn't it?' Tanzy said, looking out, too.

'I spoke with someone at Essex Police,' Byrd said.

Tanzy frowned. 'And?'

Byrd told him what John Malice had said about her.

Tanzy banged his fist off his bed, causing the man in the next bed to glance over. 'What about the hotel she's staying at?'

'Went there before. There's no one by her name staying there.'

Tanzy gritted his teeth. 'Why didn't we see it, Max?'

Byrd shrugged. 'She convinced everyone, Ori. Not just us.'

Tanzy looked away for a moment, also disappointed with himself. It wasn't his fault. It wasn't anyone's fault. She'd manipulated them all.

'I spoke with traffic division and Jennifer. Gave them the info on a blue Ford Focus we believe Dilton got into. A guy standing near the car park at the cemetery said he saw someone matching Dilton's description get in and drive away quickly.'

'If traffic don't find it, Max, she will.'

Byrd agreed and asked him how his family was.

'Pip is good. I've just been on the phone with her. She said she'd try to get here later if her mum watches the kids for a bit.'

'When are you allowed out?'

'Nurse said tomorrow.' Tanzy sighed, rolling his eyes. 'They need to keep me in because it's a head injury.'

'Just a scratch, Ori. Don't know why you're fussing over it.'

Tanzy reached over and playfully punched Byrd in the arm.

'You seen Phil yet? Andrews said he was down the hall.'

Byrd said, 'Not yet, Ori. I'm going to see him after I've left you. I need to find out why Dilton chose him. I need to find out what he's done. If he doesn't cooperate, then we'll have to bring him in.'

Tanzy winced. He hated the thought of one of their own doing something they shouldn't have. 'Keep me updated. I need to make sure he's okay.' He paused a few moments. 'I just hope whatever it is, there's been a mistake. I really do.'

'Me and you both.' Byrd leaned over and fist pumped Tanzy. 'Rest up. I'll pick you up tomorrow. You need anything bringing right now?'

'Pip will bring a few bits soon. Don't worry about me. Go see Phil.'

Byrd nodded and departed the room, taking a left down the brightly lit hallway. There was a reception desk with two nurses sitting behind it down on the right. Both nurses were blonde, around the age of fifty, looking at separate computer screens. Byrd wondered if they were sisters. One of them looked up at Byrd and smiled as he passed, the other too absorbed in whatever she was looking at to notice him. It wasn't long before Byrd reached the room and knocked twice.

He grabbed the handle, opened the door and entered the single room where the air was warm and stuffy. The window at the end was closed but the blinds were open, the sun setting over Darlington casting an orange glow across building tops. Stockdale lay on a single bed to the right. Andrews was seated on the left in a single, low-level chair, facing Stockdale. From the hanging silence between them and serious faces, Byrd got the impression they'd been talking about something important. Beside the bed, was a table with a jug of water and several plastic cups.

'Hey,' said Byrd.

'Hi, boss,' Andrews said, turning his head to the door.

Byrd closed the door, stepped forward and focused on Stockdale, who was awake, staring at the ceiling.

'How you doing, Phil?' asked Byrd.

'I'll survive, sir. You know me.' He sounded dull and flat as if he had no energy. 'They're keeping me in to see how my breathing is. Make sure my lungs are working properly.'

Byrd grabbed the spare chair next to Andrews and dropped into it.

'How long you been here?' Byrd asked Andrews.

He glanced down at his watch. 'Ever since he was brought in. I'm bloody starving.'

Byrd noticed the time. It was just after 7 p.m. 'Go and get something to eat. I think the café is still open.'

Andrews didn't need to be asked twice and left the room.

'How are you holding up, Phil?' Byrd said, this time more serious.

Stockdale looked his way with glassy eyes. 'I'm . . . okay.'

'What happened, Phil?'

Stockdale told him what had happened the night before, how he had gone out for a walk and Dilton had pulled over in the car at the roundabout on Woodland Road, asking for directions. He said he had recognised him and called Tanzy but he hadn't answered. Then he had seen Dilton walk into the park and followed him. The next thing he knew he had woken up inside the coffin. 'It was terrifying, sir.'

Byrd nodded in understanding and asked a very important question. 'Why did he pick you?'

Stockdale looked away, avoiding eye contact with his superior. The silence that filled the small room was deafening.

'If there's something you need to tell me, Phil, you need to do it now.'

Stockdale swallowed hard, then over the following five minutes, told Byrd exactly what he'd done.

Byrd was speechless and glared at him with wide eyes. 'Jesus, Phil.'

75

Tuesday morning
Police station

When Byrd had left the hospital after seeing DS Stockdale, he rang DCI Fuller immediately, telling him what Stockdale had said.

'What is it with this bloody department?' Fuller had said.

Byrd knew the question was rhetorical and allowed Fuller to vent his frustration. Fuller then said he needed to figure out a way to keep this under wraps for as long as possible.

Byrd pulled up in his X5 and parked in his usual bay. The sun was rising somewhere behind him, casting shadows of nearby cars on the tarmac below. He opened the door, stepped down onto the ground, feeling waves of sickness in his stomach. He'd missed out on breakfast which hadn't helped. He'd left Claire on the sofa in the living room accompanied with a few snacks and drinks. She told him her friend was coming over again, which was something Byrd didn't mind. It was as much Claire's house now as it was his.

He walked through the sliding double doors into reception and smiled at Julie.

'Good morning, Max,' she said, with a smile.

The office was a third full. DC Leonard was at his desk to his left, typing away quickly.

'Morning, Jim.'

Leonard turned to him. 'Morning, sir.'

'You hear about Phil?' Byrd asked quietly, knowing there'd be a chance he had but didn't want to catch the attention of others nearby.

He replied with a slow nod.

'Who else knows?'

Leonard looked to his right. Cornty hadn't arrived yet.

'Phil knows. Amy knows. A few others do. We were messaging about it last night.'

Byrd had asked PC Josh Andrews to keep it quiet so was curious as to why others knew. But it was an issue that would need addressing sooner rather than later so he'd have to accept it and move on.

'How's he doing?' Leonard asked.

'He's upset . . .'

'I can imagine.'

'I'm calling a meeting soon. I'll run through it all with everyone. It isn't pleasant but it's something everyone needs to be aware of.'

Byrd walked down the aisle towards his desk but before he reached it, Fuller opened his door as if he knew he was approaching and asked Byrd to come inside. Byrd took off his jacket, hung it on the back of his chair and went inside.

Fuller's office was warm, the open window to the left not making a difference to the humidity. On Fuller's desk was an empty mug and a scrunched up cereal bar wrapper, among a pile of paperwork and a couple of photos he'd been looking at.

'How's Phil?'

Byrd gave him a sad smile. 'As soon as the doctors give him the all- clear, we'll bring him in. Does Barry Eckles know about this yet?'

Fuller winced at the thought. 'Not yet, Max.'

'I'm holding a meeting at nine. I need to tell everyone what he told me.'

Fuller looked sceptical.

'They deserve to know,' insisted Byrd.

Fuller understood his point and agreed with Byrd, trusting his call.

'How's Orion?'

'He was okay last night. He should have been able to go home but the doctors insisted he stayed in for monitoring. He's just texted saying they're happy for him to come out. His missus is picking him up soon so he should be here for the briefing.'

Fuller nodded his approval. 'I guess I'll need to let Barry know. It won't be long till it makes the rounds.'

Byrd stood up, put the chair in slowly and made his way back to his desk. After turning his computer on, he sighed heavily.

No Tanzy.

No Linda Fallon.

The more he thought of her, the more anger built up inside him. For the next thirty minutes, he compiled a report and PowerPoint presentation for the upcoming meeting and sent everyone email alerts, letting them know where to be at nine.

He saved the presentation on a memory stick, pulled it out from the computer and stood up, before he made his way across the office towards the meeting room.

'This should be fun,' he whispered, walking down the hall, approaching the closed door on the right.

76

Tuesday morning
Police station

In the meeting room, there was a dark silence hanging in the air. Byrd closed the door and, as he walked over to the whiteboard in the centre of the nearest wall, he knew most of his colleagues had not only heard about Phil Stockdale being buried in a coffin, but that he'd told Byrd what he'd done, and more importantly, why.

'Morning,' he said loudly, building himself up for what was coming.

Everyone was there. On the email he'd sent out less than thirty minutes earlier, Byrd had also included the Forensics team, who were seated next to DCI Fuller.

Byrd looked at Fuller, who appeared physically sick, his skin a shade of white, no doubt filled with dread and anticipation on how his team would react to the news. What Stockdale had done had been horrific.

Over to the right, DI Tanzy was sitting on the end with a bandage around his head. Byrd turned to him specifically.

'How you doing, Ori?'

'All good, Max,' he said, with a positive nod and both thumbs up. He'd just arrived minutes earlier and had come straight through. Pip had picked him up from the hospital and dropped him off before taking the kids to school.

Byrd nodded and focused forward, falling into a moment of silence. He padded over to his left, opened the laptop and placed his USB stick into the slot. It wasn't long before the screen at the front lit up.

It told them today's date and time. In addition to that, it said "Urgent Meeting" underneath it. The words grabbed the attention of everyone. Byrd grabbed the small black remote, took a few steps away from the laptop, and stood beside the screen.

Everyone waited.

'Firstly,' he started, his voice clear and loud, 'I want to thank everyone for coming in on such short notice. This meeting is not only going to be about what happened yesterday involving DS Phillip Stockdale, but what role he played over the past couple of weeks.'

His words were met by a few understanding nods but equal stares of confusion. He glanced over to Fuller, who slowly nodded, agreeing that full transparency within his team was for the best.

'Yesterday, Adrian Dilton's fourth video was uploaded online. I'm aware the majority of you will have seen it.' He turned to the screen, pressing the button, showing a close-up of Stockdale's scared face. 'This video was inside a wooden box. As you can see, it's Phil. At the end of the video, we heard Dilton say the air supply had run out and he didn't have long left. We went from the time the video was uploaded and searched for local cemeteries. Luckily, our team acted quickly. By that, I mean all of you. So, before I continue, I want to thank you all for your efforts yesterday. It was your quick, decisive actions that saved his life.'

He took a breath and pressed the button again. An image of the grave he was buried in appeared.

'When we arrived, we saw Adrian Dilton standing at a grave then he fled. With the help of the gravedigger, we dug up the earth and lifted Stockdale up. We saved his life.'

He pointed around the room, his eyes serious. 'Because of *this* team.'

Fuller nodded at him, appreciating his leadership.

'DI Tanzy and Linda Fallon then went in pursuit of Dilton, climbing the wall and giving chase. It wasn't long before James and Phillip went to help, but they came back with only Tanzy, who'd been hit over the head.'

A few stared at the bandage wrapped around Tanzy's head for a moment.

'Where did Linda go?' asked Jacob Tallow, the senior forensic officer.

'At the moment, we don't know,' admitted Byrd. 'I've tried calling her. She's not answering. We've been to her hotel. No one with her name was ever staying there.'

Cornty sighed and looked down. 'What about her phone — can we not track it?'

'Already tried. Mac can't locate it.'

'Where was Linda when you were attacked, Ori?' The question came from Emily Hope, the other senior forensic officer.

'She was right behind me.'

Wide eyes circled the room as they put two and two together.

'We can't make assumptions,' Byrd said. 'But . . . based on what we know and the fact she's disappeared, it's hard not to think there's something off about this. In addition, I spoke with a Detective Superintendent from Essex Police, who informed me that Linda didn't retire. She was too mentally unstable to work anymore. There had been theories floating around regarding her helping criminals and advising them in policing matters to give them a better chance in court. Because of her, some had been freed to walk the streets.'

Byrd spotted several head shakes, those giving them obviously disgusted at her actions. It made him feel stupid for letting her help with the investigation.

'Do you think she's been helping Dilton?' Cornty asked, adjusting himself on the seat.

'It's looking very likely.' Byrd looked down at the floor for a moment to collect his thoughts, not allowing them to defeat the positive attitude he was desperate to keep a hold of.

'When Phil was at hospital, Amy and Eric went looking for Dilton. We were told he'd got into a blue Ford Focus and had left in a hurry. I reached out to traffic and Jennifer Lucas at the Town Hall with some info, hoping they'd track the car down.'

'Anything yet?' Tanzy asked.

'Nothing yet.'

'What happened to Phil?' PC Grearer asked.

'After Phil was taken to hospital, I went to see him. As we know, from the previous three victims, Adrian Dilton had left notes on their laptops asking us to look at them. According to Mac in DFU, there's a website called *attheend.com*. Mac said it's unusual because the website shows a home screen that is pretty much blank, with a box asking for a username and password, but the site contains massive memory. Something he explained is beyond the log-in page. We wouldn't know what this is if Tanzy hadn't managed to get on, using the laptop from Danny Walters' attic that had his username and password saved.' He looked over to Tanzy and nodded.

'Yeah, once we pressed enter, it took us to a screen showing a woman in a room. The floor was made of concrete and the walls were bare. Next to the camera shot was a list of a few "players". *RCarl20* was there. Who we know to be Adrian Dilton. Below that, there was a tab saying, "watchers". Next to "watchers" was a number. There were over a thousand. It then logged me out and I couldn't get back in.'

'What was it?' DC Cornty asked, frowning.

Tanzy shrugged. 'Some kind of a game. Whatever it is, I didn't have long enough on there.' He looked back at Byrd for him to tell them what Stockdale had said.

'When I spoke with Phil, he told me he'd logged on to the website, and that he was a player.'

Several gasps were heard around the room.

'What did the players do?' Leonard asked, concerned.

'Phil said that players paid a lot of money to play the game. The game was run by unknown hosts. Only five players were allowed at any one time. The watchers, Phil explained, were online users wanting to play but they had to wait for their turn. They paid a lesser amount to watch the game until the series of games finished and they'd get a chance to become a player.'

Weaver raised a hand to her mouth. 'Jesus. That's awful.'

'What happened in the games?' Cornty asked.

'They decided how the person died.'

Byrd's words sent shivers among them. They all looked at one another, astounded that Stockdale was a part of this.

'Please, Max, go on . . .' Fuller encouraged him, wanting them all to know the full story.

Byrd nodded. 'Each victim was placed in a chair, tied down, with a gag over their mouth. And each player, in turn, could tell the hosts what to do with them. He said in the first game, the victim had died in the end from fire. The username *DWalt66* had instructed the hosts to pour petrol on her and burn her.'

Weaver physically gagged but stopped herself from being sick.

The senior forensic officers, Tallow and Hope, exchanged worried looks between each other.

'Then what happened?' Leonard asked.

'The username *EricJ4* had told the hosts to put a bag over her head to starve the next victim of oxygen. The third murder involved a woman dying from water. One of the hosts, who dressed in black with a black balaclava to hide their face, placed a tightly fitting plastic bag around her head and filled it with water until she drowned, as per *Hammr33*'s instruction. Only the players had a say what happened to them. Each player had a go at each victim. So far, Phil told me, there'd been three victims. There was one more to go.'

'So, if there have been three victims in this game, and Phil was meant to be Dilton's fourth murder, what did Phil do?'

288

Byrd took a breath. 'Phil told me the hosts had a lot of props. He'd asked the host to place a plastic box with a hole in the bottom just big enough for the victim's head to fit through, and then asked them to pour soil inside so the victim wouldn't be able to breathe, then take it off just in time before they died. All the players had a say in what happened but each player had their turn to finish the victim. Phil's victim would have been the next one.'

'When do these games happen?' Weaver asked, grimacing.

'According to Phil, every Friday night. There's one coming up this Friday.'

Collective sighs swept the room.

And then something strange happened.

Tanzy and Leonard both looked at each other and narrowed their eyes.

'You thinking what I'm thinking, Jim?' Tanzy asked.

Leonard nodded twice. 'I think so . . .'

'What is it?' Byrd asked, intrigued about what they'd figured out.

'You go first . . .' Tanzy offered.

'So if user *DWalt66* had told the hosts to kill the victim with fire, it can't be a coincidence that Dilton set Danny Walters's house on fire, or that *EricJ4* had told the hosts to place a bag over the victim's head and then she was gassed out in the lift before she fell from her balcony . . .'

Byrd nodded in understanding. He looked at Tanzy.

'Or that *Hammr33* had told them to place a plastic bag over their head and fill it with water. Then she and her boyfriend died by Dilton injecting excessive water into their bodies until they internally drowned?'

The realisation of what had happened hit everyone at a similar time.

'So,' Fuller said, 'you're thinking that Dilton, who we know was playing the game with them, had somehow figured out who they were and had taken some form of revenge on them, killing them a similar way?'

Tanzy nodded. 'That's exactly what I'm thinking.'

The door in the corner opened suddenly and in came the receptionist Julie. 'Max, there's a call for you . . .'

Byrd said okay.

Julie walked in with a cordless phone that was usually sat on the desk at reception. 'She's tried to call you, but couldn't get through, so-called reception.'

'Who is it?' Byrd asked but took the phone anyway and put it to his ear. 'Hello?'

'Max. It's Jennifer from the Town Hall.'

'Hi, Jennifer. Thanks for getting back to me. What do you have?'

'I have a very good idea where to find your blue Ford Focus.'

77

Tuesday morning
Darlington

Brad bent down near Sarah and placed the tray of food near her leg. A ham and cheese sandwich, a packet of crisps and bottled water. He'd even treat her today because she'd been so good and put a chocolate bar on there too.

What a hero.

He picked up the empty tray and the empty bottle she'd squashed out of anger earlier that morning. Brad didn't blame her for it; he'd do the same. Being taken to a dark room with three friends in pitch black, then suddenly waking and finding one of them missing was no idea of fun. Especially when she didn't know where they'd gone or what had happened to them.

He stood up, looked down on her for a moment and felt sorry for her. It wasn't pleasant what they had done, or what they'd do over the next few months, but financially, it was something he couldn't turn down.

He'd been thinking over the past few days about the next victims, making a list of five for the next set of games. He'd created a fake profile and planned to meet them on Saturday.

Joanne, the one he'd been speaking to, said she would message him to meet. He would drive into town, park the blue van somewhere, and hit the bars. Once he located the women, he'd tell them there was a party at his house and on their way back, gas them out.

On his way out of the room, he closed the door and slid the bolt across until there was a metallic ping. He turned with the empty tray and made his way up the stairs.

He opened the door at the top, took a left and went through further doors until he reached the room with the computers in. He placed the tray with empty wrappers down on a table to the right, then dropped into the chair at the desk and plucked his phone from his pocket to call Mitch.

'Brad,' Mitch answered. 'How's it going?'

'Just given her some food. She'll wake up soon.'

'Good.'

'When are you getting here?'

'I have a lot on today, Brad. Are you all right holding the fort?'

Brad said he was although he had little choice. Mitch was in charge of all the money the players and watchers paid, so whatever Mitch wanted Brad to do, he would.

'How's the list coming on?'

Brad told him about Joanne and the plan to meet them this Saturday. That he'd lure them into the van and bring them here.

'Keep up the good work, Brad. I'll see you soon.'

Mitch hung up the phone and the line went dead.

78

Byrd had passed on what Jennifer Lucas had said about the blue Ford Focus to Leonard, Cornty and Weaver. It was seen on a camera leaving the roundabout on Haughton Road going up Barton Street. The only way out of the Albert Hill area was under the bridge on Cleveland Street leading to North Road. Jennifer knew there was a camera positioned high up on the side of a factory next to the railway line, facing towards North Road. She'd waited at least half an hour, looking for the car but it didn't show, nor had it gone back on itself and come back down Barton Street to the Haughton Road roundabout it originally came from.

Although she knew Darlington like the back of her hand, she had looked on Google Maps and made a list of streets within that small area. Judging by the list, it wasn't that small. There were ten in total with a few small industrial units, including a hefty number of garages where a vehicle could easily be hidden.

'Where should we start?' Leonard asked them, pressing his lips together, knowing the area wasn't as small as they'd thought.

Cornty, who was riding shotgun, looked down at the list of streets in his hand on the paper that Byrd had written for him. Weaver was in the back with her phone open on Google Maps, switching her focus between the road ahead and the electronic map in her hand.

'Could start with this one? Barton Street,' suggested Weaver.

Leonard nodded and drove on, slowly passing the timber place on the right. They were all looking around carefully and meticulously, scanning left and right.

'What year was it?' Leonard said in concentration.

'Twelve reg, Jim. N. A. 1. 2. O. P. P,' he said, referring to what Byrd had jotted down.

Over the next thirty minutes, they drove around the streets slowly, passing every house in the area. When they returned to Barton Street, they pulled over to the left. Haughton Road was roughly one hundred metres behind them.

The enthusiasm they'd arrived with seemed to have dissipated a little.

'No sign then?' Weaver noted sadly.

'Do you think if there had been, one of us would have said,' Cornty replied sharply.

The tone he used with her didn't go unnoticed with Leonard.

'Don't take it out on her, Phil.' Leonard stared at him and Cornty matched it. 'She's making conversation.'

Cornty sighed and swivelled towards the back of the car. 'Sorry, Amy. It's getting to me all this shit.'

She pursed her lips together but didn't say anything.

'It's getting to everyone,' said Leonard. 'This Dilton fucker. Fallon, wherever the hell she is. And now Stockdale is involved in this online shit.'

Cornty nodded and apologised again.

'It's fine, Phil,' Amy replied quietly.

'Looks like we'll need to—'

'Whoa!' Leonard snapped, stopping Cornty from finishing his sentence.

'What?' Weaver said, leaning forward from the back, her hands on the head rests of both front seats.

'There . . .' Leonard said, pointing down the street on the right, watching a man walk across the road further down.

'Him?' Cornty said.

He was bald, matching the height and width of the profile they had on Adrian Dilton, wearing a red T-shirt and black shorts. He took a right into Church Grove.

Leonard engaged the clutch of the silver Insignia and put the gear in first, checked for traffic in his wing mirror and pulled out quickly, planting his foot to the floor. They frantically scanned the area after they turned in search for the man who'd they just seen.

Leonard stopped in the cul-de-sac with nowhere to go. 'Can anyone see him?'

Weaver leaned back and methodically studied each house in turn. They'd been in the same street five minutes ago but hadn't seen a Ford Focus. 'I can't see him.'

'Phil? See anything?'

Cornty inspected the houses to the left. 'Zilch . . .'

'Bastard.'

Leonard asked Weaver for her phone, which she handed over. He focused on the map open on Google.

'What are you looking for?' Weaver asked.

Handing back her phone, he did a U-turn, returning to Barton Street again.

Cornty was baffled. 'What are you doing?'

'Show him, Amy,' said Leonard.

Cornty frowned and took the phone to have a look. 'What am I looking at, Jim?'

Leonard leaned over and pointed to the map. 'It's a cul-de-sac. There's no way out. I think we should sit tight and see what happens.'

'Why don't we just knock on doors,' suggested Weaver.

'Because if Fallon is helping him, she'll recognise us immediately and they won't answer the door. We haven't the manpower to burst down every door.'

Weaver made a *fair-enough* face and leaned back.

'Who you calling?' Cornty said to Leonard as he plucked his own phone from his pocket.

'To let Max and Orion know.' He paused a beat. 'We have Dilton cornered.'

79

Tuesday morning
Police station

Byrd hung up the phone and slipped it into his pocket.

'Who was that?' asked Tanzy, staring at him.

'Leonard thinks they've spotted him go into Church Grove but lost him. Reckons he's in one of the houses. They're waiting out on the road until backup arrives. Says he's blocked in.'

Tanzy nodded and stood up. 'Let's go then.'

'We'll get Timms and Grearer there, too.'

'Good idea,' replied Tanzy as they both made their way down the office.

'Timms!' Tanzy shouted. 'Grearer. Let's go.'

PC Timms and PC Grearer were seated near each other on separate desks and stood up immediately. Tanzy filled them in on the situation about Dilton and they grabbed their things, then followed Byrd and Tanzy out into the car park. Byrd jumped in the driver's seat. Tanzy got into the passenger seat and buckled up.

Grearer and Timms took one of the marked Peugeots and pulled out onto the road a moment after.

* * *

'You think it was definitely him?' DC Cornty asked Leonard as he focused on the opening to Church Grove.

'I'm pretty confident, yeah.'

'Good enough for me,' Cornty said, nodding.

'Are Max and Orion coming?' Weaver said from the back of the car.

'Yeah. Max said he'll request more backup. Once they're here, we'll go in.'

'What if they—'

'Look!' Cornty shouted, stabbing the warm air inside the car. 'Look.'

Leonard and Weaver watched the blue Ford Focus edge out and take a right, moving away from them.

'There she is, the bitch!' Leonard shouted, spotting Linda Fallon in the passenger seat.

'Think they saw us?' asked Weaver.

Leonard pulled out and quickly accelerated through the gears. By the time they hit the bend, the Focus was out of sight, somewhere along the road.

'C'mon, Jim!' Cornty shouted, tapping the dash in frustration.

Leonard planted his foot and the car surged forward. Soon they reached the traffic lights just before the bridge.

The Focus shot down the ramp, through the lights and raced up the other side, thick plumes of smoke shooting from the exhaust.

Leonard gripped the wheel tighter and pushed hard on the pedal, and the car powered under the bridge, the roar of the engine echoing off the brick walls on either side.

'C'mon, Jim!' repeated Cornty, watching the Focus reach the top of the incline and disappear.

'I am,' replied a frustrated Leonard. They sped up the hill and the car went airborne for a moment, sending butterflies through their stomachs. 'Ring Max. Tell him they're on the move!'

Cornty found Tanzy's number and pressed CALL. 'C'mon. Pick up, pick up,' he said quickly, his heart rate through the roof.

'Phil?' Tanzy answered.

'They're moving towards North Road.'

'In the Focus?'

Cornty said they were.

They watched Focus whiz by Aldi, at least sixty miles an hour. If a car pulled out, or a pedestrian crossed the road, the repercussions would be catastrophic.

'They must know we're behind them!' Weaver panted from the back seat, watching the speeding car through the front windscreen.

A red Clio pulled out of Aldi's car park just as Dilton and Fallon passed and slammed on their brakes, causing them to skid out into the road, people nearby staring at the high-screeched sound.

'Jesus!' Leonard gasped at the close call. There were no oncoming cars, so when Leonard's Insignia approached the Clio, he veered onto the other side of the road to go around it and pulled back in. The Focus took a sudden left onto North Road, its tyres screeching harshly.

'He's a nutter!'

Leonard reached the turn and realised the traffic lights were on red. Cars from the right started to shift forward.

'They've gone left on North Road, Orion,' Cornty shouted into the phone.

'Got ya!' replied Tanzy. 'We're on St Cuthbert's Way, heading to the roundabout.'

Cornty scowled at the cars coming from the right. 'Jim!'

'Hold on . . .' Leonard floored it and guided the car left. The tyres almost lost grip and the car bounced, the rubber squealing on the dry road. The driver rocked his head back in horror and slammed on his brakes, although Leonard was confident in making the turn.

Up ahead, roughly forty metres beyond the bridge, the Focus was weaving in and out of the traffic.

'He's gonna kill someone!' bellowed Cornty from the passenger seat.

'Sit tight!' Leonard approached the next car and did the same, mindful of the oncoming traffic.

'Easy, Jim,' Weaver said. 'Easy . . .'

'We need to catch them.'

The Insignia passed Skin Deep tattoo shop on the right and approached the traffic lights near the petrol station. Again, the lights were red. The Focus swung wide and powered through, flying past stationary traffic, making it over before the cars from Eastmount Road turned onto North Road.

'Shit!' Leonard panted, immediately slowing the car to thirty, quickly assessing his options, knowing cars would turn in his path.

'Orion, they're heading along North Road towards the roundabout,' Cornty said into the phone as Leonard slowed the car to a stop. 'We've lost them in traffic we'll catch up when we can.'

'Okay. We're approaching the roundabout now,' replied Tanzy.

* * *

Byrd nodded as Tanzy relayed the message and kept his eyes on the roundabout ahead, specifically the exit from North Road, knowing Dilton's Focus would appear any moment.

'There, there. There!' Tanzy screamed, pointing.

Byrd could see it. The blue car flew out of North Road onto the roundabout without a care for the traffic coming from their right. A black Fiesta suddenly came to a halt and the white transit van behind it collided into the back of it with a metal crunch.

Byrd watched Dilton pass in almost a blur but spotted Fallon in the passenger seat, who made eye contact with him for a brief moment before the car was gone. Dilton went straight over the roundabout and followed the bus route into town.

'Where the hell's he going?' snapped Tanzy.

Byrd followed them into the busy town centre, catching a flash of the Focus before it whizzed out of sight down towards Wilko's.

'Max. Put ya bloody foot down!'

Byrd scowled and lost his patience. 'I fucking am!'

Without any warning, a bus pulled out from the left, nearly forcing them onto the path over to the right but Byrd managed to somehow keep it on the road, inches from a family of five casually walking by.

The Focus took a right at the next junction, heading towards the William Stead pub. Byrd followed.

'The car is in the middle of town,' Tanzy said into the phone.

'We're not far behind,' replied Cornty from the Insignia. 'Just at the roundabout now.'

'Head straight over. Go down the bus route,' Tanzy replied.

The Focus took the right turn before it reached the William Stead pub.

'Why — what on earth . . .' Byrd whispered, slowing the X5 and followed him up the bank. The road ahead was clear. No buses. No pedestrian shoppers idly crossing the road. When the Focus went under the Cornmill, the exhaust echoed off the building.

Before the Focus reached the turn, a taxi pulled out, causing it to slow allowing Byrd to close the gap.

'Easy, Max . . .' Tanzy warned him, eyeing the speed-ometer on the dash.

'He's mine!' Byrd shouted. The Focus veered around the awkward taxi which had suddenly stopped and started to make the turn. Byrd drove around the taxi and put his foot down, surging the X5 forward.

'Max!' Tanzy shouted with wide eyes, not knowing what was going to happen. They were going far too fast.

Byrd tightened his grip on the wheel and as the Focus was mid-turn, Byrd ploughed into the back quarter, sending the Focus into the concrete flower bed. The crash was so loud, every-one around froze and stared in horror at what had happened.

Byrd's airbag came up, smashing him in the nose with the force of a hammer. Tanzy's airbag exploded too,

cushioning his face as he was jerked forward into the direction of the dashboard.

Silence surrounded them after the deafening crash faded
into the town. Nearby people glared in shock with open,
speechless mouths at the mess. Someone got their phone out
to take a picture.

Byrd didn't move. Neither did Tanzy.

80

Tuesday morning
High Row, town centre

'God . . .' Fallon whispered. 'Think my arm's broken.'

'Can — can you move?' Dilton asked, feeling a pounding in the side of his temple where he'd collided into the side window. He raised his hand and felt the warm blood gushing from the cut.

'I — I think so, Adrian . . .' Fallon struggled to say.

When Byrd had crashed into the rear of them, sending the Focus forward into the concrete flower beds, she had jerked forward, hitting her shoulder off the central console. She'd wailed in pain, immediately feeling like something terrible had happened. A bone breaking, for sure.

'Come on. We need to go.' Dilton turned around. The X5 was hard up against the rear, the bonnet crumpled and smashed up.

'Your head . . .' Fallon said, seeing the blood dripping onto his trousers and the inside of the car.

'Come on. We need to get out.'

He opened his door and, with just enough room to squeeze out, he pulled himself up onto his feet. Fallon opened the passenger door but struggled to move. Dilton noticed the front of the Focus hard up against the high concrete slab, the bonnet totally crushed.

He looked back at the white X5. Tanzy and Byrd were both leaning forward, unconscious. Dilton rushed to Fallon' door. 'You okay, Linda?'

'I'll survive.'

Dilton took a soft grip of her arm and gently helped her out of the car. 'Let's go before they wake up.'

* * *

Tanzy's eyes flickered a few times until he managed to keep them open and saw the deflated airbag on his lap. His nose felt hot and sore, like he'd just been headbutted. He sniffed hard, tasting the blood in the back of his throat. To his right, Byrd was still unconscious.

'Max?'

Nothing.

Then he heard a voice say, 'Let's go before they wake up.'

He followed the sound, the simple head movement causing a wave of almost unbearable pain. Dilton and Fallon moved down the side of the car, but Tanzy quickly grabbed the handle and threw his door open, unbuckled his seat belt and leaned out, leading with his left leg. As Dilton ran by, he kicked Tanzy's door closed, jamming Tanzy's knee between the side skirt and the door. There was a crack and Tanzy howled in agony and fell out of the car and rolled onto his back. He hadn't felt pain like it. He watched Fallon and Dilton dash across the road and run into the Cornmill Shopping Centre.

'Max — Max!' he screamed.

Byrd stirred and jerked awake a moment later, sighing something inaudible.

'Max. Here!'

Byrd swivelled his stiff neck to the left and noticed Tanzy lying on the road through the open passenger door, wincing in pain. His knee was bleeding and swelling already.

'Get them. They've gone into the Cornmill.'

Byrd pushed his door open and stepped down onto the concrete, a little unsteady on his feet, then staggered around the rear of the car to aid to Tanzy.

'Did you not hear me?'

Byrd frowned, unsure what he'd said.

'The Cornmill.' Tanzy stabbed the air in the direction of the entrance. 'Get them!'

Byrd nodded and tried to make sense of what had happened. His head was pounding. He collected himself and dashed across the road towards the entrance.

81

Tuesday late morning
The Cornmill Shopping Centre

Dilton barged into the entrance door first and almost collided into an elderly man with a walking stick in his eighties, who was on his way out. The old man jolted back a few inches and glared wide eyed at Dilton, wondering what on earth he was doing.

Fallon managed to get through before it swung back to hit her and swerved the man, who remained still, a look of disgust on his face at both of them. He shook his head and exited through the door.

'Come on, Linda!' Dilton screamed.

In jeans and heels, she wasn't really dressed for sprinting, but she was doing her best. For her age, she was quick.

Dilton hung back a little, waiting for her to level with him. 'Come on,' he repeated, and looked back at the door they'd just come through, seeing DI Byrd barge through, almost losing his balance in the process.

He grabbed her hand, and they passed the perfume shop until they had a choice to make. They could take the escalator down to the ground floor. Or they could take a left, along to the next area of shops where JD Sports was.

They swung a left, barely missing a woman walking with two toddlers, who both seemed to be around the age of five.

'Watch it!' the mother blasted in revulsion and glowered at them as they ran past.

Fallon and Dilton ran on, their heavy footsteps slapping the floor, loud enough for nearby shoppers to stop and glare at them in wonder. They sprinted past JD Sports, almost running into a group of teenagers who looked young enough to be skiving school.

'Stop them!' they heard Byrd shout somewhere close behind them.

He pulled on Fallon's arm, urging her to move quicker. They raced past Game on their left and headed toward WH Smith. Dilton's mind was doing overtime, thinking hard, wondering what to do, where to go. He knew they were being followed from his house to North Road because Fallon had said she recognised the registration on the Insignia. A guy called James she'd said. If backup was coming, they'd no doubt have the exits covered very soon. It was policing basics. So Dilton needed to think outside the box.

'Here! Take a right here,' he shouted, just before they reached WH Smith's. A set of open double doors led to a lift and a staircase down to the toilets. Dilton went through first, narrowly missing a woman in a wheelchair, dressed in a red coat and hat although it was nearly thirty degrees outside.

'Hey . . .' the woman said, sighing.

Dilton and Fallon reached the stairs, but instead of taking the stairs down, they went up, climbing them two at a time. He was much quicker than she was and reached the next level, scanning what was there. A closed door with a Yale lock.

'Shit . . .'

He went up the next level and kept going until he was four floors up where he reached the emergency exit access to the roof. Before he went through, he stopped to hear where Fallon was. The level below.

He pushed the bar, opened the door and went outside into the hot sun. It was so bright he had to cover his eyes with a palm to see what was out there. It was pretty flat in most areas, but he noticed a long, angled window, which he recognised was the skylight giving natural light for the shoppers down below. Other areas contained cubed-shaped ducting probably used for HVAC systems.

Fallon barged through the door a few moments later with a red face, panting heavily, her blonde hair all over the place.

'Linda,' he said, going back to her. 'You okay?'

'Where — where are we going to go?'

'We'll hide up here for a while . . .'

She shook her head. 'No, Adrian. We can't. Max is right behind us. We need to hide now.'

82

Byrd was two floors from the top when he stopped hearing Fallon's shoes slapping inside the stairwell, meaning she wasn't in the stairwell anymore. He was tired. His lungs gasped for air and his arms and legs were burning. He reached the top level and saw the open emergency exit door swinging gently in the breeze.

He burst out onto the roof, the light almost blinding him in the process. For a second, he shielded himself, feeling very vulnerable if Dilton had waited at the door to attack him.

Fortunately, no attack came.

He stopped and glared around in all directions.

No sign of Fallon and Dilton. He absorbed the ducting lines and small metal items. He noticed a handrail at the edge of the roof to the right, which, as he soon spotted, ran the whole perimeter of it.

He took a few quiet steps away from the open door, pulled a baton from his pocket and fully extended it. He decided to take a right and tiptoed across the roof, scanning everything around him, trying to hear for any movement.

As he stepped into the centre of the space, he realised the roof was bigger than he first thought. The view of Darlington beyond the handrails was admirable, to say the least. He soon came across a small shed made from brick, with a thick door on the front of it. There was a keycode panel at head height beside it, so wherever they'd gone, it wasn't through there. He backed away, turned and moved along the railing, looking carefully through all the ducting pipes.

Then he had an idea.

He lowered to the ground, his head still pounding from the crash minutes earlier and looked along the floor of the roof. He'd figured out the ducting sections didn't reach the floor and were supported by metal brackets an inch off the deck.

Bingo.

There they were, roughly forty metres over to the right, hiding behind a large section of the ducting.

He stood, battling against his own spinning head, and slowly made his way over. He plucked his phone from his pocket and called Tanzy.

'Max . . .'

'Hey, Ori. They're on the roof. I've got them cornered. Where are you?'

'Still outside. I can't fucking move. I think they've broken my knee. Ambulance is here.'

'Leonard. Cornty. Where are they?' he whispered, not wanting to be heard.

'Inside the Cornmill looking for you.'

'Send them up. Staircase near the toilets. It goes to the roof.'

He took a quick, sharp breath and moved over to the ducting ahead of him, slowly and carefully rounding the edge of it.

Dilton and Fallon edged away when they saw him, taking a few steps back towards the railings.

'Linda,' Byrd said. 'I don't understand.'

'There's a lot of things you don't understand, Max,' she replied, stepping in front of Dilton, as if somehow protecting him.

'Please explain.' Byrd stepped closer, but with each step, Dilton and Fallon backed away, getting close to the handrail on the edge of the roof. There were a few feet between them.

'I don't need to explain anything to you . . .'

Before Byrd replied, Dilton pushed Fallon into Byrd and made a run for it. Byrd deflected Fallon's slap and knocked her to one side, then went after him. Dilton was quick, but Byrd was no snail.

'Stop!' Byrd shouted, panting as he chased him.

Dilton ran along the side of the handrail until he reached the edge and disappeared.

'Shit!' Byrd sighed. When he reached it, he realised there was another roof next to it, roughly two feet lower, a small access ladder between them.

'Stop!' Byrd screamed at him, but Dilton didn't slow.

Up ahead, was a large dome-like set of windows. Byrd recognised it as the huge skylight above the escalators near Primark.

Dilton reached it and jumped on top, then started moving up it.

'Adrian, don't!' Byrd yelled, unsure if it was safe. 'Get off there.'

It would be engineered to withstand the weight of snow over the whole area but not necessarily the concentrated weight of a man.

Dilton ignored him and went higher.

'Max, leave him alone,' Fallon cried somewhere behind him.

Byrd ignored her plea and arrived at the base of the glass dome skylight. 'Fuck it,' he muttered. He started to climb it. Dilton was nearly at the top, and as Byrd was nearly halfway, he noticed Dilton had slowed, almost coming to a stop.

Byrd carefully went up, keeping his weight on the PVC framework instead of the glass, just in case. It wasn't long before Dilton stopped and turned to him.

'Why?' Dilton asked.

Byrd frowned. 'Why what, Adrian?'

'Why are you chasing me?'

'Because killing people is illegal.'

'I'm doing you a favour. Can't you fucking see that?'

'Well, whatever you're doing . . . it's against the law. You need to come with me.'

Byrd finally stopped on the angled pane, roughly three metres from Dilton. He glanced right and left, realising he didn't have anywhere to go.

'I'm going nowhere. There's so much more work to do . . .' he said, scowling at Byrd.

'Please, Adrian. You need to—'

Dilton lifted his right foot and stomped hard onto the glass he was standing on. The rectangular pane was large, roughly a metre by two metres.

'No,' Byrd begged, holding his palms out quickly. 'Don't do that!'

Dilton lifted his leg and did it again. Byrd knew what would happen if the glass gave way. He looked below for a second, noticed the sea of people watching them from below, their faces glaring up in horror at the crazy guy standing above them.

'Do not do—'

Dilton did it again, this time harder.

The pane of glass crunched. Dozens of paper-thin cracks shot off in all directions away from the impact of his heel. Time seemed to come to a halt when there was another crack and a sudden whoosh before Dilton disappeared through it, not making a sound as he fell.

The loud thud of his body hitting the handrail of the escalator below was sickening. His body literally folded in two and blood cascaded in several directions, followed by the screams of nearby startled shoppers.

Byrd immediately turned away and clamped his eyes closed, not wanting to see the mess below.

Slowly, he lowered himself off the dome and turned to see where Fallon was.

She had gone.

83

Tuesday late morning,
The Cornmill Shopping Centre

Byrd tried calling Fallon, but her phone was switched off. He phoned Tanzy on his way back down the stairs, who informed Byrd he was in the rear of an ambulance with a paramedic looking at his knee. He said he'd heard the screams inside but didn't know what had happened.

Byrd filled him in and ended the call. He stepped out of the toilets and ran up towards JD Sports, his frantic footsteps bouncing off the shiny, tiled floor towards the mass of people standing near the glass handrail, gobsmacked by Dilton's mangled body below. A couple of people were physically sick at the sight of it.

'I need everyone out!' Byrd shouted with his head high, so it projected his voice. 'Everyone out now.'

A couple of people turned but most were fixated on Dilton's broken body below.

'I'm with the police. Get out!'

He spotted Leonard to his right, glaring wide eyed down at the mess over the glass handrail until he recognised Byrd's voice and ran over.

'Jesus, Max! What happened?'

Byrd quickly told him, then added, 'We need everyone out. Where are the security guards? Call for backup. We need this shit cleaned up ASAP.'

Leonard took out his radio.

Byrd scanned the area, noticed Cornty on the other side, trying to get people to move. Weaver was near him doing the same, saving people from seeing the awful sight.

'What a fucking mess,' muttered Byrd to himself.

* * *

A little while later, after the security staff of nearby shops had joined in to help the police clear the place, the Cornmill was empty. It was eerie, Byrd thought, standing at the glass hand-rail in silence, looking up at where Dilton had fallen. The senior forensics, Tallow and Hope, were down below dressed in their white overalls. They'd taken photos of the whole scene, and as usual, Tallow had taken videos for later analysis.

The undertakers had been called to collect what was left of the body, and Peter Gibbs had turned up. The colour surprisingly had drained from his face as he approached Byrd.

'My goodness . . .' he said, raising a palm to his mouth.

Byrd had informed everyone what happened on the roof but had asked security if there were any cameras up there which would confirm his story. As it stood, if someone had said Byrd had pushed him, he couldn't prove otherwise.

He also wanted to see which direction Fallon had run off in. She must have slipped past Cornty and Leonard, and planned to ask Jennifer Lucas about it later to see if she could trace her movements on the town's cameras.

Their next task was to search the house where Dilton had been staying. To understand someone, especially a killer, it was best to start off in a place they spent much of their time in, because there were often clues which had been missed.

Byrd, after dealing with Fuller shouting in his face back in town, had kept his cool and told Weaver, Leonard and Cornty to go to Church Grove to find the house which Dilton was staying in. He went to the ambulance to see Tanzy who was sitting on a trolley with his leg bandaged up to see how he was doing.

'What's the damage, Ori?' he asked from the open rear doors.

A female paramedic with blonde hair in her thirties said, 'Excuse me,' and veered around Byrd, climbed into the back of the van and grabbed a small kit bag, then thanked him when she jumped back out.

'They said it could be bad, Max,' replied Tanzy, physically in pain. 'Won't know until I get an X-ray. Hopefully it's just bruised. Where's Linda?'

'I don't know. Fuller isn't a happy man.'

Tanzy sighed and waved his hand. 'He's never happy, Max. It's the way he is.'

Byrd made a fair-enough face. 'Are they taking you now?'

Tanzy nodded. 'Checking if anyone else needs any help before we go. Make me a promise, Max . . .'

'What is it?'

'Catch that bitch.'

'I'll do what I can, Ori.'

'Never a dull day in Darlington, is there?'

Byrd smiled, agreeing with him with a shake of his head.

* * *

By the time Byrd had reached Church Grove in his battered X5 which, fortunately was still driveable, the police had managed to locate the house that Dilton and Fallon had been staying in by asking neighbours and giving them their descriptions.

Cornty had kicked the door in while Leonard watched. They put overshoes and gloves on and entered with Weaver following behind. They searched the house until Byrd arrived, pulling into the street and spotting Leonard's Insignia and two marked Peugeots over in the left corner, parked in front of a nice-looking semi-detached house. Byrd got out, locked the door, and walked towards the house, feeling the stares of nosy neighbours from all directions, standing behind curtains, peeping out to see what was happening.

Byrd stepped through the broken red door and called out.

Leonard appeared at the top of the stairs with a serious look on his face. 'Come up here, boss. There's something you need to see.'

84

Tuesday early afternoon
Church Grove, Darlington

Byrd climbed the stairs and followed Leonard into a small room at the end of the short, narrow landing. It was obvious Dilton had used it as an office. A desk was against the wall to the right and, above it, dozens of photos and bits of paper randomly pinned to the wall.

Byrd looked at it, seeing photos of Danny Walters, Jane Ericson, Rachel Hammond, and lastly, DS Phil Stockdale. Next to each photograph, there were random notes pinned beside them that Dilton had made when he'd observed them over the last couple of weeks. There was a yellow Post-it Note stuck to the bottom of each photo with a single word written on them. The word *Fire* was under Walters, *Air* under Ericson, *Water* under Hammond, and lastly, *Earth* under Stockdale.

Byrd pulled his attention away from the wall, noticing an envelope in Leonard's hand. 'What's that?'

In the centre of it, in scribbled handwriting, it said *FAO Max Byrd / Orion Tanzy.*

'What is it?' Cornty asked, stepping into the room. Byrd turned it over, peeled away the sticky flap, and reached inside, pulling out multiple sheets of A-4 paper.

Byrd dropped them onto the desk and peered over them. The first page was a printed letter to Byrd and Tanzy.

To Max and Orion,

Firstly, I want to apologise for what I've done. The way I killed Danny, Jane, and Rachel wasn't pleasant. I'm glad you found Phil before he ran out of air. I left you the message at the end of my fourth video in the hope you would find him. He seemed like a genuine man caught up in something wrong, but I hoped he learned his lesson for what he did. By now, I'm sure he's confessed to what he's done and is paying the price in prison for a long time, so either way, justice is served.

I came across the website which I know you're now aware of: www.attheend.com — *it's pure evil. The people who did those despicable things needed to pay the price.*

Yes, I admit, taking an eye for an eye isn't the way it should be, but after I witnessed what they'd done and what they said, it sickened me. So, I got them back.

By now, I'm either dead or arrested. So this is my way of saying sorry for what I've done. The online games were disgusting. What they did was unforgivable. I couldn't accept it.

Now, as you know, I'm not in a position to stop this anymore. This, now, is up to you Max / Orion, to finish this. If you look on my computer (username RCarl20 *and password Dilton) and look at the program that is currently running (LocateIP). It's a special tracking program from the US. It was expensive, but if it works, it'll be worth it to save them. So far, I haven't been able to locate the source of where these games are taking place. It could be anywhere in the world. Judging by the missing four girls, I have an idea it's somewhere in Darlington.*

Open the program and see if it's worked. I'm hoping it's found the location of where the website originates from. Once it reaches one hundred per cent, their location will come up. You need to find them and stop them from causing more harm to innocent families.

Keep up the good work.
Best wishes,
Adrian Dilton

'Jesus,' Byrd whispered.

'What is it?' Leonard said.

Byrd handed the letter over to Leonard, who started to read it. Cornty leaned in to read it too.

Byrd logged on to the computer and the program appeared. The current search bar had reached ninety-seven per cent and was slowly crawling across the screen. Under the percentage number, it stated *Location not yet found* . . . in bold lettering.

'Come on . . .' he said, looking above the monitor at the notes on the wall.

'Bloody hell,' Leonard said behind him. 'He's trying to stop it.'

'In other words,' Cornty said, pushing his lips out, 'he's a hero then.'

'I wouldn't go that fucking far,' countered Leonard, who placed the paper on the desk and looked at the screen.

'Once it's a hundred, we'll know,' Byrd said.

Leonard and Cornty both nodded in anticipation.

'I'm gonna check on Weaver,' Cornty said, edging back and leaving the room. Weaver was downstairs, checking through the cupboards in the kitchen.

'Hey,' Cornty said, entering the kitchen.

It took her by surprise, and she jumped.

'Jeez . . . you got me there.' She placed a palm on her chest. 'Found anything upstairs?'

Cornty explained the letter and the location program.

'We'll nail them!' she said positively.

Back upstairs, a little over fifteen minutes later, the bar had reached one hundred per cent. It provided an IP address and coordinates. Byrd grabbed a pen and piece of scrap paper, making a note of them. He then went on to Google and typed in the coordinates that the program had given and pressed ENTER.

The location came up.

'Bingo . . .' said Leonard, leaning over him.

'Ring this in, Jim.'

Leonard took his phone out and rang dispatch as they went downstairs. Weaver was in the living room, hunting through a cabinet in one of the alcoves.

'We found a location for the online games. Just off McMullen Road. Where are Timms and Grearer?'

'Upstairs with you, I think. In the back bedrooms?'

Byrd appeared behind Leonard. 'We need to go, Amy. You go with Leonard.' He turned back to Timms and Grearer, who had heard them descend the stairs and followed them down. 'Eric and Donny, you go together.'

They both nodded.

'Where's Cornty?'

Weaver shrugged. 'He was here a moment ago.'

They went outside and found the marked Peugeot was gone.

'Where's Cornty gone?' Byrd asked.

'He asked me for our key to the car, said he wanted to check something,' Timms said.

'Someone please call him,' countered Byrd.

Timms pulled his phone from his pocket and did as Byrd had asked. They all saw the blank look on his face. 'He's not answering, boss.'

'He was literally here a moment ago.'

Byrd thought for a moment. 'Amy, you come with me. Eric, Donny, you both go with Jim.'

They nodded and made their way to the cars. Byrd edged the front door closed.

Byrd climbed in his seat and pulled his door shut. Weaver got into the passenger seat and closed her door. While Byrd turned on the engine and turned the car around, Weaver noticed a slip of paper down by her foot. She bent down, picked it up between two fingers, and scanned it curiously.

There was a list of names.

Max Byrd
Orion Tanzy
Amy Weaver
Phil Cornty
Julie Shepherd

'Boss, what's this list?'

Byrd pulled out of Church Grove and glanced her way, seeing the paper. 'List of people whose prints Forensics found on the box that was delivered to the station. One with the head in.'

Weaver frowned. 'I don't understand.'

Byrd looked her way. 'What?'

Weaver stayed silent for a moment.

'Amy, speak up. What is it?' Byrd was stern.

'I got it from Julie when it was at reception then brought it straight to you and DI Tanzy in the office.'

'Okay . . .' Byrd was unsure what she meant.

'Phil Cornty didn't touch the box while it was at the station.'

85

Tuesday afternoon
Church Grove, Darlington

'He didn't touch the box?' Byrd asked, turning onto Barton Street.

Weaver shook her head. 'No.'

Byrd grabbed the radio from the dash, pressed the button. 'Dispatch!'

'Go ahead . . .' the female voice replied.

'Can we get a location on vehicle November-Alpha-Six-Seven-Yankee . . .' His mind went blank for a second.

'PC,' whispered Weaver, helping him out.

'Papa-Charlie?' added Byrd, then nodded thanks towards her.

'Hold on . . .' replied the operator.

Byrd approaching the roundabout at the bottom of Barton Street and angled left, taking the second turn, heading towards McMullen Road. The location of the IP address the program on Dilton's computer had told Byrd was at an industrial property near Lingfield Point, close to the Tornado Way heading to the A66. He flew over the roundabout, the X5's three-litre engine roared as he put the gear into third and pushed his foot flat to the floor. The road ahead was clear which allowed him to reach seventy quickly.

Weaver straightened in her seat, grabbing the handle on the door to steady herself.

'DI Byrd,' said the female operator through the radio, 'the location of the vehicle is currently at Eastpoint Road in the Lingfield Point estate.'

'Thank you,' he replied, concentrating on the traffic lights ahead which were quickly approaching.

'Sir?' Weaver muttered, noticing he wasn't slowing down.

The lights were on red, with a line of cars waiting to go straight ahead.

Byrd didn't ease off the pedal.

Traffic from the left and right were crawling through the cross section, unaware of Byrd hurling towards them.

'Sir?' she repeated, this time louder, tightening her grip on the handle.

'Hold on, Amy . . .'

The left lane for cars turning left was empty. Weaver wondered if he was planning on taking that. The lights were less than a hundred metres away.

As Byrd veered over to the left lane and reached level with the last car in the queue waiting to go, the lights flashed amber before it went green. Byrd judged the first car would set off when they turned green, so dropped a gear and planted his foot, surging the big 4x4 onwards.

Weaver clamped her eyes closed, gripped the door handle so hard, her knuckles went white.

'Hold on . . .' Byrd whispered and concentrated hard to avoid the oncoming kerb, pulling hard on the steering wheel. The tyres skidded a little, the sound of screeching ripped through the air but somehow managed to steady the car before it levelled out.

'Sorry about that.'

She opened her eyes and smiled shyly at him.

He took a right at the next traffic lights and another right at the roundabout before they reached Eastpoint Road.

Weaver looked down at her phone in her hand. 'This is the road.'

'Keep an eye out for our Peugeot.'

She nodded and scanned around.

He decided to take a right and followed the road down until it reached a left bend, taking them around an old, abandoned building, something he'd noticed when driving along the main road a hundred times before.

Byrd carefully took the bend, cautious of oncoming traffic, when Weaver shouted, 'Hold on, hold on!'

'What — what is it?'

'Stop the car.' She pointed to a small parking area behind the small building.

'What, Amy?'

'Over there,' she said.

Byrd peered through a gap between two small buildings, spotting the car they were looking for. He followed the road and pulled up behind the Peugeot. Next to it was a blue Volkswagen Transporter Van.

'There's our van,' noted Byrd with a sigh, remembering it was the one they'd been looking for, the one the body parts had fallen out of on the A66.

Leonard's Insignia appeared behind them a minute later and slowly came to a stop beside them. Leonard wound down his window. 'What's happening?'

Byrd pointed at the Cornty had travelled in.

'Why is he here, sir?' Leonard said, clearly frustrated about the situation. 'He doesn't know where it is yet . . .'

Byrd had a dark feeling in his chest and climbed down from his car, closing his door. They all got out and looked around the marked police car Cornty had been in.

'What's he doing here?' said Leonard, looking around.

Behind them was a large factory with a set of faded yellow double doors near them. 'Did he go in there?' wondered Amy out loud.

Byrd eyed the doors, thinking it was the only logical answer.

They went over to them cautiously, studying the situation. The doors were metal and looked like they'd been there for over a hundred years, judging by the rust that had taken over. The whole building appeared ancient and abandoned.

'What is this place?' Leonard asked no one in particular.

'God knows,' Byrd said as he tried the handle on the right door, then the left. Both were locked.

'Whatever it is, it's up for let,' Timms added. 'Sign on the top up there.'

Grearer looked up for a moment, noticed the blue fabric banner.

'James . . . you got a crowbar in your car?' asked Byrd, looking his way. He nodded and went to the Insignia, opened the boot, and grabbed the crowbar. He ran back to the door and placed the sharp tip into the slightest of gaps in the door. He pushed against it, the reluctant sound of metal responding to his efforts.

'Come on!' he whispered, putting more effort in.

'Here, let me help.' Timms stepped forward and grabbed the bar at a lower point to Leonard.

'On three,' said Leonard. 'One, two, three.'

They both pushed hard. The door cracked and edged open, whatever holding it in place had shattered on the other side. Leonard stepped back, keeping hold of the bar.

'You got your flashlights?' Byrd asked after he peered inside, noticing it was very dark.

Timms and Grearer nodded and pulled theirs from the belts.

'Let me have one,' said Byrd.

Timms handed his light over. Byrd adjusted his grip on it and pulled his baton from his belt too. 'Right, let's go . . .'

86

Tuesday afternoon
Lingfield Point, Darlington

Byrd had told Weaver to stay near the door in case anyone tried to escape while they were inside. She nodded and called for more backup. They had no clue what they were dealing with so the more help available, the better.

Byrd, Leonard, Timms and Grearer went down the dark space, with Byrd and Grearer at the front holding the torches out in front, lighting up the long, narrow corridor in front of them. There were multiple doors on both sides, all of them closed.

'Hello? Police,' Byrd said loud and clear.

They moved further into the building, trying the handles of the doors they passed but every door was locked.

Byrd raised his hand suddenly. Everyone stopped and stared.

'Wha—' Leonard began to say.

'Shhhh . . .'

There was a rustling sound somewhere down the hall.

'Hear that?' Byrd whispered.

'Yeah,' Grearer replied.

'Come on.'

Slowly, they followed Byrd's lead, keeping their wits about them, trying door handles, and moving onto the next, trying to keep quiet. On the right-hand side, they came to a door Byrd was sure he heard something behind.

Byrd raised a palm again, put his head to the door and listened hard. There was the sound of a click on the other side, but Byrd couldn't make out what it was.

He tried the handle, but it was locked. He stepped back, raised a leg and kicked the left side of the door just below the handle. The door juddered but held. He did it again, but this time the door crumbled in on itself, the lock shearing with a crack.

Inside the room was bright. He slowly entered with the baton tightly in his hand, ready for anything. There was a large desk with two computer screens on top of it. Behind the screen, was a black window.

'What the fuck is this?' Leonard said as he stepped inside, seeing the computer screens.

Byrd looked carefully around the room. To the right, a thin black coat hung from a hook on the wall. To the right of that was a shelving unit with various papers on them. There was an empty chocolate wrapper and a half-drunk bottle of Pepsi on the desk, meaning whoever was here, hadn't been gone very long.

Leonard took a seat on one of the two empty desk chairs and pulled himself in. The right monitor screen showed a camera looking down onto a room. He leaned forward, squinting.

'Is that a woman?' He turned back to Byrd. 'Sir. Have a look.'

Byrd, Timms and Grearer came over immediately.

'Looks like it . . .' replied Byrd.

They saw the tab with the word "players" on it, then underneath, another tab saying "watchers".

'This is exactly where it happens,' Leonard noted angrily, hitting the desk with a palm.

The rustling sound on the other side of the door over to the left caught their attention. They all stared, exchanging quick glances with each other. Byrd wasted no time. He moved away from the desk, dashed over with the baton high up in his right hand and grabbed the handle, pulling the door inwards.

He was well aware of the dangers when opening a door, not knowing what could be behind so, through experience, he stamped his foot down near the open threshold but held off, missing the baseball bat that swung down from the right. And boy, was he glad he did. Judging by the speed and the crack when it hit the floor, it would have split his skull in two.

Leonard, Timms, and Grearer all froze, staring at the sudden sound at in the open door.

A moment later, a large man stumbled through, raising the bat high above his head with menace on his face. Byrd kept a close eye on him, watching his movements. Brad was big and bulky and Byrd knew he'd have to be sharp to avoid another one of Brad's vicious swings, which would no doubt knock him into next week.

'Calm down,' said Byrd quickly. 'You don't want to do this . . .'

The man didn't speak. He moved forward and raised the bat high above his head. Only when he was in the room he noticed Leonard, Timms and Grearer, and realised he was outnumbered, but it was clear that he'd go down fighting.

'You need to put that down,' Byrd said, louder and clearer this time.

His eyes flicked from Byrd to the others, then rested back on Byrd, as he was closer and posed a threat with the extended baton.

'Where's Phil?' asked Byrd.

The man frowned. 'Phil who — you dare come near me!' he screamed at Leonard, noticing him edge closer from his left.

Leonard threw his palms up. 'Okay. Okay. Calm . . .'

He glared back at Byrd. 'I don't know a Phil. Now fuck off.' He raised the bat higher and took a step forward.

Byrd weighed up his options. The last thing he wanted was a clout from the big guy with a baseball bat, but he was a threat that had already swung for him. If he'd connected, it would have probably killed him.

He also knew DC Cornty was somewhere in the building.

The man swung again, but Byrd was ready and dived to the floor, just missing the bat that whizzed by his head. Once he was distracted, Leonard acted quickly and charged at him, knocking Brad off balance until he hit the floor. Leonard mounted him, using his left arm to block him from swinging the bat up from the floor. Without hesitation, Leonard laid into him, relentless pounding on his face with his fists until he dropped the bat and it rolled away a few feet.

Timms pulled Leonard off and dragged him away against his will. He was like a man possessed, wriggling like an animal.

'Jim — fucking calm down!' Timms shouted, struggling to hold his frantic arms back.

Byrd had rolled away and had climbed to his feet. Leonard finally lowered his arms and regained control of his breathing and uncharacteristic temper.

'I'm fine. I'm fine,' he said, pushing Timms off him, allowing the mixture of emotions that had built up over the past few weeks.

'You got him?' Byrd asked Timms and Grearer.

Grearer nodded, pulled the cuffs from his belt, and leaned down over the big man.

Byrd went to the open door and noticed the stairway going down. He stood at the top of the stairs and, although it wasn't very well-lit, he saw someone standing at the base of them, looking up at him.

He didn't need to be a detective to recognise it was DC Cornty.

There was a sudden scuffle behind him in the room. Byrd turned quickly. Brad had managed to get up, wriggling Timms and Grearer off him, and charged through the open door heading directly at Byrd.

'Max!' Leonard screamed.

87

Tuesday afternoon
Lingfield Point, Darlington

Byrd spun on his toes and watched Brad charging right for him. He looked bigger against the light inside the room behind him, almost highlighting a rapid moving silhouette, growing bigger each passing second.

In his mind, he knew if he stayed where he was at the top of the stairs, he'd be flying down them. A hot wave ran through his body as he tensed and waited for him, raising the baton high above his head.

When he felt Brad was close enough, he did two things almost at the same time. First, he swung the baton at Brad's face. Hard. This caused him to wail in pain as the end of the baton popped his nose, causing blood to explode from it instantly. And two, he dropped to his knees and rolled to the left, hurling himself into the wall.

Brad continued to travel and went tumbling past him, bouncing off the stairs, all the way down to the bottom with a huge thud.

Byrd rolled over and stood up.

'You okay, boss?' asked Leonard, who appeared behind him and placed a hand on his shoulder.

Byrd managed a nod and stared down the stairs. There were four sets of eight or nine steps with flat areas between each flight. It must have been thirty metres down, maybe more. A long way to tumble.

The man at the bottom didn't move.

And DC Cornty had gone.

'Come on, Jim,' said Byrd. 'Cornty is down there somewhere. I've just seen him.'

Byrd went first, taking the steps quickly, sliding his hand down the railing so he could grab it quickly if he tripped. Leonard followed, with Timms and Grearer behind. As they reached the bottom it was clear that Brad hadn't moved. Byrd's light highlighted a large pool of blood underneath his lifeless body.

They stepped over him and came to a set of double doors.

Byrd pushed down the handle and entered a well-lit corridor that was twenty or so metres in length, but barely more than a metre wide. The floor was covered in a worn blue carpet that had seen better days and off-white walls, no doubt faded in time along with the rest of the place. There were doors on either side, roughly two metres apart; the last door on the right was the only one open, telling Byrd there was a chance Cornty had gone through there.

'Phil?' Byrd shouted. 'Phil. Please speak to me.'

No response.

Byrd, Leonard, and Timms moved on. Grearer had hung back and called dispatch, asking for backup and medical attention.

Byrd approached the door on the right and shone the torch inside. He could see a wall on the left, indicating the space inside wasn't very big, unless it was another corridor.

'Phil? If you're in here, we're coming in. Talk to me.'

Byrd waited for a response. When he didn't get one, he kicked it fully open, the door swinging off its hinges and crashing into a wall. Byrd shone the torch inside to see a small closet, roughly a metre wide, going back two metres at the most, filled with old cleaning equipment that hadn't been used in a long time, almost hidden under a mass of spider webs.

'Shit,' muttered Byrd.

Behind them, a little further up, a door opened quickly. They all turned and stared.

Cornty dashed out of it and ran towards the stairs, knocking Timms over, who was off balance down on one knee. Timms fell back, cracking the back of his head against the wall.

'Fucker!' Leonard screamed and turned, setting off after him. Timms followed and Byrd trailed. When it came to sprinting, Leonard was the man.

Byrd pulled his phone from his pocket and called Weaver. If Cornty made it up the stairs and through the room, there would only be Weaver blocking his path before he got out.

'Come on . . . pick up!' Byrd shouted into the ringing phone.

88

Tuesday afternoon
Lingfield Point, Darlington

'Amy . . . can you hear me?'

'See . . . for ca . . . nat . . .' Weaver crackled.

Byrd sighed, pulled the phone from his ear to see the signal. It was on one bar. He bent down to Grearer, who was holding the back of his head. 'You okay, Donny?'

Grearer nodded.

'Amy, if you can hear me, go outside, shut the door, and put the crowbar across,' Byrd shouted into the phone. 'He's coming now!'

Timms was just ahead on the stairs but Leonard was out of sight, presumably through the room on his way to the exit.

'Who . . . hu fort . . .'

'Lock the door, Amy!' Byrd shouted clearly.

'Door?' There was a crackle.

'Yes. Yes. Lock the door.'

'Okay . . .' she said finally.

Byrd ended the call and helped Grearer to his feet, checking he was okay. He said he was so Byrd took the stairs two at a time, propelling himself up with the aid of the handrail.

He stepped into the room with the computer and through the door they'd first come through, out into the long corridor. He took a left and dashed towards the exit door.

No one was there.

The door was wide open.

'Shit!'

There was commotion to the right when he reached outside. Leonard and Timms were on top of Cornty, wrestling with him, trying to keep him still while Timms attempted to put the cuffs on him.

Leonard punched him for good measure, sending Cornty into a moment of dizziness, giving them enough time to click the cuffs into place.

Byrd looked to his left to see Weaver on the floor, holding her head.

'Jesus, Amy.' He lowered to one knee and took hold of her. There was a cut to her forehead. 'What happened?'

'Fucker kicked the door open. It hit me in the head.'

Byrd looked closer, noticed the cut starting to swell. 'Backup is coming soon. You'll be okay.' He stood up, raced over to Cornty who was handcuffed on the grass on his front, bent down and grabbed his face, squeezing his cheeks so hard, his nails dug into his skin.

Cornty winced in pain, glaring up at him in defiance.

'You're going away for a very long time. Piece of shit.'

* * *

It wasn't long before the sirens were heard and backup arrived. An ambulance pulled up and two paramedics saw to the cut on Weaver's forehead and then checked on Grearer, who'd suffered a cut to the back of his head when he'd been pushed into the wall at the bottom of the stairs.

They had Sarah McKay on a trolley inside the ambulance, hooked her up with fluids and an IV line to build her strength back up. It was obvious she'd been deprived of a decent intake of food and was hours away from dying.

DCI Fuller came down to see the mess. As usual, he was less than impressed, and didn't mind showing it either.

'What a fucking shit show . . .' his final words were before getting back into his Jaguar F-Pace and speeding off, kicking up the gravel.

Byrd couldn't blame him. Fuller had been inside to see the computer where Cornty and Brad had run the games, then gone down the stairs and through a door on the right, leading to the cold, concrete room where they had found Sarah McKay asleep on a duvet covered in urine and faeces. The smell was atrocious.

Fuller was pissed off because there was only one left alive, meaning three of the missing four women had no doubt been killed. Byrd saw the positive. They'd saved one of them and in the process, stopped whatever Cornty and Brad had planned for the future games. They'd let Mac inside later this afternoon to analyse the computers to see what more information he could extract.

What had bothered Fuller the most was the room they found next to where they found Sarah. It was roughly twenty feet by twenty and in the centre of it was a wooden chair with ankle straps fitted to the legs and wrists straps fitted to the arms. To the side of it were drawers and a cupboard full of items that Stockdale had described were used in the games.

Fuller was right, Byrd had to admit. It *was* a shit show.

But the shit show was now over and they needed to be happy about that.

Byrd went over to the ambulance and asked one of the paramedics how Sarah McKay was.

'Very weak,' the man said. 'But she'll live. You've saved her life. You should take credit for that, Detective.'

Byrd nodded appreciatively before he moved away and checked in on his team, who were sitting on the grass over to the right, the afternoon sun beating down on their tired faces.

'Listen up, guys.'

Leonard, Weaver, Timms and Grearer looked up at him. 'You should be proud of yourselves today. I'm proud to have you on my team.'

89

Byrd arrived back at the station a little after 3 p.m. The sun was still bright in the cloudless blue sky, and it was hot. Probably the hottest part of the day. Byrd had put his thin black jacket on the passenger seat but even in his T-shirt, was sweating profusely. He tiredly pulled the key out of the ignition and sighed heavily, watching an elderly couple walking on the path nearby through his windscreen.

He smiled, thinking about the future. About Claire. The idea of them at that age walking along and holding hands after forty-plus years of a happy marriage. The thought faded away when he opened the door and sluggishly got out.

Leonard, Timms and Grearer had gone back in Leonard's Insignia and were already back at the station. DC Phil Cornty had been taken away by additional units that arrived after they got the cuffs on him.

Weaver had been taken to the hospital for the cut on her forehead, so he mentally noted to check up on her very soon.

The senior forensic officers, Emily Hope and Jacob Tallow, had looked inside the building, especially down in the room where they had found Sarah McKay. As she had gone missing with Lisa Butterwick, Lorraine Eckles, and Theresa Jackson, they needed to know from obtaining the DNA samples, they'd been there. They had proof that the body parts that had fallen from the blue Volkswagen van on the A66 had been Lorraine Eckles, but they needed to know if the others had suffered the same fate. They'd assumed so, but assumptions weren't to be made without evidence to back it up. They'd need to speak with Sarah when she was well enough.

Byrd went through the sliding doors into reception and felt like he had walked into a sauna.

'You okay, Max?' asked Julie, the receptionist behind the desk.

Byrd gave a weary wave and an equally tired nod before he went through the door and continued down the corridor into the office.

The round of clapping almost took him by surprise.

His eyes widened, unsure what was happening.

Fuller was standing at the end of the aisle, near the door to his office, clapping hard. Several others were also clapping, Leonard, Greater and Timms included. At first, he thought it was sarcasm, but by their looks of sincerity, and of course Fuller's too, it was genuine.

Byrd nodded at his peers in thanks. When he was close enough Fuller extended a solid hand.

'Well done, Max. We nailed the sonofabitch.'

Byrd shook his hand and was lost for words.

'Come into my office, please,' said Fuller, placing a hand on his back, guiding him in. Byrd did and took a seat in front of his desk. Fuller closed the door, made his way around to his side and sat down. The air inside was a blessing. Air-conditioned and bloody lovely.

Byrd didn't know what this was about. The last time he'd spoken with him, Fuller had stormed off.

'Max . . . I'm sorry how I went on before. It was unprofessional. A lot of how I felt was clouded by what I'd have to say to Barry Eckles.' He leaned and winced. 'You know how he can be sometimes.'

Byrd did.

'Although two of our own have proved to be on the different side of the law, it's because of you, Orion, and our team that we solved this.'

Fuller saw the doubt on Byrd's face.

'What is it?'

'We haven't found Linda,' replied Byrd. 'She was helping Dilton.'

Fuller considered that for a moment, almost as if he'd put that into the back of his mind. 'No, that's true. We haven't. But there are no more online games and there's no more Adrian Dilton. So, for that, Max Byrd, I thank you for carrying out your role and doing it the best you possibly could.'

'Have you heard from Orion?'

Fuller nodded. 'I have. Fortunately, his leg — well, his knee — is only badly bruised. It isn't broken. They've strapped it. He's coming out of hospital today.'

Byrd raised his brows. 'That's good. That's really good.'

'How are you doing, Max?'

'Tired. It's been a tough few weeks.'

Fuller agreed with a smile.

'I was going to ask about Sarah McKay — have you heard from the hospital?'

Fuller nodded. 'Yes. Just put the phone down before you arrived. She's sleeping. They've fixed her up with medicine and fluids, so hopefully, she'll be in a better state to talk to soon.' Fuller stood up and extended his hand. 'Once again, Max. I'm proud to call you one of my DIs.'

Byrd shook it, thanked him, and left the office slowly as if his body was almost shutting down.

'Have some rest,' Fuller said through the open door.

'See you tomorrow, boss.'

* * *

On his way home, Byrd phoned Tanzy, who'd told him a similar story to what Fuller had, about the injury to his knee not being as severe as it felt hours earlier. Tanzy, although he wasn't meant to and should go straight home, told Byrd he'd pop over with some flowers for Claire to make sure she was okay and to say hi.

Byrd thanked him and ended the call as he pulled up outside his house.

Karen's car was still there. They were probably on the sofa, resting up. He was glad her pills were working and equally glad she had company to cure her boredom. He couldn't wait to see her and tell her about his day. Usually, the last thing he'd want to do was sit with her and watch some crappy American show about people with less talent than a blade of grass, but tonight that's all he wanted to do. After the day he'd had, he wanted to sit, doing nothing and look at her and the little baby growing inside her.

He unlocked the door and stepped inside.

'Hello?' he said. He hung his jacket on the hook to his right, then flicked off his shoes and put them in a rack near the bottom of the stairs. There was a sweet smell lingering somewhere, but it wasn't a familiar scent, a mixture between perfume and baking. The thought of homemade cakes or scones waiting for him on the kitchen worktop caused a rumble in his stomach.

'Hello?' he said as he entered the living room.

The television was on. One of the American shows she loved to watch. Everything was in its place, apart from Claire.

And her friend.

On the small table in the middle of the room, were two glasses, half-empty. Beside them were two plates, one with a half-eaten scone on.

'Claire?' he said louder this time.

No response.

He frowned, wondering where they were. She was probably somewhere around the house showing her friend something. Another project for him, no doubt. She had mentioned a list of things she wanted to do before baby Alan arrived over the last few days. It was only natural, Byrd realised, after reading up on pregnant women wanting to change things. Nesting, it was called.

He stepped out of the room, took a left and headed for the kitchen.

The unusual thing was there was no noise anywhere. Unless they were in the garden, lapping up the sun. The doctor had told her to rest, and sunbathing wasn't exactly an exhausting task. He might join them, lap up the rest of the day's sun which would still be warm.

As soon as he entered the kitchen, he noticed the back door to his left was wide open. The cool breeze trickling in brushed his forearms where he'd rolled up his sleeves.

Then he stopped dead and glared at the floor near the back door.

'What the fuck?' he whispered, seeing all the blood.

90

Slowly, he padded across the tiled floor over to the back door. The pool of blood was thick, roughly two feet in diameter, meaning there was a lot of it.

'Claire?' Byrd shouted.

He leapt down into the garden and glared around. There were two empty sun loungers in the middle of the grass, with a folded magazine on one of them and an empty glass beside the other.

'Claire!'

He went along the outside wall of the kitchen and looked around the back. There was no one there. If her friend's car was still here, that meant she was still here.

But where the fuck were they?

He dashed back into the kitchen, noticed something red on the floor over to the left, in front of the door leading to the garage.

More blood.

'Claire?' he repeated. Still no response. He went over to the blood which seemed to lead towards the garage door.

He grabbed the handle, and opened it, not knowing what to expect.

'Jesus . . .' he said, then gasped.

In the middle of the garage floor was a woman, her eyes wide, staring up at the ceiling. It wasn't Claire. Regardless of that, Byrd panicked when he saw the enormous slit across her throat and the blood oozing from it. He jumped down and frantically looked around, but there was no sign of Claire.

'Claire!' he screamed.

He leapt back into the kitchen, took a left and ran into the hallway. He checked the dining room. Empty. Then he darted upstairs, screaming her name over and over until he reached the landing. All the doors were open apart from his bedroom, which was fully shut.

He dashed to his bedroom and opened the door.

Claire was tied to the chair, facing the door. Duct tape was wrapped around her ankles and over her mouth. She mumbled something but it was nothing more than a desperate moan.

'God . . .' Byrd said, stepping inside with his arms out to help her.

Then he froze when she came into view and stopped beside Claire, holding a bloody knife by her side.

'Welcome home, Max,' Linda Fallon said coldly.

91

Tuesday late afternoon
Low Coniscliffe, Darlington

Byrd couldn't speak as he stared at Fallon, then at Claire, absorbing the fear in her terrified eyes.

'Linda . . . I don't understand.'

Fallon smiled. 'I didn't think you would, Max.'

He went to take a step forward, but she lowered the knife to Claire's stomach, the tip of the blade touching her stretched skin where their baby was growing.

'I wouldn't do that if I were you . . .' she insisted.

Byrd threw his palms up in surrender and suddenly stopped. 'Okay. Okay.' He took several deep breaths. 'I don't understand this, Linda. Talk to me . . .'

She sighed heavily and kept the knife at Claire's stomach, knowing Byrd wouldn't dare breathe near Claire, let alone try to save her.

'Adrian Dilton was like a son to me. Because of you, he's dead, Max.'

Byrd frowned and shook his head. 'What happened to Dilton was his own fault, and his fault alone. He was the one who broke the glass and fell through it. He killed himself.'

'He did not!' she screamed, startling both Claire and Byrd.

The whole house fell silent.

'Okay . . .' Byrd said, doing his best to remain calm. 'Please explain. Go on,' he added, nodding at her. The longer she spoke, the more time he had to come up with a plan.

'Like I said, he was like a son to me. When I was a criminal psychologist, I had the job of getting into his mind, learning why he'd done the things he'd done. I got to know him . . .' Byrd nodded, waiting for her to go on. 'He's very special, Max.'

There was a lengthy moment of silence.

Byrd said, 'He killed people seven years ago, Linda. The last word I'd use to describe Adrian Dilton is special.'

Claire's eyed widened for a second, advising Byrd not to piss her off anymore.

Byrd gave her a slow nod, deciding to say nothing more.

Fallon started laughing. Byrd wondered what was so hilarious. 'You — you think that was Adrian who killed those people seven years ago?' She tilted her head to one side. 'Well, you would do. After all . . . that's what I told you, wasn't it? Oh God . . . this was so easy, Max. How could I just walk into your department like that?'

Byrd felt an anger build up inside but didn't show that her words were getting to him.

'I killed those people, Max. I did. They deserved all they got. They'd mistreated people all their lives and even killing them was not enough. I took Dilton under my wing after months of getting into his head. Yes, he'd violently attacked a man in Essex one night and had been enrolled on a programme with me, so he wasn't exactly an angel, but once I knew him, Max, I realised he was a shy, young man, who didn't respond to the world like everyone else did. I blame his upbringing. It was awful. It's not what a child should go through — don't worry, I'm not getting into it. Let's just say his first attack was him expressing himself. During the time I got to know him, I realised there was more he had to give, otherwise he'd go crazy. So, what better way to do it than to get back at people who really deserved it. You see, I know he wrote you and Orion a letter, saying he found this website online and he blah blah blah . . . the truth is, is that *I* found the website. And I contacted Dilton. I asked him if he wanted to unleash some of that frustration I knew he had deep down.'

'So, killing people is the answer?' asked Byrd.

She nodded. 'If they deserve it, yes. This website was horrible. The things they did to victims on there is something I don't want to even think about. And to make money doing it — it's utter madness.'

'How did you find the website?'

'Someone — a contact — had sent me a link. I checked it out. I joined up to find out what it was about and paid the fee. After witnessing what happened as a watcher, I knew I couldn't let this go on. You see, when I got to know Dilton, I realised he was a whiz-kid on a computer. He did things beyond my comprehension. Codes. Algorithms. Jesus, Max. You name it. I told him about it, so he joined up. He had the skills to locate the players using their IP addresses, and well . . . you know what happened after that.'

'So,' said Byrd, 'what happens now?'

'Well, now I kill your wife and the baby growing inside her. Then maybe you'll feel like I'm feeling right now.'

Byrd looked at Claire. Tears ran down her cheeks.

There was no way he could let that happen, but he didn't know what to do. In all his years in the police, he'd never come up with this dilemma. If he tried to save her, Fallon would put the knife into Claire's stomach and kill their unborn son and her too.

He took a deep breath.

Fallon was still leaning over Claire with the tip of the knife at her stomach. Byrd calculated Linda's face was inches from Claire's. He looked at the tape around her mouth, hands and feet. There was a loop of tape around her middle, holding her to the chair.

Maybe Claire could move a little, maybe just enough.

Byrd looked directly into Claire's eyes and nodded slightly.

Claire's eyes narrowed, not quite understanding, then it clicked. He needed her to do something to distract Fallon. It was the only way out of this.

As Byrd raised his hands in surrender, Claire rocked to the side and gave her best headbutt into the side of Fallon's face, knocking her off balance a little. Byrd darted forward and wrapped his arms around Fallon, not thinking about the knife, and knocked her over the bed onto the floor near the wardrobe with a thud. The knife flew from her hand and landed on the carpet. He punched her three times as hard as he could in the face, the second one popping her nose, the third one knocking her unconscious.

He jumped up, unwrapped the duct tape from Claire and held her for a long time while she cried.

* * *

After the police had come to arrest Fallon, it wasn't long before the house was filled with people. The forensic officers checked the house, particularly the kitchen and garage. The undertakers collected the body from the garage, and finally, the paramedics checked over Claire to make sure the baby was okay. Byrd and Claire grabbed some overnight things and left the house, checking into the nearest Premier Inn as they both needed to get away from the house.

Claire had explained that there'd been a knock at the door, and her friend had opened it to allow Fallon in, saying she was a colleague of Byrd's and was looking for him. Claire had asked her if she wanted a coffee so her friend had gone into the kitchen to make her some. Linda had followed and killed her. She then came back with the bloody knife, demanding she go upstairs.

Byrd counted his blessings.

He had been a single moment away from losing everything.

Once Claire was settled in a hot bath filled with bubbles, Byrd answered his ringing phone and stepped into the bedroom for privacy. It was Fuller, who'd heard what had happened. Byrd briefed him and told him he was taking a few days off and that if Fuller wanted his report doing right there and then, he was retiring.

Fuller told him to take a few days off and come back when he was ready.

'Look after your wife, Max. Family is the most important thing in the world. It's taken the last few years for me to realise that myself.'

Byrd hung up and threw his phone on the bed.

He went into the bathroom and sat down on the closed toilet seat and looked at Claire. Her eyes were teary, thin lines of mascara running down both sides of her face.

In the bath, the tip of her stretched stomach was just above the waterline. Byrd leaned forward and placed a gentle palm on it. Claire smiled and placed both her wet soapy hands on top of his.

'Everything is going to be all right, Alan,' Byrd said to the baby, then leaned over and kissed Claire's forehead. He returned to the bedroom and yawned. What a day it had been. One he certainly wouldn't forget for a long time.

His phone pinged with a text message. He picked it up. It was from Tanzy.

Heard what happened, Max! Jesus! Hope you're both okay! Love you both very much. There's never a dull day in this fucking town.

Wednesday morning
Police station

Although Byrd was taking a few well-deserved days off to look after Claire, Tanzy made it in to work just after 9 a.m. He'd dropped the kids off at school, which he seldom had the chance to do, then headed straight over, parking next to Fuller's Jaguar F-Pace.

He stepped out and stretched, looking up at the bright rising sun. There wasn't a cloud in the sky. Today was going to be a beautiful day.

He limped past Julie in reception and smiled, then used his key card to get through the next sliding doors. Down the corridor, before he reached the office, he saw DC Leonard walking towards him. There was a skip in his step and a smile on his face.

'Morning, James.'

'Morning, sir. How's the knee?'

They stopped.

'Getting there. A little bruise won't stop me.'

Leonard smiled wider.

'What are you so happy about?' Tanzy asked, curious about Leonard's grin.

'We're getting a dog,' he said. 'A cross between an Alsatian and something else, I'm not sure. She's found a place online. Place in Romania. Dog shelter type place. Getting her at the weekend.'

'You already have a dog?'

Leonard nodded. 'We do. But she needs some company.'

Tanzy nodded this time and narrowed his eyes. 'By 'she', who do you mean?'

'I think you know, boss.'

Tanzy would be lying if he said he hadn't noticed that Weaver and Leonard were close. They had been for a little while; it was obvious to see.

'Are you ready for this morning — did you get my text?'

'I did. I was coming to speak to you about it.'

They chatted a little while longer and come up with a plan, then parted ways, Leonard going to the canteen and Tanzy heading for the office. His colleagues nodded in his direction, confirming they'd received his text message earlier and understood what was happening.

Yesterday, after they'd arrested Fallon and Cornty, they'd brought them back to the station to interview them both individually. It was interesting, to say the least.

Tanzy went in to see Fuller, who was sitting behind his desk, just coming off a phone call. They discussed the plan and Fuller gave him the go-ahead. He stood up, made his way through the office and down the corridor towards IT. Mac didn't know the plan yet.

Tanzy knocked on the door.

'Come in,' Mac said.

Tanzy opened the door and stepped inside. Even though the window was open, the hot air coming in didn't help cool the room. The fan to the right of his desk didn't seem to be doing much, apart from circulating the humid, stale air. 'Morning, Mac.'

Mac turned on his desk chair and smiled, lines of sweat trailing down his temples. 'Morning, boss. What do I owe the pleasure?'

'I've realised I hadn't updated you on what happened yesterday and the plan for today?'

His eyebrows furrowed.

Tanzy moved over to the desk and pulled out the spare chair, then sunk into it. 'About Dilton, Linda Fallon and DC Phillip Cornty.'

'I heard about the arrests.'

'What did you hear?' Tanzy leaned forward a touch and tapped the desk with his right hand.

He frowned and studied Tanzy's hand. 'That Detective Cornty had been arrested. He was the man responsible for the online website I tried to access for you.'

Tanzy nodded twice. 'What of Fallon?'

'That she was working with Adrian Dilton all along . . . she helped him.'

'Good. So, the only thing I need to tell you is about the plan today,' Tanzy said.

He nodded and waited, his hands hovering over his keyboard.

'Well, after speaking with Cornty yesterday, we made some discoveries. Let's just say I was surprised by this.' He smiled and leaned back. 'You see, I wondered how he had come up with the website. How could a detective constable devise a website so intricate that *you* couldn't get in to. I couldn't fathom it out. You've got on to sites like that in the past. You're our number one man.'

'I know. But you were there. You saw me try. The web-site, had these—'

Tanzy raised a palm. 'Bear with me here . . .'

Mac fell silent, nodding.

'So, if our lead IT guy couldn't get on to a site that a detective constable created, who by the way, had no genius IT training, let alone the ability to build firewalls so complex, they were unbreakable . . . it got me thinking.'

'About?'

'That someone must have helped him set it up. They must have. Someone with vast experience and expertise in the field.'

'Like who?' Mac shook his head. 'Whoever it was, they were very talented. Whatever firewall they'd installed, trust me, was uncrackable. You saw it yourself.'

'I did, you're right. You know Denny from the Met?'

Mac nodded. Raymond Dennett, aka Denny, had worked with Mac on several occasions in the past. If there was something Mac wasn't sure on, he'd ask Denny. The Metropolitan Police didn't mind as they helped each other out.

'What about Denny?'

'I got in touch with him. Sent him over the link.'

Mac frowned. 'Did… he crack it?'

'He struggled to, but he got there in the end. You wouldn't believe it. The website had been set up on the dark web. That's why you couldn't get in. The original website was a front for the whole thing. Think of it like an onion. *Attheend.com* was only the outer layer.'

Mac nodded, intrigued. 'That makes sense.'

'The players and watchers paid via bitcoin too. It was a genius idea. Almost untraceable . . .'

Mac widened his eyes and looked down at his desk in amazement. 'That's a very clever way of doing it.'

Tanzy agreed with a wider grin. 'But . . . they didn't cover their tracks fully.'

Mac focused back on him. 'How do you mean?'

'IP address.'

'The IP address kept jumping all the time. Even I couldn't track it. What did he find?'

'Denny told me all about that. He told me if there's a trail, even something minute, there's a possibility it can be found.'

Mac waited. 'What was the IP address?'

Tanzy clapped his hands twice.

Mac frowned.

The door opened to the right. DC Leonard walked in holding a closed laptop, followed by PC Weaver and PC Andrews. Leonard placed the laptop down on the desk.

'The IP address was located to that specific laptop,' said Tanzy.

Mac stared at it and said nothing.

'The only reason you—' Tanzy raised both hands to physically show inverted commas with his fingers — 'couldn't crack the website, is because you're the one who set it up for him. You knew exactly how to get in because you designed it.'

Mac fell into a lengthy silence and looked away from the laptop he recognised as his own, focusing on the monitors in front of him. He didn't speak for nearly thirty seconds. The longest thirty seconds of his life.

Tanzy pulled a set of handcuffs from his pocket, threw them on top of the laptop. 'Put them on, Mac.'

'I — I . . .' He looked away and sighed.

'Now, Mac.'

He grabbed the cuffs and did as Tanzy asked, then Weaver and Leonard walked him out of the room.

Tanzy sighed heavily, leaned back in the chair and closed his eyes.

93

Three months later,
Darlington Memorial Hospital

Claire held tightly onto Byrd's hand, her nails digging into his skin, sending waves of pain through his body, but he couldn't stop it now. Couldn't interrupt what was happening.

Byrd could see the baby's head as he leaned over. A full head of black hair; just like his.

'I can see him, I can see him,' Byrd shouted excitedly, looking back at her red, sweaty face.

'Just breathe,' said one of the midwives, a woman bordering on the age of sixty who'd been a midwife since her twenties. 'Come on, Claire. We're nearly there. On your next one, you need to give it one last push and he'll be here. You've done brilliantly.'

When the baby came out, the midwives took little Alan over to check him out. In that time, which felt like an eternity, Claire looked over with wide, searching eyes, asking Byrd where they'd taken her baby. Once he was checked and given the okay, the midwife brought him back to them, wrapped up in a white blanket.

'Everything is okay. There you go. Congratulations.' She lowered him onto her bare chest. 'He's beautiful.'

Claire started crying. Byrd couldn't control himself and cried more than she did, his body heaving with the emotions that a parent could only endure during these life-changing moments. Byrd stroked his little head with a trembling finger, then stood up, kissing Claire's sweaty forehead.

'You did it, Claire. There he is. Baby Alan.'

A while after, once the chaos had subsided, Byrd told Claire he needed some air. Before he left through the door, Claire and Alan were both asleep, holding each other. He stood for a moment and absorbed the beauty of it, realising their lives would never be the same again.

He made his way down the corridor and left through the security door, then to the lifts, pressing the button to call the closest one. From the four lifts, the left one opened. He stepped inside and pressed 'G' for the ground floor. Once he was outside he took out his phone and paused, feeling sad it wasn't his mother or father he was ringing first to tell them about their new arrival.

He found the number he wanted and pressed CALL.

It rang three times, then it was answered. 'What's happening, Max? She must be close by now.'

'Congratulations, Ori,' Byrd said. 'You're an uncle to Alan Max Byrd, born at four twenty, weighing in at nine pounds three ounces.'

'Aww, Max! I'm thrilled to bits for you, mate. Well done. How's Claire?'

'She did amazingly, Ori. She really did.' Byrd wiped a tear from his eye.

'Well, send her my love. Send them both my love. I can't wait to see him.'

'Midwife said she's staying in overnight. Something with having a different blood type so they need to monitor him to make sure he's okay. Nothing ever simple is it?'

'Well, you know what they say, don't you?' Tanzy replied.

'What do they say, Ori?'

'That there's never a dull day in this town. And today my friend, is no exception.'

EPILOGUE

Linda Fallon was charged with murder and taken back to Essex. After the courts had viewed her case, the jury had given her a life sentence. At her age, she wouldn't see another day outside prison.

DC Phillip Stockdale, because of his involvement with the online games, taking part and telling the hosts to kill and make their victims suffer, was given twelve years. He'd be out just after his fiftieth birthday.

DC Cornty, the man responsible for running the online games and posing as Mitch, taking money from the people who logged on, and killing three victims, was sentenced to life in prison. He also wouldn't see the light of day again, metaphorically speaking.

Mac, the IT wizard in DFU, admitted to helping Cornty set the website up, and was given twelve years for his sins. Although it was him who had aided Cornty in his horrific acts, he physically hadn't killed or harmed anyone.

Tanzy, Pip and the kids decided to move to a new house. They'd had enough of where they were living and decided to move into a detached house near a great primary school in the Mowden area of Darlington. The location would be ideal for Jasmine and Eric to go there and then to a nearby secondary school afterwards. Tanzy had promised to build Eric a den for his bedroom, not that he needed reminding by Pip who, on a weekly basis, had mentioned it.

Byrd and Claire had settled at home with baby Alan, who as it turned out, didn't like sleeping. Claire spent most nights awake with him while Byrd slept, so he was able to go to work the following day. Byrd loved being a dad and recently asked Claire what they had done with all the time they used to have before he arrived. Regardless, he wouldn't change it for the world. When Alan was three months old, he got his first tooth. Claire had taken the most perfect photo of him and put it on a large canvas for the living room.

In his little village of Low Coniscliffe, the person responsible for breaking into houses had finally been caught by a security system that one of Byrd's neighbours, Jerry, had installed. It turned out to be a man in his fifties called Paul who, for some reason, had turned bitter and couldn't stand his neighbours being happy, so had gone out of his way to cause a stir. Byrd had enjoyed personally taking him to the station after seeing the CCTV footage Jerry had showed him.

DCI Fuller stepped down, admitting to Superintendent Barry Eckles that he'd had enough of Darlington, and wanted to move back to the West Midlands. Eckles asked Fuller who, from his experience, would he advise stepping up from the current workforce. Without question, Fuller told him he'd recommend either Byrd or Tanzy, and that he'd speak with them about it. If one of them decided to take on the role of DCI, it left a gap for someone to step into the role of the new DI. Eckles had also asked Fuller who he thought would be a good replacement for DS Stockdale. Without hesitation, Fuller had mentioned DC Leonard.

Let's just say things were looking good for Darlington and Durham Constabulary.

THE END

THE JOFFE BOOKS STORY

We began in 2014 when Jasper agreed to publish his mum's much-rejected romance novel and it became a bestseller.

Since then we've grown into the largest independent publisher in the UK. We're extremely proud to publish some of the very best writers in the world, including Joy Ellis, Faith Martin, Caro Ramsay, Helen Forrester, Simon Brett and Robert Goddard. Everyone at Joffe Books loves reading and we never forget that it all begins with the magic of an author telling a story.

We are proud to publish talented first-time authors, as well as established writers whose books we love introducing to a new generation of readers.

We have been shortlisted for Independent Publisher of the Year at the British Book Awards three times, in 2020, 2021 and 2022, and for the Diversity and Inclusivity Award at the Independent Publishing Awards in 2022.

We built this company with your help, and we love to hear from you, so please email us about absolutely anything bookish at feedback@joffebooks.com

If you want to receive free books every Friday and hear about all our new releases, join our mailing list: www.joffebooks.com/contact

And when you tell your friends about us, just remember: it's pronounced Joffe as in coffee or toffee!